KASEY MICHAELS

is the *New York Times* and *USA Today* bestselling author of more than sixty books. She has won the Romance Writers of America RITA Award and the *Romantic Times Magazine* Career Achievement Award for her historical romances set in the Regency era, and also writes contemporary romances for Silhouette and Harlequin Books.

GAYLE WILSON

Winner of the Romance Writers of America's RITA Award for best Romantic Suspense, the Kiss of Death Award, the Texas Gold Award, the Laurel Wreath for Excellence and the Dorothy Parker Award, Gayle Wilson has written nearly thirty novels for Harlequin and Silhouette Books. Gayle writes historical romance set in the English Regency period and contemporary romantic suspense. She lives in Alabama with her husband and an ever-expanding menagerie of adopted pets.

Kasey Michaels

Gayle Wilson

A Timeless Love

Silhouette® Books

Published by Silhouette Books

America's Publisher of Contemporary Romance

SILHOUETTE BOOKS

ISBN 0-373-21720-X

by Request

A TIMELESS LOVE

Copyright © 2001 by Harlequin Books S.A.

The publisher acknowledges the copyright holders of the individual works as follows:

TIMELY MATRIMONY
Copyright © 1994 by Kasey Michaels

RAVEN'S VOW
Copyright © 1997 by Mona Gay Thomas

Visit Silhouette at www.eHarlequin.com

Printed in U.S.A.

CONTENTS

Dear Reader,

My first romance novels were Regencies, stories set in England in the time period between 1811 and 1820. A lovely time, a sometimes terrible time, but one where I was allowed to have some very great fun concocting arrogant, witty, handsome heroes who could break a heart with a single look.

Then I started writing for Silhouette. Hmmm...what to do with my Regency heroes? I loved writing about contemporary heroes, but I longed for one of those witty, urbane, maddeningly arrogant men.

Happily, after writing a Silhouette Romance novel titled *His Chariot Awaits,* I found I had enough characters left over to write *Romeo in the Rain,* which somehow begat *Sydney's Folly*...and left me with only one character—the delicious, slightly eccentric Suzi Harper—without a love interest on the horizon. Clearly Suzi needed a delicious, slightly eccentric hero, and where better to look for him than in Regency England!

Or washed up, out of time, on a New Jersey beach...

All the best,

Kasey Michaels

TIMELY MATRIMONY
Kasey Michaels

To my niece Lorraine Charles,
because I already dedicated one to her sister,
and because she is as
wonderfully "singular" as Suzi

Prologue

The late-summer storm had been raging for three interminable days and nights, causing the *Pegasus* to be blown badly off course.

But there was nothing anyone on the ship could do, at least not until the storm began to abate. Moment by moment, the *Pegasus* drew closer to the southern New Jersey shoreline, and certain disaster.

Veteran seamen were silent under this threat of imminent death, returning from their exhausting above-deck shifts with pinched gray faces and avoiding the questioning eyes of their mates.

There was no nearby port they could head for, even if they could be assured of a welcome, and everyone knew that if the storm did not ease soon they would be food for the fishes.

And then on the third dawn, just as all seemed lost, the storm disappeared. Not eased, nor merely slowed down, showing signs of soon being over. It simply stopped. One moment the wind had been howling, rain lashing the ship, the sky a dark, menacing gunmetal gray, and the next moment the storm was gone.

The sea, formerly so violent, calmed, and a watery sun began to rise over the horizon. Gulls could be heard screaming as they perched in the rigging, and in the galley men raced to fill their bellies with something other than cold food and stale biscuits.

"I'm going up on deck," Harry announced to his companions, many of whom still suffered from seasickness brought on by the roiling waves. He had been stuck below-decks for what seemed like forever, and the notion of a little fresh air was extremely appealing.

"Don't do it, son," one of the oldest sailors warned as he stuck his unlit pipe into the corner of his mouth. Smoking had been forbidden by the captain until the storm was over, for the last thing the crew of the *Pegasus* needed was a fire on board ship. "I've heard about storms like these. It's not over. This is only the eye."

Harry smiled, pushing a stray lock of longish blond hair back off his forehead. "The eye, is it? Fascinating. Well then, my fainthearted friend, I think I shall go 'eye' it."

"Be careful," the seaman cautioned. "We've got men climbing all over the riggings. It's plenty dangerous up there, especially for a wobbly-legs like you."

"It's prodigiously dangerous down here, my good fellow," Harry countered, picking up his pouch and slinging its heavy leather strap over his head—he went nowhere without his pouch. "One more moment looking at your hangdog face and I might weep. Don't worry. I'll be back in a minute."

So saying, he bounded up the short, steep flight of steps and opened the hatch, the fresh sea air teasing his senses so that he hurriedly scrambled onto the deck and headed for the railing, intent on catching his first glimpse of the New Jersey shoreline as the land was lit by the rising sun.

How flat it all was, covered only by shrub, so that he could see that they were lying close beside an island, with the true shoreline, and what appeared to be an immense forest of pines behind it.

The breaker island, as he supposed such an area of land was called, was ringed by a wide, unbroken stretch of white sand and populated by thousands upon thousands of gulls, all of them screaming—and some of them laughing, Harry thought—as they plundered the wet sand for the treasure trove of small sea creatures that has been washed there by the storm.

It was a beautiful, inspiring scene, with the sky the clearest blue Harry could remember, and the sun glowing red from behind him, turning the ocean into a vast fairyland of shining lights.

Harry was mesmerized by the sight in front of him, his romantic soul enlivened by nature's display of grandeur, his full attention on the shoreline, and not on the men climbing overhead in the riggings, doing their best to make repairs on the mizzenmast.

"Avast aft! *Avast,* man!"

What the devil? Aft? Which way was aft? Harry had been aboard the *Pegasus* for over two months, but he'd be damned for a tinker if he'd figured out fore and aft, or port and starboard for that matter.

He wasn't a sailor; had no notion of becoming a sailor. He was only on board this ship because it was the right thing to do, the right place to be. His heart certainly wasn't in it. Only his body.

"Aft?" he yelled, wheeling around and looking heavenward just in time for the broken piece of rigging to deal him a glancing blow on the temple. It wasn't enough to kill him outright, but did serve to turn the sunny morning into darkest night as he pitched backward and tumbled, unknowing, into the sunlit sea.

Chapter One

Click. "—said to the gorilla, 'I don't know. We don't serve *ducks!*' *Beep! Beep!* Yes, indeedy, folks. Another two beeper. Too bad, Maisie from Cape May. It takes four beeps," *Beep! Beep! Beep! Beep!* "of the old car horn to make your joke eligible for our weekly drawing. So this is Annoying Arnie in the A.M. reminding you early birds out there to keep those jokes and limericks coming. The prize this week is a full, six-piece set of steak knives, compliments of WLFJ and—"

Suzi Harper frantically beat on the top of her clock-radio with both hands until she located the snooze-alarm bar and silenced the screaming Arnie. Then she fell back against the pillows, breathing heavily as she glared up at the ceiling fan above her bed.

She must have been farther out of her mind than usual. Setting her alarm for five-thirty could be nothing less than proof of an impending mental breakdown, most probably brought on by the three-day-long storm that had kept her cooped up inside her Ocean City condo.

Why else would she think it such a splendid idea if she were to rise before dawn to search the beach outside for pieces of driftwood for Mrs. O'Connell?

She closed her eyes, sighing. Poor Mrs. O'Connell. The woman had looked so pitiful the other day when she showed Suzi her collection of driftwood art—if anyone could call bits of wood stuck all over with plastic flowers and seashells *art*.

But Mrs. O'Connell, Suzi's closest neighbor, obviously delighted in the pastime, and her complaint that her arthritis kept her from combing the beach for "exquisite" pieces of driftwood after a storm before the morning beach patrol swept the area had touched Suzi's soft heart.

"And my even softer head," Suzi grumbled tiredly, throwing back the covers. "Next time I make someone a promise, first I'll be sure it has nothing to do with getting up in the middle of the night."

She glowered at the clock-radio as she turned off the alarm. All she needed now was for the snooze bar to pop again and hear Annoying Arnie's ridiculously cheerful, adenoidal tones reminding her that it was now only five thirty-*five* in the "A.M."

She slid her ruby red painted toes off the bed and onto the woven grass mat Wilbur Langley had brought her back from his last trip to Tahiti and dropped her head into her hands, pushing equally ruby red tipped fingers into her chin-length ash blond hair.

"C'mon, Harper, you can do this. Just get with the program," she admonished herself as she stood, doing her best to open her eyes and focus them on the brightening dawn just outside her window.

Except all the vertical blinds were still tightly shut against the scary streaks of lightning that had kept her awake past two o'clock last night, so that she couldn't see much of anything.

Padding to the window while clad only in an emerald green silk camisole and matching tap pants, and yawning prodigiously as she went, she pushed back the blinds and blinked several times as the rising sun cut through the morning mist, giving her a dose of brightness she hadn't expected.

"At least the storm's finally blown over," she said to Patchwork, her five-year-old calico cat, who was still blissfully, annoyingly asleep at the bottom of the queen-size bed. "And sure enough, there's the driftwood, just like Mrs. O'Connell promised. Driftwood, and a helmet crab—ugh, without the crab, and—" she wrinkled her small pert nose, "—sixteen tons of sickening, slimy, mussel-stuffed seaweed. Oh, joy."

She was just about to turn away from the window when something else on the beach, something just at the water's edge, caught her eye. Too big to be driftwood, too solid to be seaweed, it resembled... "*A man!* Dear Lord. Patchwork—it's a *man!*"

Call 911, call 911, her brain screamed to her as she ran out of the ground-floor bedroom and raced toward the spiral staircase that would take her upstairs, to the telephone in the kitchen.

She had her foot on the second step from the top before she remembered that she hadn't had the phone hooked up. For the month she had planned to spend in Ocean City, a total disconnect with modern communication seemed to be a good idea—or at least had at the time.

It figured. Every stupid thing she'd ever done in all of her thirty-two years had seemed to be a good idea at the time.

Suzi retraced her steps and fumbled with the dead bolt. Throwing open the door at the side of the condo, she sprinted toward the beach, her bare feet slapping against the cold, hard, wet sand.

The sun was just creeping above the horizon, turning the sea to gold, and she had no difficulty in making out the location of the man's body as it lay half in, half out of the water.

Not his body, you idiot! she admonished herself as she ran, forgetful of the fact that she was still in her night-clothes. Her fairly skimpy, revealing nightclothes. *He's not dead. Please, don't let him be dead. What on earth would I do with a dead body? Decorate it with plastic flowers and seashells?*

Breathless, she dropped to her knees on the sand, beside the man. He was lying on his stomach, his hands beside his head, his long legs at the mercy of the still angry waves that broke farther out on the beach, then foamed up onto the shore.

He wasn't moving—unless she counted his legs, which were almost floating. His face, the small bit of it she could see, was a ghastly gray beneath his dark blond hair. She took only a moment to consider the man's unusual dress.

His woolen pants, shrunk up to just below his knees by the seawater, and his white shirt, its long, full sleeves plastered against his arms, were not exactly the usual outfit of vacationers.

"Oh, who cares, Suzi? This is no time to play fashion police!" she berated herself, pushing both hands against one of the man's shoulders and heaving him over onto his side. It wasn't an easy job, for he was tall, and rather muscular, his body heavy with seawater and the sand that caked him head to toe, but at last she managed it.

"Ugh. He's dead, all right," she said, sitting back on her haunches, shivering and shaking her hands to rid them of the feel of his solid, cold body. "Real dead. Real, *real* dead."

But then, as Suzi was not the sort to give in gracefully, she took a deep breath and narrowed her eyes, her small, fairly belligerent chin lifting a notch as she decided that she hadn't raced outside in her camisole to give up without one hell of a fight.

She laced her fingers together tightly, almost as if in prayer, trying desperately to recall the public service program she had seen recently on cardiopulmonary resuscitation. Then she decided she remembered at least *some* of it.

First she should give him a good crack between the shoulder blades, just to let him know she was there. That seemed reasonable—or was that what she should do to a choking victim? No. That was what people *used* to do to choking victims. Now they performed that squeezing thing called the Heimlich maneuver.

Well, too bad. She'd already hit him. She'd hit him once, then twice, just for good measure. It had been like hitting lead. Cold, solid lead.

Then, her hands shaking violently, she pushed him all the way over onto his back and, while prudently looking the other way, cautiously stuck one finger in his mouth, believing she should check to make sure his windpipe wasn't obstructed.

Stupid rule, she thought, her finger scraping against the man's upper teeth. *It isn't like he's got a herring stuck down his gullet or anything.*

Only once she was satisfied that she'd followed all the instructions she'd seen in the public service program did she pull at the strap of the leather pouch the man had draped over his shoulders and throw the thing onto the sand. Then she began tearing at the buttons on his shirt, revealing his broad, slightly golden chest.

Golden? she thought, belatedly realizing that his entire chest, now exposed to the sunlight, was covered with a blond down that, although crusted with sand, was soft to the touch.

"That's the ticket, Suzi, waste precious time admiring

the guy, why don't you,'' she told herself, knowing she was speaking aloud so that the only sounds coming to her ears were not those of the waves and her own rapidly beating heart. "Go to it!"

After giving herself that order she straddled the man at his waist, hating the feel of his cold wet clothing against the inside of her thighs.

Placing her hands on his chest just below his neck, she measured down three handspans until she believed she had found the correct spot, then laid one hand on top of the other and pressed down—hard.

Going up on her haunches in order to gain leverage, she repeated the movement, counting aloud for five beats, then leaned forward and, holding his nostrils pinched, puffed into his mouth five times.

She didn't know if five was the correct number, or if she was in danger of killing the dead man —*how do you kill a dead man?*—but at least she was doing something, which had to be a whacking lot better than doing nothing.

Alternating the puffs with the chest compressions, Suzi worked for what seemed like forever, although she hadn't been performing her peculiar version of CPR for more than a few minutes the man suddenly coughed, then moved his arms.

"Yes!" Suzi screamed, slapping his face as she bounced lightly on his pelvis, caught between exhaustion and an exhilaration close to euphoria. "That's it, mister—breathe. *Breathe!*"

Eyes the color of the ocean at dawn opened wide and looked straight up at her for a moment before he unceremoniously pushed her away, turned onto his side, and began to retch violently onto the sand.

He was sick for some moments, which didn't bother Suzi, who was busy jumping up and down on the sand, offering high fives to any imaginary onlookers who might be applauding her performance.

She had done it! She—silly, flighty, airheaded Suzanne Harper—was an official, bona fide, card-carrying *heroine*.

Who said she was only good enough to write book reviews and look good while dangling from some man's arm at trendy Manhatten cocktail parties? She was *woman,* damn it—and she had just saved a man's life.

She stopped jumping up and down, remembering that the man was far from saved. He was still lying on the beach, and he was still, she noticed, looking as pale as the underbelly of a fish. Now she knew where that expression had come from, she thought randomly as she dropped to her knees in the sand and looked at her patient.

"Are you all right now?" she asked, ducking her head so that she could see beneath the hair that was hanging in his face, nearly obscuring his features. "I mean, do you think you're done being sick?"

He collapsed onto his back and raised one arm to shield his eyes from the sun. "Ow!" he said immediately, then gingerly touched a hand to his temple. "That's quite a lump. What happened?"

"You're asking *me?*" Suzi scrambled to her feet, holding out a hand to help him rise. He stood slowly, leaning heavily against her, one arm around her shoulders.

Her knees nearly buckled under his weight. "Hey, who do I look like, Superwoman? Come on. My house is right here. Try to help yourself a little bit, okay? You've got to be over six feet tall, and I'm a full foot shorter, and about one hundred and twenty pounds lighter—and that's not counting the fact that you're sopping wet and piled with sand."

He took a single step away from the beach.

"Well," she said, grimacing, "it's a start. Look, I could leave you here and go call the authorities. The tide's going out, so you'd be in no danger of washing out to sea again. Maybe that would be better."

Suddenly the man showed her a strength she hadn't supposed possible. "No. Not the authorities. I'll be all right, I assure you. Just let me hold on to you. I can make it."

"Great, now he thinks *he's* Superman!" Suzi mumbled, helping him as slowly, one small step at a time, they made their way back up the beach and onto the path leading to the condo.

They entered through the still-open door and Suzi steered him toward her bedroom, which was the only way she could steer him. She had learned as they made their way up the beach that he was like every grocery store shopping cart she had ever used—he might be capable of forward movement, but he could only make right turns.

Using her last possible burst of energy she propelled him toward the unmade bed, where he collapsed onto his back, immediately making a soggy mess of her freshly laundered sheets.

Patchwork, highly put out to see she had a bedmate, hopped down and exited the room, tail held high.

"Am I in heaven?" the man asked almost reverently as he looked up at her.

"Right," she answered curtly, sinking to the floor, her chest still heaving with her exertions of the past ten minutes. "And I'm the angel Gabriel. Don't worry, you're not dead. You just feel like you ought to be. So do I. I should get ten merit badges for this one! Now just let me catch my breath and I'll go call for help."

"No!" he commanded tersely, although his eyes were closed, as if he was too weary to keep them open. And his voice did have an unmistakable note of command, especially for somebody who, at the moment at least, most closely resembled a drowned rat. "You'll be well rewarded for your assistance—as well as your silence."

Her silence? She wasn't going to call Annoying Arnie and have it put out over the airwaves for a set of steak knives. All she wanted to do was call for help. What was with this guy, anyway?

"Look, mister, you've been injured. You've got a lump on the side of your head I could hang my hat on. You have a concussion, at the least, and might even have a fractured skull, which can be very dangerous. I'm no doctor, so it only makes sense for me to—"

"Stifle yourself! Good Lord, woman, is your tongue hinged at both ends?" he interrupted, frowning fiercely, then touched his chest, his neck, obviously searching for something. "My pouch. What have you done with my pouch, madam?" he asked a moment later, struggling to rise. "I must have my pouch!"

She wanted to kill him. She should be allowed to do that. It only seemed fair. After all, she had been the one who had saved him. Her tongue hinged at both ends, indeed. Who did this guy think he was—Wilbur?

"It's still on the beach," she told him, taking some small pleasure in the notion that her news wouldn't please him.

He turned his head to look at her, darn near pinning her to the floor with the heat of his gaze, then raised his hand to his temple and closed his eyes once more. "What is it doing there? Why did you leave it? Fetch it to me at once!"

"Fetch it yourself, bucko. I gave at the office," Suzi responded, rising to begin brushing the sand off her arms, her bare thighs. Damn, couldn't the guy at least say thank you?

What was in that pouch, anyway, his life savings? The man should be down on his knees, kissing her feet, grateful to be alive. "I'm going to take a quick shower in the guest bathroom, then call someone to take you away. You should have a doctor look at that bump on your head."

"Get me my pouch, woman!"

"Hey, now look—" Suzi began angrily, jamming her hands down on her hips. Then he opened his eyes once more, those gorgeous, black-lashed, heavenly blue-green eyes, and she knew she was beaten.

As she watched, he struggled to rise, only to fall back onto the pillows once more, exhausted. "Oh, what the hell," she said, shaking her head. "All right, I'll go get the thing. What's in it, anyway? And it better not be drugs!"

"Drugs? What would I do with drugs? I'm not an apothecary. It's my—my manuscript," he answered, curling his long body against the mattress. "Just fetch it. Please. And then let me rest here for a moment. Only for a while. Then I'll be on my way. I—I won't be any trouble. Any trouble at all."

"It's too late for that promise," Suzi told him, but he was asleep, his chest rising and falling rhythmically, his color already much improved.

She really should call the police, or at least go next door and phone for an ambulance. A couple of paramedics might come in handy. Yes, that's what she should do. Call for help. Lots of help.

But, as she retrieved the pouch from the beach—and picked up a couple of pieces of interesting looking driftwood for Mrs. O'Connell while she was at it—Suzi thought once more about the man's strange clothes, and his decidedly British accent. There was something very strange, and very strangely exciting about this whole business.

Maybe she should wait. After all, he was in no condition to hurt her. He couldn't lick his weight in sand flies at the moment.

She'd just take that shower she'd mentioned, brew a pot of coffee, and take a look at the guy's manuscript. A writer? Had he faked this whole thing so that she'd look at his work and maybe put in a good word with Wilbur or some other publisher?

It seemed like a pretty desperate act, but just look at that guy who had threatened to fly his private plane into one publisher's office a dozen or so years back. Stranger things had happened.

But a drowned man landing on her beach with his manuscript conveniently strapped to his body? It was just too farfetched. Nobody would believe it.

"Yes, they would, Suzie," she told herself as she dropped the pouch on the foyer floor and headed for the bathroom. "That's the great pity of the thing. You're *just* the sort of person these crazy things happen to—and it's beginning to get pretty darn boring!"

Chapter Two

Harry woke to the aroma of freshly brewed coffee, immediately aware that his stomach was empty and he was more than a little hungry.

He had barely eaten anything during the course of the storm, especially once the cook had slipped in the galley and broken his leg as the ship pitched in response to one of the larger waves.

The cook had spilled the pot of soup as he'd grabbed for a handhold as he went down too, which had been a damnable shame, for that soup had been intended for their supper.

But the sea was calm now, so the storm must be over at last, and none too soon.

He moved his legs tentatively, realizing that he was on a bed and not lying in the too-short hammock that had been his berth on the *Pegasus* for two months. He must be in the captain's cabin, although how he had come to be there he had no idea.

Yes, yes, he did. He had gone above decks, to take a

look at the coastline. He remembered that. He also remembered someone calling a warning to him, and then—and then?

Harry frowned, the action immediately sending a wicked pain through his skull. He lifted one hand to his temple and felt the lump that was just in front of his hairline.

That was it! He'd taken a whack to the noggin—a bruising blow, if he was to be considered any judge in the matter—and toppled overboard. Now, after being fished out of the sea, he was tucked up in the captain's cabin, recuperating.

But he was still all wet, even though someone had thought to throw a blanket over him. Ah, well. At least he was out of that miserable hammock.

He shifted slightly on the mattress, enjoying the decadence of crisp, clean, sweet-smelling sheets, then slowly forced open his eyes, intending to take an assessing look at the lap of luxury he'd just landed in.

"Bloody hell," he said a moment later, staring up at the circle of sharp metal blades hanging against the ceiling. What sort of ridiculous invention was that?

He turned his head to the left, to see that he was in a very large room—too large to be a ship's cabin—and it was filled with delicate white furnishings he immediately identified as being of Imperial French design.

French? Where the devil was he? And this wasn't just any room. It was a lady's bedchamber; he was convinced of it.

He turned to his right, his heart beginning to beat rapidly, and saw wedges of light coming through strange, narrow shutters, then blinked twice as he saw the painting on the wall directly across from the bed.

It was an enormous portrait of a young woman, a rather ethereally beautiful young woman who had been painted as she half reclined on some large boulders close by the sea, her hands braced behind her, her blond hair blowing in the breeze.

She looked like a fairy sprite, her pink-and-white flowered gown just skimming the tops of her bare feet, a large straw hat decorated with roses lying beside her on the rocks.

But it was her face that struck him, jabbing at his brain, mocking him with her laughing blue eyes.

Am I in heaven?

Right. And I'm the angel Gabriel.

"Bloody hell!" Harry exclaimed again, bolting upright, a reckless move that sent all the bells of Westminster Abbey to mercilessly clanging in his head at one time.

"Oh, good, you're awake. You've been sleeping for hours. I thought the smell of my special coffee might do the trick, although I think you should hop in the shower before you eat. Those wool slacks are beginning to smell. I'll probably have to buy a new mattress, but I suppose that's a small price to pay for being a heroine. Here, I ran out to one of the boardwalk shops that opens at eight-thirty and picked up some clothes for you. Even underwear. Your clothes are past saving, you know. The guest bathroom is that way, on the other side of the foyer."

She stopped talking for a moment, most probably to catch her breath. "Oh, and by the way, I'm Suzanne Harper, although I suppose you can call me Suzi, seeing as how you've been sleeping in my bed."

If the portrait hadn't jogged Harry's memory, the young woman's propensity for long-winded speeches would have served his purposes just as well.

She was dressed very informally in a vibrantly striped green-and-white dressing gown of some nubby material, her hair tied up on her head with an emerald green ribbon, her feet barely covered by strange, thonglike slippers.

She had worn green before, on the beach, although he

seemed to remember that she had been nearly naked, her long, straight legs visible for his inspection—not that he had been in any mood for seduction.

"You—you're the one who pulled me out of the sea, aren't you? I remember now. No one on the ship rescued me. You did. And you're an American, of course. I can tell by your accent. Where are we? Who holds control of this stretch of land—you, or us? Silly question. We don't control much of anything anymore, at least not below Canada. Not since that debacle at York. Have you rescued me simply to turn me over to your soldiers?"

"Oh, good. Oh, yes, this is good. This is just great," the woman who had introduced herself as Suzi said, backing toward the door, her hands held out in front of her as if preparing to ward him off if he should attack. "I've rescued a nut case! Why me? Why is it always me? Why not? Why should this time be different?"

She halted beside the open door and picked up a strange-looking bag, tossing it to him so that he instinctively caught it, then set it aside.

"Now listen, fella. I'm not looking for trouble. Here's your clothes. Just put them on and get out of here. Your pouch is on the foyer floor. I didn't even open it, promise! I'll be out on the beach—me *and* my purse—counting to one thousand. If you're not gone by then, I'm sending for the cavalry. You got that?"

"Wait!" Harry called out as she turned to make her escape—as if he was going to hurt her or something. He had to say something. Something that would make her stay. Something that would convince her that he meant no harm. If he left the safety of her house now, without any preparation, he'd be in an American prison before nightfall.

"I haven't thanked you yet, Miss Harper," he went on, deciding he'd attempt to be charming, which wasn't easy, for he felt like death. "You did a brave thing, rescuing a drowning man. You have my eternal gratitude."

"Well, I should most certainly hope so!" Suzi declared, turning back to look at him once more. He grinned, knowing his smile was rather endearing—or so many women had told him—and watched as she relaxed her guard slightly. "You know, I thought you were dead. But that CPR stuff is really something else. I'm rather proud of myself, actually."

"CPR? And what, Miss Harper, is CPR?"

"Oh, never mind. Um—look. You had quite a knock on the head, and I shouldn't be surprised if your brains are a little scrambled. Just forget what I said a moment ago. Take your time. Have your shower while I see about getting you something to eat. Use my bathroom—it's just through that door over there. Then you can be on your way. All right?"

Harry shoved back the constricting blanket, levered his legs over the edge of the bed and pushed himself to his feet. He had gone up on deck sans his boots and must have lost his stockings in the water, so that his legs were bare to the hem of his breeches.

Even his shirt had been torn open, so that he drew the edges of cloth together over his chest, doing his best to make a decent, nonthreatening appearance. After all, he still had quite a headache, and he didn't want to set her off again.

Not that hers wasn't a pleasant voice. He just didn't need to hear her talk so much—although he didn't mind looking at her. It had been well over two months since he'd been in the company of a beautiful woman.

"Thank you once more, Miss Harper," he drawled in his most congenial tone, pushing a hand through his drying, sea-salt sticky hair. "And perhaps you might be persuaded to have one of your servants draw me a tub as well. If it wouldn't be too much trouble, that is."

He watched, amazed, as her eyes nearly popped out of her head. "Servants? Draw you a *tub?*" She seemed to lose any fear she might have of him as she advanced once more into the room, shaking a finger at him—a finger painted a bright, vulgar red very much in contrast to her petite, blond beauty.

Had he ended up in the household of a well-financed courtesan? And, was that so bad? He could have washed up in front of a bear cave or something.

"Now look, mister," she continued heatedly, "fun's fun and all that, and I suppose you've got some sort of lingering concussion or something, but it's time to give it a rest. You're not in jolly old England now."

"I know," he answered, liking the way she challenged him, either unaware or uncaring of the fact that he was so much larger and stronger than she, and capable of silencing her with one hand. "I'm in America and, since you were the one to discover me, your prisoner, I suppose."

"My prisoner?" Suzie asked him, frowning, her arm dropping to her side. "My prisoner of *what,* for crying out loud?"

And she questioned *his* sanity? "Your prisoner of war, of course, madam. You have heard that we just recently captured one of your frigates, haven't you? I believe it was called the *Chesapeake.*"

"Uh-huh," Suzi mumbled, beginning to back toward the doorway once more. "The *Chesapeake.* That would be during the War of 1812, I believe, having just reviewed a really *dreadful* book on the subject. I gave it a scathing critique, too, now that I recall. Just because it's history, it doesn't have to be unremittingly boring, you know. I think I'm beginning to understand now. This is all some sort of twisted joke, isn't it? You wouldn't happen to be Professor Jonathan Blakeheart, would you? I mean, I've heard of some really rotten stunts being pulled by authors who got their noses in a snit because of a bad review, but—''

"You do enjoy listening to the sound of your own voice, don't you?'' Harry offered affably, slowly advancing toward her. "And a most lovely voice it is, too, not that I understand half of what you're saying. My name is Harry. Harry Wilde. Of Sussex. I'm a writer of sorts, even a historian, but most certainly not a professor. At the moment, however, I am a soldier, and your prisoner.''

"Uh-huh,'' she said again, her monosyllabic answers beginning to tear at his nerves even more than her earlier marathon speeches.

"Yes, well, I shan't be boring, shall I? But what's this about a war of 1812, Miss Harper? You speak as if it's already concluded. This is 1813, and we're still engaged in hostilities, although I don't believe either side has ever really had its heart in the thing. We English have enough on our plate with Napoléon still running about Europe unchecked.''

"1813,'' she repeated, picking up a hairbrush and brandishing it in front of her like a weapon. "Uh-huh. Sure it is—if you say so. And Napoléon, too. That's good, very good, tossing old Boney in there for good measure. I'm impressed. Really. Although I thought you people all believed you were Napoléon. Go on, Professor Blakeheart. Tell me more. I'm all ears!''

She was looking at him as if convinced he was mad— or some sort of impostor—a circumstance that was beginning to make him angry.

"Yes, and very lovely ears they are, although I don't believe there's anything of any great import between them,'' he countered, wishing he still didn't feel so damnably weak. "What's the matter with you, woman? It's 1813, just in the first days of August, although I've rather lost track these past few days, what with the storm raging about our heads and all. I'm English, you're an American—and our two countries are at war.''

"At war. America and England. Uh-huh," Suzi said again in that maddening singsong way he'd heard employed on children telling their elders whopping great fibs about ghosties and dragons they'd espied out under their beds in the middle of the night. She pointed toward the corner of the room and a strange, glass-fronted box that sat on a white pedestal. "And what's that?"

"What is what? That?" Harry shrugged, unable to understand her point. "That, Miss Harper, is some sort of box. A container for your personal belongings, perhaps? And enormously ugly, if you really desire my opinion. It clashes badly with the remainder of the room. Madam, what *are* you about?"

"It's a television set, you idiot—a *television*— and don't you go telling me it's a box!" Suzi all but screamed at him. "Just watch, as if you don't already know what's going to happen," she demanded, still brandishing the hairbrush as she skipped across the room, picked up a much smaller black box, this one in the shape of a flattened rectangle, and aimed it at the larger box. He heard a small *click.*

Harry flinched, expecting an imminent explosion, then looked, startled, as the larger box seemed to come to life, a colorful drawing appearing inside it. The drawing resembled a sailor, although he barely seemed human.

"I'm Popeye the sailor man," the drawing sang, swinging its large, grotesquely out of proportion arms, "I'm Popeye the sailor man—"

There was another slight *click* and the large box seemed to flicker once more, then go dark.

"All right, buster," Suzi challenged, stepping into his line of sight, blocking out the box. "I've got you now. So, tell me again. Is it 1813?"

"God's teeth, what a fascinating trick!" Harry, truly impressed, unceremoniously pushed her to one side and dropped to his knees in front of the box, placing his hands against the cool, dark glass.

"Where did he go?" he asked, turning to look at her, not sure if he should be frightened or impressed with this show of American ingenuity that was so much advanced of English shadowboxes, which were small, and handheld, and not nearly so clever. "What did you do with the sailor? And how did you make him talk?"

"You—you don't know?" The small rectangular box dropped to the floor. "No, of course you don't. Nobody could be such a good actor—especially not a professor. And you don't know what a shower is, do you? That's why you asked me to have a servant draw you a tub. Oh, you poor man. You need a doctor! You—you really do think this is 1813. Don't you?"

"Of course I do, because it *is*. It's 1813, and I just fell overboard from my ship after a storm. I say, Miss Harper, is there anyone else about I might speak with? Someone in authority? Your nurse—your *keeper?*" Harry said, then sat back on his heels and looked at her levelly, immediatey sorry he had insulted her. She didn't look too well all of a sudden; her cheeks were pale and her lovely blue eyes very wide. "Miss Harper? Are you all right?"

"He thinks it's 1813," Suzi said, as if to herself. "He doesn't *look* crazy. But he *has* to be crazy. Because if he's not...if he's *not*, then he really *is* from...but now he's *here*...and I'll have to tell him where he is...*when* he is—and—oh, dear Lord!"

She seemed to sway where she stood, so that Harry went to her quickly, taking hold of her upper arms just as her eyes rolled up in her head and she fell forward against his chest.

Chapter Three

Suzi came awake all at once, instantly realizing that she was lying on damp sheets.

What had happened to her? Had she fainted? Well, of course she had fainted! Who wouldn't faint when presented with the theory that the man she had saved from drowning was actually some sort of time traveller? Fainting was the least she should have done, with screaming and then running for her life still a viable second option.

"Ugh!" she protested, rolling onto her side, feeling the room spinning around her.

"Lie still, woman, or else you'll swoon again," Harry warned from somewhere above her. "I have enough on my plate as it is without that."

"Harry? You're still here?" Suzi asked, opening her eyes to see the handsome blond Englishman sitting on the edge of the bed. "I—I had rather hoped this was all some sort of nightmare and you'd be gone. But I should have known better. I wouldn't be that lucky."

She motioned for him to move aside and sat up, looking

straight at him. "Sorry I fainted. I'm not usually that sort, which is a pity because, if I could learn to swoon at will I could get myself out of some boring parties a lot easier."

Realizing she was babbling—something he obviously did not like, she shut up, remembering that she had something extremely important to tell him. But how?

"Harry?" she nervously ventured at last, deliberately avoiding his eyes. "Um, Mr. Wilde—there's something I have to tell you. Something I don't think you're going to want to hear. You see, although at first I thought you were pulling my leg, and then I thought maybe you were just rowing without both oars in the water, now I think that maybe, that just *maybe*—"

"I already know, Miss Harper," he interrupted her, so that she looked at him curiously.

"You already know? You already know what?"

"I know that this isn't 1813," he answered, running his fingers through his hair. His strong, well-shaped fingers. His romantically long dark blond hair. His wonderfully made body. His extremely handsome, appealing face.

Good Lord, Harper, what are you thinking? Are you out of your tiny mind? He's still all wet and caked with sand. And he's alone with you in your bedroom! Get up! Get out of this room before something terrible happens!

"How—how do you know that?" she asked, suddenly glad she had put her beach wrapper on over her bikini in order to go up on the boardwalk to buy her time traveler some underwear.

She couldn't imagine what might have happened—what sort of shock she might have placed on his nineteenth-century system—if she had walked into the room half-naked.

As it was, he probably thought she was a streetwalker, or a loose woman, or a camp follower, or whatever it was they called prostitutes in Regency England.

And so what if he did? It wasn't as if he'd be interested in her romantically. She was thirty-two years old, young by her standards, but positively ancient to a man who came from a society where any woman over the age of twenty-one was considered an old maid without a prayer of marriage. He was thirty-five if he was a day, and just right for her, age-wise—not that he'd think so.

Right for me? What am I thinking? Did I faint, or have some sort of mental collapse?

"Harry?" she repeated shakily when he didn't answer her question, but just sat there, fondling her remote control. "*How* you do know?"

"How? It's rather obvious, don't you think? Your very different-looking house, that box with the sailor inside it? I've never seen anything like either of them. You Americans might be inventive, but you aren't that much ahead of us. But, to be truthful, I used this," he said, holding up the remote control.

"You turned on the television? I'll bet that was a shock," Suzi inserted, giggling nervously and wondering if she shouldn't faint again. It seemed a reasonable alternative to what was taking place at the moment in her bedroom.

"Yes, it was, rather. I pushed the button labeled Power which seemed a logical choice, then a few other buttons, and a man inside that box over there told me. You called it a tele-vision machine? Interesting use of the language, I suppose. I don't know where the sailor man went. But it's not 1813. It's 1994."

Suzi rolled her eyes, wondering if, since it didn't seem as if she could faint, she might give some serious thought to taking up drinking. "Oh, brother, Harry. You *do* know."

"Yes, Miss Harper, although I don't quite understand the expression, I agree. *Oh, brother.*" He looked at her and laughed, rather endearingly, she decided.

"And it's August 4, 1994, to be precise about the thing,"

he told her incredulously. "The temperature at the Atlantic City Airport—he did say airport, I'm sure of that, not *sea*-port, so I imagine you Americans have mastered balloon flight, which was little more than a hobby in my day—is currently eighty-one degrees, the winds are out of the southwest at two knots and high tide is scheduled for three o'clock this afternoon. And, oh yes, there will be a buffet dinner tonight at an establishment called Jocelyn's, with all you can eat for a single price. Do you like shrimp? We'd have to peel it ourselves, but, I suppose that's a reasonable concession, considering we can eat until we're bilious."

"Oh, Harry, you poor man!" Suzi took hold of his arm, hurting for him. "You're frightened, aren't you?" she asked, knowing she would not be behaving half so well if she had been put into his position. Not her. She'd be racing around the room, crying for her mother! "Are you going to be all right?"

He placed a hand over hers. "I'll be fine, Miss Harper—Suzi. Just fine. I think."

He scratched his upper arm. "Although I still would like that tub. I'm beginning to offend myself, and I ache all over, as if I tumbled head over heels along the sea floor all the way from 1813. God's teeth, do you hear me? I should, by all rights, be dead. But I'm not. I'm alive, and I'm in 1994! What a grand adventure! It's astounding. Simply astounding!"

Oh, he was cool, Harry Wilde was, Suzi decided. A real stiff-upper-lip Englishman and all that sort of rot. But he had to be dying inside, just *dying!*

"Pick up that bag and follow me," she told him, scoot-ing off the bed and heading for her bathroom. "If you think the television machine is something, you're going to *love* my shower massage attachment!"

In the end, Suzi had to turn on the shower for him, adjust the temperature and then, after removing the tags from

Harry's new clothes, stand outside the door, waiting for him to finish.

That took some time, and probably most of her hot water, so that she decided against another shower herself and hid in her walk-in closet while she stripped out of her bikini.

She then dived into underwear and the single dress she had brought with her from Manhattan, and was back standing in front of the closed bathroom door a good five minutes before Harry popped his head out.

His hair was still wet, although he had brushed it back from his forehead, its length nothing out of the ordinary, thanks to current styles.

And he was smiling again, so that she could smell her minty toothpaste on his breath. She always kept a supply of guest toothbrushes at the condo, because friends who visited her from New York rarely arrived with them. She had decided it had something to do with living in the center of the world, where everything from antipasto to ironing boards was readily available from room service.

"So that's a shower, Miss Harper? Outstanding! Really. One minute it's there, warm and wet, and with the push of a knob—presto!—it's gone. I'm extremely impressed. However, grateful as I am for all your kindnesses, I don't believe I can wear these—these articles of *clothing* you've purchased."

"Why not?" Suzi inquired blankly.

He sighed, rolling his eyes, then stepped out into the bedroom and turned in a full circle in front of her.

His long, straight, golden hair-dusted legs and really A-1 rear end certainly did justice to the white duck shorts, and the navy blue muscle shirt bearing the words It's Better in Ocean City showed off his slim waist and broad shoulders—not to mention his blond hair—to advantage.

In short, Harry Wilde was a hunk, no matter what century he'd hailed from.

"So?" Suzi asked, wincing as she heard the nervous squeak in her voice. "Where's the problem?"

"Don't be obtuse, Miss Harper." Harry bit out the words, once more rubbing the bruise at his temple. "I saw the man in the box—in the tele-vision machine. He wasn't outfitted in such a ramshackle manner. He had on a shirt, a jacket and some odd sort of wildly dotted neck cloth. It wasn't precisely like that of the Four Horse Club, but then I've always thought that outfit and the membership in general, to be a trifle overdone. In any event, he didn't look anything like this."

"Oh, good. The man's a prude," Suzi said, wrinkling her nose.

"And what's this?" he went on, pulling at the white, ironed-on print on the front of his shirt. "*What's* better in Ocean City? And where—I must add—is Ocean City? Why would anyone call a city after an ocean? Seems to smack of a lack of imagination, don't you think?"

"*This* is Ocean City, Harry," she answered, beginning to see the humor in the thing, "and I suppose you're right. The founding fathers could have called it Stratford-on-Atlantic, or something equally romantic. And I'm sorry about the shirt."

She imagined he had never come across T-shirt advertising and manufacturer's logos on clothing from his time. Beau Brummell, she was convinced, would never have approved. "Everyone wears shirts like that while they're on vacation." She giggled as he rolled his eyes in exasperation. "Just be happy I didn't get you one of the raunchier ones."

"Go on, Miss Harper. Indulge yourself to the top of your bent at my expense. Enjoy yourself. You may believe it is acceptable to parade about with newsprint all over you, and showing your limbs to all and sundry, but *I* do not."

"Yup. A prude."

"Don't look down your nose at me, madam. I don't wish to call attention to myself, reveal my dilemma, until I have sufficient time to take stock of my situation, as—priding myself in the notion that the countryside isn't littered with century-hopping Englishmen—I have no wish to become some sort of scientific oddity. Therefore, I suggest you go out to these shops you mentioned once more, and this time return with something more suitable."

"If you go out on the beach in a business suit you might as well set off a few flares as well, shouting to everyone that you're out of place. And, Harry, you really do have to stop ordering me around. It's beginning to wear thin, okay?"

His smile turned her knees to water.

"Look," Suzi ended quickly, pushing him toward the spiral staircase in the foyer, "I know this is difficult to understand, but Ocean City is a resort, and people come here because they don't have to wear suits or ties—outfits and neck cloths to you."

She led him upstairs and pointed toward the living room, which she had only recently redecorated in lovely eighteenth-century reproductions, which should have made him feel somewhat at home.

"Open the door that leads onto the deck—um, the porch? The balcony? The portico?" she instructed, madly groping for the correct term. "And I'll join you outside in a moment with our coffee. While you're waiting, take a look at the people down on the beach. You'll get the idea soon enough."

Suzi waited until he had pushed back the sliding screen, then raced into the kitchen, pouring out two cups of coffee from the percolator.

Then, as she had never purported to be a gourmet chef, she quickly toasted two iced strawberry Pop-Tarts, threw them on napkins and headed for the deck, their makeshift breakfast on a plastic tray she'd already equipped with containers of cream and sugar.

"How are you doing?" she asked, her back to him as she placed the tray on the glass-topped round table. Turning, she saw that he was standing at the far railing of the deck, alternately looking down at the beach and to the wide variety of beachfront condos lining the area as far to the north and south as he could see.

"I don't believe it," he said, his voice awestruck. "I don't bloody believe it! When I saw this place from the deck of the *Pegasus* it was nothing but sand and brush and birds. Have you Americans wrought a miracle, or cut a swath of destruction? Is this paradise—or hell?"

"Hell?" Suzi glanced to her right and left, then frowned. "I don't get it. You're looking at some of the choicest, highest priced real estate in Ocean City—and I've got the property tax receipt to prove it. Why would you think this is hell?"

He turned to her, grinning. "Well, not hell, precisely, and I suppose I shouldn't be surprised to see some development after one hundred and eighty-one years."

"Yes," Suzi said, noticing the way the sun lit small golden fires in his long hair, "we have managed to invent a thing or two."

"Of course. After all, my parents had never seen a gaslight, or water closets, in their youth. Each new generation does bring progressive thinking with it. But this place does smack of Sodom and Gomorrah, doesn't it, of a future run amuck? For instance, does everyone in America traipse around in public in their underclothes?"

Suzi shrugged. "Are you still complaining, Harry? Just think about it. You could have traveled *backward* through time and ended up in the seventeenth century. Which do you prefer—looking like a blond cover model, sure to be drooled over by all the voluptuous young women you see on the beach below us, or being surrounded by women dressed all in ugly gray wool from their toes to the tops of their heads, and then summarily being burned at the stake as some sort of warlock?''

"You have a point, madam, although I don't understand that term—cover model," Harry said, giving one last, rather interested look toward the beach and the half dozen bikini-clad young women playing volleyball on the sand. "Perhaps it is better in Ocean City after all. Would that by chance be my coffee?"

She followed him back to the table, deliberately seating herself in the shade of the umbrella stuck into the center of the glass top, because she was a natural blonde, and her skin tended to burn whenever she was even close to the sun.

"That's a pastry, sort of," she told him, pointing to the Pop-Tart. "Try it, you'll like it. But don't worry that you'll starve to death. I've already decided to phone my house-keeper in New York and have her come stay with us, be-cause I don't think you're ready to eat at Jocelyn's—or any public place—at least not until you get used to being here."

Harry was already finished with his pastry and eyeing hers, so that she pushed it toward him. "Agreed," he said, taking a sip of coffee. "Do you think I'll be *here* for long?"

Suzi sat back against the orange-and-white director's chair and crossed her legs.

"Be here long? Cripes, Harry, how should I know? I don't know the faintest thing about time travel—because that's what you did, you know—travel through time. Unless I *have* gone bonkers, and a figment of my fertile imagina-tion has just downed two strawberry Pop-Tarts in sixty sec-onds flat."

"I think it had something to do with the storm," Harry told her, ignoring her suggestion that he might not be real.

"One of the sailors said I was to stay belowdecks, to keep out of the 'eye,' but I didn't listen to him."

"Yes, that's a failing of yours I already recognize," Suzi said, smiling.

He wagged his finger at her as if trying to put that finger on the solution to his journey from 1813. "That's it, of course. That strange storm. Everything has an explanation, if you only look for it. However, as I don't intend to brave any more storms from the deck of a ship, I suppose I am here to stay. There is no one in Sussex who will miss me, as I was an only child and my parents are deceased these last five years. I will just build myself a new life here in America. Yes, I believe I can live with that answer."

"I don't think you have a heck of a lot of choice, Harry, considering that you're stuck with having to make sense of the impossible or else lose your marbles. The real question is—can *I* learn to live with that answer?" Suzi teased, grinning openly now.

Really, Harry Wilde was a dear man. A little autocratic, but very dear. "However," she continued, "since we have no other choice but to work with the idea that you're here for keeps I'll have to get cracking. You can't live in that single outfit. And you don't even have shoes, just those thongs. I guess there's a silver lining to everything, Harry, because now I get to go shopping."

"Allow me to correct you, Suzi—please don't mind the informality, but you have, you know, been addressing me as Harry all morning long—*we* must go to the shops. I don't believe I care for your taste."

"You don't care for my—hey! The door's open downstairs, Harry, old sport. Feel free to leave at any the time. I'm sure you'll do just great out there on your own, with no money, and without the faintest idea how to behave."

He reached out and took her hand, sending a curious

shiver up her arm—as if he didn't know that! "Now, Suzi, don't cut up stiff on me. I meant no harm."

She continued to glare at him, wishing he weren't so handsome when he smiled, wishing she wasn't such a gullible fool, wishing he was a nice, safe investment banker from the upper East Side with his own apartment and a Volvo whom she could take home to mother— if she still *had* a mother, which she didn't, so what did it matter, anyway?

But he *was* so very handsome, and she *was* a fool more accustomed to being tumbled around in the middle of an adventure than being boring and safe, and she was stuck here in her Ocean City condo with a romantic-looking, arrogant Regency hero in a muscle shirt.

Besides, hearing him say "Suzi" in his crisp English accent tickled her senses. Only slightly, of course. She wasn't the sort of female to go goo-goo over a man because of his accent. Was she?

No matter what, she might as well relax and go with the flow. After all, just like Harry, what other choice did she have?

"Look, Harry," she said, sighing. "Let's be reasonable about this, all right? You're not, as they say, really ready for prime-time playing yet, okay? So you just stay here— there's a television set in the living room you can watch while I'm gone—and I'll go buy you some more clothes. I'll even rustle up a couple of sandwiches—that's meat on bread—to hold you over until lunch."

"I would appreciate that very much, Miss Harper—Suzi. I feel as if I haven't eaten in a century, or perhaps two centuries."

"Very funny. Maybe you have a future as a comic. But don't worry. If you're lucky, Mrs. O'Reilly will be here before dinner tonight, so you won't starve. Between now and then, I'll take you on a tour of the condo, show you the light switches and all that stuff—don't ask, I'll explain later—and clue you in on a few things so you don't goof up and give yourself away. All right?''

Harry stood, and sliced another longing look toward the beach and, Suzi thought, bristling, the tanned, giggling, *bouncing* volleyball team. "Agreed, Suzi. Consider me your servant. Lead me to your tele-vision machine."

"You called me in Tokyo to ask me *what?* And at this hour of the night? Suzi, I've known and loved you for a long time, and I have tried with, I will admit, only varying levels of success, to understand how your mind works. I did my best to understand why you put a red rinse in your hair and served borscht at your dinner party after reading *The Hunt For Red October* as a way of showing appreciation for the book.''

"I know, Courtney," Suzi said into the telephone she'd reluctantly had hooked up to service the day after Harry's appearance in her life, "and I'm grateful. But it wasn't just a dinner. It was my try at performance art, and you don't have to tell me how terrible it turned out. I had to wash my hair twice a day for a month to get rid of that rinse.''

"Yes, well. That's only one example, Suzi. There's more. I didn't say anything when you took up skydiving because you thought it would be a good way to meet men who didn't still live with their mothers. And I refused to listen to Adam's rather biting remarks on the Op-ed piece you wanted to publish in the *Times* about favoritism toward the right-handed in today's society. But this tops Adam's list of 'the ten most unexplainable things Suzi's ever done!' And another thing—"

Suzi rolled her eyes at Harry and smiled at the receiver as she held it away from her ear. "Bad connection," she whispered, covering the mouthpiece, and Harry nodded, then pressed the remote control, once again on the lookout for the weathergirl on Channel Seven.

Suzi would be jealous, if she cared about Harry in "that" way, but as she didn't—well, she kept telling herself she didn't—she didn't mind that the weathergirl reminded him of someone he knew a long time ago. One hundred and eighty-one years ago, to be precise.

She placed the receiver against her ear once more to hear her good friend, Courtney Blackmun, bestselling novelist and wife of Adam Richardson, the senior senator from New Jersey, end with a sigh, "And why would you want to write a time-travel novel in the first place? You've always said the last, the very *last* thing you'd ever want to do is write a book. You said that it's far easier to be a reviewer and stand back launching grenades into the literary world than it would ever be to step onto the battlefield itself so someone like yourself could take potshots at you. That is what you said, isn't it?"

"Did I?" Suzi asked, pulling a face. "That sounds entirely too militaristic for me, Court. But listen. I apologize again for not thinking of the time difference, but I really do need help with this synopsis I'm writing. You did get my fax, didn't you? The one where I outlined my idea?"

"Yes, Suzi, I got it. But it's two a.m. here, and I'm exhausted. Can't I phone you in the morning? Adam has to meet with one of the Japanese foreign ministers, and I'll be free until four."

"Oh, sure," Suzi said, grimacing. "But by then it will probably be the middle of the night *here,* so that wouldn't work. Look, Courtney, old buddy, I said I'd never be so mean as to ever hold it over your head that I was the one who found Adam for you—"

"You loaned me your condo because I was suffering from writer's block, Suzi. *I* found Adam."

"Yeah, well, that's just semantics, isn't it? Like the way

I took Sydney off your hands so you could be alone with
Adam until you figured out he was right for you, even
though *I* knew that the first moment I laid eyes on him. I
did tell you how your dear daughter ran poor Mrs. O'Reilly
bonkers with her practical tricks, didn't I? Not that I'm
complaining, especially now that Syd's married and settling
down, but you'd think, after all these years, that you might
consider that you owed me one *teensy-weensy* little favor—"

"Break the connection, Suzi," Harry ordered imperiously, clicking off the television set. "Begging is beneath
you, and most unbecoming in a lady of your age."

Suzi quickly covered the receiver and glared at Harry.
Did he always have to harp on her age? Anyone would
think she was old enough to be his mother!

"Will you please be quiet? This is women's business.
It's how we operate. I'll have her wrapped around my little
finger in three seconds flat. I—" She yanked the receiver
back to her ear. "What did you say? Oh, Courtney, you're
a doll! You want to know what? How long I've been working on this idea?"

She winced, looking to Harry, who was beginning to
look more at home in her living room than Patchwork, who
had shifted her loyalty to the newcomer and now slept at
the foot of his bed. "Oh, about three weeks," she said,
biting her bottom lip. "It's been going along pretty well so
far, but now I've come to a sticky part."

"Trying to find a way to get identification for your time
traveler," Courtney said. "Yes, I saw that in the fax. It's
a tricky question. In fact, the whole notion of dealing with
a man from another time is tricky."

"You don't know the *half* of it, Court," Suzi responded
feelingly, looking toward her "tricky question," who was
just then slipping on his sneakers, as if planning to go out
on the beach without her—something she had expressly

forbidden him to do. Not that her threats had stopped him
yet.

The next time she went shopping she was going to buy
him a leash! She covered the receiver yet again and barked,
"Harry—*sit! Stay!*"

"Suzi? Do you have someone else there with you?"
Courtney asked.

"Someone else with me?" Suzi parroted, smiling grimly
as Harry winced at hearing her words and, for once, obeyed
her. "No, Court. That's just the television. But I turned it
off now. So, don't keep me in suspense. If you were writing
this book, how would you handle the problem of identification?"

"I asked Adam," Courtney told her, and Suzi, hearing
those magic words, immediately reached for a pen in order
to take notes.

To Suzi's mind, asking Adam was almost on a par with
anything to be found written on clay tablets—sensible, be-
lievable, and as safe as money in the bank. After all, not
only was Adam a senator, but he was being touted as a
vice-presidential nominee in the next election.

"Go on, Court," Suzi urged as Harry rose and came
across the room to stand behind her, bending down to look
over her shoulder at the still-blank piece of paper lying on
the eighteenth-century English design mahogany desktop.
"Tell me what he said. Tell me everything."

"Adam *said*," her friend informed her, "that for any
alien—that includes your time traveler, Suzi—to gain identification without going through the normal immigration
channels is illegal."

Suzi wrote it down: *illegal.*

"I can see now why he's such a trusted friend, Suzi,"
Harry sarcastically whispered into her free ear. "It takes a
brilliant, top-rate mind to deduce that what we're asking to

do is in violation of every legal precedent. I heard that term on CNN the other night," he added, smiling.

"Would you *please* put a lid on it," Suzi mouthed quietly, levering her free arm backward to give him a push. The man was a dedicated television junkie, and had learned more about her world in the past three weeks than she had cared to absorb in thirty-two years.

"However," Courtney went on, "as this is purely a fictional situation, as everyone knows time travel is nothing more than a romantic imagining..."

"Yeah, Court, pure fiction! You got that right," Suzi said brightly, once more turning her back on her resident fictional character.

"Yes, well," Courtney went on as Suzi began to feel *really* impatient with her friend, "seeing that it couldn't hurt to use such a device in fiction, Adam told me the best way for your hero to get bogus identification is through a criminal specializing in such things. There are probably a couple dozen people in that line of work in Manhattan alone, or so Adam told me. It's a problem he's trying to deal with in Washington."

"Really?" Suzi wrote: *problem.*

"Yes, indeed. The government is attempting to crack down on the practice at the federal level, and Congress wants to impose really stiff jail penalties for anyone who fakes an identification. Suzi? Are you still there? Did you hear me? Are you writing this down?"

"Sure, Court. Every word," Suzi promised, sitting stock-still, her pen frozen in her hand, her stomach suddenly relocating itself somewhere near her toes as she saw herself in prison stripes. "Every single word."

Chapter Four

Harry watched Suzi as she walked out of the ocean and pulled off her ridiculously flowered bathing cap, shaking her head so that her blond hair fell free and rearranged itself in a sleek curtain around her face.

A modern-day Venus rising from the sea, he thought, sighing, wondering if any artist, past or present, could do her justice.

Then his eyes fell to her figure, and the bright green bikini that had become the centerpiece of his daydreams these past two weeks or more, since she'd let him out of the house after their first, chaotic week of trying to get used to the idea that he had arrived in New Jersey direct from Regency England.

And it wasn't the house, but the *condo,* he corrected himself punctiliously, for he was always working, always concentrating on trying to become the complete gentleman of the late twentieth century.

Except when he was concentrating on Suzi's bikini, that was, and how she would look without it.

Thirty-two. The number was enough to boggle the mind. Ladies of two and thirty were supposed to be matrons, happily raising their children and bedeviling their husbands for gaming too deep, or on-the-shelf spinsters, definitely past their last prayers, and wearing silly white caps that tied beneath their chins.

Not that he'd say anything remotely like that to Suzanne Harper, who didn't seem to have the slightest notion that she was an old maid.

"Ah! That felt good! The water's always beautifully warm in August," Suzi declared, dropping to her knees on the blanket, dripping water everywhere.

"You are a creature of sensations, aren't you, Suzi? The texture of fudge against your teeth, the smell of the ocean, the feel of the waves breaking against your body. You're almost childlike sometimes," he commented, wiping stray droplets of water from the pages of the book he'd been trying, without much success, to read.

Watching Suzi jump the waves was far more interesting than history.

"So what? Don't patronize me, Harry. Really, you ought to try it, instead of roasting here on the blanket, reading Professor Blakeheart's book. No matter how you slice it, the war ended in a draw. Although I still think it stinks that you guys burnt down our capital."

"Why? From what I've seen on the news programs, your own citizens are doing a pretty good job of destroying the entire city, one block at a time. Aren't you chilled?"

He looked at her as she unashamedly knelt in front of him; her hair delightfully mussed, her small nose sun-kissed, small rivulets of water lazily running down her body, along her feminine curves, sliding beneath the slick green fabric just at the enticing curve of her breasts.

A single droplet leisurely made its way lower, toward her navel, coming to rest in that delightful indentation.

He really wished she wouldn't sit so close. She was beginning to interfere with his breathing.

"Cold? No, not really. Oh, I get it. You want me to cover up, don't you? You're such a gentleman, Harry, if a bit stuffy sometimes." Suzi obligingly slipped her head and arms into the green-and-white striped caftan and wriggled its length down over her hips before sitting back on the blanket. "There. Better now?"

Harry swallowed once, trying to bring some moisture into his suddenly dry mouth. "Much. I know I've attempted to conform to your American mores, and I agree that you are wearing nothing out of the ordinary, but for the life of me I can't seem to become accustomed to this practice of parading about half naked. My friends and I used to watch ladies descending from their carriages, praying for a glimpse of ankle."

As he said the words his mind conjured up a mental picture of Suzi as she would appear in Regency dress. Her small, slim body fashionably clothed in dainty sprigged muslin, a large straw hat fetchingly tied beneath her chin, a silly parasol shading her little nose from the sun as she sat up beside him and they tooled his horses through the park for the promenade.

He swallowed again, the thought doing more to excite him, and his imagination, than the reality of Suzi in her bright green bikini.

How strange. How exceedingly strange.

"You know, Harry," Suzi said, interrupting his uncomfortable thoughts just as he was imagining what it would be like to shock the *ton* by kissing Miss Suzanne Harper in the middle of Hyde Park, "we'll soon have to go back to Manhattan. I'd only planned to stay at the condo until the end of August, and although I could do my reviews from here, I've got a few social engagements for September that I simply can't get out of. Especially Wilbur's dinner party. Nobody misses one of those."

"Wilbur," Harry repeated, nodding. "That would be Wilbur Langley, head of Langley Publishing. He's the one you said might be able to help us get identification after you all but hung up on your friend Courtney the other night without listening to what she had to say. How would a publisher know about such things?"

Suzi rolled her huge, beguiling eyes. "Wilbur, dear Harry, knows something about *everything*. That's a large part of his charm. I don't know why I didn't go to him in the first place. Wilbur's a real Renaissance man, with a lovely touch of Phineas T. Barnum thrown in. Phineas T. was a showman—you know, a circus master?"

"He puts on horse shows, like at Astley's in London?" Harry was confused, not an unusual circumstance these past three weeks and two days, but one he was becoming used to. "I don't understand."

Suzi ran a hand through her hair, a habit she had whenever she was thinking deeply. "Wrong analogy. Sorry about that. I keep forgetting that your English and American English are sometimes two different languages. No, he doesn't show horses."

"You'll have to explain."

"I'm trying, Harry. Wilbur is—well, Wilbur is just Wilbur. He's crowding seventy now, although you'd never believe it to look at him. He's got more money than almost anyone I know and only dabbles in the publishing business anymore, allowing his ex-son-in-law, Daniel Quinn, to take care of everything. You'll love Daniel and his wife, Joey. She was once his chauffeur—his coachman—but now she's a bestselling author. They have four of the most wonderful children…"

She raised a hand to wave off his questions. "Never mind. It would be impossible to explain. Besides, I'm get-

ting off the point. Wilbur is a patron of the arts, knowl-
edgeable in politics and finance, and a lover of fine foods,
although he's also got a puckish love of mischief in his
soul. He dresses like something straight out of GQ, that's
a man's fashion magazine, and still has women falling all
over him.''

Suzi sighed. "I guess you could say he's a Regency gentleman. Yes! That's it! Wilbur's a cross between Beau
Brummell, Lord Byron and your Prince Regent."

"He's sounds extremely interesting, if a bit intimidating." Harry stood and shook out the blanket, as Suzi gathered up her belongings in preparation for a return to the
condo. "When can I meet him?"

"Meet him? You've been out in the sun too long." Suzi
laughed out loud, a lovely, trilling laugh that Harry had
already learned he enjoyed hearing. "Good Lord, Harry,
I'd never let you *meet* him!"

They trekked back through the hot sand, heading for the
condo. "Now I am confused," Harry admitted, opening the
door and taking hold of Suzi's arm, keeping her from heading straight for the shower. "Why can't I meet the man?
Are you afraid I'll give myself away? I didn't raise anyone's suspicions last night, when you took me to that
strange restaurant."

"Oh, yeah. Right. You asked for a finger bowl, Harry,
for crying out loud. At a place with golden arches outside.
Harry, at a fast-food restaurant that doesn't even include
plates with the meal, didn't you think you might have been
pushing things just a little?"

"All right. So I made one simple mistake," he conceded,
remembering the look on the attendant's face when he'd
asked for the finger bowl after being forced to eat his french
fries with his hands.

And he would admit he was still having some difficulty
resigning himself to the idea that people would wish to

wipe their mouths with paper rather than finely pressed linen, too, but he wouldn't bore Suzi with that complaint again.

"But," he persisted, "this Langley fellow sounds like a fine sort, a man of the world. We'd probably rub along together extremely well."

"Uh-uh. No. Not in this lifetime. Trust me in this, Harry. We don't want Wilbur within ten miles of you. I'll just use the same story on him that I used on Courtney. And you have to admit it was a brilliant idea. Good old Court fell for it without a hitch, and I see no reason for Wilbur to sniff out a problem."

"Really, my dear? And I had so thought you believed me to be penetratingly astute. How sad."

Both Harry and Suzi whirled to face the still-open door.

"Wilbur!" Suzi exclaimed, quickly shaking her arm free of Harry's grip. "Darling! How good to see you." Her eyes narrowed speculatively as she took a single step toward the man standing in the doorway, then stopped. "Er, exactly *why* am I seeing you, Wilbur?"

Harry stood by silently, taking his measure of the tallish man who, with a wave of one manicured hand and a slight bow of his silvery head, wordlessly asked permission to enter the foyer of the condo, then allowed Suzi to kiss his cheek.

Now here was a man who knew how to outfit himself, Harry decided, instantly impressed with the publisher's light gray, double-breasted suit, the startlingly white, highly starched shirt with collar edges as sharp as knifepoints, the mauve silk neck cloth—his *necktie,* he mentally corrected—exquisitely arranged and neatly accented by a small diamond stickpin.

"You're seeing me, dear Suzi, because our mutual friend and your self-appointed guardian, Courtney, telephoned me from Tokyo begging me to come to this backwater because *our* mutual friend—that would be you, Suzi—is once more showing signs of having perhaps taken an unfortunate, brain-scrambling blow to the head. From what I overheard as I arrived, I'd say Courtney has once more proven herself to be the next best thing to a soothsayer. Was it a topple down those ridiculous spiral stairs that did the damage this time?''

Sensing Suzi's panic, and not the sort to comfortably fade into the background, Harry stepped forward, his right hand outstretched, a bright smile on his face, and said bracingly, ''Mr. Langley, how very good to meet you. Allow me to introduce myself. The name is Wilde. Harry Wilde, on holiday from Britain. Please excuse my ramshackle attire. Won't you please come upstairs to the sitting room? Mrs. O'Reilly, Suzanne's housekeeper, is not in at the moment, having discovered a kindred spirit in Suzanne's neighbor, Mrs. O'Connell, so that she spends the majority of her time with the lady. But I am convinced Suzanne is up to brewing us a pot of tea. Suzanne?''

''Hmm?'' Suzi questioned distractedly, looking to him with naked appeal in her large blue eyes. ''I missed something. What did you say, Harry?''

''He said,'' Wilbur intervened smoothly, winking at Harry, ''that you should run along now to have your shower and put on your prettiest dress so that we might allow my chauffeur to drive us to Atlantic City for dinner. You're rather sandy, in case you haven't noticed, and smell of the sea. Harry will join me upstairs, where we men will somehow manage to make our own tea sans Mrs. O'Reilly's assistance. Take your time, my dear. I am convinced Harry and I will be able to entertain ourselves in your absence. He can bathe and dress later, while you and I catch up on all the New York gossip you've missed.''

''Oh, no,'' Suzi protested, grabbing Harry's arm as if afraid he was going to immediately announce that he was a traveler who was visiting from Britain, all right—from nineteenth-century Britain. "That can't be what Harry said, Wilbur. I mean—"

"Suzanne." Harry bit out the word through clenched teeth, his tone heavy with meaning, which he knew might frighten her, but then there were times when a gentleman had to assert himself. "Please go do as Mr. Langley says. We'll be just fine."

Harry felt sorry for Suzi, he really did, but he had a strong urge to be alone with Mr. Wilbur Langley for a few minutes, to engage the man in conversation—if only to test himself on what he believed to be his rather excellent acclimatization to the twentieth-century world.

Besides, if he could learn the name of the man's tailor it would go a long way toward reconciling himself to his temporary, and totally unsuitable Ocean City wardrobe. At the moment, he was feeling decidedly underdressed in his bathing trunks and the same muscle shirt Suzi had presented him with that eventful morning three short weeks ago.

"Oh, all right," Suzi declared at last, looking as if she was about to burst into tears. "But don't you dare say anything—" she sneaked a quick look at Wilbur, then blurted, rather helplessly, Harry thought "—anything about *us*."

"Ah! Do I sense a blossoming romance?" Wilbur inquired, waving a blushing Suzi on her way and motioning for Harry to precede him up the spiral staircase. "How very intriguing, to say the least. I never pictured Suzi with an Englishman. A fortune-hunting race car driver or globetrotting polo player perhaps, although I suppose that wouldn't preclude the man's being English."

Harry bit on his bottom lip, knowing he should say nothing about the glaringly obvious fact that, at thirty-two, Suzi was more than a little long in the tooth to interest him, and led the way up to the sitting room. No. The *living* room.

Had he already slipped, and referred to it as the sitting room? That would be too bad. Really, he must monitor his tongue every moment if he and Suzi were to carry this off!

"As it's already gone five, I don't believe I should mind a glass of sherry as a substitute for tea," Wilbur said as he settled himself into a chair as if very much at home in the condo. "Suzi keeps some for me, as I recall, for I am always finding myself summoned to this place, tending to various crises in the lives of all my favorite people. Courtney and her Adam, her darling daughter, Sydney, this past year, and of course to visit with Daniel and Joey and my grandchildren. I must consider purchasing my own domicile on the beach. It is rather relaxing here, isn't it, in its own small way?"

Harry sought out the sherry and three glasses, smiling noncommittally as he took up a chair across from Wilbur's. "So, Mr. Langley," he said after a long moment during which he could feel the older man inspecting him, "you've heard from Miss Blackmun? Was it something to do with Suzi's desire to write a novel?"

"Ah, you know about that, do you? It would prove extremely interesting—a novel written by our dearest Suzi. Although I don't believe I'll ever see the completed manuscript." Wilbur's vivid blue eyes narrowed as if measuring him in some way. "That would place you in this condo for some time, wouldn't it? Did you meet on the beach? A romantic place, the Ocean City beach, if my past experience with beautiful New York women transported to its smooth sands is any indication."

Harry looked into his glass, deliberately avoiding Wilbur's all-too-intelligent eyes. "Yes, as a matter of fact, Mr. Langley, we did meet on the beach. Just at dawn. It was highly romantic, actually."

"Yes, Suzi is very into romantic situations. Also bizarre situations, as I know to my sorrow. She can't help it.

Things just seem to *happen* to Suzi. Strange things that would never happen to anyone else.'' He paused for a moment, definitely, Harry decided, for effect, then asked, "Are you a strange thing, Harry?"

Suzi had been right this time, Harry decided, hiding a grimace. He shouldn't have come within ten miles of Wilbur Langley. "Strange, Mr. Langley?" he repeated, trying to chuckle. "In what way?"

Wilbur smiled. "Time will tell, won't it, Harry? And, please, call me Wilbur. Everyone does."

"All right. Wilbur." Harry knew the man was trying to put him at his ease, and he fought the sensation to allow him to succeed. "You mentioned Atlantic City earlier, Wilbur. I believe Suzi mentioned something about games of chance in that city. Do you gamble?"

"I'm in publishing, Harry. That, in my humble opinion, is always a gamble. To take someone's idea, someone's vision of reality, and turn it into a successful piece of fiction—I do adore fiction, you understand—is always a gamble. Do you read, Harry?"

Harry closed his eyes for a moment, doing his best to recall the name of a contemporary author he'd seen on a television talk show the day before. It wouldn't do him much good to name Shakespeare, or Milton, or Sheridan, as his favorites, and it might do him great harm.

"Grisham," he said at last, smiling as his mind captured the name. "John Grisham. He's quite interesting, don't you think? And extremely successful."

"Immensely," Wilbur answered, taking another sip of sherry. "Although my taste runs more to romantic fiction than legal thrillers. Are you, perhaps, like Mr. Grisham, a lawyer?"

Very neat, Wilbur, Harry thought. You pry, but you pry discreetly. "No," he answered, smiling. "For my sins, I,

too, am a writer. Although I have not as yet seen any of
my work published.''

''A writer? A novelist, perhaps? Perhaps I have stumbled
on something. Perhaps you are a novelist attempting to
write a novel on *time travel?* That would make more sense
than trying to believe that Suzi has decided to dabble in
science fiction.''

Harry felt his hackles beginning to rise. ''I am not attempting to use Suzi in order to establish a career, Wilbur.
I am not without my own resources.'' He said this last
without flinching, although he knew whatever ''resources''
held in his name in his London banks and on the Exchange
had long since gone either to his third-cousin heirs or the
Crown.

''Dear boy, whatever makes you think I am suggesting
anything of the kind? It can only be a coincidence that you
have taken up residence here with Suzi—and you have
taken up residence here, haven't you? It can only be a coincidence that you are a writer and Suzi is a well-known,
respected reviewer with ties to many of the most prestigious
publishing houses in Manhattan. No more than serendipity,
I'm sure.''

''Here I am!'' Suzi announced breathlessly as she all but
stumbled from the spiral staircase, her hair damp from her
shower, and still working to close the topmost buttons of
the dress she had worn the first day she and Harry had met.
''You can take your shower, Harry,'' she said, glaring at
him meaningfully. *''Now.''*

Harry, grateful for her timely, if heavy-handed rescue,
quickly excused himself and headed downstairs, brushing
past Suzi as he went, but unable to look her in the eye.

But don't you dare say anything—anything about us.
She may only have been trying to warn him to keep his
mouth shut, but on a scale of one to ten, it still had to be

about the *stupidest* thing Suzi believed she had ever said. And to say it within earshot of Wilbur Langley? Well, that took the statement out of the realm of stupid and pushed it straight up to completely idiotic!

Throughout the drive into Atlantic City and most of dinner, Wilbur had been looking at her oddly. It was almost as if he was torn between wanting to congratulate her for finally falling in love with a man who appeared somewhat normal—ha! if Wilbur only knew!—and wondering if she was in some sort of trouble.

How could she be in trouble? Just because she was harboring an alien, planning to procure him illegal identification and then still be at a total loss as to what to *do* with the man once he was no longer in danger of being deported?

Why would anyone consider that trouble?

And if she had begun to look at Harry Wilde in an altogether other light, one that had a lot more to do with her personal feelings for him than her worries over his problems, well, what of it? It wasn't as if Harry were falling in love with her. He couldn't be.

According to the rules of society in Harry's time, she was older than the flood, and good for nothing more than sitting in a corner with an ugly purple turban on her head, knitting slippers, or whatever it was old maids did in Regency England.

In Harry's Regency-era mind, an eighteen-year-old bride was his desired mate, which was just about the silliest thing Suzi could imagine. What eighteen-year-old could possibly pull off marriage to a man who still didn't "get" the distinction between the rock star Prince and the Prince of Wales?

And why did Wilbur have to show up, anyway? Wasn't it just like Courtney to smell a rat in that phone call she'd made to Japan, and then send Wilbur running hotfoot to investigate? What did they think she was? Helpless? Accident prone? Capable of getting herself into trouble at the drop of a hat?

Okay. So maybe she didn't have such a great track record. Maybe she did tend to bite off more than she could comfortably chew once in a while. Maybe she did seem to have a penchant for trouble, for odd situations, for jumping into water that was over her head.

She had been on her own since her early twenties, when her wealthy parents and only uncle had died in a plane crash, but she hadn't frittered away her considerable inheritance or married the first ski bum she'd met.

She had finished college, graduating with honors, no less, and gotten work at *Literary Lines,* a damn respectable book review magazine, and if she only free-lanced now, taking more time for herself now that the remainder of her trust fund had been turned over to her at the age of thirty, she still hadn't done anything ridiculous.

She was simply a free spirit, a woman who liked her independance and enjoyed trying new things.

Like bungee jumping from a West Virginia bridge.

Like meditation, in India.

Like tofu hamburgers at her dinner party to which Senator Adam Richardson had brought an unexpected guest— the president's nominee for attorney general.

What was so wrong with any of that?

"Suzi?"

She shook herself mentally and brought her mind back to attention, having slipped away into her own world halfway through the main course at the casino restaurant.

What in the world was the matter with her? She couldn't afford to lose her concentration for an instant when Wilbur and Harry were talking. At any minute Harry could make some mortal slip, like telling Wilbur about his near speed-record-breaking monthlong ocean crossing from Portsmouth. "Yes? What did you say, Wilbur? I'm afraid I was woolgathering."

"That's quite all right, my dear. Young love does have a way of muddling the brain," Wilbur said, smiling at her so that she longed to kick Harry under the table. Why hadn't he disabused Wilbur of the idea that the two of them were lovers? A better question—why hadn't she?

"Wilbur suggested we visit the casino, Suzi," Harry said, his eyes positively glowing with interest. Damn the man. Was there ever a Regency dandy who didn't like to gamble? Whose money did he think he'd be spending? He certainly couldn't pull out one of the pile of gold pieces he'd had stuffed in his pouch!

"How lovely," Suzi said, her smile more of a grimace as she looked at Harry, dressed in the navy blue sports jacket she had bought him, his blond hair tied back at his nape.

He did look wonderful, even with his long hair. He looked wonderful, intriguing, sexy, and if he didn't stop smiling at her she was going to pick up her butter knife and stab him! "I suppose I wouldn't mind losing a few quarters in the slot machines."

"Slot machines. Ah, yes, I understand. Slot machines are a female's quaint notion of gambling, Harry," Wilbur said informatively, his smile taking any sting out of his words. "Actually, Suzi, Harry and I are going to try our hands at the baccarat table."

"Baccarat?" Suzi felt her heart taking the express elevator to her toes. "Was that inven—that is, does Harry know how to play?"

"I've explained the rules," Wilbur told her, "and Harry is extremely interested."

"I'll just bet he is," Suzi muttered under her breath.

"Shall we get you a few rolls of quarters and let you play while we men investigate our options?" asked Wilbur.

"Harry has volunteered an interest in the blackjack tables as well, you understand, so we might be a while."

"Oh, goody," Suzi said, her smile painful.

"Now, now, Suzi. Don't pout," Wilbur scolded genially. "You two talk it over while I go settle the bill, all right? I'll meet you at the main entrance to the casino floor."

Suzi's smile stayed glued in place until Wilbur had placed his arm around the young waitress's slim waist and guided her toward the cash register, before turning quickly to Harry, her eyes narrowed dangerously. "Harry Wilde! Are you out of your *tiny mind?*"

He patted her hand comfortingly, an action that made her want to scream at him. "Now, Suzi, don't go flying into the treetops. Wilbur and I are rubbing along together quite famously. And I'm not about to stumble now and do anything revealing."

"If I were a betting woman—which I am *not*— I wouldn't put a bent nickel on your odds of keeping Wilbur from becoming suspicious."

"You're in danger of becoming overset, Suzi, and for no reason. I didn't say anything when I saw that vehicle he called a limousine, did I? It's nothing like your car, and it even has a television machine. You Americans can't do anything without a television machine close to hand, can you? Not that I'm complaining. If it weren't for all the news programs I've been watching I wouldn't have known how to answer when Wilbur questioned me about our new prime minister. He has quite an impressive smile, doesn't he? Do you suppose he uses that toothpaste that makes teeth whiter and brighter?"

Suzi placed her elbow on the table and sighed, resting her forehead against her hand. The man was a walking commercial, and a fountain of misinformation ever since he'd discovered the daily soap operas. To Harry, all the world was filled with political tyrants, partisan politics, commercials for everything from hemorrhoidal creams to personal computers and now, the sexual adventures of daytime television.

"Harry," she said—pleaded—looking up at him through her lashes. "I don't know how much more of this I can take. Honestly. No, you didn't go all bug-eyed when you saw Wilbur's limousine. However, he might have suspected a little something out of the ordinary when you first saw the lights of the casinos and wondered aloud how many *gas lamps* it took to make such a glow."

He waved his hands in front of his face, pushing away her objections. "I'm on familiar territory now, Suzi. There wasn't a gaming house in London I didn't visit, and I am, I must say with all modesty, fairly good with the cards. I'll just watch Wilbur for a while, and take my cues from him. You have nothing to worry about. Honestly you don't. I promise that I won't let the game out of the bag. And I'll repay you from my winnings—with interest."

He accepted the money she handed him, then stood behind her and held out her chair. "That's let the *cat* out of the bag, or give the game *away*, Harry. Just stick to your own language, okay? American English is still beyond you. And you're right. Your modesty overwhelms me. Oh, and stop being so nice to me. Wilbur's ready to send out invitations to the wedding."

She froze, turning hot and cold by turns, as Harry bent forward and placed a lingering kiss on her nape. "Harry!" she exclaimed, startled, looking into his smiling face. "We're in public, for crying out loud, where anybody could see you. Why did you do that?"

He took her hand and led her through the maze of tables and toward the casino. "You walk around in *public* half naked and ask me why I believed it permissible to kiss you in a darkened restaurant? You Americans kiss all the time, and even go to bed in public."

"That's not what I meant and you know it. And we don't go to bed in public. How many times must I tell you that those are actors in a soap opera."

"Then you're really asking why I kissed you," he said pleasantly, waving to Wilbur, who was waiting for them, already holding several rolls of quarters. Obviously he intended to get Harry to himself for a while, shunting her off to the slot machines.

"All right," Suzi answered grudgingly, shrugging her shoulders. She really didn't want to discuss the subject anymore, but she was still interested in his answer. "Why did you kiss me?

She nearly tripped on the smooth rug when Harry answered calmly, "I kissed you, dear Miss Suzanne Harper, because I'm slowly beginning to understand the attraction American men have with older women. Something about them becoming not older, but somehow *better*."

Chapter Five

Suzi stood at the edge of the driveway, a wide smile pasted on her face as she and Harry stood arm in arm and waved goodbye to Wilbur.

Then, as the limousine's softly glowing taillights disappeared down the street and into the night, she took off Harry's arm, whirled around on her heels and stomped back to the condo.

Harry raced after her, not convinced she wouldn't slam the door in his face, leaving him to sleep on the beach. He slipped into the foyer just as she was pushing on the door and took hold of her arm.

"Oh, no, you don't," he warned, pulling her toward the staircase. "You're not going to look daggers at me all the way back from Atlantic City and then disappear into your bedchamber without an explanation."

"That's bedroom, Harry—not bedchamber," she bit out angrily, then shrugged. "Oh, very well. You want to hear why I'm upset? You really want to hear it? Okay, buster, I'll tell you. *Boy,* will I tell you!"

Giving him a none-too-gentle shove in the center of his chest, she pushed past him and made her way upstairs and into the living room, where she nearly threw herself onto the couch.

She was like a child giving into a tantrum, and she was infinitely appealing.

He followed after her, more than a little amused by her outburst of temper, and took up a chair across the room, motioning with his hand that she was now free to lambaste him with her complaints.

"You won over six thousand dollars, you idiot!" she exclaimed, obviously beginning with her most important complaint, sitting forward as if she had been turned into a spitting cat ready to spring.

Was that all? He grinned, still rather pleased with himself. Using today's exchange rate on the financial news, how would that translate into pounds, he wondered idly, his grin fading as Suzi went on the attack once more.

"Don't look so damned pleased with yourself, Harry Wilde! Do you know what would have happened if Wilbur hadn't stepped in and said that he'd won that money and you were only helping him carry the chips?"

"No, Suzi, I don't. But I am confident that you will not allow that lack of knowledge to continue."

"Oh, don't be so bloody British! And you're darn right I won't! The IRS would have asked you for your social security number, so that you could pay taxes on your winnings—that's what would have happened. Only you don't *have* a social security number, do you, Mr. Harry Wilde? So now not only does Wilbur have to pay taxes on *your* winnings, but he smells a rat—he smells a *big* rat."

She beat her closed fists on the cushions on either side of her. "Lord, I could cheerfully murder Courtney for calling him and asking him to check up on me! Why does everybody think they have to help me? Do they think I'm incapable of doing anything myself? And don't you dare to answer that question, Harry. Not if you want to sleep here tonight!''

Harry frowned, trying to concentrate on Suzi's main argument. ''The IRS?'' He shook his index finger, trying to remember where he'd heard those letters before. ''Oh, yes. That would be the Internal Revenue Service. Your government's collecting arm for taxes, isn't that correct?'' He frowned. ''How much revenue will they require from Wilbur? I'll have to reimburse him, of course.''

Suzi rolled her eyes, still looking as if she wanted to punch something. Or somebody. He was glad he had chosen to sit across the room. ''Sure you do. And exactly how do you plan to do that, Harry? Send him a check? You don't have any checks, Harry. You don't have a bank account. And do you know why? I'll tell you why *Because you don't exist!*''

She fell back against the cushions, folding her arms across her stomach. ''Of course, that's the least of our problems. Wilbur's on to us now, Harry. You can count on that. He knows you're illegal—boy, are you illegal! He may have said he bought my story that it would be easier for him to claim all the winnings as his because he's an American citizen and you're a British subject, but he was only playing along.''

''Playing along?''

''Yes, pretending to believe that there's nothing the least bit strange about you. Count on it, Harry. Wilbur might be gone, but he'll be back. He's probably on his car phone to Scotland Yard right now, checking to make sure you aren't some escaped ax murderer I decided to bring home to dinner.''

''You are overreacting,'' Harry declared, bravely going over to sit beside her on the couch, and fighting the niggling feeling that she might be right.

"Really? Okay, wise guy, convince me." Suzi dared, glaring at him.

"Wilbur doesn't believe you to be that poor a judge of character, for one thing. Otherwise, he would never have gone back to Manhattan tonight."

"Who says he's gone?" Suzi countered. "I'll bet you the tax we owe the man that he's off the phone with Scotland Yard and is checking himself into that new luxury hotel down the street even as we speak. Oh, Harry," she wailed, laying her head against his shoulder, "we're in for it now."

The possibility that they might be in trouble disconcerted Harry, but not nearly as much as Suzi's presence excited him. Slipping his arm up and around her shoulders, he used his free hand to pat her bare arm, promising, "I won't allow Wilbur's suspicions to upset you, Suzi. I'll leave immediately."

Her head shot up and she stared at him, her wide blue eyes shocked as she pressed a hand against his chest. "Leave? But you can't leave. Where would you go? The local New Jersey retirement home for nineteenth-century time travelers? Harry—don't be ridiculous!"

This was nice. She didn't want him to leave. She also was sitting very intimately pressed against him. That was also nice. Very nice. Almost inspiring.

"You want me to stay, Suzi?" he asked, lifting one side of his mouth in a smile he'd been told by one forward young Mayfair miss was "rather unnerving, Harry, truly."

"Don't go reading anything into this, Harry," Suzi warned, although she didn't pull away from him. "I'm kind to dumb animals, too."

"Really? You must tell me about these ignorant animals. Do you also pay their gambling debts?"

Now she did move away, only far enough so that she could give him a playful swat. "No, silly. I give them something to eat and send them on their way. The way I should have done with you.''

"Feed them? Now that you mention it, I *am* a little hungry.'' He leaned forward and began nibbling on her ear. "Um, that tastes good.''

"Harry! Stop that!'' Suzi protested, although he was quick to notice that she didn't pull away but, rather, only tilted her head slightly so that he could gain even closer access to her throat, the sweet smell of her hair, the tantalizing texture of her skin. "Really, Harry,'' she whispered huskily, "you must stop that.''

Harry was feeling nothing if not amenable. He'd stop nuzzling her neck. Gladly. Because if he stopped nuzzling her neck he would be free to kiss her lips.

Her soft, pouting, cherry red lips.

Did they taste of cherries as well? Or would they taste of heaven, of delights that would take him above the problems of the earth?

He decided to find out.

Pressing Suzi back against the cushions of the couch, he levered himself forward, then turned to face her, placing a finger beneath her chin.

"Harry?'' Suzi fairly squeaked. "You don't want to do this. I—I'm too old for you, for one thing—''

Harry concentrated his vaguely amused, definitely appreciative gaze on Suzi's slightly open mouth. "I've been thinking about that. Allowing for my trip through time, dear heart, I'm two hundred and sixteen. You couldn't possibly be too old for me.''

He watched, entranced, as the corners of her mouth lifted in amusement. "You have a point, Harry,'' she said softly, and he felt her hand cupping the back of his neck. "Maybe I'm too *young* for you?''

He lowered his head another fraction. "I don't think so,

Suzi. But you do talk too much,'' he chastened gently before closing the gap and touching his mouth to hers.

Harry didn't know if his reaction was so strong and immediate because he had been without a woman for the two months he had been at sea, or if it was because he had been without a woman for one hundred and eighty-one years, or if it was because Suzi Harper was the woman he was kissing.

He didn't, couldn't, know what was making him feel as he did now, as if he could kiss this woman until the world came crashing down around him and never be sorry.

He only knew that Suzi Harper was in his arms, her mouth sweetly open beneath his, her body curved intimately against his, her spread hands pressing against his back, her acceptance of his kiss at once startling and somehow natural, as if this moment was meant to be. Had always been meant to be.

Br-r-ring! Br-r-ring!

''Ignore it,'' he grumbled against her lips as she stiffened in his arms. Harry appreciated the immediacy of modern communication such as the telephone, which was certainly an improvement over the penny-post, but there were times when there was a lot to be said for the slower pace of what Suzi insisted upon terming Regency England.

She pushed her hands against his forearms. ''I can't, Harry. It's Wilbur.''

He collapsed against the couch cushions, his breathing disturbingly ragged, as she struggled to her feet, stepping over his legs as she made her way to the telephone. He couldn't seem to recover from their kiss as rapidly as she, and prudently remained on the couch.

''How above all things wonderful!'' he managed to say. ''Not only is she beautiful, but the woman's clairvoyant as well.''

The phone rang again, insistently.

"Put a sock in it, Harry," Suzi ordered, smoothing down the skirt of her dress as she lifted her chin, ready to do battle. "I'm not clairvoyant. It just figures that it's Wilbur, checking up on me."

Silently agreeing that Mrs. O'Reilly, who had temporarily moved in with Mrs. O'Connell in order to lend the old woman some company during a flare-up of her arthritis, left much to be desired in the way of a chaperone, Harry nodded, agreeing with Suzi's conclusion.

"Hello!" Suzi said, rather breathlessly, Harry noticed with a smile as she pointedly turned her back on his amusement. So, she wasn't so unaffected after all. That was nice.

He listened during Suzi's silence, as if he could somehow hear the conversation taking place at the other end of the telephone.

"Wilbur, that's so sweet of you!" Suzi exclaimed at last. "You've what?" She turned toward Harry once more, shaking her head. "They don't just rent? They actually *sell* the apartments? How, um, how perfectly *wonderful* that you should be considering the idea!" Her grimace was comical. "Yes, I do know the place. It's a lovely building...and the units are completely furnished?"

She shook her fist at Harry as he began to laugh, any thoughts of romance now effectively fled with Wilbur's telephone call. What? Suzie was saying. "Breakfast? *Tomorrow?* Just you and me? You want to discuss Harry's problem? What problem. Harry doesn't have any problems. Oh. Oh, I see. All right. If you want to be nasty about it, yes, Harry does need some identification. Well, I don't—"

Harry fell head down lengthwise on the couch, prudently stuffing his face into one of the pillows as his laughter escaped him. Watching Suzi try to sidestep Wilbur Langley's obvious insistence that they meet tomorrow morning was better than having a box seat for the farce at Covent Garden.

He felt a slap on his back.

"You can come up for air now, Harry," Suzi told him as he turned onto his back and looked up over the edge of the throw pillow and into her clearly angry features. "Wilbur's going to tell us how to get you identification. He says," she hesitated a moment, then went on, "Wilbur says we can do it ourselves, without involving anyone else. He says—"

Harry jackknifed to his feet, staring at Suzi across the coffee table. "How does he know I've traveled through time?"

"He doesn't," Suzi said, turning for the stairs. "He simply thinks you're here illegally and has given you the benefit of the doubt that there is a good reason behind what you've done—sneaking into the country. He *likes* you, if you can believe that, and thinks you're a good, honest man at heart."

"And since I'm so good and honest, *he's* decided he's willing to break the law for me?" Harry asked, hurriedly following after Suzi as she made her way down the spiral staircase.

Something about Wilbur's reasoning didn't ring true, but for the moment Harry was far more concerned for Suzi. "He'd allow *you* to break the law? A man who is so obviously protective of you. Why?"

Suzi stood just inside her bedroom, her face small and pinched, her eyes like saucers. "Because my old friend Wilbur's a firm believer in the course of true love running smooth, or words to that effect," she answered dully. "Personally I think he's finally going senile. Love has nothing to do with why I want you to get identification. Absolutely *nothing!*"

Before Harry could play the cad and remind her that she had appeared to be a willing, if not yet loving, participant in the lovemaking that had barely begun before Wilbur's call had so importunely interrupted, the door slammed in his face and he heard the lock turn.

Smiling in pleasant bemusement, and reflectively scratching his head, Harry retired to his own bedchamber— *bedroom*— feeling pretty much in charity with the entire wild and wonderful world he had been transported to three short weeks ago.

It was hot, even for New Jersey at the end of August, and Suzi wished she had thought to bring an insulated container of ice tea with her. A jug, and perhaps a map. Most certainly a flyswatter. The place was simply crawling with mosquitoes and other bugs she preferred not to give a name to.

This was the third cemetery they'd checked, she and Harry, and it looked as if they would soon have to pile back into her car and find a fourth. And all because Harry was being such a royal pain in the neck!

"I still don't believe I'm doing this!" she exclaimed, stopping beneath the shade of a tree and turning to glare at her stubborn time traveler. "We found one in the first cemetery, and two in the second. What's your problem anyway, Harry? *Why* can't you be satisfied?"

She watched as he bent to look at another headstone, his skin bronzed from the sun, the nearly white dusting of hair on his arms and legs almost giving his body a golden glow.

For a guy who had claimed not to like modern dress, he was doing a great impersonation of a golden beach boy in his shorts and muscle shirt. And if he ever cut his hair, that glorious, sun-streaked blond hair, she just might strangle him.

But she didn't, as Wilbur had supposed, love the man. At times like these, when he proved to be so infuriatingly pigheaded, she wasn't even entirely convinced she particularly *liked* him.

"The name has to be exactly right," he said as he stood once more, shaking his head. "Not just the year of birth, but the name. I refuse to spend the remainder of my life as an Ignatius or a Frank."

"Or a Johann," Suzi said, stepping back out into the sun in order to follow him down the next row. "I know, I know. You want a good, solid, English name. Like *Harry,* as if it was the be-all and end-all of great names. Personally, old sport, I'm not all that cracked up over it."

He was bending down once more, balancing himself on his haunches. "If I'm going to have to take on a new identity, I have to feel comfortable with it. It's not enough that the person was born in 1959. Now, here's one that might suit."

She dropped to her knees beside him and leaned forward to peer at the small heart-shaped stone. It wasn't easy, for the remote graveyard was rather old and run-down, the grass even in this relatively newer section grown up around the stones as if no one cared about this place, about what it meant.

"William Robert Arthur," she read, squinting to make out the words. "Born June 10, 1959, died June 11—oh, Harry, that's so sad!"

"Only a single day on this earth. One small boy, one small day." He levered himself backward and into a sitting position, his forearms resting on his knees as he stared at the stone. "I feel like a ghoul," he said, lowering his head. "Isn't there some other way?"

Suzi had pulled out a few weeds with shaking fingers, mindlessly doing some crude housekeeping of the small grave. "It's the only way, Harry. Wilbur says we apply for a new birth certificate in the name of—of William Robert Arthur," she said, her voice catching. "Then, when it arrives, we use it to get you all sorts of identification. A social security card, a driver's license—"

He laid a hand on her arm, stilling her in the process of tracing the carved "W" in "William" against the stone. "I'm sorry, Suzi. Sorry you ever got involved in this. But you're right. Wilbur's right. It's the only way."

Suzi sat on the deck chair at noon, staring into space, oblivious of her surroundings. For two weeks more she had kept Mrs. O'Reilly and Wilbur close to her, for protection, or so she told herself.

After all, she had invited a strange man into her house— a *very* strange man, indeed.

Just because he was bright, and amusing, and devastatingly handsome, didn't mean that she should be so trusting. Why, he could be a nineteenth-century version of Jack the Ripper. Or had Jack the Ripper actually lived in the nineteenth century? Yes, he had. Well, scratch that analogy.

Still, it simply wasn't prudent to be alone with Harry Wilde.

He was much too tempting.

And she was much too vulnerable to temptation.

Not that there had been a repeat of that mind-blowing kiss the first night Wilbur had been in town. Oh, no. Suzi considered herself to be much too smart to get involved *that* way!

She had sent to *Literary Lines* the very next morning, requesting some galleys that she would be reviewing for the fall issue, and had done everything but closet herself in her bedroom for ten days, leaving Harry to blunder through conversations with a curiously unwilling-to-move Wilbur and to spend endless hours watching what Suzi had begun to term "that damned tele-vision machine."

If he asked her one more time if they could visit this wonderful place called "a theater near you," she was going to scream!

But for the past six days, since Wilbur had reluctantly

left Ocean City—a place he had once said was only suitable for giggling toddlers and weary parents—and returned to Manhattan for the opening of a new art gallery, Harry had been transcribing his manuscript. He had written the original in his own form of code—or shorthand, as Suzi called his chicken scratches when she saw them—and had scarcely spoken to her.

Harry was a man with a mission, or so Mrs. O'Reilly had commented when she carried his untouched lunch tray up to the kitchen. The woman was right. When Harry watched television, he watched intently. When he played, he played intently.

But now, now that he was working on the thick manuscript that had been wrapped in oilskin and therefore had suffered little damage for its dunk in the Atlantic, he was like a man possessed.

Not that Suzi cared. She had her own work to do. Really. She couldn't have cared less if Harry never spoke to her again. If he never smiled at her in that silly, one-sided way of his. If he never touched her arm, or teased her, or walked hand in hand on the beach with her, or kissed her—

"Damn!"

"I so admire your clever way with words," Harry said from behind her, startling her into dropping the galley she had been reading without really comprehending, so that it slid off her lap to the floor, losing her place.

"Go away, Harry," she grumbled, not turning to look at him. After all, if she looked at him, if she saw his engaging smile, if she were to gaze into his laughing green-blue eyes, if she were to remember once again how very wonderful his arms had felt as he had held her close in their single embrace, their single kiss—well, if she were to keep remembering things like that it could be dangerous, that's all.

"If you insist, madam," he answered, his tone as well

as his words mocking her. "I hear you older ladies can be a tad crotchety now and again."

"Harry Wilde!" Suzi exclaimed, turning so swiftly on the deck chair that it nearly tipped over. "You promised not to call me old ever again!"

"Hello, dear heart," he said, grinning, as she looked up at him. "It's not so difficult gaining your attention, if one only takes the time to go about the thing correctly. Would you like to read the mail that's just arrived? This one," he offered, holding up an official-looking envelope and waving it in front of her intriguingly, "might prove interesting."

"Your birth certificate!" She lunged for the envelope, grabbing it out of his hand. With trembling fingers she tore the envelope open and pulled out the certificate bearing the name William Robert Arthur. "Oh, Harry," she said, her nerves on edge as she leapt to her feet, "it's happening. You're on your way to becoming a whole new person."

He screwed up his face and scratched at a spot just behind his left ear, a habit that alerted her to the fact that he was going to say something she'd hate hearing. "Harry?" she prompted, replacing the certificate and clutching the envelope to her breasts.

"Would you care to take a stroll on the beach?" he asked, avoiding her eyes.

"No, I wouldn't," she answered warily. "I don't think that would be a good idea. You see, if you say something I don't like, I may be tempted to drown you."

"And Wilbur," Harry added, wincing.

"Wilbur? What's he got to do with anything?" Suzi didn't like the feeling she was getting in the pit of her stomach. It reminded her much too much of the feeling she'd had in her stomach that first morning, when Harry had told her it was 1813.

"First things first," he said taking her hand and quickly

leading her toward the steps that led down to the path leading to the beach. "Let's walk, and let's talk about William
Robert Arthur."

For all his insistence that he needed to speak with her,
Harry kept curiously silent until they had traveled along the
water's edge for some time, concentrating on kicking at the
small wavelets that danced around their ankles.

Finally, just as she knew her nerves were about to tear—
because he was still holding her hand—why did it affect
her so much whenever he held her hand?—he said, "I can't
become William Robert Arthur."

Suzi stopped dead, so that Harry was forced to halt as
well or else chance having his arm torn out of its socket.
"You can't *what?*"

He grinned at her. Oh, how dare he grin at her at a time
like this?

"I said, I can't become William Rob—"

"For heaven's sake, don't repeat yourself. I heard you
the first time, and it was bad enough then!" Suzi exploded,
dropping his hand as if it might burn her. She then pushed
the fingers of that hand through her hair and glared at him.
"Harry Wilde, if I had a stick, I'd hit you with it—repeat-
edly! *Why* can't you use the name?"

He stepped closer, so that his bare, fuzzy gold thighs
were against her smooth skin, immediately giving her a
panic attack of claustrophobia. "Because, Suzi Harper, I
like the way you say 'Harry Wilde,'" he told her simply,
resting his hands on her shoulders. "I like it exceedingly,
and I should miss it. Very much."

"Oh, Harry," Suzi groaned, laying her head against his
chest, not knowing whether to be angry or if she should
burst into tears. "You stubborn, pigheaded, arrogant, wonderful Englishman. What in the world am I going to do
with you?"

She heard the rumble of his soft laughter as she remained

pressed against his chest. "Well, that brings us to Wilbur, doesn't it, dear heart?"

Suzi raised her head, unable to step away from him, because he was still holding fast to her shoulders. "It does? How?"

"Wilbur says that, to be safe, I should give serious thought to marrying myself an American citizen," Harry explained, his smile partly sheepish, partly intoxicating to her senses. "We've had several long talks on the subject and, although he still believes I am only an Englishman who has entered the country illegally, he was quite adamant about it."

"Marry an American citizen," Suzi repeated dully, her heart pounding so loudly she could barely hear herself speak. "But why? It isn't as if you were trying to get a Green Card—or whatever it is aliens need to live here and apply for citizenship. You'll be William Robert Arthur, and already a tax-paying citizen—if I can figure out what sort of job you could do, that is. I don't get it."

"I don't, either. Or at least I don't understand all of it. Wilbur says I'd be hedging my bets. If we attack the problem from two angles, we might just confuse the authorities if ever they decide to investigate me for any reason. That's when I realized, not unhappily, that we could confuse the authorities even more if I kept my own name. I could still remain your Harry Wilde."

At last Suzi succeeded in moving away from Harry, which might not have been a good idea, for her head was spinning and she wouldn't be surprised if she toppled headfirst onto the beach. "Marry. Keep your own name."

She looked at him quizzically, realizing that she was still holding the birth certificate, had been carrying it with her along the beach without realizing it. "But how would we change the name on this?" she asked, waving the badly creased envelope in front of her.

He lifted her chin with his hand and dropped a kiss on the tip of her nose, a move that turned her knees to limp seaweed. "Wilbur is convinced you're an inventive puss. You'll think of some way," he said, taking her hand once more and leading her back up the beach toward the condo.

"Oh, yeah. Right. Suzi will think of something. Suzi has larceny in her soul. No wonder he went back to Manhattan. He knew I'd go nuclear if he'd dared to suggest such a thing in person! Tell me, Harry, did Wilbur make any 'suggestions' as to where you're going to find this willing American citizen who'll marry you just so you won't be deported to oblivion one fine day? You can't go back to England, you know. You're not a man without a country— you're a man without a *century!*"

Who would Harry marry? As if there could be any other woman—not counting Mrs. O'Reilly, of course. As soon as the question was out of her mouth Suzi had longed to take it back. Of course Wilbur had had a woman in mind. The sneak! That wonderful, romantic, mischief-making *sneak!* The man plays Cupid for his son-in-law, then Courtney, then Countney's daughter, Sydney—and now he thinks he's got a corner on the market.

They had reached the outside steps when Harry finally answered her question. "Wilbur suggested you, naturally," he said, stepping aside so that she could precede him up to the deck. "And that's when I first knew I was right to want to keep my own name—the moment Wilbur tried the name Suzi Wilde out loud and then asked me if I thought that it should be considered a name or a description."

"I hate you," Suzi declared feelingly as she turned at the top of the steps and glared down at him. "I hate you, I hate Wilbur, I hate men in general. You in particular, but all men in general. Is that clear?"

"Partially. Would that be a 'no' then, Miss Harper?"

Harry asked, his wide, infuriating grin revealing his confidence in her answer.

And it was that confidence that made her balk. "How do you know I'm not in love with someone? For all you know I might be in love with a half-dozen men! Or didn't that occur to you?"

"You?" Harry appeared to be amazed, and then he grinned. "I would have thought you were past the age for—"

"Don't you finish that sentence, Harry Wilde," Suzi threatened. "Don't you even *think* it!"

"I wouldn't dare, madam," Harry answered, so that she knew he was deliberately teasing her, trying to make the moment easier on them both. Harry was a dear man, really he was. And he'd be lost without her. Absolutely lost.

But he didn't love her. He had never mentioned, or even hinted, at the word *love*.

There was a short, uncomfortable silence between them before Harry asked, "So, all things considered, and realizing that I am asking you to sacrifice that freedom you modern women so cherish—should I take your lack of answer as a 'no'?"

"Yes, damn it! I mean, *no!* I'll marry you." She held out her hands in warning as he moved to take her in his arms. "But only because you'd be totally helpless without me, Harry Wilde—and because it's the best way I can think of to make your life a misery!"

And with that she was off, running for the condo and the safety of her bedroom.

Chapter Six

Harry had been in his bedroom working on transcribing his manuscript when Suzi had called for him to join her in the foyer. Something in her voice, a bubbling enthusiasm not unmixed with wonder, told him he was about to be amazed. He didn't know if he was going to be *happy,* but he was going to be amazed. Suzie Harper constantly amazed him.

He wasn't disappointed.

He was amazed, and he wasn't happy.

Suzi Harper, a strange young woman he was fast beginning to believe was the mother of all invention, had tossed his precious, bogus birth certificate into the fully loaded washing machine!

"I first got the idea while looking at the certificate, and saw how it was all creased from the way I had been holding it," Suzi explained as they stood in the foyer, the open bifold doors that usually concealed the automatic clothes washer and dryer behind her.

The clothes washer was in the process of its spin cycle

now, or so Suzi had informed him a moment ago when he had closed his gaping mouth and decided he could listen to her without throttling her, and Harry could feel his nerves tightening, wondering what sort of dastardly crime he had committed in his lifetime to be punished in this bizarre way.

"You see, Harry," Suzi was saying, "I've often left something, sometimes a piece of paper—sometimes a couple of dollars—in my pocket, so that it ended up going through the washer. Even the dryer, once or twice. It makes a hell of a mess."

He was beginning to understand, not that he put much credence in her belief that her plan would work. "But will it cover up the fact that you changed William Robert Arthur to Harry Wilde? That white liquid you painted over the original name was quite magical, but a discerning eye could still see that the certificate has been altered."

"Oh, ye of little faith!" Suzi exclaimed as the washing machine gave a small click, a slight sigh, and slowed to a stop. "It'll work just fine. Trust me."

"It would appear I do not have any other option, doesn't it?" Harry said, leaning against the curved banister of the spiral staircase and wishing he could will himself to be stern. But it was difficult not to be infused with Suzi's almost childlike optimism.

She tipped back the lid and reached into the washing machine, giving Harry a delightful picture of her long legs peeping out beneath her bright pink short-shorts. He did the gentlemanly thing, and turned away, then gave into temptation and indulged himself in admiring the view.

They were going to be married.

And optimism was optimism.

His luck hadn't been unremittingly bad.

Three days had passed since Suzi had accepted his ramshackle proposal of marriage, two of those days spent mostly in uncomfortable silences interspersed with covert looks and nervous smiles. Suzi had concentrated on her own work and he had walked the beach, unable to focus on transcribing more than a few pages of his manuscript before his mind returned to thoughts of Suzi and their up-coming nuptials.

A marriage of convenience. An accepted practice in his time, perhaps, but not in hers. Americans most especially married for love, and only for love. Not for convenience. Not for money. Not for titles or position. And most defi-nitely not to obtain an identity.

But Wilbur had been adamant. He had vowed that the only surefire way to elude detection was to marry an Amer-ican citizen. Wilbur had said that Suzi should settle down, that marriage might be the making of her, and that her "biological clock," whatever that was, was ticking away at a mighty pace, and if there was ever a woman who should be surrounded by her own children it was Suzi Har-per.

Children. Harry raised one eyebrow as he watched Suzi searching through the small collection of wet beach towels, on the lookout for the birth certificate.

Would there be children?

A better question.

Would there be love?

There was already desire, on his part.

There was already compassion, on hers.

Could there be more? Could he believe, trust, in the promise of more?

"Ta-da! Mission accomplished. Harry—come look!"

He shook his head, trying to clear it of questions, those never-ending questions that had kept him from his rest these past two nights, and obediently pinned a bright smile on his face. "You've wrought a miracle, Suzi?" he asked, taking the soggy paper from her.

There were several fold marks visible, and the paper was dangerously delicate in its saturated condition, but it was still legible—if you looked carefully. What was missing was the former pristine white newness of the paper, so that Suzi's alterations were no longer apparent.

He looked at her in genuine admiration. "Have you ever considered counterfeiting as an avocation, dear heart?" he asked, watching her as she tried without noticeable success to hide her elation in this latest victory. "I believe you might have a true calling to larceny."

"What can I say, Harry?" she asked, skipping past him, her grin devilish. "You bring out the worst in me. Now, come on. We have to shower and dress while the certificate dries. We were just lucky I could have my own certificate expressed here from Manhattan in time. The local licensing office closes at four and won't open again until Monday. There's a three-day waiting period for marriages, you know, and we still have to get our blood tests."

Harry stood very still for a moment, considering her words, and feeling his feet slowly going numb. "Blood—blood tests?" He'd been examining the television machine late last night when he couldn't sleep, using the remote control to "channel-surf," as Suzi condemned the practice which she decried as having something to do with his male genes and not the century in which he was born.

At three o'clock in the morning he'd discovered a channel devoted to subjects in a medical vein—vein? was he going to be required to open a vein?—and had watched a heart transplant surgery in mingled horror and fascination until he could summon the power to click to another channel.

Modern medicine made submitting himself to the quacks and leeches and tooth-drawers of nineteenth-century England seem preferable to anything the modern world had conjured up in the name of "progress."

"Um—Suzi?" he ventured, clearing his throat. "Precisely what is a blood test? How do they test it? For what perverted, ungodly purpose do they test it? And lastly, and most definitely most important to my peace of mind—how do they acquire this blood in the first place?"

Suzi turned in the act of entering her bedroom and looked at him quizzically. And then she grinned. It was an evil grin. She held up her hands in front of her, about a foot apart. "How do they get it, Harry? Why, it's simple. They use a needle—about *this* long!"

Harry knew she was enjoying herself at his expense, but could not keep from asking, "What sort of needle? A sewing needle? A knitting needle?"

"I don't believe this!" Suzi exclaimed upstairs fifteen nauseating minutes later, after she had instructed him in the ways of modern bloodletting—using drawings to explain her explanation. "You're whiter now than when I fished you out of the ocean. Harry, it's only a small needle, and it only pinches for a second. Honestly. I wouldn't lie to you."

"Yes, you would," Harry said firmly, his arms folded against him, protecting the vulnerable crooks of his elbows. He'd never been ill a day in his life—except for that embarrassing bout with measles when he was fifteen—but he'd seen physicians in action, and knew he'd rather face an entire fleet of American warships than submit himself to their ministrations. "Not only would you lie to me, but you'd enjoy yourself while you were about it. Have you ever had one of these blood tests?"

"Everyone has, Harry," she told him as she led the way to the spiral staircase once more, her tone shifting from amusement to exasperation. "Don't worry. I'll go first, and you can watch me. All right? Now hurry up. If we don't go through with this now I may get cold feet."

"The thought of marrying me is that daunting?" Harry

asked, forgetting the coming horror of the blood test as his attention was once more brought back to the fact that Suzi was marrying him, but for all the wrong reasons.

"No, silly," she told him, once more heading for her bedroom. "As an old maid more likely to be struck by lightning than to find a husband, I'm getting rather used to the idea of being a wife. It's the clerk in the licensing office I'm worried about. If we can't pull this off this afternoon, Harry, I'll be spending the next few years in jail. And I don't even want to *think* about what might happen to you! I saw a movie once where scientists discovered a mermaid on land and wanted to dissect her!"

One short hour later Harry was to remember Suzi's words as they stood on the other side of the counter from a rather overwhelming, overbearing woman in her early sixties who insisted upon staring him down overtop her heavy gold-rimmed reading glasses as if he had just recently crawled out from beneath a nearby rock.

"Don't you know how important this paper is, Mr. Wilde?" the clerk asked him accusingly, gingerly holding on to the still-damp certificate with her fingertips, as if it might contaminate her in some way.

"Indeed, madam, I do," Harry answered earnestly, and in his best schoolboy English. "But I was so in a rush to marry Miss Harper here that I inadvertently left the certificate in my trousers and her housekeeper placed them both in the washing machine. I—" he continued, inventively, he thought, when she continued to glare at him "—I have been carrying the certificate with me for weeks, in the fervent hope Miss Harper would honor my suit."

He put an arm around Suzi, drawing her stiff, tense body close against his. "When my dearest heart finally agreed to the marriage, my elation must have done war with my common sense, and lost the battle." He smiled at the clerk, hoping to dazzle her. He'd always had a way with older ladies.

Except for this one.

"If you were born in New Jersey, what are you doing with that English accent?"

"Harry's parents were diplomats, and traveled extensively. He was educated at Oxford," Suzi explained proudly—and rather quickly—as she gazed up at him adoringly, her fib much more convincing than his, he thought meanly. "Weren't you, my darling?" Then she, too, looked to the clerk and added in a near whisper, "I believe the man exaggerates his accent to impress me, but I don't care. I think it's adorable! Don't you think it's *absolutely* adorable?"

The clerk sniffed, clearly less "impressed" than Suzi with Harry's accent. Then she inspected the certificate again before placing it on the counter and picking up a pen and glaring at Harry. "Occupation?"

"Lieutenant, His Maj—"

"Freelance writer!" Suzi fairly screamed, effectively drowning out his verbal slip as she delivered a sharp, painful kick to his ankle.

"Writer, is it?" the woman scoffed. "So's my brother-in-law, who's been sponging off my sister Winifred these thirty-some odd years. How about I put down unemployed? It's the same thing."

Longing to reach across the counter and cuff the woman's ears—an action that would probably end badly—Harry only smiled and nodded his head.

"Social security number?"

Harry and Suzi exchanged horrified glances. He didn't have a social security number. They hadn't thought he'd need it simply to get married.

It was Suzi who came to the rescue again, rattling off a

series of numbers Harry knew she was making up as she went along, and the clerk scribbled on the form once more.

"Can't he speak for himself?" the woman asked, pointing her pen at Harry.

"Suzi believes me incapable of dealing with anything the slightest bit numerical," he offered in explanation. "And she's correct, of course. You know how it is with people of an artistic bent—we have no head for mundane, everyday matters."

"You can say that again," the clerk agreed grudgingly. "Winifred's husband couldn't find his own way home from the corner market at high noon. This your birth certificate?" she asked, taking the paper Suzi offered her. "Well, at least I can read this one."

"This isn't going well," Suzi whispered out of the corner of her mouth as the older woman turned to a table behind her to pick up another form. "I think she's on to us, Harry."

"On to us? You mean, she suspects something is wrong? How?"

Suzi tugged on his arm, moving him three steps back from the counter. "I don't know how. Just keep your mouth shut and let me handle her. Okay?"

Harry was beginning to feel extremely frustrated, and not a little out of his depth. He didn't want Suzi to "handle" the situation. He, after all, was the man, the strong one. He would be the one to save them, if they needed to be saved. He'd show the woman that he was as American as she was!

He shook off Suzi's hand and returned to the counter as the clerk picked up her pen once more, obviously ready to ask another penetrating, hard to answer question.

"How 'bout them Phillies?" he piped up in imitation of the rather sloppy grammar of the gas station attendant he'd seen on one of his rare outings, briskly slapping his hand against the counter, calling on his scant reserves of knowledge about the major league baseball team he'd been watching perform on television. "Dropping three in a row to St. Louis! They're going to blow the pennant if they keep this up."

"I don't like sports. As a matter of fact, I *detest* sports," the woman said crushingly, her beady brown eyes narrowing. "Charlie, my ex-husband, liked sports. The little squirt watched sports night and day. Baseball. Hockey. Football. Basketball. Anything with a ball, or a hoop, or a goal. That's *why* he's my ex-husband, and why I'm standing here earning my own keep rather than working in my garden."

She turned to Suzi and wagged a finger at her. "You'd better rethink this, little girl, if your fiancé is anything like my ex. Take my word as gospel on this one—he'll break your heart."

Suzi flashed Harry a triumphant smile. "Oh, but he's so *cute!*" she exclaimed, launching herself at him, sliding her arms up and around his neck and lifting her feet off the ground, so that he nearly stumbled. "Isn't he cute?" And then, as she literally hung suspended from his neck, and to Harry's mingled surprise and pleasure, she kissed him.

"Dear heart," he said in all sincerity long moments later as he attempted to catch his breath.

"Sweet darling," Suzi crooned with syrupy sweetness, running one hand through the long hair that lay against his nape. "My own little sugar snookums. Look at him! So cute! So cute, so cute, *so cute!* Oh, I can barely wait until we're married. I simply can't keep my hands off this gorgeous hunk of man another minute! I'm *crazy* about him!"

"Crazy? A mutual condition, I agree," Harry said, nuzzling her throat as she molded her small, delightful body against him.

He didn't know what she was doing, but he wasn't so bacon-brained that he was about to push her away and demand an explanation. Not while she was pressing short, hot kisses on his cheeks, his mouth, and going on and on about the romantic heart-shaped hot tub to be found at their honeymoon cottage in a place called the Poconos.

Only vaguely did he hear the mad frenzy of stamping behind him as the clerk placed official seals on the small pile of documents on the counter. "Here!" she then exclaimed nervously, her voice fairly trembling with disgust. "Take these and get out of my office."

Suzi whispered in his ear, which was a simple matter of logistics, for she happened to be nibbling on it at the time. "Pick me up and aim me toward the counter," she instructed, her breath warm against his neck.

He was almost beyond hearing her. He had, in fact, almost forgotten where they were, why they were there and even who he was. All he could concentrate on was Suzi's mouth, Suzi's roaming hands, Suzi's ardor.

But, somehow, he managed to respond to her order. Suzi relaxed her grip on him long enough to scoop up the papers and, a moment later, they were heading for the door, Suzi still held high against his chest and gurgling, "Oh, yes, Harry. *Yes!* Take me home! *Now!*"

"...just about the most disgusting display I've ever witnessed in all my born days," the clerk was muttering as they exited the licensing office. "I get them all in here! Can't tell whether to issue the idiots a license or throw a bucket of cold water over the pair of them. Why, in my day..."

Much to Harry's confusion and regret, once the door was closed behind them Suzi's ardor abruptly cooled and she wriggled out of his arms just as he was about to kiss her once more. "Thanks for going along with me, *sugar snookums,*" she said, fumbling with the papers as she attempted to locate the all-important marriage license application.

Then she smoothed down her fairly rumpled lime green blouse in a coolly businesslike "that's that" demonstration of dismissal and grinned up at him impishly. "I thought that went quite well, didn't you? She couldn't wait to get rid of us and our embarrassing display of libido."

Harry believed he could feel Charlie's ex-wife's bucket of cold water pouring over his head and all over his "libido." So Suzi's little exhibition had all been for effect? He took a deep, steadying breath and willed his features into a noncommittal expression. Of course Suzi had been only putting on an act, playing a part. He knew that. He'd known it all along. Now, if he could only control his ragged breathing.

"Are we legal now?" he asked, looking down at the papers.

She shook her head as they made their way back to the parking lot and Suzi's car. "Not yet. Once we have the blood test results I'll have to come back here one more time and get the final papers. You don't have to come along for that, thank goodness, or we might have to repeat our performance if the dragon lady is on duty."

"Yes. That would be tragic, wouldn't it." Harry stepped in front of Suzi as she went to walk around to her side of the car. "Was that all it was back there, Suzi? A performance?"

"What else would it be, Harry?" she asked, looking in his direction, but not directly at him. "We both know why we're doing this. I rescued you, so in a way, I'm responsible for you. We're stuck with each other, unless you plan to announce to the world that you've traveled through time. We have to live together, so we might as well be married. Left on your own you'd be a menace to society and yourself. Harry, we've been over all of this already."

"Yes, of course," Harry agreed, watching her as she went around the car and opened the driver's side door. Her reasoning was good, but her voice lacked conviction. He took heart in that thought. "Although I won't lie and say

I didn't enjoy the exercise, *sugar snookums,*" he ended daringly as she was about to slide onto the seat.

"Oh, Harry!" Suzi exclaimed in what he decided was nervous exasperation, her head hastily disappearing into the car, so that he quickly got in himself and watched her as she struggled with the seat belt, doing his best to look sheepish and appealing at the same time.

"Oh, Harry!" he parroted, smiling as a becoming tide of pink rose into her cheeks, then settled back in his seat. "And, *oh, Suzi!*"

She started the car, staring daggers at him, and pulled out into traffic, a move that still chilled him to the bone. Although his former idea of speed had been pleasantly shattered with his first drive in Suzi's car, he knew he would feel more comfortable with the reins—the wheel—and his life, in his hands rather than in those of a mere female who should be sitting beside him, gushingly complimenting him on his expertise.

"I'll just bet the laboratory technician will be able to wipe that self-satisfied smirk off your face," Suzi told him, turning into another parking lot located beside a building labeled Medical Laboratory.

"Ah, yes," he countered smugly, for he was still feeling rather smug. After all, a woman who truly detested him would have found some other way of diverting the clerk than by throwing herself in his arms and therefore throwing convention to the four winds! "But I am equally convinced that you will be able to kiss away my pain."

"I hate you, Harry Wilde," Suzi declared as she slammed the car door.

"No, you don't," Harry said, taking her hand as they made their way to the front door of the office building. "You seem to delight in saying so, but you don't hate me. As a matter of fact, I believe we are rubbing along together tolerably well. We certainly *rubbed* together to advantage in front of that most delightful clerk. Ours should be an interesting marriage, don't you think?''

"Shut up, Harry," Suzi ordered. "Just do us both a favor and shut up." However, he noticed with a happy, hopeful heart, she did not let go of his hand.

Suzi relaxed on the lounge chair, the cares of the day behind her as she watched the stars appearing one by one in the clear, darkening sky.

If only the worries of tomorrow, those of all her tomorrows once she and Harry were married, could disappear as simply.

For tomorrow she and Harry Wilde would be married. Irrevocably joined. Man and woman, husband and wife, time traveler and flighty female.

Only she wasn't flighty. She wasn't! *Quixotic*. That's what she was. And Harry was lucky to have found her. Who else would have believed the man had traveled through time—yet alone helped him cover his tracks by marrying him? Only her, that's who. The quixotic Suzi Harper.

She sighed, looking out over the ocean, listening as the waves broke against the beach below, and remembering that embarrassing, enlightening scene in the clerk's office. "How 'bout them Phillies?" Could he have been any more transparent? How had the absurd idea of kissing Harry to keep him from saying anything else entered her head? And, better yet, why had she acted on the impulse?

Harry had to know now that she was not indifferent to him. Indifferent? Hah! She was fascinated by him. He was handsome. He was intelligent and endlessly curious. He was very handsome. He was sweet, and polite, and kind, and very, *very* handsome.

Good grief! She was hooked. Why didn't she just admit

it to herself, even if she'd die before she told Harry how very much she wanted to be married to him.

Married. Tomorrow. In less than twenty-four hours. Suzi Wilde. Suzanne Wilde. Mrs. Harry Wilde. *Oh, Lord!*

All their plans had already been made, not that there were many of them. It would be a small wedding in a small town away from prying eyes, a legally binding ceremony before the justice of the peace and with Mrs. O'Reilly as their sole witness.

Suzi supposed she should be grateful for "small" favors. She had never wanted a large wedding anyway, although anyone who thought they knew her would most certainly be excused if they imagined otherwise.

But, for all her love of pomp, she had always imagined her marriage to be a very private thing, perhaps with her vows being whispered in a shady glen, with only the minister, her soon-to-be husband and the birds in the trees to hear them.

Besides, she decided with a rueful smile, how could they possibly have a large wedding? Who'd sit on the groom's side, for pity's sake? And another thing. She wouldn't have to be made nervous by the obligatory weekend visit to meet Harry's relatives. That would have been an impossibly long trip, wouldn't it?

Suzi's small smile turned into a wide grin, and soon she was giggling, which was a good thing, because anyone who might stumble out onto the deck would mistake her tears for those of mirth.

But, then, didn't all brides cry before their weddings?

Harry stood on the moonlit beach, his hands stuffed deep in the pockets of his rolled up white-duck trousers, his long blond hair blown around by the sea breeze, his bare feet being lapped at gently by the small wavelets that crept along the sand at the water's edge.

He'd be married in the morning. Married to Suzanne Harper. His rescuer. His mentor. The thorn in his side. The angel in his dreams. The woman who had offered so much, sacrificed so much and asked for so little in return.

How could he do this to her? How could he allow her to throw her life away on a man she barely knew, a man who had only recently come to her from a world so different from hers he might as well have landed here after half a lifetime on some distant planet?

How would he support her? With his writings? Did Suzi's world care about the adventures and musings of a nineteenth-century dreamer turned reluctant soldier in a war he neither believed in nor could turn his back on and still call himself a man?

Would a man live on the largess of his wife? Many of his contemporaries had done so, and bragged about it. But not him. Not Harry Wilde! He'd have to find a way to support Suzi. Support their children.

Their children. Harry sighed, watching as the movement of the ocean turned the path of moonlight shining down on it into a fragile stairway to the heavens. It was terribly romantic, this Ocean City beach. But he was out here alone, and Suzi was avoiding him.

Suzi knew what their marriage tomorrow would mean. Neither of them had said the words, but they both knew. This would be a marriage of convenience—even of necessity—but it would not be a marriage in name only.

Suzi deserved children. She deserved love and honor and loyalty. She deserved kindness, and gentleness, and the sweet romance all women seemed to crave, all of which had been glaringly missing in their relationship thus far.

He couldn't go to her, tell her he loved her, and have any chance of being believed. He wouldn't believe it, either, for their association was still too new, too bizarre, to really know much of anything. But he did care for Suzi. He cared for her deeply. He desired her.

He wouldn't rush her, he wouldn't too assiduously pursue the blossoming of mutual trust, the mutual—he was sure—desire, the promise of mutual love. It would all come to them, in time.

Time. Was it their friend, or their enemy? If only he could suppress the feeling that there was something potentially dangerous about his strange voyage to the twentieth century that still alluded him. Some future problem he wasn't seeing.

He picked up a flat, broken seashell and sent it skipping across the waves.

He wouldn't think about problems now.

After all, he should be happy, on top of the world. He was getting married in the morning.

Chapter Seven

Suzi, who couldn't remember ever being upset with the long-suffering Mrs. O'Reilly, felt close to shaking the woman. She had been dawdling, and delaying, and offering one lame excuse after another as Suzi attempted to get her to the front door of the condo.

"Wait!" Mrs. O'Reilly said now, just as Suzi thought she had settled all the housekeeper's questions and opened the front door in anticipation of the three of them leaving for the office of the justice of the peace.

"Now what?" Suzi complained. "And don't tell me you have another run in your stocking, Mrs. O'Reilly, because I don't care if you do. The justice of the peace is waiting for us—if he hasn't retired and moved to Florida after giving up on us, that is."

"Perhaps she's politely showing us that she doesn't wish to bear witness to the ceremony?" Harry suggested, broadly winking at a becomingly disconcerted Mrs. O'Reilly before turning to once more inspect his appearance in the mirror beside the door.

He had been admiring himself all morning, Suzi knew. And she didn't blame him. He was gorgeous to look at in his new double-breasted suit, the sort of man who was born to wear designer clothes as naturally as some men wore jeans and T-shirts.

"No, no, Mr. Wilde. It's nothing like that, as well you know, you scamp. I've grown rather fond of you, you know." Mrs. O'Reilly turned and headed for the spiral staircase once more as Suzi silently and incredulously mouthed the words "you scamp" under her breath. "But I think I may have left the kettle on the boil. That would never do, would it? Can't go burning down this lovely house, especially when you consider that I've just scrubbed it from top to bottom. I'll be right back, Miss Harper, I promise."

"Where have I heard that before?" Suzi groused, rolling her eyes. "Oh, I give up!"

"Morning, all. Quite the perfect day for a wedding, isn't it? The drive from Manhattan was glorious, if a bit delayed by a last-minute errand."

"Wilbur, come in, " Harry said in greeting, not looking at all surprised by the publisher's appearance in the doorway. "Lovely to see you again, dear man. Once more you have put my own attempts at sartorial splendor firmly in the shade. My compliments to your tailor."

"Hallelujah! Er, that is, never mind about the kettle, Miss Harper. I remember now—I turned it off just after breakfast," Mrs. O'Reilly piped up happily, and in obvious relief, as Wilbur Langley strolled through the doorway and into the foyer, his uniformed chauffeur following after him, carrying an enormous white box decorated with a huge pink ribbon.

The housekeeper brushed close by Wilbur as she relieved the chauffeur of his burden, and whispered to the two men, "My stars, what I've been through trying to keep her in one place! I thought you'd *never* get here," and with a heavy sigh, headed for Suzi's bedroom.

Suzi shook her head. It didn't take a rocket scientist to figure out that, although Mrs. O'Reilly might be on her payroll, she had been working for Wilbur Langley for at least these past few weeks. "Wilbur, you're impossible, incorrigible and a bit of a traitor, now that I think about it," she said without anger, going up on tiptoe to kiss his cheek.

"Yes, I am, rather, aren't I?" The publisher turned to Harry and the two men shook hands, each equally happy to see the other. "Now that I've played deliveryman, you won't mind if I come along to give the bride away, will you, Harry?"

"I should be delighted, sir," Harry responded, his sea blue eyes twinkling. "I hope it wasn't too much of a bother, procuring my bridal gift? I shall reimburse you from my gaming winnings, as promised. Was it very difficult to have my design implemented?"

"Not at all. The seamstress had no problem, or so she assured me. I haven't yet seen it, but I am convinced everything went well."

Now Suzi was confused. Had Mrs. O'Reilly phoned Wilbur in Manhattan and spilled the beans, or had Harry? "I didn't know you'd mastered long-distance dialing, Harry," she said, part of her wanting to know everything that had been going on behind her back, and another part of her longing to rip into the big white box and see her unexpected present. She didn't know what it was, but it was bound to be beautiful. Both Wilbur and Harry had excellent taste!

"Oh, yes," Harry answered calmly. "And just the other day, the overnight mails and the fax machine as well. Mrs. O'Reilly has been endlessly helpful."

Suzi bristled, forgetting the present. "Anyone in skirts wants to be 'endlessly helpful' to you, you sneak. So the two of you have been running around behind my back, carrying tales to Wilbur? Why aren't I surprised? You and Wilbur might have been cut from the same bolt of natural fiber silk! What was the fax for?''

''To send me the sketch of his requirements for your bridal gown, of course,'' Wilbur told her, taking her by the elbow and guiding her toward her bedroom. ''Not that you don't look lovely in the ensemble you have chosen, my pet—a *Donna Karan* unless I miss my guess. Now why don't you be a good little bride? Toddle off and allow Mrs. O'Reilly to assist you in dressing. We're already running late, you know.''

''My—my wedding gown?'' She looked to Wilbur, who was making shooing motions in her direction, and then to Harry, who was standing there looking so maddeningly innocent, so adorable.

Suzi was going to cry. She just knew it. She was going to stand here and start blubbering like some emotional baby, making a complete fool of herself. ''Harry, you bought me a wedding gown?''

''It's not the more traditional bridal gift of pearls, I agree, dear heart,'' Harry said rather formally, as if he, as well as she, was suddenly operating under some emotional strain. ''However, I felt the need to indulge myself in a small fantasy. You will, I hope, do me the pleasure of honoring my wishes in this matter.''

Indulge a small fantasy? What had Harry meant by that? ''I suppose so,'' Suzi told him hesitantly, looking to Wilbur, hoping something in his expression would tell her whether Harry's gift would delight or dismay her. ''As long as there isn't a spinster's cap or some such English monstrosity in that box.''

''Oh, for shame, Suzi,'' Wilbur said in slightly bored tones, pulling back his French cuff to glance at his gold Rolex. ''Time's a-wasting, my dear. Go after Mrs.

O'Reilly. You can be impolite to us all again later if you feel the need.''

Knowing when she was beaten, and now more interested than ever in seeing the contents of the box, Suzi gave up the fight and returned to her bedroom, only taking time to slam the door to show that she didn't much like being or-dered around like a misbehaving child.

''Oh, my goodness!'' she exclaimed as she slowly walked across the room to the bed, where Mrs. O'Reilly was lifting the gown from a small mountain of tissue paper. ''It's lovely!''

The gown was simply made of some sort of soft, natural fabric, a pattern of extremely tiny, delicately stemmed pur-ple flowers scattered across a white background. The neck of the gown was a modest scoop, the design high-waisted, banded just below her breasts by a thin purple velvet rib-bon, then flowing softly down to ankle-length, where it ended in a small ruffle much like those that edged the short, cap sleeves.

''There's gloves, lovely white satin shoes in your size and a bonnet the likes of which I haven't seen since I was a girl in Brooklyn and my mother bought us all new bon-nets for Easter-time. I think we should pile your hair up high on your head, the way you did for that dinner at the Metropolitan Museum last winter, and well—Miss Harper, I think you should see this for yourself,'' Mrs. O'Reilly said, holding out a small velvet box.

''Thank you, Mrs. O'Reilly,'' Suzi said absently as she took the jeweler's box, still staring at the gown. Harry wanted her to look like a Regency Miss, if that was the correct term for a young lady of his time. He wasn't in-sulting her; he was indulging in a ''small fantasy.'' The gesture was sweet, touching and very revealing. Harry was treating her as if she was his affianced wife, and not just the woman circumstance was forcing him to marry.

Now she knew she was going to cry.

She became aware that she was holding the jeweler's box and snapped it open to see Harry's signet ring inside. He had been wearing it the day he'd voyaged through time and into her life, but she didn't remember seeing it on his hand this past week.

The ring was solid gold, a small, elaborately curved and swirling *W* engraved on its small oval surface. How had it come to be in with the gown Wilbur had brought from Manhattan? Oh, yes. Harry had "mastered" the overnight mails, hadn't he?

She lifted the ring from its velvet bed and experimentally slipped it onto the third finger of her left hand. It fit perfectly.

"I sent along one of your own rings in the same box, so Mr. Langley could get it sized right," Mrs. O'Reilly explained, dabbing at her eyes before loudly blowing her nose. "Isn't it lovely? Mr. Wilde has been planning this for more than a week. It's like something out of a fairy tale, that's what it is. Isn't Mr. Wilde the most romantic, considerate man you ever met?"

Suzi looked up at the housekeeper, so blinded by tears she could barely make out the woman's broadly grinning face.

It took the better part of an hour for Wilbur to satisfy himself as to the arrangement of the small truckload of flowers he'd ordered for the justice of the peace's shabby living room, excluding the time he'd spent rehearsing the justice's wife as she played that old sentimental standard, "Because," on her out-of-tune piano.

During that time, the happy couple had been told to amuse themselves as best they could. Suzi, who had barely spoken except to shyly thank Harry for his gifts, had asked to sit alone in the office.

Harry, not sure if Suzi was avoiding him or merely playing the bride who should not risk bad luck by seeing the groom too close to the ceremony, paced the small, depressingly brown garden behind the justice's office.

As he paced, he tried to tell himself it was only natural that he should have been shocked spitless by Suzi's appearance. The gown had worked like a magician's trick, seemingly transporting him back to Mayfair and the world he had left. A world he had thought to see again if he did not die in battle. A world he knew now he would never see again.

Suzi, by the simple act of donning that gown and its complementing straw bonnet, would have dazzled London society with her presence! Blond, petite, with skin as pure and smooth as marble, and with blue eyes as large and guileless as Caroline Lamb's, she would have taken the town by storm, becoming the sensation of the Season.

Why, if Suzi Harper had been a debutante in 1813, he wouldn't have gotten within fifty yards of her, having been cut out by every titled gentleman who could pen an ode to her eyelashes or dazzle her with his box at the opera.

If Suzi Harper had been a debutante in 1813, he might never have been able to do more than worship her from afar as she went down the dance at Almack's, then retire to his club to drown his sorrows in a bottle.

But Suzi Harper was not a debutante and this was not 1813. All thoughts of London, of his past life, receded without another moment's regret. For Suzi Harper was here, as was he, they were about to be married—and Harry felt more nervous than if he were some green as grass looby straight from the country about to face his first evening in London society.

Would Wilbur ever be done fussing and stage-managing the business so that they could get on with the ceremony? Much as he admired the man for his many talents and appreciated his gift of the flowers, Harry knew he was within seconds of bodily removing Wilbur Langley from the scene so that the justice of the peace could pronounce the vows and have done with it!

At last Mrs. O'Reilly opened the back door and loudly "Yoo-hooed" at Harry, motioning for him to come inside. Harry took a deep breath, collected his composure and followed the housekeeper into the living room, doing his best not to laugh at the woman's choice of headgear—a small box of a hat decorated with a single red rose that insisted upon jiggling up and down with every heavy tread of her sensible-shoe clad feet.

Wilbur had wrought a miracle, turning the small living room into a woodland glen, more than a dozen tall, leafy plants bordered by baskets of daisies, and violets, and white-as-snow roses obscuring any sight of the furnishings.

The justice of the peace stood beneath a ceiling-high horseshoe-shaped white wooden trellis that was dripping with wisteria much the same shade as the violet flowers in Suzi's gown. And, much to Harry's quiet amusement, it appeared that the man's suit had only recently been pressed, his gravy-stained tie replaced by a clean one.

"You're to stand over here, Mr. Wilde," Mrs. O'Reilly told him, waving him to the right of the trellis with the hand that clutched a bouquet of daisies. "That's it. I have to go into the other room, then come out again, just like a real matron of honor. It was Mr. Langley's idea. Now, don't go away."

"I wouldn't think of it, madam," he said, grinning as the justice's wife began murdering the piano. It was nice to learn that Wilbur wasn't infallible.

And then Harry didn't think much of anything at all, because Mrs. O'Reilly appeared once more—minus the rose-topped hat—her wide Irish face beaming as she took the scant half-dozen short strides that brought her to the trellis. She stepped carefully to one side, then turned to look back at the doorway, and Harry followed suit.

Suzi entered on Wilbur's arm, dressed as he'd already seen her, but now wearing the bonnet and carrying a nosegay of violets, her eyes demurely downcast. The baby's breath nestled among the violets trembled because her hand was trembling...because she was nervous...because she was about to throw her life away on a man she only recently had met but could not avoid...had bravely decided she could not allow to face his new, unknown, unknowing world on his own.

Harry wanted to run, to take himself off before Suzi could sacrifice herself, before she was eternally bound to him, a man she did not know, could not love. At the same time he wanted to be a gentleman—be a man!—and refuse to give in to this sudden madness that told him that if he ran from Suzi Harper now he would be the biggest coward in eternity.

And then Suzi raised her gaze, saw the towering green plants, saw the flowers, saw the trellis—saw Harry.

She saw them all.

And she smiled through the tears standing in her eyes.

"Wilbur, how did you know?"

"I pride myself on knowing everything, my pet," he answered, finishing his last bite of wedding cake in the small private dining room he had hired for the postwedding luncheon. "However, if you are referring to my decorations for the ceremony, I would remind you that you were rather vocal on the subject after dear Sydney's lavish affair last fall."

Suzi averted her eyes. "That's right," she said, blushing. "I had a few glasses of wine that day, didn't I? It was wonderful—watching Courtney's daughter walk down the aisle—but a little scary as well. I mean, when my friends' children are getting married and I'm still—''

"But now you're an old married woman," Wilbur interrupted, "and have been for nearly three hours. Are you happy, my pet?''

Suzi looked across the room to see Harry returning from the small balcony overlooking the ocean, Mrs. O'Reilly on his arm. He was being kind to the housekeeper, because it was in his nature to be kind. It had also been in his nature, at the conclusion of the ceremony, to kiss his new bride until her toes curled inside her new white satin shoes. "Oh, yes, Wilbur. I'm happy. I'm probably also certifiably *nuts*. But I'm happy."

"Good," Wilbur said decisively, then struck when she was least suspecting an attack. "Now, why don't you be a good little girl and tell me who Harry really is."

Suzi's blood ran cold, something she had formerly imagined only happened in bad novels. Toying with the handle of her coffee cup, she mumbled, "Who is he? He's Harry Wilde, an Englishman I met here in Ocean City. I don't know what you mean."

"Never mind," Wilbur assured her smoothly, too smoothly, motioning for the waitress to bring the check. "I shouldn't have asked. Shall we head back to your condo for a few minutes? Then I shall have to be on my way. There's another art exhibit I have promised to attend this evening in the Village—a boring but necessary chore."

Suzi looked at Wilbur from beneath her eyelashes. "You aren't going straight back?" she asked, a sinking feeling in her stomach telling her that her old friend wasn't finished asking questions. He was just going to interrogate someone else. Someone like Harry.

It was nearly six o'clock before Wilbur's limousine backed out of the driveway with Wilbur and Mrs. O'Reilly inside. Wilbur had suggested that he transport the house-keeper back to Suzi's Manhattan condo, leaving the new-lyweds on their own for a short honeymoon before they, too, returned to the city.

Suzi watched the limousine pulling away, fighting the urge to run after it and drag Mrs. O'Reilly back.

How could Wilbur have done this to her? He knew her quick marriage to Harry was due to strange circumstance, knew there was something strange about Harry himself. Wilbur knew everything.

So why had he abandoned her and taken her comfortable, live-in chaperone along as well?

"Hungry?" Harry asked, slipping an arm around her waist and guiding her back to the condo. "Mrs. O'Reilly said she left a meal for us in the refrigerator. Or would you rather walk down to the boardwalk and nibble on some pizza? Of course we'd have to change first. As you've said so many times, the best way to elude unwanted attention is to blend with the crowd."

Suzi sensed Harry's nervousness, and the realization comforted her. And then she was struck by inspiration. A terribly romantic inspiration, at least to her mind. "Harry, take off your jacket and tie," she said suddenly, pulling him into the foyer.

"Well, that's true enough, Suzi. There is a third alter-native." His one-sided smile as he quickly stripped off his suit coat nearly caused her to race for her bedroom, bolting the door behind her.

"That's not what I meant!" she hastened to explain as Harry expertly worked the knot out of his tie and slowly slid the tie from beneath his collar. "I just thought we could walk on the beach, that's all. I've always wanted to walk on the beach in a long gown, the hem hovering just above the water as if I couldn't care less about getting it wet."

"Ah, yes," Harry said, laying the jacket and tie over the

banister. "I've seen the commercial on your television, I believe. The man and woman walk hand in hand along the water's edge as the sun goes down, the two of them barefoot—the man's trousers rolled up to his knees—as someone I can't see talks about stocks and bonds and preparing for something he called 'golden years.' Or perhaps the sun is rising? Do you think that matters?"

"No, Harry. It doesn't matter." Suzi thought she'd die of embarrassment. "Never mind. It was a lousy idea, and the dry cleaning bills would be sky high." She turned to go into her bedroom but he stopped her by placing his hand on her arm.

"No, dear heart," he contradicted, his voice low and faintly husky. "I believe it to be a sterling idea, truly. Just give me a minute to roll up my trousers and we'll be on our way."

She watched as Harry sat on the stairs and removed his shoes and socks. She had to swallow down hard on a rapidly rising excitement as he rolled up his pant legs to just below his knees, exposing tanned, golden hair-dusted calves, then stood and unbuttoned the top two buttons of his snowy white shirt. His hair had come free from the thin black ribbon he'd used to secure it at his nape and he used both hands to sweep it back from his face.

Damn the man anyway! If he got any more gorgeous he'd be declared illegal in all fifty states.

"Just a minute!" she said excitedly, racing to her bedroom to strip off her panty hose. There was nothing very romantic about walking in the ocean unless her legs were bare. She hesitated a moment before rejoining Harry, taking time to pick up her straw bonnet and take it along with her, holding it by its trailing satin ribbons. All the best romantic scenes included a large straw hat being carried by the beautiful heroine.

She would have checked her appearance in the mirror

over her dresser, except that she was sure that if she did she would immediately remember that she was *not* a sweet, young, romantic heroine but nothing more than an over-thirty spinster who had hooked a husband only because he didn't have any other choice.

"Here I am," she called breathlessly as she stepped outside the condo to see Harry standing at the edge of the path, his fists on his hips, the breeze off the ocean ruffling both his long blond hair and the rolled-up sleeves of his dress shirt. She was struck by how much he suddenly resembled the man she had rescued on the beach, then shook her head, banishing the thought. Harry Wilde was no longer a stranger on the beach. He was her husband.

And she was scared to death!

Harry held out his hand to her and she took it, keeping her gaze directed toward the ground as they made their way across the wide stretch of sun-kissed sand and headed south along the shore, away from the boardwalk.

The beach was nearly deserted at this time of day, with the vacationers who rented the beachfront condos either eating their evening meal or dressing for a night on the boardwalk. In fact, except for a few die-hard body surfers and an elderly couple using metal detectors to sweep the sand for lost coins and jewelry, Suzi and Harry had the beach to themselves.

Neither of them spoke for at least five minutes as gulls screamed above their heads, the two of them concentrating on the scenery, their feet surefootedly finding the hard, cool, wet sand as wavelets curled around their ankles.

Then one larger, unexpected wave broke closer to shore and Suzi got her wish—her hem was suddenly soaked! "Oh, Harry, look what I've done!" she called out in disgust, shaking her hand free of his and running back up the beach a few paces, her hem clinging to her shins. "It's ruined. How could I have been so stupid?

"Nonsense, dear heart," Harry told her, pulling her back into the shallow water. "I find it most becoming. All the most daring young debutantes in Mayfair dampen their muslins."

Suzi felt a bubble of laughter rising in her throat as her jangled nerves calmed under Harry's sweet good humor. "They did, did they? And did all the most daring young bucks go wading with their trousers rolled up to their knees?"

"Our breeches were already *at* our knees, if you'll remember my water-soaked state when we first met," Harry reminded her, nudging her deeper into the water. "And I haven't been a 'young buck' in some years. I am—was— a Corinthian, a lover of sport and good wine, and beautiful women. Of course that is all behind me now."

"Because you hit your head, fell overboard and ended up in the twentieth century," Suzi said, her heart aching for him.

"No, dear heart," he answered, bending down to splash a fine spray of seawater on her skirt. "Because I am now a married man with sober responsibilities. I imagine I shall have to confine myself to watching sports, like Charlie, the clerk's lucky ex-husband, and concentrate on weightier matters."

Suzi ran a few paces ahead of him, then turned to hold up her skirts and kick a small fountain of water in his direction. "What sort of weightier matters would those be, good sir?" she asked, feeling suddenly carefree and, strangely, most remarkably beautiful. There *was* something to be said for walking along the ocean in a long gown, a large straw bonnet hanging from her arm by its satin strings, her hair free of its pins and curling about her face thanks to a gentle sea breeze.

Harry scratched at a spot behind his left ear as he grinned at her. "Allow me a moment to refine on that, sweet lady.

I suppose,'' he said, taking her hand and turning her back in the direction they had come, "that I should concentrate on securing a comfortable future for my wife—that would be you. Strange, isn't it, how we, too, are speaking of 'golden' futures, just like the commercial? And then, of course, I shall have to go about setting up my nursery,'' he ended, pulling on her hand so that she had no choice but to follow him into the waves that now reached their knees.

His nursery? Suddenly Suzi was all out of snappy patter, her usually agile tongue cleaving to the roof of her very dry mouth. It was only when the next wave to hit the beach broke against her thighs that she shrieked and asked, "Harry, are you trying to drown me?''

He scooped her up in his arms at once, holding her high against his chest, the skirt of her gown plastered against her legs, clinging to the fabric of his pant legs. "Never, dear heart,'' he said, his expression so serious, his gaze so intent on her face, that she realized she was dangerously close to tears. "I'd never want to lose you. I was merely attempting to cool my ardor, for I know I should be hanged for what I'm thinking at the moment, husband or no husband.''

"Oh, Harry.'' She laid her head against his broad chest, sighing, as he carried her back up the beach to the condo.

To the condo. To her empty condo. To her empty bed.

"You're not supposed to think, Harry,'' she said at last, daring to stroke his cheek with the back of her hand, daring to press a kiss against the intriguing hollow at the base of his throat. "Neither one of us is supposed to think. If we did, we would be left with no other choice but to run, screaming, into the sea.''

Chapter Eight

Moonlight streamed in between the slats of the vertical blinds, spilling onto the bed. Patchwork, who had been spending her nights on Harry's bed, had taken up a place at the foot of the mattress and was curled into a small ball, sound asleep and contentedly purring.

Suzi's blond hair was spread fanlike around her head as she slept on her side, the sheet covering her to her hips, her right arm flung across Harry's waist.

As for Harry, he was propped against the pillows he'd pushed against the headboard, still awake, and caught somewhere between the greatest happiness and the most profound sadness he'd ever known.

He hadn't been the first, just as there had been women for him before Suzi. That was all right. He had been in twentieth-century America long enough to know that Suzi could not have been a virgin in this modern society unless she had been living alone on a mountaintop for the past thirty-two years.

Her lack of virginity didn't bother him; nor did her stam-

mered explanation of a "stupid mistake" she had made in
her mid-twenties, believing herself to be in love with a man
when she had only longed to be in love.

What saddened Harry was the thought that he had missed
being with Suzi for all of those thirty-two years.

He had missed her at the age of five, when all the world
was a wonder.

He had not been privileged to know her at eighteen, with
the world before her.

He had not been there to hold her hand, comfort her, be
strong for her, when the world of her dreams and the world
of reality had combined in her early twenties, when her
parents had died and she had been forced to face that world
alone.

But now he was here, and that was what filled his entire
being with happiness, a golden glow of contentment, a
fierce devotion, a vow to himself and to Suzi that she would
never be alone again.

He looked down at her sleeping form, adoring the way
her long lashes cast small shadows against her cheeks, the
way she seemed to smile in her dreams. She was a marvel.
Soft one moment, shy and deliciously nervous, responsive
and burning with desire the next.

All her passion for living, all her endless enchantment
with the world had centered on him as he had carried her
in from the beach, laid her down on the bed, then joined
her as he took that first, sweet kiss from her sea-kissed
mouth.

His hands had trembled as they sought her, found her,
molded her slimness, her sweet valleys, her soft, mounded
curves.

And then the fire. The sweet fire. The all-consuming
blaze that had simmered between them for so long had
exploded in a white-hot heat that had left them both breathless, in awe, and unable to speak.

He closed his eyes, taking a deep breath, wondering what he had done to be so blessed, wondering when he would summon the nerve to do more than love her—to tell her how much he loved her. To put into words all that he had tried to say with his hands...his lips...his worshiping body...

"Harry?"

He looked down at Suzi, to see her in the process of tugging the sheet up over her bare breasts. "Yes, dear heart?" he asked, running a finger down over her nose, then playfully rubbing her soft bottom lip. "Have you wakened to realize that we have somehow neglected to partake of our evening meal?"

"Partake of our evening meal? Ah, Harry, how I love it when you talk Regency." She held his hand in place and began nibbling on the tip of his finger with her small, white teeth. "Is that what I'm feeling, Harry?" she questioned him, gazing up at him teasingly with those great, blue eyes. "Hunger?"

"Wretch!" he exclaimed, sinking fully down onto the mattress and taking hold of her, rolling her over on top of him. "You know, of course, that you are an extremely forward little minx?"

Her smile dazzled him. "Would you have me any other way, good sir?"

He threaded a hand through the silky hair at her nape, pulling her toward him. "I'd have you any way I could get you, madam," he admitted, reveling in the feel of her bare breasts against his chest, unsurprised by his quick arousal. "For the moment, however, and for the next fifty years or more, I'd much prefer having you just this way, in just this place."

She pressed quick kisses against the side of his throat, her fingers splayed against his chest, burrowing in the golden hairs she had only recently told him fascinated her beyond all reason. "Hmm, how nice. Please, sir, tell me more. I'm all ears."

"No, you're not," he told her, sliding his hands along her back, to the curve of her small waist, then lower. Deliciously lower. "Although they are most attractive, your ears, dear heart, are definitely not your most appealing feature. This, for instance, is very nice," he went on, curving his hands against her buttocks, then smoothing one hand upward to cup one perfect breast, "and I believe I have developed a definite preference for many of your other feminine attributes."

"Ah, more Regency talk. So formal, yet so deliciously sexy! More, Harry. Tell me more," she teased, her own hands becoming busy as she levered her body slightly to his right, exposing him to any liberty she might wish to take.

She took several, with both his unspoken agreement and his eventual breathless encouragement, before he rolled her over onto her back and straddled her. His kisses were hot and insistent, his heart pounding as he both felt the moment and anticipated the next moment, until he could stand it no more and took her, took himself, on their second journey in as many hours to the special heaven made for lovers.

And then they slept in each other's arms, this loving couple, without ever speaking a single word of love.

For now, for the moment, for this first night, words didn't seem to matter.

But what would happen, Harry asked himself as he finally drifted off to sleep, if all they would ever have were moments? What if he had come into Suzi's life for some sort of cosmic "moment" and could just as easily and unexpectedly fade out of it again?

"It's Yorkshire pudding."

Suzi watched as Harry eyed the concoction suspiciously.

"Uh-huh," he said, obviously trying very hard not to laugh at her latest culinary effort. "Of course it is, dear heart. I should have recognized it at once—if it weren't so very, um, *fluid*."

She allowed the pan to drop a full two inches onto the ceramic tabletop. "It's not just fluid, Harry. It's *liquid*." She took off her oven mitt and threw it in his general direction, then returned to the stove and the cookbook that lay open on the counter. "Two eggs?" she read aloud, trying to refresh her memory. "Did it. One cup milk? Yup. We're all right so far. Two cups flour? *Two?* Does that say *two?*"

"Do I detect a hint of surprise in your voice, dear heart?" Harry asked, coming up behind her and slipping his arms around her waist as he laid his chin on her shoulder and peered at the page in the cookbook.

"Oh, put a sock in it, Harry," Suzi ordered, bending her knees so that she could slip out from under his chin, disconcerted by his closeness. They had been married for nearly two weeks, had made love every morning and evening ever since, but she was still as skittish as a young colt whenever Harry indulged in any friendly closeness. It was silly of her, darn near stupid, but she couldn't help it. They were great in bed. That didn't make them great anywhere else.

Maybe she was just trying too hard. Experimenting with recipes, trying to impress him with her domestic skills—a nonexistent talent to this point in her life—hoping to show herself as the perfect wife. It wasn't like her to play pretend, at least not with something so very *real*, and she should have given up the ghost on the project days ago, when she had accidentally broiled that chocolate cake.

She busied herself carrying the prime roast of beef into the dining room, secretly pleased that it smelled and looked heavenly, and called for Harry to join her.

He pushed the pan of ruined pudding to one side and held out her chair, once more complimenting her on the table decorations as he took his own seat.

"The centerpiece was a gift from Mrs. O'Connell next door. A wedding present. She gave it to me this afternoon," she said as she affectionately eyed the small piece of driftwood decorated with pink plastic flowers, the names Suzi and Harry having been spelled out along the base in seashell chips. "I think I know now how my dad felt every Father's Day when I handed him another tie I'd picked out myself. Poor Mrs. O'Connell. She means well. But you know something, Harry? I wouldn't sell that centerpiece for a million dollars!"

Harry laid a slice of beef on a plate and held it out to Suzi. "One Christmas when I was nine or ten I presented my father with a rack for his pipes, a truly homely trifle that I'd stuck together from odd pieces of metal the smithy allowed me to work on at the forge. Papa always treasured it, as we shall treasure Mrs. O'Connell's gift. I hope you enjoy your beef rare, dear heart."

Suzi sat up very straight and eyed the beef over the rim of the plate. She liked her prime rib rare. To her, it was the only way to eat it, and she often ordered the dish at *Charlie O's* before going to the theater. "Oh, Lord, and it looked so good on the outside, too," she said miserably, slumping back down in her chair. "That's not rare, Harry. That's raw. I'm surprised it didn't *moo* at you when you sliced into it."

"I know a simple remedy for our dilemma." Harry picked up the platter and disappeared into the kitchen. A few moments later Suzi heard the oven door open and close. Then Harry returned to the dining room and stood behind her, to help her from her chair. "I suggest we find something else to occupy us while the oven does its magic.

It's all but impossible to ruin a good joint of beef, dear heart. We need only to be patient.''

She looked over her shoulder at him. ''Doesn't anything get you rattled, Harry?'' she asked, fighting back tears of frustration. ''I mean, isn't it boring being so damned British all the time? That stiff upper lip thing only works for so long, especially when you're hungry. You and that patience of yours could starve to death before your incompetent wife learns how to cook.''

She stood and he pushed in the chair, then turned to smile at her. ''I didn't marry you for your domestic prowess, dear heart. You possess other skills much more to my liking.''

Suzi picked up the bowl of crushed corn and the dish of salad and headed for the kitchen to put them away, feeling her cheeks beginning to flush. That was the first time he'd even obliquely referred to their stunning compatibility in the bedroom *outside* of that bedroom, and he was making her nervous again, damn him.

''Maybe I could take another stab at making some Yorkshire pudding while we're waiting?'' she suggested, her throat tight.

''Or we could take a walk on the beach, I suppose,'' Harry said, bringing in the single nearly raw slice of beef that he'd already carved and adding it to the roasting pan already in the oven. ''Although Mrs. O'Connell says the neighbors on the other side of our condo have complained to her that they don't entirely appreciate hearing giggles coming from the beach at midnight.''

''It isn't midnight, Harry,'' Suzi said, trying to tell him that he was crossing a line she didn't want breached. Their lovemaking was not to be spoken of, to her mind, not when so much of their lives remained unsettled.

Didn't he remember why they had married in the first place? Didn't he remember that they weren't just another married couple enjoying their honeymoon, but two near strangers indulging in a mad, impulsive adventure that could end badly?

Or didn't he see what she saw? Perhaps he didn't. And she wasn't about to discuss it with him. She refused to worry him about her anxiety late at night as he slept beside her, the nagging fear that was with her all day and that turned to stark terror in those long, dark hours after midnight.

The fear that she might wake up one morning to find him gone, returned to his own time.

"I think a walk on the beach would be wonderful," she said at last as he waited for her to answer, carefully pinning a smile on her face. "You see, I didn't want to say anything to you, but I think we should leave for Manhattan tomorrow. Other than the fact that I miss Mrs. O'Reilly's cooking, I really do have to go in to the office, deliver my reviews and pick up some more galleys."

She glanced up at him and winced inwardly, for he looked so solemn. She would have thought he could read her mind and knew how frightened she was. Or was he disappointed that she had all but slapped his face for speaking of their lovemaking? "Harry? Is something wrong?"

"Not a thing, dear heart," he said, his handsome face splitting in a grin. "I can hardly wait to see Manhattan. To take a bite out of the Big Apple. To walk along the Great White Way—Broadway. To visit Times Square, which sounds much like Piccadilly Circus was in my day. And Wilbur has already promised to take me on an extensive tour of Langley Publishing."

Suzi was pleasantly surprised with Harry's ready agreement to their move to her New York condo—right up until the moment he'd mentioned Wilbur's name. That's when she began to smell a rat. "When did Wilbur invite you to Langley Publishing?"

Now it seemed to be Harry's turn to avoid *her* eyes. "I'm not completely sure. He could have issued the invitation shortly after he asked me if he could take the portions of my manuscript that I'd already transcribed back to Manhattan with him."

Suzi thought her eyes were about to pop out of her head. "He took the—you *gave* him the—and *I* haven't even been allowed to *look* at it? I knew it that day! Oh, yes, I knew. I could smell that he was up to something. That miserable little *sneak!* Turn my back for one minute, one *single* minute, and he—*damn,* you, Harry Wilde!" She gave him a swat somewhere in the vicinity of his left shoulder. "How *could* you?"

"I do so adore it when you become incomprehensible," Harry said, ruffling her hair before taking hold of her hand and leading her toward the spiral staircase.

She used her free hand to slap him on the back. "Never mind that now, Harry. Why did you give him your manuscript?"

"He asked," Harry told her with maddening calm. "If you had asked, I would have given it to you. You didn't. Wilbur did. It's that simple."

"Harry, *nothing* Wilbur does is 'simple.' Not *ever!*" Suzi informed him tightly as she nearly stumbled on the curving staircase. "But he doesn't fool me. Not for a moment. He's looking for clues, the *sneak!*"

Harry stopped at the bottom of the steps and turned to take hold of Suzi's waist as she stood on the second step. "Clues? Clues to what, dear heart? You may say that I watch entirely too much television, but it seems to me that you're the one who's sounding like an installment of that show on lawyers I enjoy on Thursday nights."

Suzi bobbed her head several times—rather in the way of a person doing her best to hold on to her temper until the other person would shut up and she could have her say.

"Oh, yeah? Oh, yeah?" she bit out the words sarcastically. "Well, a fat lot you know, Harry Wilde. The day we got married, while you were romancing Mrs. O'Reilly out on the restaurant balcony, Wilbur was asking me who you are. Who you really are. Did you catch that, Harry? Wilbur wanted to know who you *really* are. *Now* what do you have to say for yourself?"

Harry was quiet for some moments, remembering Wilbur's questioning glance when Harry had stumbled and referred to his trousers as breeches, then sighed. "First, I should like to offer you my apologies. Secondly, dear heart, I'd say that tomorrow might not be soon enough for us to travel to Manhattan."

If Ocean City had surprised and delighted Harry, his initial look at the island of Manhattan had transported him to ecstasy.

Nothing he had seen prepared him for his first sight of the metropolitan skyline as viewed from the front passenger seat of Suzi's car. He didn't know where to look first, and he asked questions of Suzi, then barely waited for her answers before pointing in another direction to demand she tell him what he was seeing now.

But the ride through the long, white-tiled tunnel threaded deep beneath the river silenced him as he sat in awe of this feat of engineering, Suzi's explanation that a similar tunnel was being constructed to link England with France almost more than he could comprehend.

For centuries, England's safety had been measured in the miles of stormy channel water between itself and Britain's on-again, off-again enemies on the continent. Why would Britain ever want to militarily compromise itself in such a way?

He asked Suzi, who answered simply, "With today's missiles and jets and smart bombs, Harry, it doesn't matter anymore that the English Channel is even there. Besides, England and France have been allies for years and years. Now, don't ask any more questions for a while, Harry, okay? If you thought the New Jersey Turnpike was bad, you ain't seen nothing yet! I've got to concentrate on getting us through this traffic in one piece.''

He obeyed easily, for he was struck speechless as he held on to his seat with both hands, watching bug-eyed as Suzi threaded her car into narrow streets clogged with cars, and trucks, and taxicabs, and people walking straight into the flow of traffic seemingly without looking, without caring that they were making a bad situation worse.

The narrow streets were lined on both sides with structures taller than he had ever seen except for St. Paul's Cathedral towers—some of the structures appearing to be made entirely of glass, some of them so old and black with soot that they had lost any beauty they once must have had. It was as if the buildings had blotted out the sun, and the world was reduced to this single street and its hulking buildings.

And then there were the signs. Huge, garish advertisements of every vice known to man—and several rather bizarre entertainments Harry considered to be beyond the realm of possibility.

People of all colors and persuasion crowded the sidewalks.

There were men dressed in everything from sober business suits to casual clothing such as Harry had observed on the Ocean City boardwalk, to decrepit creatures who appeared to be wearing everything they owned, none of it worth a bent penny.

He saw women in skirts so short and shoe heels so high that both seemed painful to wear, others clad in summery dresses, and still others wearing what appeared to be gentlemen's suits, only the bottom half of their legs were bare.

And everyone he saw was obviously in a great hurry to reach their destination.

The cacophony of blowing horns, and screeching brakes, and high-pitched screams, which Suzi told him were sirens, and hawkers crying their wares, and even one man haranguing a crowd of people stopped at one corner, warning them that doom was at hand, melded together into one, great racket, so that Harry was at last forced to raise the window to shut out the heat and the dust and the noise.

"Suzi?" he asked, not knowing whether to be impressed or disgusted. "Is all of Manhattan like this?"

"Not all of it, Harry," Suzi answered, pointing to her left. "See, down this street? And over there?" She pointed to her right, nearly poking him in the nose. "We're in the theater district now. In a dozen or so more blocks we'll be out of the worst of it. Hey!" she yelled, jamming her foot on the brake while pressing on the disk at the center of the steering wheel, so that Harry heard a horn blowing very close to his own ears as he held on to the dashboard, in fear of his life. "Where'd you get your license, buster? Mail order? Did you see that, Harry? That idiot cut me off!"

"Suzanne," Harry said tightly once they were on their way again. "Now that I'm, as you refer to my status, *legal*, would it be possible for me to learn to navigate an automobile?"

She sliced him a quick look from behind her huge, bright red-rimmed sunglasses before pulling around a large truck loaded to the gills with garbage. "I suppose so. Why do you ask?"

He scratched at a spot behind his left ear. "Because, dear heart, much as I admire your courage and determination, I do not believe I will be able to continue sitting idly by in this seat while allowing you to take my life in your hands."

"Is that your stuck-up way of inferring that you don't approve of the way I drive?"

"Why, yes, dear heart," he answered, grinning. "I do believe it is. I am the man in this small family of ours and, speaking both for myself and for Patchwork—" he glanced into the back seat to see the calico cat cowering inside her small plastic wired cage "—I must say that I would feel much more comfortable with the reins—that is, the *wheel*— in my hand."

"You didn't complain when we were in Ocean City," Suzi said, her lower lip stuck out, her pout adorable, Harry thought.

"And I once allowed a young lady—her brother was a notable whip and had taught her how to tool the ribbons— to drive my curricle in Hyde Park for the Promenade. That does not, however, mean that I was so paper-skulled as to trust her to thread her way down Bond Street at noon," Harry pointed out, he thought, reasonably.

Suzi frowned for a moment more, then grinned at him. "Don't worry about it, Harry. I don't drive in Manhattan. A person would have to be certifiable to do this every day—which explains a lot of our cabdrivers, I suppose. I drive into and out of Manhattan, on my way to New Jersey or to visit my friends Daniel and Joey Quinn in Pennsylvania, but I don't drive in the city. For the most part, all this car does is collect dust and ridiculously high parking garage fees. Happy now?"

"Momentarily mollified, Suzi," Harry corrected before once more becoming interested in the changing scenery outside the car. The street were wider now, and less crowded with trucks, and there were even small islands of green to be seen here and there. The garish signs were gone, and he felt as if he had just driven from Piccadilly into the comfortable neighborhoods of town houses and stately mansions known as Mayfair.

"Good Lord, what's that?" he asked, pointing to his left once more. "I know you don't have royalty here in America, but that building could do competition with Prinny's Carleton House."

"That, Harry," Suzi informed him, "is the New York Metropolitan Museum of Art, better known as the Met. And stop talking about America as if you're just a visitor. As far as anyone except Wilbur is concerned, you were *born* here, remember? Okay, here we are—home sweet home," she said, pulling the car over against the curb and stopping. "You can help Fred, he's the doorman, with our luggage, and then Fred will deliver my car to the parking garage."

Harry opened the passenger door and went to assist Suzi from her seat, only to jump back quickly as one of the yellow taxicabs blew by him, horn blaring. This Manhattan was going to take some getting used to, he decided, prudently retreating toward the curb as the independent Suzi maneuvered herself past the gearshift and climbed out onto the sidewalk.

"Are you all right, sir?" a man in an elaborate uniform asked, taking his arm. "Gotta watch it around here, you know. Those cabs fly past here trying to make the turn and pick up fares at the Met. Gotta keep your eyes open every minute, isn't that right, Miss Harper?"

"Absolutely, Fred," Suzi said, looking at Harry as if to inspect him for injuries. She then introduced him to the doorman, whom Harry had for a moment believed to be a member of the military. He held out his hand to Fred, who hesitated for a second, looking both surprised and flattered by the gesture, before his face split in a grin as he shook Harry's hand.

"So our little Miss Harper is married?" Fred exclaimed, beaming as he energetically pumped Harry's arm up and down. "Well, that's something Mr. Langley didn't tell me when he and the lady arrived a little while ago and Mrs. O'Reilly buzzed him on through.''

Suzi and Harry exchanged quick glances, Suzi saying, "I phoned Mrs. O'Reilly yesterday to tell her we were coming. Damn it, Harry, I'm going to make that man make my quarterly payment for her withholding tax, considering that she's as much in his employ as she is in mine. Come on. Grab a couple of suitcases and let's get this over with!''

"Fred said Wilbur had a woman with him," Harry said, following after Suzi.

"Yeah, he did, didn't he," Suzi shot back, her blue eyes glittering. "And I'll bet my single Picasso sketch that the woman's name is Courtney Blackmun. I'm thirty-two years old. Isn't it time everyone stopped treating me as if I couldn't find my own way out of Bloomie's?"

"I'm sure Wilbur is simply concerned—" Harry began before Suzi cut him off.

"Concerned? Get real! *Nosey* is what I'd call it! Damn, Harry, I love my friends, but there are days—"

"Is something wrong, Miss Harper—er, that is, Mrs., Mrs.—gosh, I forgot!"

"Wilde," Harry reminded Fred proudly after opening the trunk and tossing the car key to the doorman. "Mrs. Harry Wilde. The name suits her down to the ground at the moment, don't you think? But don't worry, everything's fine."

He then pulled five heavy cases out of the trunk, watching as Suzi picked up two of them, then slammed the trunk, grabbed the three remaining cases and took off after his irate bride as she walked beneath the canopy, heading for the front door.

He wasn't accustomed to following where any female led, but in Suzi's case, and knowing that Wilbur was upstairs waiting for them, he didn't see that he had any other choice. Although Harry did take a moment to admire Suzi's legs as she glided along in her short skirt and delicate high-heeled shoes, believing that, if nothing else, the varied women's fashions of the twentieth century might make up just a little bit for the modern man's loss of superiority.

Not that he'd ever say as much to Suzi. She'd only give him another lecture on something she called "equal rights," then reel off a list of women who'd climbed mountains, fought in wars, become great judges and doctors and corporate presidents—and even flown into space, all while raising children, keeping a neat house and reminding their totally helpless husbands where they had left their car keys.

He entered the elevator behind Suzi, only his third elevator ride to date, so that he watched the buttons in admiration as he was lifted seemingly effortlessly to the eighth floor. He didn't have any other choice, actually, because Suzi was standing face front, her chin at a belligerent angle, almost as if *daring* him to say anything, just so she could tell him again, "I *told* you so!"

Chapter Nine

"Plague and Pestilence? Oh, no, Suzi. Don't tell me Sydney's been using her pet names for her brothers in public. The twins are fine, believe it or not. They're still at computer camp, driving their counselors wild, I suppose," Courtney Blackmun said as she sat at her ease on the long white couch in Suzi's living room.

Harry stood beside the small, portable bar, an untouched glass of wine in his hand, knowing himself to have been favorably impressed with the bestselling author the moment he first saw her as she came forward to wrap Suzi in an enthusiastic bear hug.

Courtney was a beautiful, sophisticated woman, one Harry could not believe to be the mother of a married daughter. And, of course, he liked her immediately because Courtney liked Suzi, and Harry would always like anyone who appreciated his very singular wife.

Not that Harry was at his ease, for Wilbur was also in the room, looking his usual elegant self, but with a sparkle in his eye that was most disconcerting.

While Suzi and Courtney chatted together, Suzi proudly showing off her wedding ring and regaling her friend with details of the marriage ceremony, Wilbur discreetly crooked a finger in Harry's direction, then disappeared into the kitchen.

Harry looked to Suzi, who was describing the trellis Wilbur had ordered installed in the living room of the hapless justice of the peace, and knew he would not get any help from her. She was deliberately ignoring him, wordlessly telling him that he was the one who had gotten them into this latest trouble by giving Wilbur the manuscript and he was darn well the one who would have to find a way to get them out again!

And she was right. Dealing with Wilbur Langley and the man's "inquiring mind" was his problem. Setting his glass of wine on the bar, he took a steadying breath, squared his shoulders and headed for the kitchen, feeling as if he were fourteen again and on his way to the headmaster's office to be read a lecture on the foolhardiness of keeping a monkey in his rooms.

"I've read your manuscript, my boy, and enjoyed it immensely," Wilbur said without preamble, which was the very last thing Harry had thought the man would say, and which was a move that put him totally off his guard.

Wilbur liked his work? He really liked it? Harry hadn't held out much hope in that quarter, firmly believing that his scribblings would not be attractive to anyone born after 1800.

"Really, Wilbur?" he asked, trying not to preen outwardly at the publisher's praise. "But you haven't seen more than a quarter of it—not that it's totally finished in any case. The section on my—that is, the character's varied adventures during his reluctant service during the War of 1812 is incomplete."

Good Lord! Why couldn't he guard his tongue? A few

words of flattery and he was acting as if his brain was to let—a vain popinjay with no consideration for his safety, for the safety of Suzi and their shared secret.

Wilbur leaned a hip against the countertop, his fingers laced together in front of him. "Ah, Harry, that's true enough. But I've been in the business for a long time. I know brilliance when I see it. It's a fascinating coming-of-age story, only with a twist, that twist being that I haven't read anything so startlingly *real* in some time. Even your spelling—so imaginative, so much in the way of the period—is an added fillip."

Harry merely smiled politely, determined not to say anything else until he felt more sure of himself, or until Suzi rescued him, which he was fairly certain she would not do.

"You know," Wilbur went on, "I believe I would want to keep the spelling as it appears now, rather in the way Stephen King's publisher printed page after page of *Misery* as if it were a real, typewritten page from a manuscript. It was an ingenious if expensive device, complete with handwritten letters to make up for the character's supposed difficulty with a malfunctioning typewriter. Not that keeping the spelling will add to our costs, even if it will give our proofreaders fits. Yes, yes. That's settled. The spelling will remain as it is."

"You—you're going to publish my work?" So much for holding his tongue, Harry thought, knowing Wilbur was drawing him in, deliberately trying to gain his confidence. But the possibility of seeing his words in print was so heady, so intoxicating, that he longed to hear more.

"Publish it? Dear boy, I will *produce* it! I will tout it, push it, and then step back modestly and watch it climb to the heights of the bestseller's lists, where it will remain for a long, long time. Harry, dear man, you have succeeded in relating a most wondrous tale of a young Regency gentleman's journeys in the world. The work is not fanciful, like

Byron's, but very real, and touching, and rather humorous as well—as well as curiously relevant to today's youth. I haven't read such disbelief dispelling fiction in twenty years!''

"Fiction?" Harry smiled, letting his pent-up breath out slowly. So he was wrong. Wilbur didn't suspect anything. "I've always enjoyed fiction, Wilbur," he said, relaxing. "Although I never thought to be compared with George. When I read his *Childe Harold's Pilgrimage* this past spring I was bowled over by its beauty, its power."

"Just this past spring, Harry? I would have thought Byron would be required reading in all English schools," Wilbur said, looking at him closely, so that Harry knew he had put his foot in it again.

"Oh, I read Byron in my youth, surely," he improvised quickly, "but not with any great relish. It is only now that I am older that I appreciate his brilliance in anything other than breaking female hearts. You know how it is with young lads, Wilbur."

"Vaguely. There are times I don't believe I ever was young. Then again," he added, smiling, "there are those who would say I never grew up at all. Very well," he added, pushing himself away from the counter. "We'll leave mundane things like contracts and advance payments until another time and rejoin the ladies before they take offense at our absence, but we do have an agreement, don't we?"

Harry couldn't believe it. He wanted to grab the publisher and kiss him on both cheeks. Not only was he now an American, but he was married to his adorable Suzi, and now he would be able to support her in the manner to which she was already accustomed! "You're really serious, Wilbur? You really want to publish my manuscript?"

Wilbur smiled and patted Harry on the shoulder. "I am always serious, Harry, when it comes to literary pursuits.

Just ask Courtney if you don't believe me. Or my dear daughter-in-law, whose work mirrors your own, if in more modern terms. By the bye, Harry, is Byron half as handsome in life as he is depicted in his portraits?''

"Oh, yes. George is definitely most hand—'' Harry said, then froze in the act of turning toward the living room. Suzi had been correct. Wilbur Langley was a *sneak*. "You *know*,'' he accused, eyeing the publisher in trepidation. "Bloody hell, Wilbur—how long? How long have you known?''

"Since that first evening, I suspect,'' Wilbur answered coolly, although Harry noticed that the older man's usually pale white skin had gone rather gray, as if he had hoped he would not be proved correct. "I still don't quite believe it, but I've always known it.''

"From Courtney's phone call?''

"You mean the one telling me that Suzi had rung her up in Japan in the middle of the night to share the harebrained scheme that she was going to write a time-travel novel and needed a way for her hero to gain legal identification? Yes, that did have something to do with raising my suspicions. Quite a bit to do with it, as a matter of fact. At first I thought she had become the dupe of an illegal alien wishing to use her to gain resident status in America, but after meeting you I began to consider something entirely different, although I decided to pretend I believed Suzi's explanation. Not that I'd even entertain such a farfetched notion as time travel if it had been anyone but Suzi. The most outlandish things do happen to that girl,'' he ended, shaking his head.

"And you're not upset?'' Harry asked, looking into the living room to see that Suzi and Courtney were still deep in conversation, Courtney balancing a pile of manuscript pages on her lap. "You don't object? No,'' he then added consideringly, "you couldn't object, could you, my friend?

Otherwise you wouldn't have helped us procure identification, and you most certainly wouldn't have given our
marriage your blessing.''

Wilbur gestured toward the living room with one well-
manicured hand. "Look at her, my boy," he demanded
imperiously. "Suzi is one of a kind, rather like you. And
she is rapturous and even more beautiful than when I first
met her nearly a decade ago. How can I object to anything—to anyone—who gives the dear girl such happiness?
As her friend, as your friend, I would not do anything to
hurt either of you.''

He turned and looked at Harry, ending sincerely, "You
may face an uncertain future, but if you love enough, any
problem can be surmounted. All I ask is that you be good
to her, my boy. For if you ever deliberately hurt her I shall
be obliged to destroy you.''

Harry extended his hand to the older man, his expression
equally serious. "You have my word as an English gentleman, sir," he promised. "Suzi may not yet be aware of it,
but I love her with all my heart. As you say, she is one of
a kind. A most singular woman.''

Wilbur smiled as if satisfied with Harry's answer, then
abruptly changed the subject, as if he had said and heard
all he wished to say and hear on the matter of Suzi's future.

"I'll want the journey through time put into your book.
Not this one, but the next work of *fiction*. You see, I do
plan for you to have a long, successful career, as do most
all of Langley Publishing's discoveries. Not that you aren't
good, and deserving of any success, but in a country that
could make pet rocks a national phenomenon, it is not very
difficult to promote an author to temporary fame and fortune with the right marketing plan. It is keeping himself
popular for several decades that is the true test of the great
writer. I believe you will pass that test.''

"Thank you, Wilbur," Harry said, knowing he was

beaming with pleasure at the man's kind words. What a wonderful place this America was—so different from the time and place he had come from! He had heard that America was the land of opportunity—or so many emigrants from Ireland and Northern England had thought in his day, but Wilbur's plans for him exceeded all his expectations, all his greatest hopes.

To write, to communicate what was in his mind, his heart, with others had been his dream since his late boyhood, even though his father had not been receptive to the plan. Neither had the few publishers he had contacted on Paternoster Row, for they were much more interested in fanciful, romantic tales such as those penned by Byron and Sir Walter Scott.

That was how he had come to be aboard the *Pegasus* in the first place, having succumbed to the notion that he could please his late father's soul by serving with the forces sent to America after his service with the army against Napoléon had been limited to those of one of Wellesley's many clerks, tucked safely away from the fighting and the glory and the adventure Harry's sire had deemed so necessary to the building of a young man's character.

Would his father be proud of him now, now that he had achieved a measure of "adventure" even his sire could never have dreamed possible? Now that he was on the threshold of "glory" thanks to the possibility of some success with his work?

Harry believed his father would be proud, if he could only know. And who was to say that he didn't know? After all, who would have said it was possible to travel through time? *Anything* was possible!

"Harry? Why are you standing there grinning like you just won the lottery?"

Harry blinked and shook his head, surprised to see that

Wilbur had joined Courtney in the living room and Suzi was now standing beside him in the kitchen.

He smiled as he looked down at his wife, wondering if she knew how wonderful she was, how beautiful she would always be in his eyes, and how very much he loved her. But when he opened his mouth he heard himself say, "He knows."

"He? Wilbur? He knows? What does he know?" She placed a hand on his arm. "Harry, has the trip been too much for you? I know I'm not the best driver in the world, but I already told you I don't drive in Manhattan. And if you need to lie down or something I have to tell you that you don't have time for that right now. Something's happened, and I have to talk to you—just as soon as we can convince Courtney and Wilbur that we want to be alone."

Harry belatedly noticed that Suzi was looking a little pale, rather in the way Wilbur's complexion had whitened as he learned for certain that Harry had come to America from sometime in 1813. Something had happened in the living room, something between Suzi and Courtney. Did the bestselling author also suspect that Harry had traveled through time?

"He knows, Suzi," Harry repeated in a whisper, believing Suzi should learn all of the truth at once. That way, if she decided to faint with shock she would only have to swoon the once, and not again and again. "Wilbur knows I traveled here from Regency England."

Suzi looked into the living room, to where her two friends were gathering up their belongings in preparation of leaving, then glared up at her husband. "That's not funny, Harry," she whispered back fiercely.

"And I am not attempting to be amusing," Harry countered in a low voice, deciding that Courtney had not been made privy to Wilbur's suspicions before their visit. "He has suspected as much almost from the beginning, or so he said, but he tricked me into admitting the truth just a few minutes ago.''

"*Tricked* you?'' Suzi pulled him farther into the kitchen and repeated, her voice once more lowered, "Tricked you? Oh, really. And how did he do that, Harry? How did Wilbur *trick* you into spilling your guts about the most *important* secret you'll ever have to keep? Honestly, Harry, people say *women* can't keep a secret. Well, those people haven't met *you* then, have they? Luckily it's Wilbur. He wouldn't tell a soul, because he adores knowing something no one else knows, and because he knows I'll *pulverize* him if he so much as hints to anyone about how you got here. But do you know how lucky you are that it's only Wilbur? I mean, Harry, how could you have—''

"He bought my manuscript,'' Harry broke in, just to see if Suzi would react and because he didn't need any lectures from his wife when he already knew he had blundered, badly.

She didn't disappoint him. Her anger dissipated in a heartbeat and her features softened, her huge eyes glowing with pride. "He bought it? Wilbur bought it? Oh, *Harry!*'' she exclaimed, then went up on tiptoe to all but crush his neck in her exuberant embrace.

He slipped his arms around her waist, not so blockheaded as to ignore a chance to hold his wife, and caught her mouth with his own.

The explosion of passion he had come to associate with any intimate encounter with Suzi pulsed through his body and Harry further indulged himself by running his hands along his wife's spine, pulling her closer against him. All thoughts of his book, Wilbur's revelation, even the presence of Courtney Blackmun, fled his mind along with any remaining nineteenth-century notions of proper public behavior as Suzi melted against him.

It was only as he heard a door closing somewhere in the

distance that he broke off the kiss and buried his mouth against Suzi's throat. "Might I surmise, dear heart," he asked in a low, amused purr, "that you are tolerably pleased by this news?"

She pushed herself away from him, placing her flattened palms against his chest. "Idiot! Of course I'm pleased. I'm more than pleased!"

"And, being pleased, your first instinct was to kiss me? I cannot tell you how gratifying that is, when I consider that the sun is still high in the sky and all forms of affection have to date been relegated to those hours between dusk and dawn."

"Harry," she answered, taking his hand, clearly having taken the bit between her teeth and anxious to run, "don't start. Not now. Besides, I kiss complete strangers when I'm happy—or I would, if I ever was happy enough and around a stranger at the same time. Come on, I want to talk to Wilbur. I've never acted in the role of agent before, but I know how it goes, and you do need representation, even with Wilbur. Why, this may be the beginning of a whole new career for me—"

She stopped just inside the living room, frowning. "They're gone!"

Harry pulled her close against his side. "Yes, I thought I heard the door close a few moments ago. A discreet pair, Courtney and Wilbur. Either that or your very public display of affection embarrassed them."

"Court and Wilbur embarrassed by a kiss? Get real," Suzi admonished, pulling him over to sit on the couch. "Courtney was just being polite. And I'll bet you she had to drag Wilbur out of here. He always said he'd give several thousand dollars to see me in—"

She clapped her hands over her mouth, her eyes wide as saucers.

"To see you in what, Suzi? To see you in the institution

of marriage? To see you kissing in the kitchen?'' Harry asked teasingly, moving close beside her on the couch, believing this to be a day made for revelations. ''Or, could it be something else? To see you in *love,* perhaps?''

She concentrated on the design in the Oriental carpet. ''I have a big mouth,'' she groused, then looked up at him. ''It seems we have more in common than we thought. Mr. and Mrs. Big Mouth, that's us.''

Harry felt his face splitting in an unholy grin and was slightly surprised his wife didn't hit him. ''Then you do love me?'' he asked, knowing the answer.

''All right. Yes. I love you. I don't know why, because there's no real reason I should, and you are the most infuriating mixture of Regency stuffiness and the worst of what you've learned watching that stupid television—but I do love you, Harry Wilde,'' Suzi said, her small body fairly shaking with fury. ''Are you happy now?''

''Happy? Yes, I believe I am. Happy, elated, delighted, even overjoyed. Rapturous, actually,'' Harry said, tipping up her chin with his fingertips. ''You see, dear heart, I quite adore you, and always will. You have the most generous, unselfish heart of any woman I ever met. You're never still for a moment, I never know what you're going to do next, and you're the most potentially *dangerous* cook in creation—but I love you, Suzi Wilde.''

''Oh, Harry!'' Suzi exclaimed, throwing herself against him, so that he lost his balance and the two of them toppled back onto the cushions. ''That was the most wonderful thing you've ever said to me!'' And then, abruptly, she hopped to her feet, leaving him lying alone and disappointed on the couch. ''However, we have a problem. We've had it all along, ever since the beginning—we even talked about it that first day—but now we have to *really* talk about it. Even if the subject scares me to death.''

Harry shook his head, trying to clear it of thoughts of

Suzi and the wide bed where he had only an hour earlier
deposited their mountain of luggage. But he had already
admitted he never knew from one minute to the next what
Suzi would do, so he took a deep breath, saying, "I'm at
your service, dear heart. Now, what is our new, yet old,
problem? I feel able to solve any difficulty at the moment."

"Well, good luck on this one." She picked up some
papers, those he remembered Courtney handling earlier.
"It's in this, Harry," she said, waving the pages in front
of his nose. "You're not going to believe this, Harry, but
I've inspired Courtney! She brought this along to show
me—a copy of the working synopsis for her next book."

"That's nice, Suzi," Harry answered, reaching into his
pocket for one of the slim cigars he had discovered at an
Ocean City convenience store. Suzi's enthusiastic embrace
had bent it nearly in half, but it was still smokable, so he
straightened it as best he could and slipped it between his
teeth. "Not as nice as nibbling on your ear while I carry
you into the bedroom, but nice. Go on."

"Don't be a spoilsport, Harry," Suzi warned, then
sighed dramatically. "She came to me for advice on how
to end the book, wondering if I had thought of how sticky
the ending could get. You see, this is only a partial synopsis. Courtney hit what she thinks is a roadblock to the
happily ever after all romance novels require."

Striking a match, Harry took several quick puffs on the
bent cigar, then looked up at Suzi through a haze of blue
smoke. "And she came here today to ask you to help her?
I thought you said she was a bestselling author. Why would
she need your help, not that you aren't brilliant? And adorable. And desirable. Not only that, but you love me. Are
you quite sure you wouldn't want to go to bed?"

Suzi rolled her eyes. "I'm not getting this out right, am
I? Hmm, I love the smell of a good cigar—and you look
so sexy with it! Lord, I can't believe we just told each other

that we love each other and now we're just sitting here, stuck in another problem. Just don't inhale, all right? Cigars aren't good for you.''

"Neither is physical frustration, dear heart, I imagine, but you don't seem to be worrying overmuch about my health on that score," he pointed out, grinning around the cigar. He'd let her finish whatever it was she was trying to say, then toss her over his shoulder, if necessary, and adjourn to the bedroom. "But Courtney did want your input?''

But Suzi wasn't listening. She was rereading the last few pages of Courtney's notes again, and her expression was becoming more and more anxious. "Sort of, I suppose," she answered absently, "not that she wouldn't eventually think up something plausible for her made-up heroine, who traveled to Victorian England after slipping down a rabbit hole, sort of like *Alice in Wonderland,* but with a twist. That's the beauty of fiction. You can make up your own reality. Only we can't can we? Court was just talking, and probably wondering if I'd thought of the problem when I decided to write my own book, which I'm not going to write because you'll probably write it, which is fine with me, except if we don't solve this problem you might not write it after all. Harry, get the luggage. I'll ring for Fred to bring the car around, and then I'll explain as I drive. We're going back to Ocean City.''

"The devil you say!" Now Harry leapt to his feet, snatching the pages from Suzi's hand, all thoughts of romance fleeing his mind as he mentally sorted through Suzi's delightful ramblings and realized that she was truly upset. "What's in here, anyway?" He scanned the pages quickly, glancing at his wife every few moments. "Courtney is writing a novel about a character that travels through time?''

Suzi was already busily scribbling a note to Mrs.

O'Reilly, who was out shopping. "Yes, darn it all anyway. And I already told you that, or at least I think I did. She got the whole idea from me, actually, which should flatter me, which it doesn't. She said she knew darn full well I'd never *really* write a novel—and she's right, not that I appreciate her knowing me that well—so that I wouldn't mind if she tried her hand at one. They're very popular right now, you understand. Time-travel novels, that is."

Harry continued to read as he listened to Suzi's garbled explanation with one ear. "Go on. I've yet to see a problem."

"That's just because you didn't get to the last page. You see, Courtney realized that the reader had to be assured that whoever traveled through time was going to *stay* in the time he or she landed in, because otherwise there couldn't be any happily ever after."

She picked up her purse, laying the strap over her shoulder, then turned to Harry, her blue eyes glistening with unshed tears. "I thought I was the only one who had thought about that. About—" her voice broke for a moment "—about how long you might be here."

Harry closed his eyes for a moment, then crossed the room to take Suzi in his arms. "You're not the only one, dear heart," he told her, pressing her close against his chest, wishing he could think up something brilliant to say, something that would end her fears. "I've thought about it, too."

Suzi pushed him away, lifting her chin defiantly, as if deliberately deciding to be courageous. "I know. We did talk about it a little bit that first day, but it didn't seem to matter then. But it matters now. We didn't come to Manhattan because I had to get back to work. We came here because I thought taking you away from Ocean City, away from the place where you traveled through time, might keep me from losing you. Well, now that I know that's not going to work, I think the only thing we can do is go back. There's a local museum in Ocean City. If we can find something, some record from 1813 that mentions the *Pegasus* and what happened to it, maybe we'll discover the proof we need to believe that you're here for keeps.''

"And if we don't?'' Harry asked, already mentally agreeing to the drive back to Ocean City. "What then, dear heart?''

She gave him a watery smile. "Then, Harry,'' she told him, "I will just have to find a way to travel back in time with you. Because you're not going to get away from me, Harry Wilde. Not now that I know I couldn't possibly want to live without you.''

Chapter Ten

The storm broke just as Suzi turned the car onto the Ninth Street Bridge leading onto the island, the twilight sky unnaturally dark this early in the evening.

Thunderstorms on the island were never placid affairs, with the breeze from the ocean stilling and a hot wind beginning to blow off the land just before the first violent streaks of lightning lit the sky.

Suzi remembered her first encounter with an Ocean City storm. She had been walking the boardwalk with a crowd of Fourth of July tourists when the air had stilled, then become warm as the wind shifted. A murmur went through the crowd, those vacationers and natives who knew what was going to happen already taking their children's hands and heading down the boardwalk in either direction, intent on finding one of the ramps that led to the street.

Suzi had stood at the railing, still nibbling on a cardboard stick twirled around with fluffy pink cotton candy, watching the people—novices like herself, she'd later realized—watching the sky.

And then the breeze had accelerated into a wet wind, heavy raindrops pelting the boardwalk, lashing the people who were now all running down the length of the boardwalk, Suzi among them.

Thunder rolled, lightning cracked and the rain was so heavy she might as well have been running in a swimming pool, for she was that wet. The cotton candy congealed on the stick, turning into a hard, dark pink blob, so that she tossed it away in the nearest trash can at one side of the boardwalk, then shielded her eyes with her hand as she looked back at the crowd behind her.

It was a scene out of a Saturday-afternoon matinee from her checkered youth, Suzi had decided, watching as hundreds of people loaded with jackets and baby strollers and bags holding purchases made at the boardwalk shops ran past her, some of them loudly calling to their children to hurry, all of them taking time to glance behind them as the storm pressed down on the shore. If *Godzilla* had suddenly appeared beyond the tall streetlights positioned on the beach side of the boardwalk Suzi wouldn't have been a bit surprised.

This, she knew, was one of those violent, invigorating, vaguely frightening summer storms.

Very much like the one that had brought her Harry Wilde.

Would this one take him away again?

Was Harry thinking what she was thinking? That she had brought him back to Ocean City just in time for fate to take him away from her?

"Can you see to navigate, dear heart?" Harry asked as he used a paper napkin to wipe the steamed-up windows. "Perhaps it might be wise if you pulled over now that we're across the bridge and wait for the storm to abate a little? Damn it all, Suzi, I feel so useless!"

Suzi shook her head, battling the rain that made her

windshield wipers almost useless, wishing the defroster could better clear the windshield of the fog their combined breaths had caused, narrowing her eyes to squint through the unnatural darkness and find the signpost that marked Wesley Avenue. "We have to get home, Harry. I have to get you inside, away from the storm."

"I don't melt in a little rain, dear heart," he assured her, patting her arm.

She shot him an angry look, then silently berated herself for believing, if only for a moment, that he wasn't aware of what she was thinking.

She gripped the steering wheel tightly with both hands. It wasn't fair. It wasn't fair! She had waited thirty-two years to find her love, and now she might lose him!

She turned the car into the short driveway in front of her condo and they both ran for the safety of the overhang above the front door, hesitating only as Suzi searched her key ring for the correct key. "Damn, damn, *damn!*" she muttered as the ring fell from her hands, sobbing now in her terror.

Harry bent to retrieve the keys then, instead of opening the door, took her hand and led her along the path leading to the beach.

"What are you doing? Are you nuts?" she called to him above a loud clap of thunder. "The beach is the last place you want to be at a time like this."

She kicked off her high-heeled pumps before they were pulled off by the deep, sucking sand, then tripped up the outside stairs to the deck, Harry still in the lead and holding her hand. He pulled her down onto her knees on the rain-lashed wooden boards, facing him, the three-foot-high walls of the deck doing little to protect them from the wind and rain.

He held her against him tightly, their bodies pressed together from knee to chest. Then he cupped her face between his hands, and looked deeply into her eyes, his handsome, deadly serious face lit by another wild streak of lightning. "Did you really mean it, dear heart? If a storm brought me to you, and a storm will take me away, do you really mean to go with me? Do you love me that much?"

"Yes!" Suzi cried, finding it difficult to see him in the darkness, holding on to him so tightly she could barely tell where her body left off and his began. They were one person now. Now and forever. She would never let him go. "Oh, yes, darling. *Yes!*"

And then, still holding her, he slanted his mouth against hers as they fell back against the wooden deck floor, the wrath of the storm and their combined fears and deep love for each other only adding to the fury of the night as they dedicated themselves to each other with their words, their hearts, their very souls.

She kissed his rain-wet body, molded his hard muscles beneath her fingers, strained with him and against him as sodden clothes disappeared and they dared the elements with their nakedness, their passion.

Suzi had never felt so alive, so elementally female, so free to express her desires and likewise free to accept anything Harry might ask of her.

Their coming together was fierce, raw and fraught with tension, fraught with a fury that matched that of the storm raging all around them.

And when it was over, as the thunder faded into the distance and the lightning died, leaving behind only a watery moon and gentle, blessing rain, they lay contented on the wooden deck, together and, at least for this one night, this one storm—triumphant.

Harry didn't know why he felt drawn back to the small, overrun cemetery where they had discovered the headstone of William Robert Arthur, but early the next morning he insisted that Suzi drive them there so that he could have another look around.

As he had told Suzi, not without pain, the fact that they had survived one storm together did not necessarily mean that they had found a way to accomplish a happily-ever-after ending to their worries.

Last night's storm had not been the same as the one that had brought him into Suzi's life. There had been no "eye," no instant calming of the storm. In fact, it was still gray and drizzling as Suzi turned the car into the graveyard and switched off the engine.

"I think William Robert's grave is over there," she said, pointing to a row of headstones that was the last before the cemetery seemed to deteriorate into several rows of considerably older stones. "That is what you wanted to see, isn't it?"

Harry took her hand as they exited the car and began picking their way through the puddles in the rutted gravel driveway. "I'm not sure," he admitted, feeling once more the eerie sense of déjà vu that he had experienced upon his first visit to this cemetery.

At the time, he had thought it only meant that this would be the cemetery where he would discover his new identity, and had not mentioned his reactions to Suzi. But now—well, there was something, some nebulous something, that had drawn him back, was still drawing him, so that he continued to walk, not sure of his destination but confident he would find something.

And there it was, in the last row of the cemetery.

A thin headstone sunk almost sideways in the sandy ground, nearly submerged in shore grasses that waved to him in the breeze.

He dropped to his knees in front of the stone, his fingers nearly numb as he parted the grasses in order to read the faded inscription, "Here lie the earthly remains of Harry

Wilde, an English sailor presumed lost from the warship *Pegasus* and washed ashore, drowned, 4 August 1813. Interred in this place through the sweet charity of the Daughters of the Revolution.''

"My God, Harry—you did drown!"

He glanced up at Suzi, who was looking at him as if she'd just seen a ghost. A ghost? Was he a ghost? He didn't feel like a ghost. He didn't even believe in ghosts. Of course, he hadn't believed in time travel until a few weeks ago, either.

"I don't know," he said quietly, still staring at his headstone. It was very queer, looking down at his own headstone, reading about his own death. Not the sort of thing to cheer a man, to be plain about the thing. "What do you think, dear heart?"

"I think," she said, tugging at him so that he was forced to stand, "that it's time we acted on *my* idea. It's time we played the tourists and took a tour of Ocean City's historical museum. Come on, darling."

Neither of them spoke on their way back to the island, although Harry was convinced Suzi's mind was as crowded with questions and suppositions as his, none of them comforting. It was only as they had parked the car and were walking toward the small building containing artifacts of Ocean City's history that Harry dared to put one of these thoughts into words. "Can ghosts father children?" he asked, taking Suzi's hand in his.

"You're not a ghost, Harry!" Suzi all but shouted at him. "My life may be bizarre, but I refuse to believe I married a ghost. Time travel I can live with. It's off the wall, but somehow explainable—sort of. But a ghost? That's going too far, Harry, even for me."

Harry nodded, accepting Suzi's logic, not as if he had a multitude of choices. He could be a figment of Suzi's imagination—or Suzi and her world a figment of his—or he was

a ghost, or he had left his mortal body, traveled through
time with a new body, and might just take another flit in
the next storm. No. There wasn't a whacking great lot to
choose from. "Scared?" he asked Suzi as he stepped forward to open the door to the museum.

"Petrified," she admitted, then smiled at him, so that he
knew that, no matter what they found inside the museum,
he had already discovered everything in the world that
meant anything to him.

The museum was interesting, or would have been if
Harry could only relax as he walked through rooms filled
with relics of Ocean City's past, including some of the
salvage from the wreck of the *Sinda,* a merchant ship that
had long ago come to grief off the shore of the island.

"There's nothing here from the *Pegasus,*" he remarked
to Suzi, who had become interested in a display of china
dolls and other toys she said had been popular when her
mother had been a girl.

"The *Pegasus?*" a pleasant-faced older woman repeated
as she laid down her knitting, left her chair at the side of
the room and walked toward them, patting at her gray bun
that was slipping badly. "Now why does that name seem
familiar to me? Hello, folks. Are you enjoying your stay in
Ocean City?"

"Very much," Harry answered, bowing to the woman
who reminded him very much of his childhood nanny, who
was forever knitting something, although she never seemed
to finish any of it. "I am a teacher," he lied easily, because
it had always been easy to fib to his nanny, who had constantly amazed him with her easy credulity, "and I have
been instructing my students in the War of 1812. There
was an English ship during that war—the *Pegasus*—and it
supposedly sailed the waters just off Ocean City. As my
wife and I are visiting your city on our vacation, I
thought—"

The woman slapped her forehead, as if that might jolt her memory. "Of course!" she exclaimed happily, looking to Suzi. "That's where I heard the name. That's where poor old Harry hailed from—the *Pegasus!*"

"Poor old Harry?" Suzi questioned, and Harry could tell by her tone that she was amused to hear him spoken of in such an easy, familiar way. "Oh, please, I must hear more about poor old Harry!"

The woman clasped her hands together in front of her and began, "Well, as I remember hearing it, there was a terrible storm at sea, and on the island as well, and the *Pegasus* was caught in it. It didn't come to grief, the way the *Sinda* did, but one of its sailors was apparently washed overboard and drowned. His body was found on the beach, somewhere up around the Twenty-eighth Street beach, I believe. Of course it wasn't the Twenty-eighth Street beach then, but just a stretch of sand, for the island was barely populated."

Harry and Suzi exchanged bemused, expectant glances. Suzi's beachfront condo was located on Wesley Avenue, just at Twenty-eighth Street. "Go on, please," Harry said, his heart pounding as he listened to the woman tell him about his own death.

"There isn't too much more to say, actually," the woman said, shaking her head. "There was a collection made by the good women of the area and the man was buried on the mainland—I don't recall which cemetery—and that was the end of it. Except for the pouch, of course. That's here."

"My—the pouch?" How could his pouch be here, in this museum? His pouch was packed in his luggage and safely locked up in Suzi's condo. "What sort of pouch, ma'am?"

The woman turned, motioning for Harry and Suzi to follow her into the next room, and Suzi took his hand, squeezing it comfortingly.

"It's just a pouch. You know, a purse? A knapsack?" the woman offered, standing just inside the door, her hands on her hips as she surveyed the crowded room. "Poor old Harry was wearing it when he washed ashore. It probably would have been a good idea to take it off so that it wouldn't weigh him down, but then I remember reading that lots of sailors couldn't swim a lick in those days, so maybe it wouldn't have mattered anyway. Now where is it?"

"The pouch was heavy?" Suzi asked, walking around the perimeter of the room, scanning the shelves for the pouch. "Was there something in it?"

"Yes, yes," the woman answered distractedly, still searching the shelves with her anxious gaze. "There was some gold coin, a packet containing the man's identifying papers—that's how we know he was poor old Harry—and another thick bunch of papers written all over in some sort of code. The seawater had made a muck of most of it, but I remember someone telling me that even what they could read didn't make a lick of sense. Now where is it hiding? Honestly, ever since we moved here from our old quarters I've been searching for things that were misplaced. But I could have sworn I've seen that pouch right in this room. It was just there on the second shelf, right where that empty space is, but now it's gone. Now, why would anyone want to steal poor old Harry's pouch?"

Harry smiled at Suzi, sure she was thinking what he was thinking. No one had stolen the pouch. No one had because it belonged to him, was precious to him, and he had somehow retrieved the pouch and brought it with him through time, a kindly nature or heavenly intervention reversing the death he had supposedly died one hundred and eighty-one years previously.

His grave would be empty now, too. He would be willing to wager his last gold coin on it!

He had always been meant to survive his fall overboard, because he had always been meant to meet Suzi Harper and fall in love. He had always believed he would meet a woman he could love. He just hadn't thought it would take him one hundred and eighty-one years to accomplish the feat!

The woman turned to them, spreading her hands apologetically. "I'm so sorry. Either I'm wrong about seeing it here, and the pouch was lost in the move, or it was stolen. Not that it matters, for sure as I'm standing here someone will hear about it and make up some fanciful story—like all the other stories about poor old Harry."

"Other stories?" Harry repeated as Suzi came to stand beside him. "I don't understand."

The woman gave a wave of her hand. "Oh, there's a million of them around here. Why, you can buy books on all our New Jersey ghost stories at most any shop on the boardwalk. Poor old Harry's just one of them. Let me see, how does it go? Oh, I know!"

Harry could feel Suzi's excitement as she stood beside him, fairly dancing in her anxiety to hear what the woman had to say.

"Well," the woman said consideringly, walking with them back toward the entrance, "it seems that, as far as the story about poor old Harry goes, he appears on the beach just before dawn every August fourth—that's the day he was found, you understand. If you were to get up very early, and look very hard, you can see him lying there, just at the water's edge, suspended between life and death, waiting for someone to come save him.

"Only there's a hitch, of course," she went on as Harry tried to concentrate upon remembering to breathe. "By the time anyone who sees him can get to him, poor old Harry's gone. Poof! Disappeared into the early-morning mist.''

She smiled as she held open the door, allowing in the bright sunlight that had at last broken through the clouds, just in the way the storm pelting the *Pegasus* had stopped and the sun had come out over the ocean.

"You know, it's a pity the story isn't true," the woman said, sighing in the way of a young, romantic girl. "Just think how lovely it would be to rescue poor old Harry from his watery grave. Ah, well, it's just one of those old legends, isn't it? We have a million of them! But it is odd about that pouch. Very odd.''

"Odd?" Suzi exclaimed, grabbing the woman and kissing her on both cheeks. "It's not odd at all—it's *wonderful!* Thank heaven for Mrs. O'Connell and her driftwood! And thank you, you sweet, adorable woman. Thank you *so much!* Come on, Harry, we're going home!"

"Harry?" the woman questioned, her voice little more than a squeak, looking back and forth between Harry and Suzi. "That would be a coincidence, wouldn't it?" she asked, smiling weakly and she looked around behind her for a chair.

"Absolutely, madam," Harry told her joyfully, also kissing her on both cheeks. Suzi had been right—if she were ever happy enough, and in the company of a stranger, she would kiss that stranger, and just had. Harry felt the same way. He wanted to kiss everyone in the whole, entire, wonderful world!

But, mostly, he wanted to kiss Suzi. He wanted to kiss her, and hold her, and thank her for rescuing him from the limbo he had unknowingly inhabited for the past one hundred and eighty-one years, waiting for a stubborn, headstrong, singular woman like Suzi Harper to come along and defy the fates by snatching him from that limbo and taking him into her life, her heart.

"Wilbur was right, dear heart," he told Suzi as he led her back to the car at a near run. "I'm going to be a very good writer. After all, I have such intriguing stories to tell! But first, I believe I am going to spend several uninterrupted days and nights with my bride."

"Oh, Harry," Suzi said, pushing him back against the front fender of the car and sliding her arms up and around his neck. "It's unbelievable. We've done it, haven't we? We've found our 'happily ever after.' I love you, Harry Wilde. I love you so much!"

"That's good, dear heart," he told her as he lowered his head to hers, his gaze intent on her smiling mouth, "because you're going to have me around for a long, long time."

Epilogue

The seventh annual Wilde beach party, slated each year for the fourth of August, was in full swing.

Senator Adam Richardson, whose twins, Pete and Paul, were now in their second year of college, had flown in from Washington during the Senate recess to be with his wife, Courtney, who still returned to Ocean City each summer to work on her yearly novel. *Twice Upon A Time,* her best-selling time-travel romance, had been such a hit five years ago that she had finally agreed to do a sequel. More than once she had walked up the beach to confer with Harry, who was always pleased to give her the benefit of his own "research" into the subject that had landed his second book, also a time-travel novel, on the *Times* list for over a year.

While Adam modestly accepted Daniel Quinn's congratulations on being named to the Judiciary Committee, Daniel's father-in-law, Wilbur Langley, sat on the deck with Joey, Daniel's wife, discussing his planned redecoration of his Ocean City condo. Wilbur was always redecorating something, and this year the condo had been on his list, and Joey was trying not to smile as Wilbur discussed the Early Egyptian motif he was considering.

Rick, Daniel's son by his first wife—Wilbur's deceased daughter—was also on the deck. He had just finished his first year of residency at the Hospital of the University of Pennsylvania and was now playing a board game with his young sisters and brother, and losing badly.

That left Sydney and Blake Mansfield, who were still down on the beach with their twin girls and their infant son, who had been born just this past spring. Sydney was lying in the sun, her long, slim body already a golden tan, while Blake was allowing himself to be buried by the giggling twins, who considered this attack on their father to be a yearly ritual.

Mrs. O'Reilly stepped out onto the deck, her hands full, holding a tray of freshly cut up fruit, and nearly tripped over William Wilde—the "great" Billy Wilde, as the blond, blue-eyed youngster preferred to be called—who was lying on his belly, tickling the feet of his baby sister, Elizabeth, who was cooing in her infant seat.

"Billy, my boy, you'd be better served to take yourself down onto the beach with your brother Robbie rather than to lie about like a beached whale. He's helping to bury your Uncle Blake at the moment," Harry advised, kissing his wife's hand as she passed by him to pick up their daughter. Robert, aged three, was the blondest of the three children, his hair so fair it was almost white, and both boys were already showing signs of being as tall as their father.

"Oh, I don't know," Suzi said, winking at her husband. "You never know what might happen to you if you just 'lie about like a beached whale,' Billy. Why, you might even discover your own true love."

"Yech! Mom, that's *gross!*" Billy exclaimed in the disgust only a six-year-old could feel about the subject of true love. "Sorry, Mrs. O! I didn't mean to trip you," he hastily apologized to the housekeeper, then scrambled to his feet to thread his way through the mass of deck chairs filled with the people he had come to know as his extended family and raced down the steps to the beach.

Suzi deposited Elizabeth in her doting father's lap and collapsed into the chair beside Harry, smiling in real contentment. "It never rains on August 4 anymore, does it, darling? We've had brilliant sunshine every year for our party." She leaned close to him, whispering, "This is the one day of the year Wilbur finds himself frustrated. He's the only one who knows why August 4 is important to us, and he can't tell anyone. He must feel as if he could burst!"

Harry kissed his daughter's turned-up nose, then repeated the gesture with his wife. "Wilbur would never burst, dear heart. It might ruin the line of his suit. Although he did seem to puff up a bit with pride as he told me about the advance sales on my latest book."

"Don't brag, darling, it isn't polite," Suzi warned, ruffling his long blond hair, which she had adamantly refused to allow him to cut more in the fashion of the day. "But, if you can blow your own horn, I imagine I can tell you that I made the cupcakes this year. All by myself, too. Mrs. O'Reilly didn't even help."

Harry rested his forehead against his daughter's and told the child confidentially, "Yes, my little namesake of her esteemed Royal Highness, I know. I saw the boxes from the bakery, too. But I won't tell if you don't."

"Harry Wilde!" Suzi exclaimed, giving him a playful tap on the shoulder. "You weren't supposed to know."

"Know what?" Courtney asked, pulling up a chair and sitting down beside them. "Never mind," she added, sighing. "It's a lovely day, isn't it? I never tire of Ocean City."

"Neither do we," Harry said, taking hold of his wife's

hand and bringing it to his lips. "It's a very special place. Almost magical, isn't it, dear heart?"

"Harry," Suzi said warningly, and then she smiled, because Harry was right. Ocean City had been magical, for Courtney, for Sydney, and just seven wonderful years ago, for her.

And she wouldn't have believed any of it, if it had happened to anyone else but her.

* * * * *

Dear Reader,

I was so delighted to learn that Harlequin was reprinting *Raven's Vow*. This story is very special to me for many reasons.

For one thing, the ancestry of John Raven, like mine, contains the blending of two warrior people—the Scots and our Native Americans. I can't conceive of a more interesting mix.

Secondly, it was in this story that I discovered how powerful sexual tension can be.

And finally, I've always thought that the English Industrial Revolution was a pivotal era in human history. The men of vision who lived then virtually created the modern world as we know it. This is the story of one such man and the woman he loved.

And to my former world history students, I have only one thing to say, "See, I told you the Industrial Revolution was exciting!"

Gayle Wilson

RAVEN'S VOW
Gayle Wilson

For my beloved sister Joy

Prologue

London, 1826

"What you need, Mr. Raven, is a wife."

The tall man at the window turned, a slight indentation deepening the corners of the hardest mouth Oliver Reynolds had seen in his seventy years. He had learned through experience that the look John Raven was now directing toward him was intended to indicate amusement.

"A wife?" the American repeated, that amusement now touching the rich tones of his voice as it had marked the stern lips.

"Unless, of course," the banker continued with the merest trace of sarcasm, "you have a duke hidden away somewhere in your family tree. Or an earl. Short of that, sir, I'm afraid…" The old man let the suggestion trail off. He had made his point, and he knew his client's ready intelligence needed no more prompting.

Oliver Reynolds had been paid, extremely *well* paid, to guide this American nabob through the perils of London society, and the solution he had just broached to John Raven was really the best advice he had to offer.

"Three of my grandparents fled Scotland after the '45,

half a step ahead of Cumberland's butchers,'' John Raven confessed. The mockery lurking in those strange, crystalline blue eyes proved his very New World lack of embarrassment over the mode of his ancestors' departure from the Old. He had been born on the edge of the American wilderness and had watched the influx of settlers move across the land, always westward toward the great river. His country was changing, the vast forest tracts gradually giving way to farms and communities, the conquest of its wildness the result of the hard work of people like his parents and his grandparents.

''In that case—'' the banker began, only to be cut off by the sardonic voice.

''My paternal grandmother, however, was a princess.''

''A princess?'' Oliver Reynolds repeated carefully. ''Royalty, Mr. Raven? And from what dynasty did this fortuitous ancestor spring? Despite its supposed sophistication, the British nobility still finds a certain fascination in foreign royalty.''

''The Mauvilla, Mr. Reynolds.''

''Mauvilla,'' the old man repeated, trying to think. ''I don't believe I'm familiar with that particular family.''

''They defied de Soto, virtually destroying themselves in the process. My grandmother was the last of the royal line.''

''De Soto?'' the banker questioned. He had heard the name, of course, in conjunction with the exploration of the American continent. Surely, Mr. Reynolds thought, those who had defied him would not be mentioned in the context of royal families.

''Indian?'' He spoke his sudden realization aloud, his voice rising. But even as he did, he acknowledged that the heritage John Raven had just confessed would explain so much. The American's coloring, for example—the bronze skin that offered such a striking contrast to the clear blue eyes. And his hair, of course. "Indian," the old man said again, an affirmation that put so many pieces of the puzzle John Raven had represented into place.

Raven's dark head inclined slightly in agreement. The small upward tilt at the corners of his mouth increased minutely. "Indian," he agreed softly. "Do you think they'll be impressed?"

"I should think," the banker began, wondering how to warn him without being too offensive, "that you should be damnably certain this noble mob never finds out about your grandmother."

"Not royal enough for our purposes?" Raven suggested easily as he moved back to the chair he had carlier occupied.

Watching his client traverse the short distance, Oliver Reynolds inventoried his recent accomplishments. The American's shoulders were now shown to advantage by Weston's expert tailoring, the coat of navy superfine covering their broad width without a wrinkle. Underneath, a striped French silk waistcoat was discreetly visible. Fawn pantaloons stretched over the flat stomach and accented the firmness of long, muscular thighs. Tasseled Hessians fashioned by Hoby's master hand completed the picture of elegance that finally matched the vast wealth the American had brought from the East into the English capital.

On his arrival in London, John Raven had sought Reynolds's advice and had, surprisingly, followed it to the letter. Except for one thing, the banker thought with regret. The only concession he had been able to wrest from his client regarding the length of his hair was compromise satisfactory to neither. The American had agreed to secure the dark strands, their blue-black gleam rivaling the feathers of the bird whose name he bore, into a queue tied with a black silk ribbon. He had adamantly refused to cut it, and given, of course, the startling revelation he had just made, Reynolds at last understood.

"If words gets out about *that*, Mr. Raven, you won't need a wife. A fairy godmother, perhaps. Or a guardian angel."

"A fairy godmother who'd wave her wand to make me acceptable? An angel to ensure that my many faults are hidden under the splendor of her wings?" the American jeered quietly, not bothering to hide his frustration.

Damn them, John Raven thought bitterly. He'd come to England to build. Instead, he had found the doors to those gracefully proportioned drawing rooms and exclusive clubs where the real power resided closed to him because he was an outsider.

The arrogant, pompous bastards. He had visited their tailors and their boot makers, and Raven knew—because he was certainly no one's fool—that he was as well dressed as any man in London. And as wealthy. Still they refused to deal with him. Because he wasn't a member of their bloody ton.

"I've told you before. You'll never find a more closed or closed-minded circle in the world," Reynolds said. "They'll back the outrageous schemes of the most profligate bounder, drunkard or scoundrel of their own class, but an outsider? You had as well have stayed in India and attempted to do business from there as to try to force your way in. You can't make them invest."

"They won't even meet me. Polite refusals is all I've gotten. If only they'd listen, they would know that what I propose is not only advantageous to Britain, but profitable for investors as well. Why the hell won't they listen?"

"Because you don't belong. Birth is the only membership in this society, and yours is unacceptable. You need a wife whose place within the ton is so secure that she will be able to win you a grudging entry by virtue of her own connections."

"How do you propose that I convince this paragon to marry me? Introduce her to my grandmother?" Raven countered with savage politeness.

"The usual procedure is to offer enough money that her family can't refuse."

"Buy her, do you mean?"

"It's done everyday. Not in those terms, of course. However, that is the general idea. You certainly have the funds. All we need to do is find some impoverished noblewoman whose family is willing to marry her off in return for a guarantee of financial security for themselves for the rest of their lives."

"I thought slavery in Britain disappeared with the Saxons," Raven commented bitterly. "I damn well don't intend to buy a wife. I wouldn't want a woman who'd be willing to sell herself."

"I suppose," the banker said carefully, recognizing the truth in the American's argument, "that most of them aren't."

"I beg your pardon?"

"Willing," Oliver Reynolds explained regretfully.

"Good God," Raven said with a trace of horror. "And they would call my grandmother's people savage. I won't buy a wife, Mr. Reynolds, willing or unwilling. If the mines and railroads I came to Britain to build don't become a reality, then the bastards will have only themselves to blame."

Fighting to control his anger, John Raven descended the stairs that led from the old man's office. If buying a wife was what it would take to succeed in England, he would damn well find somewhere else to invest his energies.

Raven moved from the narrow flight of stairs onto the

street with an unconscious grace, a smooth athleticism that had already attracted attention in the capital. More than one pair of female eyes, accustomed to the sometimes delicate fragility of the gentlemen who set the mode for London society, had on occasion during the last month followed that purposeful stride.

The feminine voice that attracted his attention now, despite the bustle of traffic that rushed past the bank, did so by the sharpness of its tone, and not because of Reynolds's suggestion.

"If you strike him again, I shall have my groom take that stick from you and apply it to *your* back."

The peddler paused in his determined attempts to move the pitiful creature fastened between the wooden tongues of his overloaded cart. Unable to pull the burden up the inclined street, the small donkey stood shivering and flinching under the blows from the rattan stick the man was using as encouragement.

The words had stopped the cruelty momentarily, but the face of the man who turned to confront the girl on horseback reflected neither embarrassment nor regret for her reprimand. Instead, the coarse features were reddened with anger.

The gleam of pure hatred that had shone briefly from the mud-colored eyes made John Raven take an automatic step closer to the scene. His forward progress was halted when the lady's groom swung down easily from his saddle. Although not up to Raven's size, he certainly appeared to be of a bulk sufficient to handle whatever threat the wizened driver represented.

"Lighten the load of your wagon," the girl ordered. "He can't possibly pull that heap." The truth of her statement was obvious to the onlookers, but until she had stopped the beating, none of them had considered the unfairness of the man's actions.

"I don't have time to be coddling him. Lazy is what he is, my lady," the peddler said, removing the shapeless felt that served as his hat. "He can pull the load. Always has. It's just temperament," the man assured her, his ingratiating smile revealing blackened teeth. "Nothing to concern your ladyship."

"If you beat your animal to death in the public street, it should be of concern to *someone*," the girl said, giving no quarter, and at the same time controlling the skittering side steps of her restive mare.

The thin lips of the American lifted slightly in admiration of that assessment, and the shrewd blue eyes took their own inventory. The black habit the girl wore was heavily frogged with silver, the darkness of its high collar and the matching cravat stark against the porcelain of her skin. Strands of dark auburn hair had escaped the modish hat and veil to curl around her heart-shaped face. Despite the perfection of her features, it was her eyes that held Raven's fascinated gaze. Clear russet, they were the exact color of leaves turning under the touch of autumn's chill. At this moment, they were fixed with determined concentration on the hawker, totally unaware of the interested bystanders.

"It be necessary 'times to prod him, ladyship. Animals don't feel the blows like we do. Don't trouble yourself about the beast. He'll pull it, I promise, 'ere I've done with him."

As an accompaniment to his last words, he turned back to the small animal, raising the stick high in the air to bring it down again in the whistling arc that had first attracted the girl's attention. This time its fall across the trembling back was arrested, the thin rattan captured by a slender gloved hand.

"I said no more. Unload the cart," she ordered. The fury in her eyes brooked no defiance.

"I've no time to be unloading. And who's to guard what

I leave? You're thinking my goods will still be here when I return, are you? This ain't Mayfair, your highness.''

At the taunting incivility, the girl's lips tightened. She gestured to the groom, who took the captured stick from the peddler's hand and broke it quickly across his knee.

"How much?" she asked.

The vendor paused, seeing his livelihood threatened, but at the same time greedily calculating what he could get from the lady. "For the donkey?"

"Donkey, cart, load. Whatever it takes to free the creature," the girl suggested. There was no trace of impatience in her voice now. She watched the man's devious expression impassively.

"If I sells my kit, I've no way to make me living."

"The donkey then."

"But without me donkey—" he began to argue.

"Get the constable," the girl ordered her groom, who turned almost before she had finished speaking, his intent too clear for the man to doubt that he would do exactly as she'd commanded.

"Two quid," the peddler suggested, a ridiculous amount.

"All right," she agreed. "Give my groom your name and lodging and he'll bring it round to you this afternoon. Get the donkey, Jem," Catherine Montfort ordered, turning her mare away from the scene, already late for her appointment in Hyde Park.

The peddler began to protest as the groom efficiently dealt with the traces. "You'll not be taking property without paying me. How do I know you'll send him with the money? How do I know this ain't a plot to steal a poor man's livelihood? I'm the one who'll be calling the constable, I think, if you take the beast. I knows me rights, nobs or no," he finished belligerently, pulling against the line the groom was using as a lead rope. "Here, you, give me back me donkey."

Catherine Montfort's lips tightened in frustration. She had no money with her, of course, and she doubted Jem would be able to come up with that much. Glancing at the groom, who was still in control of the exhausted donkey, she saw him shake his head in response to her unspoken question. She had no option but to send home for the amount and try to stop the hawker from leaving in the meantime.

"If I might be allowed to offer assistance," a deep, accented voice at her elbow suggested.

She glanced down into the bluest eyes she had ever encountered. The clear, rare color of a summer sky, they were set like jewels in the golden skin surrounding them, emphasized by small, white lines radiating around the crystal blue and the black sweep of lashes.

A man who'd lived a long time in a climate where the sun left its mark, she thought briefly. He was very tall, tall enough that she needn't look down far to be lost in those blue depths. She watched as his hand, lean, long fingered and remarkably graceful, automatically smoothed the sweating neck of her impatient mare. He whispered something, the words too softly spoken for Catherine to make sense of the soothing sibilants, and Storm's ears flickered with interest.

Amazingly, as he continued to whisper, Catherine could feel the tension caused by the street's commotion and the delay in the promised run leave her mount. Storm turned to nuzzle those strong fingers, and Catherine found herself watching their caress with something approaching fascination. "Two quid, I believe," the stranger said.

Still disconcerted, Catherine nodded. She watched him give Storm one last competent stroke and then walk to the waiting peddler. If Jem's intimidating size had affected the man, he had given no sign of it, but his response to the American seemed one almost of fear. His instinctive recoil when the tall man held out his hand brought a brief reactive movement to those thin lips. Raven waited patiently until the peddler had worked up his courage to take the money and restore his cap to his head.

Slipping between the wooden tongues in the donkey's place, the vendor awkwardly turned the heavily loaded cart so that it was now headed down the slight incline. The three watched as the wagon gathered momentum on the slope and the usual street sounds again intruded into the stage where the drama had been played out.

Raven turned back to the girl to find her eyes no longer watching the merchant's retreating figure, but on him. She was questioning the color of his skin, he supposed, or his hair. Making her fascinated distaste apparent. He didn't know why her frank appraisal bothered him. He had certainly grown accustomed to the stares he'd attracted in London in the last few months.

"Thank you," she said simply, her eyes meeting his. She held out the small gloved hand that had caught the peddler's stick. Not to be kissed, Raven realized, but to be shaken.

Her hand was almost lost in his, but her grip was pleasantly firm. He controlled the quick amusement at the sight of those slender fingers captured by his hard, dark ones.

"If you'll give Jem your address—" she began.

"Consider him a gift," he interrupted softly, and watched her eyes flick quickly to the animal he'd just bought. Head drooping, the donkey stood patiently waiting for the next blow to fall. In several places where the stick had cut, blood oozed.

The girl's lips tightened and she took a deep breath. For the first time an emotion besides anger tinged her voice. "Damned bastard," she whispered. Realizing that she'd spoken the epithet aloud, she glanced quickly at the American. The russet eyes swam with tears, but before they could overflow, she blinked, a fall of impossibly long, dark lashes concealing feelings Raven read quite clearly.

"Thank you," she said again, looking down into that strong-featured face. Something in the crystalline eyes had changed. And he made no response to her gratitude.

"For my gift," she explained softly, her lips lifting into the smile that had set masculine pulses hammering since she'd turned fourteen. Catherine Montfort thought of all the presents she had received from suitors in the last three years, not one of whom had, of course, thought to give her an abused donkey.

There was no response in the still, dark face. Not handsome, Catherine thought; it was too strongly constructed to be called handsome. But there was something, some indefinable something in the hawklike nose and high cheekbones that was very appealing. And in his eyes, she thought again. She had never seen eyes that shade of blue.

Raven became aware suddenly that she was talking to him, but he didn't have any idea what she had said. Something about a gift. Something... He took a deep breath, realizing that air was a necessity he had neglected in the last minute. The perfection of the heart-shaped face floated before him against the background of clouds and sky.

"Angel," he said softly in his grandmother's tongue, although the word's connotation there was not exactly the same. Oliver Reynolds had told him he'd need a guardian angel. The stern line of John Raven's lips tilted upward at the corners.

Catherine Montfort found that her hand was still resting in his and her throat had gone dry. The small movement of his mouth fascinated her until she recognized the expression for what it was—he was smiling at her.

Sensing her inattention, Storm sidestepped suddenly, and the pull against their joined hands broke the spell. Reluctantly, Catherine disentangled her fingers. She had thanked the man twice, and there was really nothing else she could say. She didn't even know his name. She might never know it. She'd never seen him before and would, in all probability, never see him again. He was certainly not a member of the select group, the London ton, with whom she associated, the only people with whom she had associated since her birth. What had happened today was simply a chance meeting with a stranger on a crowded London street.

Raven stepped back, clearing the way for her departure. Her boot heel touched Storm in command, and, her back flawlessly straight, Catherine Montfort directed her mount around the donkey and back on the course of her normal activities.

John Raven watched the slight figure until it was lost in the throng of riders and carriages. Realizing that he had been staring far too long for politeness, he turned back to find the groom carefully inspecting the animal's injuries.

"Shall I find him a home?" Raven asked, wondering what her ladyship would do with a donkey in Mayfair.

"You think she'll forget him?" the groom asked, not bothering to look up from his examination. "You think she bought him on impulse and will forget him before she gets home?" The rude sound that followed was indicative of his opinion of what Raven had suggested about the girl.

"Then she won't?" Raven asked, the slight smile again marking the hard mouth.

"If I don't have him back in the stables and these injuries tended to by the time she returns, she'll serve my head to the old man with his supper."

"The old man?" Fear stirred suddenly in Raven's gut.

"Montfort," the groom informed him, as if, that said, there was no other explanation needed. He moved to the other side of the donkey to run skilled hands over the protruding ribs and to pick up a trembling foreleg to examine an untreated cut.

"Montfort," Raven repeated, feeling like Echo.

"The Duke of Montfort," the groom said, glancing up at last to assess a man who was so ignorant as not to recognize *that* particular name. "The Devil Duke, they call him. Not out loud, of course," he said, remembering his employer's temper. The sobriquet was well earned and well deserved.

"Who is she?" the American asked, his gaze moving back to the street down which the girl had disappeared.

"The Devil's Daughter," Jem said, noticing for the first time the style of the foreign gentleman's hair. The groom's eyebrows climbed slightly, but it was not his place to question his betters. "Lady Catherine Montfort. The Duke of Montfort's only heir."

"Thank you," Raven said, and reaching into his waistcoat pocket, he flicked a coin to the groom. The man smiled his thanks and then turned back to his careful survey of the donkey.

John Raven crossed the street and, taking the narrow stairs two at a time, retraced his path to Reynolds's office. The old man looked up from his notations in a leather-bound ledger.

"Lady Catherine Montfort," John Raven said, his wide shoulders filling the doorway.

"Montfort?" the banker repeated, wondering again, as he had when he'd first met the American, if he were more than merely eccentric.

"Is Lady Catherine Montfort angelic enough for our purposes?" Raven asked calmly.

The old man stared blankly for a moment, wondering how his client had come up with that name.

"Is she?" Raven prompted, knowing that the banker's reply really didn't matter. The die had been cast in the middle of a crowded London street, but at least Reynolds's approval would provide an acceptable excuse.

"Catherine Montfort is bloody well the entire seraphic choir," the old man acknowledged truthfully. He watched the smile that touched the American's mouth again deepen the indentions at the corners. "But I'm afraid that the Montforts—"

"You said one only had to offer enough money."

"Montfort's one of the few men in London even *you* couldn't buy. And I must tell you…" The banker's voice trailed off. He really hated to offend the man, but he knew that the duke would never accept John Raven as a suitor for his daughter's hand. His only daughter. His only surviving child and heir. Reynolds's mind having dealt too long with the prospects of profit, he briefly allowed himself to consider those combined fortunes being handled by his bank. And why not? Was his not the oldest financial establishment in the city? The bank had financed the East India Company's venture into the Russian market in the sixteenth century. He cleared the tempting visions from his mind and shook his head regretfully.

"He'll never allow you to even present your suit. Forget Catherine Montfort, John. You'll never convince her father, and I must warn you that it would be dangerous even to try. Montfort's as proud, cold-blooded and arrogant as any of the old aristocrats. His was a generation that made its own rules—whatever they wanted, whether legal or moral, they took, consequences be damned. There's nothing you can do to win Montfort's daughter. You have nothing to offer the girl that she doesn't already have."

The blue eyes rested on the seamed face of the old man a moment, their farseeing gaze untroubled by the obstacles Reynolds had just thrown in his path.

John Raven had believed he had come to London to make money. The call had been so strong that he had left India in the middle of an incredibly successful mining venture. His intuition had directed his journey to this city as surely as it had previously drawn him to Delhi, leaving the profitable exporting business he'd founded in New York to be run by his assistants. Wherever there was money to be made, John Raven could sense it. He could feel it moving in his hands as clearly as he had felt the reality of the rubies and sapphires he'd mined in India. He thought he had been drawn to England by the growth of the mining industry and the possibilities offered by the new developments in the locomotive.

Now he knew that his arrival in London had had nothing whatsoever to do with that. *What you need is a wife,* Oliver Reynolds had told him, almost exactly the words his grandmother had said to him when he had last seen her more than five years ago. He wondered how many prayers had accompanied the sacred white cedar smoke directed to the All-Spirit in the intervening years. And with amusement Raven found himself wondering if, in one of her dream trances, his grandmother could possibly have envisioned anyone like Lady Catherine Montfort.

Chapter One

"I didn't come out to be pawed. I came for a breath of air that wasn't contaminated by a hundred perspiring bodies wearing too much perfume," Catherine Montfort said, wondering why the lovemaking of this extremely handsome and highly acceptable suitor left her so cold. She moved out of the attempted embrace of her escort, who released her with a small laugh.

The Viscount Amberton watched as Catherine leaned gracefully against the stone railing of the balcony. He knew she was as unmindful of the nearly priceless material of her gown as if she had been wearing sackcloth. Of course, none of the tedious hours of beading that had gone into its creation had been performed by her hands. She propped her chin on fingers covered in the finest kid and stared out into the darkness that hid the garden.

"Admit it, Cat. You're bored. Too many ballrooms. Too many dinner parties attended by the same people. Too many suitors declaiming their undying love. Why don't you name the lucky man and put them all out of their misery?" the viscount suggested.

Since Amberton was well aware that he held the inside track, with the duke, certainly, if not with the daughter, he was becoming increasingly impatient with Catherine's refusal to accept the necessity of matrimony. Especially when he considered all the diligent toadying to the old man it had taken to acquire that inside track. The viscount was not nearly so impatient as his creditors were, however. The only reason they had held both their tongues and his bills was that they, too, were well aware of how this game was played. The faintest hint that Lord Amberton needed Montfort's money, and he'd never see a guinea of it.

"All of *them?*" she questioned mockingly, slanting a quick smile at him over her shoulder.

"All of us, then," he conceded. "You know my heart's yours. It always has been. You are very well aware of that fact."

"But the problem is in *my* heart," Catherine said softly.

"Not being in love is not generally considered to be a hindrance to marriage," he assured her. Indeed, they both knew how rare a love match was in their circle.

"I keep thinking there must be a man who won't bore me to tears after the first month."

"You're such a wonderfully spoiled chit, my dear. There are worse things than boredom," Gerald suggested lightly, knowing she wouldn't understand just now the truth of his statement. But she would. One day soon she most certainly would. Then she might long for boredom, Gerald thought with a touch of malicious humor.

"I doubt it," she said, but she smiled again.

"You're eighteen, at the end of your second season. The Duke of Montfort's only child, and he wants a grandson. He's not going to wait much longer."

"I know." She'd heard the same arguments all too often, from both Amberton and her father. She had begun to be afraid the duke would brush aside the promise he'd made two years ago to consider her wishes in the selection of her husband.

There was no need to base that decision solely on the amount of the marriage settlements. And no one unsuitable by birth would be so absurd as to offer for Montfort's only daughter, so her father had seen no reason not to give her the assurance for which she had so charmingly begged. But now he was growing impatient. Her refusal to choose was becoming a source of discord in what had always been, despite the duke's notoriously volatile temperament, a loving relationship.

"Give in gracefully before you're left with no choice at all," Gerald suggested smoothly. *And before I'm clapped into Newgate,* he thought bitterly.

"Give in," she repeated, with her own touch of bitterness. "Always to be at someone else's command. Forever hemmed in by his wishes and desires. Governed by his—"

Amberton's laugh interrupted her litany of complaints. "And you, of course, believe that you should be the exception to those restrictions, allowed to make your own decisions."

"To a certain degree. Why not? I've not made so many errors in judgment that I must always be constrained to accept a husband's guidance in every decision," she argued.

"And if you *have* made errors, your father has been remarkably willing, and certainly more than able, to extricate you from situations that were, perhaps, not in your own best interests. Such as a certain clandestine journey to the Border."

Catherine had been only sixteen, and the fortune hunter who had arranged that elopement had been handsome and charming enough to turn older and wiser heads. However, his carefully selected target had been, almost from his arrival in London, the Duke of Montfort's daughter.

"Don't," she ordered softly, her humiliation over the

incident still acutely painful. "I shouldn't have told you about that. And you promised never to repeat it."

"Your secrets are safe with me, my dear. Especially if you agree to favor my suit," he suggested truthfully, smiling at her. "Then I'd have a vested interest in protecting your reputation."

"Such as it is," she finished for him. "Blackmail, Gerald?"

"Not in the least. Simply another heartfelt avowal from quite your oldest suitor."

"Oldest?" she repeated, laughing, relieved to be back on the familiar ground of flirtation. "You've forgotten Ridgecourt."

"Then earliest, my love. I think you know that we'd rub along together very well. And I promise to permit a certain amount of freedom. Not, I'm afraid, that I'm willing to give you as long a tether as your father has allowed."

"Tether!" she echoed despairingly. "Oh, God, Gerald, that's just the sort of thing I'm talking about."

"Simply a figure of speech, my dear. There's really no need to pounce on every idiom as if I'm trying to imprison you."

"That's exactly how I *do* imagine marriage. I'm already surrounded by enough restrictions to enclose an army. Don't ride too fast. Don't dance with the same gentleman more than once. It's not seemly for unmarried females to wear that color or this style. God, I'm so sick of it all. Even my father has lately taken to issuing dark warnings about my being left languishing on the shelf, despite the fact that he's received at least three offers in the last week."

Eventually, the viscount knew, she would have to succumb. Everyone did. And Amberton intended to be prominently at hand, conveniently under her father's nose and eminently suitable, when she did. But she had damn well better hurry. He had heard the wolf howling at his door too often to have any peace of mind.

"There is a solution," Gerald reminded her.

"Marriage. To exchange one prison for another. To give *another* person the right to correct, criticize and chastise. Do you know, Gerald, that there are men who beat their wives if they don't obey them in every instance? How would I know—"

He held up his hand, palm out, and vowed, "I shall never beat you, Cat. There are better ways to achieve control over a recalcitrant wife than violence. Far more pleasant ways." There were methods that he'd be delighted to demonstrate to this girl, who was seriously endangering his plans with her stubbornness.

"Really?" she said with a touch of haughtiness, disliking the suggestive undertone of that declaration.

"Marry me, my sweet, and I shall be delighted to demonstrate the controlling power of love."

"No," she said simply, returning to the contemplation of the garden that stretched below her in the darkness. "I don't want to get married. To anyone."

"But eventually—" he began.

"Not tonight, please. I don't want to think about that tonight. Go away, Gerald. Let me just enjoy being alone. I have a feeling that the days when I control my own destiny are dwindling, which makes each more precious. My days of freedom may be numbered, but I'm not at your beck and call yet. Nor any man's. Not yet," she said with an almost fierce resignation.

Amberton watched the slight heave of the slender shoulders as she took a deep breath, but smiling still, he obeyed.

Let her enjoy the illusion that she had some choice in the matter as long as she was able, he thought. The Season was coming to an end, and her days of freedom *were* certainly numbered. Like it or not, Catherine Montfort would have to choose, forced to that decision by the demands of her father and of society. Amberton knew that there was not another of her suitors who enjoyed the rapport he had so carefully cultivated. Soon she, and more importantly her fortune, would be under his control, and there were a few lessons that he would delight in teaching Catherine Montfort, proud and stubborn as she was.

With Gerald's departure, only the calm of the night sounds and the drifting music from the ballroom surrounded her. Propping both elbows on the stone railing, she interlaced her fingers under her chin and sighed again.

Unbelievingly she heard behind her the sound of a pair of hands slowly clapping. She turned to see a tall figure standing in the shadows at the edge of the balcony.

"Bravo," the intruder said softly. "A remarkable declaration of independence. I applaud the sentiment, even if I doubt the possibility of your success in carrying it out."

"How long have you been there?" she demanded.

"I believe you were being pawed. And objecting to it."

"How dare you!"

"*I* didn't. That was Gerald."

"You were listening to a very private and personal conversation. You, sir, are obviously no gentleman."

"Obviously," he said agreeably.

Now that she was over her immediate shock, she had begun to notice details of his appearance. He was far taller than any of the men she knew—over six feet tall. Several inches over, she accurately guessed. And very broad shouldered. Massive, really.

As he moved into the light from the windows, she became aware of bronzed skin stretched tautly over high cheekbones and lean, smoothly shaved cheeks. Dear God, she thought in disbelief, it was the man who had bought the donkey. The man with the eyes—crystal blue and piercing, set like jewels among the uncompromisingly strong angles of his dark face.

She swallowed suddenly, fascinated again by his sheer foreignness. No fashionable cut scattered curls over the high forehead. His black hair was pulled straight back and tied at his nape, the severity of the style emphasizing the spare planes of his face and the strong nose.

She realized that she had been staring. Angry with her display of near country simplicity and still embarrassed at having been caught in such a compromising situation, she turned back to the railing, trying to regain her composure.

The silence stretched, only the muffled strains of the music invading the quietness. She had expected some reaction—an apology for his intrusion, a reminder that they'd met before and that she was in his debt, something. He was certainly not responding as Amberton or any of her other courtiers would have reacted to her very deliberate lack of attention.

Almost against her will, she turned back to face him. He was standing exactly as he had been before, watching her with those strangely luminescent eyes. Those damnably beautiful eyes. Even as she thought it, she wondered what was happening to her. She was surely sophisticated enough not to fall tongue-tied at the feet of a stranger because he had blue eyes.

"I'd like to talk to you," he said. The accent was marked, and she wondered why she hadn't been aware of it when he'd spoken from the shadows. Probably because she'd been too mortified by the idea that he'd witnessed Amberton's attempted lovemaking.

"If I don't want to talk to Gerald, who is a very old friend, it should be obvious that I don't wish to talk to you."

"I'm not Gerald," he said, unmoving.

"I beg your pardon?" She had gaped at him like the

veriest schoolroom miss. Yet she didn't intend to be treated like one.

"I'm not Gerald," he repeated obligingly.

"I know what you said. I didn't mean that I didn't hear you. I meant..."

He waited politely for her explanation. His hands were relaxed at his sides; his face perfectly composed.

"I meant I don't know *why* you said that—that you're not Gerald. Obviously you're not Lord Amberton."

"My name is Raven," he said calmly.

"Mr. Raven," she said sweetly, acknowledging the information. Raven? What kind of name was Raven?

Raven inclined his head, not the least bit taken in by her politeness. She was certain by now to be wishing him in Hades.

"Go away," she responded, turning once more to the railing.

Behind her she heard his soft laughter. He was laughing at her. Whoever he was—whatever he was.

"I'm not accustomed to gentlemen who refuse to do as they've been requested," she said with frigid politeness.

"I didn't imagine you were," he said reasonably. "However, I have some business to discuss with you. I believe that this is an opportunity I may not be offered again."

She could still hear the amusement in the deep voice.

"Business?" she repeated, turning once more to face him. "I assure you that I do not discuss *business* with strange men."

"But I'm not a stranger. We've met before. I thought you might remember."

"Of course I remember. I believe that I *did* thank you for the donkey. And now, I really must insist that I be left alone. If you would be so kind." She didn't understand why she was trying to drive him away. She was honest enough to admit that his image had intruded frequently in her brain during the days since their first encounter. She had even envisioned meeting him again, but not while baring her soul on a dark and isolated balcony where no well-brought-up young lady should be found.

"I have a proposition to offer you," Raven said, completely unperturbed by her repeated attempts to dismiss him.

She turned back to face him, appalled beyond words, feeling her skin flush hotly. He had witnessed Gerald's very improper embrace and apparently believed that she would entertain...

"My father will have you horsewhipped," she threatened.

The line of his lips tilted upward at the corners. "Not *that* kind of proposition," Raven corrected. "And I'm shocked that a gently reared young woman would believe that I'm about to offer her carte blanche. I *am* surprised at you." He made a small *tsk*ing sound, shaking his head. The anger he'd felt watching the blond Englishman hold her was beginning to dissipate. She was obviously not the kind of flirt he'd feared when he'd followed the pair from the crowded ballroom.

"What do you want? Please state your *business* and then go away," Catherine ordered. "You have the manners of a barbarian."

"American," he admitted pleasantly, knowing that she was probably correct—at least by her standards.

"Ah," she said, giving him a mocking smile of agreement. "That explains so much." American. No wonder he was unusual.

"I hope so," Raven replied graciously, as if there had been no trace of sarcasm in her reply. "I'm not very familiar with the apparently intricate courtship rituals of your circle. So forgive me if I fail to say all that's proper. I'm a man who believes in cutting to the heart. I'd like you to marry me.''

Despite her genuine sophistication, Catherine's mouth dropped open slightly. She made a small strangled sound and then, controlling her shock, began to laugh, in honest amusement that he should believe he could appear out of the shadows—a stranger with all the panache of a red Indian and the physical presence of a prizefighter—and offer her marriage.

Raven made no outward reaction to her amusement. He hadn't expected her to laugh, despite the fact that she knew nothing about him. Few people ever laughed at John Raven. If nothing else, his sheer size was too intimidating. But, he remembered, Reynolds *had* tried to warn him.

The American waited with only a calm patience evident in his features. Eventually her laughter began to sound a little forced, even to her own ears, and she allowed it to die away.

His lips lifted slightly in what she was beginning to recognize as his version of a smile. A mocking smile.

''I'm glad I've amused you. I imagine you haven't found an occasion for such a prolonged bout of laughter in months.''

''You *are* amusing,'' she taunted, knowing he'd seen through her. Could he possibly realize how he'd affected her at their first meeting? She forced sarcasm into her voice. ''I can't tell you how deliciously ridiculous I find you. And your suit. Quite the most unconventional suitor I've ever had, I assure you.''

''At least I'm not boring you,'' he suggested softly.

She realized with surprise that he wasn't. She was not—definitely not—bored and had not been for the last few moments.

''There are worse things than boredom,'' she retorted mockingly, unconscious that she was repeating Amberton's statement, which John Raven, of course, had certainly over-heard.

"I doubt it," he responded, exactly as she had. "At least we agree on something."

"I would imagine that's the only thing we are ever likely to agree on," she said, opening her fan and moving it gracefully.

His eyes watched the play of her hands a moment and then lifted to study her features. He'd never seen a woman as beautiful. Despite her coloring, there was no scattering of freckles across the small, elegant nose. The long lashes that surrounded the russet eyes were much darker than the auburn hair. Almost certainly artificially darkened, he realized in amusement.

Catherine was glad of the covering darkness that hid the slight flush she could feel suffusing her skin at his prolonged examination. Her acknowledged beauty, which had been her heritage from her mother, had attracted the usual masculine attention, but he was tracing each individual element of her face as if he were trying to memorize them.

"And I believe there are other, more important considerations about which we are in agreement," he said finally, the piercing crystal gaze moving back to meet her eyes.

"Such as?" she asked indifferently.

"Such as the idea that a woman need not be at the beck and call of her husband. That she should enjoy a great deal of personal freedom. With a few necessary limitations, of course."

You have nothing to offer the girl that she doesn't already have, Reynolds had told him, but Catherine Montfort herself had given him a key, an inducement that might tempt her to consider his proposal. She had said that she wanted freedom, and perhaps, if he promised her that...

"Of course." She smiled tauntingly. "But there are those limitations—those very *necessary* limitations."

"I'm offering you almost unlimited wealth. Enough money to become the most fashionably dressed woman in London. You'll have your own household, furnished and staffed exactly as you desire. An unlimited account for entertainment. And the more lavishly you entertain, the better it will suit me. Jewels, horses, carriages, travel—whatever appeals to you will be yours to command."

She smiled again, almost in sympathy at his naiveté. "And if I told you that I already enjoy all of those enticements? What do you have to offer that I don't already possess?"

He studied her upturned face a moment. "Freedom," he said again, and laughing, she simply shook her head. "Freedom from being courted by men you abhor," he continued, as if she'd made no response. "Freedom from society's restrictions. Freedom from your father's demands for a grandson."

"Ah," she said, mocking again, "but to achieve that particular freedom..." She let the indelicate suggestion fade.

"I don't need a mistress," Raven responded softly. "What I need is a hostess." She wanted his assurance that he didn't intend to make physical demands on her, and although her rejection of that aspect of his proposal had not occurred to him before, he knew that he would do whatever was necessary to ensure that Catherine Montfort would be his. Even if it meant restraining for a time his very natural inclinations to do exactly what Lord Amberton had been attempting moments ago.

A platonic marriage was definitely not what John Raven had in mind, but he was a very patient man. He had been carefully trained in that stoic patience since childhood. He could wait for what he wanted, for the kind of relationship he intended to have with this woman.

At his rejection of her taunt, Catherine was surprised to

feel a tinge of regret. *Good God,* she thought, examining that emotion. *Why the deuce should it matter to me if he has a dozen mistresses? A hundred mistresses.*

"Then how should I answer my father's demand for a grandchild?" she asked. "Or will your mistress handle that, too?"

"Our marriage would answer for a time. And eventually—"

"Eventually?" she interrupted, smiling at the trap he had created for his own argument.

"He'll decide you're barren or unwilling to share my bed—whichever version you prefer to put about. I assure you I couldn't care less."

She hid her shock at his matter-of-fact assessment of her father's probable reaction. "You won't require an heir for this unlimited wealth you intend to put at my disposal?"

"Eventually," he said again, as calmly as before, the blue eyes meeting hers. "But you may take as long as you wish before satisfying that desire." The word hung between them, its sexual connotations implicit in the context of their discussion. "You will surely begin to feel maternal stirrings before I require you to carry on my family line," he continued. "After all, I believe you're only eighteen. Or was Amberton wrong about that, too?"

"And how old are you?" she wondered aloud.

"I'm thirty-four," he said.

Almost twice her age. Older by several years than most of the eligible suitors who had approached her father. Except, of course, for the highly unsuitable—like the Earl of Ridgecourt, on the lookout for his fourth wife, someone to preside over his shockingly full nursery, the production of its inhabitants having brought a swift and untimely end to his first three wives.

"Why do you need a hostess?" she asked. She didn't understand why she felt such freedom to delve into the intricacies of the patently ludicrous proposal he'd made. Maybe it was his willingness to discuss any aspect of his plan with her, despite its nature. He didn't seem to be shocked by her questions. On the contrary, he had treated them as legitimate attempts to solicit information necessary to make her choice.

"I've already made investments in British industry—"

"What kind of investments?" she interrupted.

"Coal," he said, thinking with pleasure of the mines that were already producing a far greater tonnage than he had thought possible when he'd bought them.

There was a spark of something in the crystalline depths of his eyes, and she could hear the same quality of possessiveness in his deep voice that one sometimes heard in the voices of women discussing their jewels or, more rarely, their children.

"I buy coalfields," he continued.

"Why?"

"So I can build railroads from them."

When Catherine shook her head slightly in confusion, he smiled that small, controlled smile. "Coal is going to fuel what's beginning to happen here, and the man who controls the coal..." His explanation faded away and he simply watched her face.

"You've made investments in coalfields and railroads?" she questioned carefully. Again she felt a sense of unreality that she was standing in the darkness with a stranger discussing coal.

"And foundries. To make iron. However, most of the men who will be instrumental in deciding on the direction British industry will take in the next few crucial years belong to the circle you frequent. I need to talk to them, to influence them in ways that will increase the value of my investments. But I have no access to those men. I need a wife who does."

"What men?" she asked, interested despite herself. There was some strange compulsion in listening to his deep voice.

"Men like your father. Men of power and influence. The men who control the House of Lords. Who control the land and property of this country."

"Men like that don't discuss business over the dinner table," she told him seriously, falling in with his fantasy.

"And after dinner? Over their port and cigars? With the ladies safely out of the way?" Raven questioned. It was what Reynolds had told him.

"Perhaps," she was forced to admit.

"But first…"

"First they must agree to *come* to dinner."

"Yes," he said simply.

She studied the lean, harshly defined planes of his face.

"I can't marry you," she said finally. She paused, thinking about all he'd offered. "Even if…" She carefully began again, wondering why she was making an explanation. It was almost as if he had constrained her to consider his proposal seriously. "Even if I wanted to."

"Freedom," he invited softly.

"With limitations," she reminded him. And then, remembering, "I never heard the limitations." Almost against her will she responded to the small movement of his lips. Seeing his smile, her own was given with a warmth usually reserved for old friends.

"No lovers," he said. Raven wasn't exactly sure of the conventions of her society, but he'd seen little since he'd been in London to reassure him about the morality of the ton. And he knew that he wouldn't allow another man to touch her. No matter what he'd promised about freedom.

"What?" Catherine gasped in shock, her smile vanishing.

"No lovers," he repeated, trying to think of an excuse

she'd believe, something other than the truth—that he couldn't endure the thought of any other man touching her. "I won't leave what I've worked so hard to acquire to some other man's—"

"How dare you?" she interrupted before he could finish.

"Other than that, I can't really think of any additional limitations," he continued smoothly. "You would be free to come and go as you will, to spend as much of my money as you possibly can, provided you bring to my house the men I need to meet to successfully carry out my investments."

"You're free to have a mistress, but I'm not allowed to have lovers. Is that the arrangement you're suggesting?"

"Unless you have some other plan for satisfying my physical needs," Raven said, wondering how he would manage to control those needs if, by some miracle, she did agree to marry him.

"And what about my needs?" she countered angrily. This was exactly the sort of thing she hated about the restraints imposed by society. It was perfectly acceptable for him to have a mistress, but she was to be bound by his "limitation."

"I hadn't intended to make that a requirement."

"What?" Catherine asked. She must have missed something.

"I would, of course, be delighted to satisfy your needs," Raven agreed, fighting to control his amusement. "However, I—"

"How dare you!" Catherine repeated scathingly. "I assure you that I don't want you to..." She couldn't believe where he'd led her, or what she had been about to say.

"I never assumed you did," he agreed, deliberately clearing any trace of humor from his voice. "What I'm offering is a simple business proposition. You have to marry. You'll be forced to do so, and you are very aware

of that. You want freedom to do *exactly* as you please. I'm
offering you that freedom, with one restriction. A very reasonable restriction. And in exchange, you provide me an
introduction into this society I should never be allowed to
enter without your help."

"Do you think you can discuss these arrangements—"

"You're very well aware of the considerations we've
discussed tonight. The understanding of them is implicit in
most marriages. You and I have simply put all the cards
on the table, open and aboveboard. That's also a freedom
you'll enjoy if you agree to marry me. I promise you I'm
unshockable. You may say to me whatever you wish. You
may ask whatever questions occur to you. About anything.
I will endeavor to answer them honestly."

"However appealing that may be—" she began.

"Then you do find something in my proposal appealing?" he questioned softly, wondering if he dared hope.

"Freedom." She repeated the tantalizing word. "But..."

"But?" he urged at her hesitation.

"My father would never entertain the idea of you as a
son-in-law. He would never consent."

His lips twitched again with that slight upward movement. "How much?" he asked.

"How much?" she repeated blankly.

"To convince your father that I'm a suitable suitor. Marriage settlements, I believe is the proper term."

"Are you proposing to *buy* me?" she asked incredulously. "Surely you don't believe that the Duke of Montfort
would simply sell his daughter to a coal merchant? You
really are incredibly ill informed." There was, she knew,
some truth in his ideas about how such things were done.
She wondered suddenly just how much it *would* take for
her father to agree to what this man proposed.

"You don't have that much money," she said bitingly.

"You might be surprised," Raven suggested calmly. There was no challenge in the quiet avowal.

"My father is a very proud man. Of his name and heritage."

"I understand pride," he answered, his eyes still watching her reaction. "I, too, am proud of my heritage." He remembered the quiet strength of the loving family he'd left behind in the haze-shrouded mountains of Tennessee when he'd begun his long quest. "I assure you it wouldn't sully the purity of the Montfort stock. In horse breeding they make such matches to inject new blood, to add vigor to bloodlines that are outworn."

"Are you suggesting—"

"I'm suggesting that what has existed as the standard for judging a man's quality is about to change in England, as it has already changed in the New World and in France. I believe you are intelligent enough to grasp that concept, even if your father will not. A man's titles and the nobility of his lineage will soon matter less than his intelligence, his hard work and his ability to create, to forge new ideas and turn them into practical applications for the benefit of all. Your father's day is drawing to a close. As is his society's. The world is about to change, and it will never again be the same."

She blinked to clear the spell woven by the conviction in John Raven's voice. Whatever the validity of those views, he certainly believed them. There was no doubt he sincerely thought her world was about to disappear. But she, having known no other, was unprepared to accept that assessment.

"I'm sorry," she said softly. There was nothing else she could offer a man who had revealed to her a dream she could not accept. For in doing so, she would admit that this society, into which she fit as well as her slender fingers fit into the gloves that had been cut to their exact measurements, was doomed. In admitting the reality of *his* vision, she would be forced to deny all the security *she* had ever known.

She brushed by him, leaving John Raven, an alien in the world she understood so well, in the darkness of the balcony, choosing instead to return to the brilliant light of a dozen chandeliers and the elegant music and the endless restrictions.

Chapter Two

The enormous black was entirely suitable. On anything less magnificent, its rider might have appeared ridiculous, but the black *was* magnificent and, therefore, exactly right for John Raven's size. Catherine supposed she should not have been surprised, on the morning after the ball, to find the American approaching her out of the mist that had not yet been burned away by the sun. The vapor swirled around the gleaming forelegs of the black as the man cantered to where she had reined in her mare.

Raven slowed the stallion, controlling the powerful animal with sure horseman's hands. "May I join you?" he asked.

"I'm waiting for someone," she answered truthfully, her voice deliberately cool.

"A gentleman given to puce waistcoats and horses too long in the tooth and too short in the shank?" he asked.

Recognizing all too readily, from his very accurate description, her intended companion for this morning's exercise, Catherine laughed. She watched the corresponding upward tilt in the corners of that forbidding mouth. "Yes," she said, still smiling despite her earlier intent to keep her distance.

"He's not coming. Unavoidably detained, I should say."

"What have you done to Reginald?" she asked, fascinated.

"Reginald?" Raven repeated, allowing disbelief to creep into his deep voice. "Gerald and Reginald," he added, shaking his head. "My God," he said under his breath, and then clearing the derision from his voice and the mischief from the blue eyes, he shook his head again.

"I assure you I had nothing to do with it." Not exactly the truth, he admitted to himself, but all's fair in love and war. "He seemed to be having trouble with his animal, but I promise you, he won't be joining you this morning."

Although, through visible effort, Catherine had managed to control her lips, her eyes were still laughing. They were deep amber in the morning light, darkened with flecks of the same rich auburn that gleamed in her hair, which was almost hidden under the modish hat that matched the dark green habit she wore. The garment, although cut very fashionably, was relatively free of decoration, designed for riding, Raven was pleased to note, rather than parading.

His eyes answered the amusement in hers, and for a moment a decided jolt of power from their crystal depths curled upward inside her body, fluttering against her heart. Catherine swallowed suddenly, dropping her gaze to her gloved hands that were perfectly relaxed over the reins. There was a moment of silence, and then she once more directed her mare onto the bridle path she'd been following before she'd paused to admire the stallion. Long before she had recognized the rider.

Taking that for permission to join her, Raven guided the black alongside, and they rode without speaking for a while.

"He's magnificent," she said finally. Surely horses were a safe topic and apparently one they both appreciated.

"He's a brute with an iron mouth and a heart as black

as his hide," Raven answered without a trace of annoyance, "but we're beginning to understand one another."

"Then you haven't had him long?" There was no evidence of anything but perfect understanding between horse and rider. If the black was a brute, he was keeping his temperament hidden.

"Since this morning," Raven said calmly.

"This morning?"

"Tattersall's, I believe, is the name of the establishment where I found him."

"But…" She paused, glancing at that dark face to see if he were teasing her.

Raven turned at her hesitation and met her eyes, his brows raised slightly, questioning her surprise.

"It must be…it's barely daybreak," she finally managed to say.

"I needed a horse," Raven said, as if that explained it all.

"They aren't open this early," she persisted.

"They are today," he assured her. Then, closing the subject of the power of his money, a subject he had never intended to open, but which had just been demonstrated, Raven asked, "Would you like a run? I haven't had a chance to see if he lives up to the promise of his looks or if he's all flash and no substance."

"Here?" she asked, looking at the narrow, tree-lined path.

"Is there a *rule* against it?" he questioned, almost mocking.

"Probably," she answered tartly, but even as she said it she touched the mare with her crop.

Catherine had caught him by surprise and was therefore able to maintain her lead for a short distance, but, of course, they both had known that the black had a decided advantage, by size if by nothing else. She was forced to admit that his rider also had an edge. Although she was widely acknowledged as one of the finest equestrians in the ton, John Raven seemed to be one with his horse, blending with the reaching effort of the black and almost adding energy to the stallion's powerful motion.

Recognizing defeat and feeling nothing but admiration for the pair who had beaten her, she slowed Storm until eventually they were moving again side by side, at a pace that almost demanded conversation.

"Is this where you always ride?" Raven asked, thinking with sympathy how constricted the area was for a horse-woman of her skills. He wished they could race over the vast lowlands along the great river called Mississippi, space and time unlimited.

Catherine wondered if the American was planning on joining her each morning. She had been forced in the past to give some sharp setdowns to suitors who believed she would welcome company on her early morning excursions. She did occasionally allow very old and trusted acquaintances like Reggie to join her, because she could be sure that they would fall in with any suggestion she made as to the speed or duration of the ride. But, except for her groom, following behind, this was a private time.

"It's the only place in London for a gallop."

"A gallop," Raven repeated derisively. "If that's what you call a gallop."

"No, it isn't, of course. But there's really nowhere else. This *is* a town, you understand—streets, houses, people."

"We have towns in America," he answered, and she knew he was laughing at her again. His face didn't reflect his amusement, of course, but he was laughing just the same.

"And in which one do you live?" she asked sweetly. She tried to dredge up the names of some of those distant cities. New York and Washington. Boston. And Baltimore, of course.

"I haven't been home in several years," Raven answered.

"I thought you'd only recently come to England."

"There are other parts of the world besides England."

"And in which parts were you?" she asked almost sharply. She didn't know how he could make her feel so provincial. He was the one who should be aware that he was lacking polish, and instead, when they were together, she ended up feeling very much out of control of the situation. That had never before happened to her where men were concerned.

"China and then India. For the last five years," he said.

Images of the East as she imagined it to be floated through her consciousness. The old lures of silks and spices. Jewels and precious metals. Ivory and drugs.

"Is that where—" She broke off, realizing the rudeness of her question.

"Where I acquired my money?" he finished easily. "I told you that you might ask me anything. There's no reason to guard your tongue with me. Most of it came from the East, but I have interests in America also."

"What kind of interests?"

"Shipping, which led naturally to my contacts in the Orient. I became fascinated by the cultures. And there, too, fortunes were to be made."

"Too?" she repeated.

"As there will be here."

"In coal and railroads?" she said, remembering.

"And in iron and steel. For the machines."

"What machines?"

"All of them," he said, his lips flickering upward. "Machines for everything," he offered, wondering if she could really be interested.

"I don't understand."

"The world is changing. What has been man-made is about to become the province of machines. To build machines, there must be iron. And to make iron…" He paused, glancing at her face.

"There must be coal," she repeated, as if it were a lesson she'd learned. As indeed, she had. "And the railroads?" she asked. "Why are you building railroads from your coalfields?"

"Because to make iron you must bring the coal and the ore together. The iron ore. So I buy the coalfields, employ the power of machinery to improve the mining techniques, and eventually I'll carry the coal to the foundries by rail," he explained patiently.

"But won't that take a long time? To build railroads from the mines?"

"Yes, but the process can be speeded up by the cooperation of the men who matter in this country. Or it can be slowed down by their refusal to cooperate."

"And that's why—"

"I need a wife. The kind of wife I described to you."

He waited for her response, but it seemed that she'd finally run out of questions. The only sounds that surrounded them were the brush of the wind through the leaves of the trees above and the soft impact of the horses' hooves over the loam of the bridle path. She had no more questions, and so he asked the one that remained unanswered between them.

"Have you decided about my proposal?"

"Mr. Raven, I'm sorry, but you must realize that I can't marry you. My father would never agree, and even if he did, we should not suit. Please, I beg you, don't mention it again."

"I think…" he began, and then stopped. He certainly couldn't tell her that he believed they'd suit extremely well.

That he believed he had been deliberately led to her by the efforts of an old woman who was very far away. He'd been led to Catherine Montfort exactly *because* she was the woman who would best suit John Raven's needs. All his needs.

She looked up quickly at his hesitation. He had always seemed so sure of what he wanted.

"It doesn't matter if we suit," he continued, but she was aware that was not what he had begun to tell her. "If you'll remember, ours isn't to be that kind of marriage. I promise that I will leave you strictly alone, free to make your own decisions and to follow your own desires, with the one exception we discussed. Other than that, you need consider me no more than a business partner who happens to live in the same house."

"A *mariage de convenance*." Smiling, she identified for him the term for the kind of arrangement he had described. One that was certainly not unheard of in the ton.

"In the truest sense of the word. At your convenience. I shall not interfere in your life."

"And you expect the same noninterference in yours?"

"Of course," he responded smoothly. "Nothing more than a business deal. No personal involvement whatsoever." *At least for the time being. At least until I've convinced you that you want to belong to me,* he promised silently. "Other than that involvement necessary to give the ton the opinion that we are united in our social contacts."

Catherine Montfort was unused to men who treated marriage to her as a business arrangement. She was more accustomed to men who made ardent vows of undying devotion. Raven, on the other hand, had in no way suggested that he was attracted to her—other than as one of his machines needed to perform a certain task.

"No," she said softly. She wondered at her sense of disappointment at his clarification of his original proposal.

"It's quite impossible, and you might as well understand that now. My father would never allow such a match."

"Then you have no objection to my approaching him?"

"You intend to approach my father?" she repeated unbelievingly, incredulous that he didn't seem to understand the width of the gap that lay between them.

"Yes."

"With that proposition?"

"Not couched in precisely those terms," he said, the amusement back in his voice. "Simply as an offer for your hand."

"He'll have you thrown out," she warned.

"Will he?" he asked, sounding interested. "I wonder how."

"By the servants," she responded with deliberate bluntness, finally angered at his continual mockery of the reality of the world she lived in. Coal merchants, however wealthy, did not ask for the hand of the Duke of Montfort's daughter.

"I should like to see them try," Raven suggested softly, and found that he really would. He'd damn well like to see them try.

He inclined his head to her and turned the black away from the path, touching the animal's gleaming sides with his heels. Catherine wondered if that had been anger she'd read in his voice, but the statement had been too quietly and calmly made. It had sounded like a simple declaration of fact.

She watched horse and rider until they disappeared into the line of trees across the park, and then, disgusted with her attention to the American nabob, she once more touched Storm's flank, breaking into what passed for a brisk gallop within the careful restraints of London. And she didn't even wonder why her morning's ride was so bitterly dissatisfying.

* * *

Two days later, returning from a particularly dull afternoon musicale, she was approached by the duke's butler as she entered the door, his agitation obvious.

"His grace requests that you join him, if you would, my lady. He's awaiting you in the salon."

"Thank you, Hartford. I'll only be a moment. Please convey that message to my father, and tell him—"

"I think…" the servant interrupted, and then paused, unaccustomed to denying her ladyship's requests. "If you would be so kind, my lady, I believe you should join him immediately."

Catherine considered the man before her. Hartford had never before shown her the slightest sign of disrespect, so she decided that whatever had distressed him enough to cause this small breech of his usually careful manner might really need her immediate attention.

"Thank you, Hartford," she said softly and walked to the wide doorway of the town house's formal salon.

Her father greeted her appearance with something that sounded like relief. He was dressed with his usual elegance, every white hair in place, but because she knew him so well she could sense his annoyance.

"This…gentleman," he said sardonically, the pause clearly deliberate, "insists he's an acquaintance of yours."

The duke's disbelief was patent. His thin hand moved to indicate the man standing at his ease before the straw-colored sofa. He had not, of course, been asked to sit down on it.

Catherine felt an absurd urge to smile at the picture John Raven presented. He, too, was perfectly dressed: his cravat, faintly edged with fine lace, flawlessly tied; his expertly tailored coat of Spanish blue stretched over wide shoulders; his silk waistcoat and pantaloons revealing the strong lines of his muscled body. And yet he looked as out of place in the genteel confines of this room full of priceless family heirlooms and fragile furniture as her father would look in a coalfield.

"Mr. Raven," she greeted him, her amusement at the image of the duke in the middle of a coalfield still showing in her eyes. There was a gleam of reaction to that amusement in John Raven's eyes, and then he inclined his head as regally as royalty was wont to do at an audience. If he felt any unease at being in the Duke of Montfort's elegant salon, he hid it very well indeed.

"You do know him?" her father asked, apparently finding it hard to believe his daughter was confirming Raven's claim.

"Of course," Catherine said easily, advancing across the floor to present her hand to Raven. He glanced down at her fingers, as if contemplating their cleanliness, and then, at the last second possible to avoid outright rudeness, he took them in his own and conveyed them to the line of those straight lips. She was briefly aware of the warmth of his breath above her skin for a second before he released them. His fingers had been hard against the softness of hers, their callused strength very unlike the well-cared-for hands of the men she knew.

"Lady Montfort," he said, controlling his anger at her amusement as impassively as he had at Montfort's rudeness.

"Mr. Raven," she answered, smiling. "How delightful you could visit today. No coalfields up for bid?"

An almost indiscernible reaction moved behind the crystal eyes, which were taking on the glint of ice. "No, I'm confining my bidding to other properties today," Raven mocked, his meaning apparent only to her.

Good God, she thought, *he* has *come to offer for my hand.*

"Coalfields?" Her father repeated the word as if he'd

never before had occasion to use it. Or as if he couldn't quite believe he had just heard his daughter employ it.

"Mr. Raven is a coal merchant," Catherine said, reducing all he had taught her to an object of derision. How dare he embarrass her before her father? He had probably told the duke that they'd discussed marriage settlements. She had *told* Raven how impossible this was, but here he was, determined to humiliate them both and to anger her father in the bargain.

"A coal merchant?" Montfort repeated.

"I'm an investor," Raven said simply. He'd be damned if he'd let the two of them belittle honest labor. He certainly wasn't ashamed of what he did.

"In coal," Catherine interjected helpfully. "And railroads."

"In locomotions?" Montfort's voice rose.

"Locomotives," John Raven corrected quietly. He wondered if he could have been so wrong about what he had seen before in Catherine Montfort's eyes. She was deliberately trying to embarrass him before the duke, but there had been no derision in her voice when she'd asked him to explain his businesses to her.

"For carrying the coal," Catherine continued. "Or was it the ore? I'm afraid I've forgotten which. And I'm sure it was very useful information. I was thinking only today how I might work that into a conversation at some dinner party. I'm sure—"

"Are you serious?" the duke interrupted.

"Perfectly," she said. "I assure you I have it on the best authority, even if I'm a trifle unclear on the details. I'm certain Mr. Raven would be willing to explain it again. He seems to feel everyone else finds coal as interesting as he does."

"I find human progress interesting," Raven said simply. There was no trace of answering amusement in his voice.

"Indeed," Catherine said primly. "How...interesting."

"Is there a reason," the duke began, looking at his guest, "for your call today?"

Catherine could almost see her father mentally repeating the phrase she'd used, as if fixing it in his mind. *Coal merchant.* She could imagine the laughter at his club tomorrow when he told his cronies about it. And she, of course, was only making it worse. Humiliation was inherent in the situation; that was why she had tried to warn the American. But he had been so sure that what he'd suggested was as reasonable as he'd made it sound.

She glanced at Raven's face and found he was watching her instead of her father. A muscle tightened briefly beside his mouth, and then even that was controlled. His eyes moved back to the duke, and he said finally, despite her warning, what she had known he would say from the moment she had walked into the room.

"I've come to offer for your daughter's hand. I would like your permission to marry Catherine."

Her father's face quickly drained of color, and then, his eyes never leaving those of the man who had made that ludicrous suggestion, it suffused with blood, purpling with rage.

"You—you would *what?*" he sputtered.

Raven drew papers from the inside pocket of his coat and unfolded them as if he had all the time in the world. "One of these is a listing of my assets. The other is a marriage agreement that the man of business I employ here in London believed might be appropriate in such a merger. As you will see, the death settlements are extremely generous, and I require nothing from you except your permission for the match to take place. Not the usual contract in matters such as these, I'm aware, but my financial success has given me the liberty of not having to be a stickler for the conventional terms. Your daughter's hand is dowry enough, I assure you.''

Raven had just uttered more words than Catherine had heard him put together in their previous conversations, except when he was talking about coal. The speech had had a rather endearing charm, if one thought about it—not that her father would.

''How dare you!'' the duke said.

Although the old man certainly presented no physical threat to the American, his fury was rather awe inspiring— to Catherine at least. She couldn't remember seeing her father this enraged since she'd run off with the fortune hunter. Resolutely, she turned her mind away from that memory.

''Listed here also are the properties I am willing to settle on your daughter after our marriage,'' Raven added.

Catherine wondered if she were to be given a coalfield as an inducement to marriage. The words *with my worldly goods, I thee bestow* ran fleetingly through her mind.

''Get out,'' her father said ominously.

''Or a cash settlement if you prefer,'' Raven offered reasonably. Reynolds's warnings began to stir darkly in the back of his mind. Because the settlements were indeed extremely generous, he had believed that a man of the duke's intelligence would immediately see the advantages for his daughter. *Not of his class,* the banker had counseled. *Notorious for his temper,* the groom had suggested. And Catherine's own advice, given almost with regret, he'd believed: *My father would never allow such a match.* All the warnings Raven's pride had ignored were repeated in the old man's features.

The Duke of Montfort stalked across the room to ring the bell, which Hartford answered too quickly. The butler must have been standing in the hall in case of just such an occurrence.

"Get out of my house," the duke repeated.

"Your daughter has voiced no objection to the match," Raven averred calmly.

Not exactly the truth, Catherine thought, but he was certainly not easily discouraged.

Her father, however, had apparently had enough. "Throw him out," he said, gesturing to Hartford.

The butler walked up to John Raven, who turned those remarkable eyes from the contemplation of her father's face to the servant's. As the duke's had, Hartford's features lost color, but for a different reason altogether. The American's controlled smile appeared briefly at the man's hesitation, and then he turned and walked around him.

There would be no advantage to Raven in a meaningless confrontation with Montfort's butler. Fighting with the servants would only make him appear more ridiculous than he already had.

However, he didn't resist the impulse to issue his own warning. He turned back in the doorway to speak to the duke.

"I intend to marry your daughter, your grace. Nothing that has been said today has changed that. I have never done business this way in the past, and I believe it was a mistake on this occasion, but because I'm a stranger here, I allowed others to influence my actions. You may name your price, but I mean to have Catherine. You can be certain of that."

The duke's shock held him motionless a moment. Raven's eyes moved back to meet Catherine's. He nodded to her and finally, mercifully, he turned to leave.

Something in that last challenge to his authority, his pride or his honor had broken Montfort's control, never particularly reliable under the best of circumstances. He rushed after the departing American, almost shouting in his fury. "You'll marry Catherine over my dead body. You'll not bring your sweat-stained lucre into my family. You're another damned fortune hunter, and you're not fit to *speak* my daughter's name. I'll see you in hell before you insult her with your proposal again. You stink of sweat, and your stench offends my nose!''

Raven turned back to face the duke, and for once the warrior Scot in his heritage overcame the hard-learned Indian stoicism.

''If my money's stained, it's with my own sweat, your grace. Not that of the peasants your family robbed for hundreds of years. Mine's a far cleaner stench than yours, sir,'' he said bitterly. ''And as for being a fortune hunter, I assure you I'm not interested in your money. It's Catherine I want, and I intend to have her. I assure you I meant no insult to your daughter. I have made her the most honorable offer she's likely to receive. Even if you're both too insular to understand that.''

''Insular?'' Montfort shouted. ''You colonial jackanapes, don't you dare call me insular.''

His gaze found the crop Catherine had left on the hall table that morning after her ride. It was not her custom, but she had apparently forgotten it when she had stopped to examine the calling cards in the salver that rested there. The crop's position proved far too convenient for her father's fury.

In his fit of blood lust, he grasped the whip, flying across the narrow space that separated him from his unwanted guest, to slash a blow across the mouth that had spoken those insults.

Raven wrenched the crop from the duke's fist, but a slim, feminine hand caught his wrist, just as it had caught the rattan stick. Although he could have easily freed himself from the grip of Catherine's fingers, Raven hesitated, another emotion interfering with his anger. She had touched him, slender fingers resting on the bare skin of his wrist, and he could feel the results of that realization beginning to move through his body, replacing the involuntary flood of adrenaline with a different, but just as uncontrollable, response.

"He's an old man," she begged. "Please don't hurt him."

Raven's eyes, filled with a fury that matched her father's, moved down to meet hers. Somehow, at the sight of russet eyes full of regret and apprehension, he found control.

She took a deep breath as she felt the rigidity gradually leave the upraised arm. "Just go away," she whispered. "I tried to tell you this would happen. Please, just go away."

Catherine's fingers slipped across the back of Raven's hand, and he allowed her to take the crop he could never have used against the old man. The welt her father had raised across his face was beginning to change from livid white to angry red. He raised his own fingers, which to his disgust trembled slightly, to explore it. The upper end was the most heavily damaged, a crimson thread there beginning to overflow and spill across his high cheekbone. He brushed his hand over the welling blood, feeling the fighting fury of his ancestors build again.

Catherine could hear the harshness of Raven's breathing. She was close enough even to smell him. There was no cloying perfume, but rather a pleasant aroma composed of the starch that had been used in his cravat, the fine leather of his boots and the warmly inviting, totally masculine scent of his body.

She lowered the hand that now controlled the whip and found, surprisingly, that she was fighting an urge to touch the brutal stripe her father had laid across his face. She knew that the duke's rage was not really directed against John Raven. This blow had been struck in revenge for another insult to his daughter, for another man who *had* been exactly what Montfort had accused the American of being.

What had happened here this morning was not what she had wanted, but she knew very well her mockery had played a role in what had occurred. Raven would never know how deeply she regretted that.

"I'm sorry," she offered softly.

It seemed almost as if he didn't hear her. Finally the blue flame of his gaze focused again on what was in her face. His lips were white with the pressure he was exerting. The small, throbbing muscle jumped again in his jaw.

"Tell him," Raven ordered, reading the look in her eyes—the look he had seen there before. He had *not* been mistaken.

"Tell him what?" she asked, truly not understanding what message she was supposed to give.

"That you're mine. And that he might as well get accustomed to that reality."

John Raven had disappeared into the street, slamming the door behind him, before she could think of an answer.

Chapter Three

In the ensuing days, her father said little about the confrontation with John Raven. He had grudgingly admitted, knowledge assuredly gained from his friends at White's, that the "coal merchant" was exactly what he had claimed to be.

"Rich as Croesus," the duke acknowledged. "They're calling him the American nabob, but I am led to understand that most of his wealth was accumulated in the East."

"China and India," Catherine agreed, remembering their ride.

The old man's eyebrow lifted. "God's teeth, Catherine, exactly how well do you know this damned miner? Surely you must realize what you're doing by this ridiculous delay—making it appear you *desire* the attentions of men like this American. Choose a man of your own class, suitable for your birth and position, and do it damned quickly. I'll not be accosted by any more importunate jackanapes with coal dust under their fingernails." The duke's slender, elegantly erect frame shuddered dramatically, illustrating his distaste.

"Importunate?" Catherine repeated. "I should think that would be one adjective that wouldn't apply in this case.

He's hardly the fortune hunter you called him.'' Recalling her father's fury over the disastrous incident of two years ago, she added, ''I should think you'd be glad you don't have to worry about that with Mr. Raven's proposal. Actually...'' she began, savoring the rather exciting bluntness of that proposal.

''Don't press me, Catherine. You think to wind me around your finger as you've always done, but I warn you, girl, this is no trifling matter. Pick a husband, or I shall do it for you. And be damned sure that I will, Cat. Damned sure.''

The problem was that she knew very well his temper might cause him to do exactly that, regardless of his promise to her. Despite her father's warning, she had found herself reliving that last encounter with John Raven more times than she wished, mentally watching her crop descend across the high cheekbone. The memory that was most clear and, to her disgust, most often repeated in her mind, was what he had said just before he'd departed.

Tell him, John Raven had said, *that you belong to me.*

Once more in the midst of a crowded ballroom, Catherine forced her thoughts away from the remembrance of whatever, besides anger, had been in Raven's eyes that afternoon. She was still not certain of the emotion that had called forth his declaration. Fury at being denied what he wanted, certainly. And at her father's treatment of his suit. But she had begun to believe that she had seen something else stirring in that blue flame.

Resolutely she broke off her fruitless attempt to identify that fleetingly glimpsed emotion and tried to focus on what her partner was saying. She wished he'd simply let her enjoy the waltz, but he seemed to think that *he* must entertain her rather than allowing the flowing movements of the dance and the pulse of the music to do so. She allowed her lids to close over eyes that were beginning to glaze with boredom, and there appeared before her, in her mind's eye, John Raven's face. That had happened far too frequently lately, and she had found herself at too many social engagements unconsciously seeking that dark head which she knew would tower above those of the room's other inhabitants.

Guilt, she had finally decided. Guilt over the role she'd played in her father's brutality that day. By her mockery she had thrown Raven to the wolves when, she knew, she could have handled the situation differently, perhaps even have mitigated the duke's fury. Apparently she wasn't going to be given a chance to explain or apologize. John Raven seemed to have disappeared from London as quickly as he had appeared. Unconsciously, she sighed.

"Bored, my dear?" Gerald asked solicitously.

Good God, she thought, shocked at that familiar voice. She had changed partners in such a perfect fog that she'd been unaware until that very moment that she was floating across the floor in Amberton's very capable arms.

"Tired," she offered, wondering what she'd said to him before, while she was thinking of the American's strong features.

"It's nearly over. The Season is winding down and—"

"Don't," she ordered with something of her old spirit. "Don't tell me what's going to happen after that. I assure you I don't intend to repeat the argument we had two weeks ago."

She began to take her hand from his, resolving, since he seemed determined to remind her, to move away from him. But his fingers tightened over hers, controlling.

"You really are too accustomed to having your own way. I don't think public humiliation, my dear, is on tonight's agenda."

She turned in surprise at his unexpected masterfulness.

Smiling smugly, he ruthlessly swept her back into the rhythm of the waltz, holding her far closer than was acceptable.

"Let me go," she demanded imperiously.

"Quit behaving like the spoiled chit I called you. We're in the middle of the dance floor, for God's sake. Don't you dare try to walk away from me."

Furious, she struggled again, and his fingers ground into hers more strongly, hard enough to bruise.

"You've had your own way too long, my pet. But I think you'll not find me so easy to deal with as your ever-indulgent parent. You really have no option here, and you must know it."

Catherine was forced to realize the unpleasant truth of his assertion. She could literally fight him for her freedom, here under the eyes of the gossiping old tabbies of the ton, or she could give in gracefully and finish the set. She couldn't imagine what had come over Gerald, but in this instance she recognized the validity of what he had said. As much as she hated the admission, she really had no choice.

Finally the music ended, and with what she hoped was an icy dignity, she allowed him to lead her from the floor. Still furious, she had said nothing after his unconscionable behavior. She was relieved to find that her next partner was an old and trusted childhood friend, Lord Anthony Dellwood. Gerald released her with what appeared to be satisfaction with his mastery, and she nodded coldly before he turned away.

"I'm sorry," she said as soon as Amberton had moved out of earshot, "but I'm feeling a trifle unwell. Do you suppose you might find my father, Tony? I really would like to go home."

She dealt charmingly with his expressions of concern and was infinitely relieved when he left her alone in the small

sheltered alcove to which he had taken her to wait while
he saw to the arrangements. It was not just Gerald's bizarre
behavior, it was everything. The Season *was* coming to an
end, and with its conclusion, her father's repeated ultima-
tums for her decision had increased. And the only man with
whom she could imagine...

The thought impacted like fireworks in her brain. The
only man with whom she could imagine spending the rest
of her life was not Gerald, nor any of the other perfumed
and pompous members of her set, but... Surely she couldn't
be contemplating marriage to the coal merchant. The words
you belong to me echoed again in her brain, causing their
own small explosion of sensation. My God, she wondered,
could he possibly be right about that? "The bride was conveyed to her wedding by locomotive," the *Morning Post*
would say.

Catherine's lips slanted suddenly as she remembered
Raven correcting her father. She doubted whether anyone
else in his very long and noble life had had the gall to point
out the duke's obvious errors to him. No wonder her father
had been so furious that day. John Raven certainly did not
play by the rules that had been set down for members of
this society to follow.

"I'm sorry, my dear, but your father seems to have been
called away. Some unexpected emergency. I'm sure a very
minor one, but I've ordered your coach brought round and
will very gladly escort you home," Dellwood offered gal-
lantly.

"There's no need for that, Tony. You know how short
the distance is. And Tom's perfectly reliable. He's been in
my father's service for years."

"I insist. I'm sure your father would much prefer that I
come with you. He probably already made arrangements
for you to be conveyed home, and I've inadvertently coun-

termanded them. I would never forgive myself if anything were to happen.''

"And what do you imagine might happen to me between here and home? This is London, you know, not the wilds of America."

He laughed cooperatively at her feeble attempt at humor, while she wondered why that particular analogy had leapt into her mind. Obsessed with things American, perhaps? she questioned herself mockingly.

"I really insist on being allowed—" her escort began, and was quickly interrupted.

"And I must insist that I'm better off alone. Please. I really am not well, and I'm afraid this pointless argument..." As an added inducement, she pulled her small lace handkerchief from her glove and pressed it delicately against her lips.

Although still worried about the impropriety of allowing her to depart without escort, Dellwood was forced to agree. As Catherine had logically pointed out, this *was* London. What could possibly happen to the Duke of Montfort's daughter while being transported to her home by her father's own coachman?

The rain that had been a shower at the beginning of the evening had turned into a deluge, but through the solicitude of Lady Barrington's servants, Catherine was put into the coach, suffering no more than a drop or two spotting the emerald silk. She sat morosely in the darkness of the swaying carriage, listening to the pounding fury of the storm against its roof. She was angered and bewildered by Gerald's attempt at domination tonight. And, she was honest enough to admit, to herself at least, she was again disappointed that she had not at some point in the evening found two piercing blue eyes meeting hers with unusual directness. She missed the excitement her encounters with the American had added to her existence, and if she were com-

pletely honest, she knew that she also missed the man himself. Her lips moved into a slight smile, again remembering.

The small jolt of the carriage as it drew up to its destination pulled her attention from those memories, and she
gathered her skirt in preparation for the descent into the
driving rain. The door was opened and an enormous black
umbrella held over her to shelter her from the deluge. Hurrying down the steps the coachman had dropped, she ran,
head lowered against the force of the blowing rain, toward
the welcoming glow that shone into the dark street from
the door of the town house.

She heard it close behind her as she was shaking raindrops from her ball gown. She turned to hand her gloves
and reticule to Hartford and found she was standing in the
foyer alone.

In a foyer she had never seen before in her life. It took
a moment for the reality of that to sink in. She was not in
her father's town house. There had been some terrible mistake.

"Good evening," a deep voice intoned from the shadows
at the end of the enormous hallway. She glanced up to find
John Raven standing there, quietly watching her. His voice
had echoed slightly across the empty expanse of softly
gleaming black and gray squares of Italian marble that
stretched between them.

She swallowed against the fear that constricted her
throat. He had brought her here to avenge himself on her
for what her father had done. She turned to the door behind
her and began struggling to open it, her fingers trembling
uncontrollably.

Before she could manage the intricacies of the unfamiliar
lock, his beautifully shaped hand, which she had admired
caressing Storm that day, gently closed over hers and removed them from the door. He turned the key that was in
the lock and, removing it, placed it in his waistcoat pocket.

Catherine's fear was reflected in the strained face she raised to his, so he smiled at her before he spoke. "I'm not going to hurt you," Raven promised softly. He hated making her afraid, especially afraid of him.

"What do you want?" she whispered past the unfamiliar tightness that threatened to block her throat.

His mouth moved slightly, the corners deepening. "I *thought* I had made that perfectly clear. Even your father finally managed to understand what I want," he answered, and she was allowed to read his amusement.

Catherine was beginning to calm down, Raven's quiet humor making her believe that he really didn't intend her harm. There was no anger in his tone or posture. Apparently he didn't intend to seek revenge for the father's insult by ravaging the daughter, but she could still see the mark the crop had made that day faintly lined on his cheek.

Raven let her study his face a moment, and then he said, "There's nothing to be frightened of here."

Somehow, she found herself believing him. But he must know—surely he must know, even stranger that he was—what being found in such a situation would do to her reputation.

"Why did you bring me here?" she asked, and then wondered for the first time how that had been accomplished. "And how? That was my father's coachman. I saw him quite clearly before, at Lady Barrington's. He would never—"

"He has an invalid wife and a multitude of children."

"You *bribed* him?" she asked, unable to believe that Tom would betray her for money.

"He was very concerned about you. But I gave him my word that you would come to no harm at my hands."

"And he believed you?"

"Of course. He seems to be an excellent judge of character. He likes you very much, but he thinks your father's a bastard.''

"You and the coachman discussed my father?" she asked. This must be some sort of nightmare. Soon she'd wake up, and she would still be on the dance floor, safely waltzing through another evening of deadly sameness. *Safe,* she thought longingly.

"Not at length. But we found ourselves in perfect agreement, I assure you."

"Why did you bring me here?" She was beginning to be able to control her fear. To be able to think.

"I wanted to show you something. Two things, really. Both of which I thought you should see."

"You abducted me to *show* me something?" she repeated carefully. "And when I've seen whatever it is?"

"Then I'll arrange to have you taken home. If you decide that's what you want."

"If I decide...?" Her voice rose. "What else do you imagine I would want?" She paused and took a breath, again seeking control. "Of course I shall want to be taken home."

"Perhaps not. We won't know until we've completed our business."

Business, she echoed mentally, wondering with irritation if that was all John Raven ever thought about. Apparently he had kidnapped her to discuss business. She felt a spurt of fury. She'd been abducted by a man whom, she admitted, she was fascinated by, and all he wanted to do was to talk business. As if she were some solicitor or shopkeeper instead of what she was—the acknowledged toast of the last two London seasons. The final thought was reassuring in light of his disinterest.

She glanced up and realized he knew exactly what she was thinking. His amusement was obvious in that dark face.

His eyes, which were warmer than she had ever seen them, displayed a clear understanding of her disappointment.

"Then why don't you show me whatever you've brought me here to see and let me go home? The sooner the better, I assure you," she said decisively.

Raven inclined his head in agreement and gestured with his hand, urging her ahead of him down the wide hall. She hesitated a moment and then swept up her damply clinging skirt and proceeded in the direction he'd indicated.

On her left was a vast salon, perfectly proportioned from the sweep of its tall Palladian windows that lined the wall to the graceful Adam fireplace and the finely executed plaster medallions overhead. And perfectly empty. Catherine wandered in, wondering what she was supposed to do. She turned, allowing a small sarcastic lift of one beautifully shaped auburn brow.

"And?" she said.

"This way," he commanded and, shrugging, she followed.

It was exactly the same over the entire lower level of the mansion: elegant rooms of stately design and size, completely unfurnished. Raven didn't comment as he led her through the vast dimness, their footsteps echoing over the bare floors. He took her finally into a small study, sparsely furnished with a huge desk and chair, another chair facing the desk, and a tall cabinet. The surface of the desk was cluttered with ledgers and papers.

"I had thought, if you didn't mind, that I would leave this as it is. To serve as my office. And there's a small bedroom that I've left as I found it, simply for convenience. However, if you have any objections, I assure you I won't stand in your way in redecorating those. I myself have little interest in such things. A chair and a bed and I'm perfectly happy."

"This is your house?" Catherine asked, beginning to

make some sense of this mysterious tour. "You're living here."

"A rather Spartan existence at present. But soon, I hope—"

"In *my* redecorating?" she interrupted, having just registered the gist of his explanation. "You expect *me* to redecorate?"

"I promised a house you might furnish as you pleased."

"This... You intend that I... That you and I..." Despite several attempts, she couldn't seem to complete the suggestion he once again appeared to be making. Apparently her father had not convinced him that he couldn't have what he had decided he wanted. "Mr. Raven, you must realize—"

"They tell me it's rare that such a property becomes available in Mayfair. That such houses as this seldom change hands. It was the first one they showed me, and I must confess, I felt it to be perfect. However, you know far more about such matters than I. If you think—"

"Mr. Raven..." She broke in again and then found herself at a loss. Nothing she said seemed to make an impression. Nothing her father had said or done seemed to matter at all. John Raven was without a doubt the most obstinate man she'd ever met.

"Then it won't do?" he asked in the sudden silence.

"It's not the house. It's wonderful. You must know that."

"The original furnishings are in storage, until you've had the opportunity to choose any of them you wish to keep. Or you may discard them all and begin anew. My solicitor assured me there are some very fine pieces among them, however. I'll make arrangements for you to see everything as soon as—"

"Mr. Raven," she interrupted, more strongly than before.

He stopped. The small depression at the corner of his lips deepened, but his expression was otherwise under perfect control, the blue eyes resting on her face with polite interest.

"I can't marry you," she said softly.

He glanced down briefly at the toe of his evening shoe, which gleamed softly at the bottom of his impeccably cut formal trousers, and she saw the breath he took before he spoke.

"Then perhaps I should show you the second thing I brought you here to see," Raven said.

"Perhaps that would be wise," Catherine agreed. "And then you promised to have me returned to my father's house. I can only hope that he hasn't already found that I'm not there."

"Your father won't be home for at least another hour."

"How can you possibly..." The realization was as startling as the idea that he could simply bribe her father's trusted servant to do whatever he wished. "You arranged for my father to be called away. So you could bring me here."

"If things don't turn out tonight as I hope they will, it seemed the safest way for you. No one will know that you've been here. Tom will take you home, and nothing will ever be said about your visit. If you decide that's what you want."

"*If* I decide?" she questioned.

"After you've seen what I would like to show you now."

There seemed to be nothing to do but let him play out this fantasy, whatever else he had in mind. Whatever else he had to show her. Jewelry? she wondered, trying to think what he had mentioned in the original offer.

Turning, he chose a paper from the clutter on the desk and held it out to her.

Catherine had hesitated in the doorway, somehow reluctant to enter the suddenly too small confines of the room, which he seemed to dominate simply by standing, completely unmoving, waiting for her to take the paper he offered. In the dimness, his eyes shone in the spare, rugged beauty of his face.

Beauty? She repeated that incredible thought, wondering at her own description.

Shaking her head slightly to break the spell he always cast over her senses, she walked forward, laid her gloves and reticule on the desk and took the proffered sheet. She looked down at what she held, expecting a deed or some bill of sale, some added inducement to all that he had already offered. Something to sweeten the pot. And yet...he had never offered her the one thing she was beginning to realize she really wanted from him, the one thing that she knew would affect her decision.

She started to read, scanning what was written on the paper. One more obstacle to be overcome, and then he had promised to have her conveyed home.... She stopped suddenly, some sense of what she held finally dawning, and her eyes flew back to the top of the page to carefully peruse what she had only glanced at before: "...His Grace, the seventh Duke of Montfort, is pleased to announce the forthcoming marriage of his daughter, Lady Catherine Montfort, to Gerald Blaine, third Viscount Amberton."

"That's to appear in the *Post* and the *Gazette* tomorrow," Raven said.

"How did you get this?"

"Most things are for sale—given enough money. I was afraid your father might try something like this, so I took precautions against it." Raven had offered her freedom, the only thing she did not have, and he could only pray that she would desire it enough to escape the trap they had devised for her.

Catherine felt the sickness growing in the pit of her stomach. Her father had broken a promise to her for the first time in her life. He was going to give her to Amberton without in any way considering her own wishes. And then, even more disturbing than that betrayal, came the remembrance of Gerald's behavior on the dance floor. As if he were already certain of his control over her. As, of course, he had been, she realized—assured of that control through her father's treachery.

Unconsciously she flexed the bruised fingers the viscount had gripped so painfully earlier tonight. "But he promised," she whispered, fighting the urge to give in to the tears that she so seldom shed. Her own father had forsaken her.

"I'm sorry. I believe my proposal probably played a part in his decision, at least in the timing. You *did* try to warn me."

She looked up at the unexpected confession, surprised to find what appeared to be a look of concern on his face. It was almost immediately replaced by the controlled expression John Raven's features always bore. So quickly did the change occur that she was forced to doubt her identification of the emotion she had seen. How could he possibly know what she was feeling—this sense of betrayal and despair over the fate her father had arranged?

"It's not your fault," she admitted, because in all fairness it wasn't. "I suppose I've always known this was inevitable. And Gerald..." she began, again remembering his actions tonight. She had held to the illusion that if she were forced to choose from the men she knew, Gerald at least offered some possibility of rapport. Until tonight. Tonight he had seemed almost a stranger, determined to force her to his will.

"There *is* another option," Raven said, interrupting her despondency.

She glanced up from the announcement her father had had composed. An option. Freedom and wealth. *Rich as Croesus.* At least she would never have to wonder if John Raven had wanted her for her father's money. No, she remembered suddenly, he wanted her for a far different reason. His promise of noninterference in her life was to be in exchange for her becoming his hostess, for arranging his entry into the ton. A business arrangement. If only he had offered…

She banished that ridiculous thought, trying to decide if accepting Raven's proposal could possibly provide a way out of the trap Amberton and her father had so blithely created. A marriage trap—weighed against the promise of freedom.

"Freedom?" she questioned aloud. And as if he had been following the convoluted path of her reasoning, he nodded.

"You have my word. Within the constraints of our contract. You invite to this house those men who would certainly not come otherwise, entertain them so well that the invitations to dine here become the most fashionable in London, and you refrain from taking lovers. Other than those responsibilities, you may do entirely as you wish. I promise that I will never censure you," he vowed, and again she found herself believing him.

"You must know my father will disinherit me," she warned.

"The fewer ties you have with your father, the better pleased I shall be," Raven admitted. His gut twisted at the remembrance of what the old man had said. That insult had cut far more deeply than the gash across his face.

Catherine hoped that, like her father's coachman, she was a good judge of character. "All right," she agreed softly.

Raven said nothing, relief and exultation blocking his

throat, a reaction as automatic and uncontrollable as that which tightened his stomach muscles and stirred painfully in his groin. She had just agreed to become his wife. Against everyone's assurance that she never would.

Because he didn't respond, Catherine was unsure that he had heard her whisper. She looked up and said it again. "All right, Mr. Raven. I accept. And now, how do you intend to bring this off, in light of the announcement tomorrow of my betrothal to Lord Amberton?" Somehow she had no doubt he had already devised a plan to handle the practical aspects of their wedding.

"I had thought…" Raven paused, trying to gauge her mood. There had been too much pain in those beautiful eyes. Pain quickly hidden beneath her pride.

She met his searching gaze with her face deliberately cleared of emotion and her chin unconsciously raised. Once committed, she was prepared to burn her bridges spectacularly.

"You intend to let my father find us together?" she guessed, realizing that he certainly didn't know the duke as well as she. "Hoping that he'll then consent to our marriage?"

"Would that work?" Raven asked, amused at the scenario she'd suggested. Far more melodramatic than what he'd planned, but when he considered the possibilities it offered…

"I'm afraid not. He'd shoot you, or hire someone to do it, and then cover it up. He also has a great deal of money."

His lips moved slightly, and she knew she'd amused him.

"Then do you suggest I tell him that you've agreed to become my wife?"

"He'll shoot you, or hire someone to do it, and then—"

"I see." He interrupted her repetition of the outcome. And he was still amused. "Then perhaps you have a suggestion."

"Gretna Green," she said decisively, fighting memories of another run for the Border. Another man, very different from this. "Shocking, I know," she forced herself to continue, "but it's really the only way."

"And your reputation?" Raven could imagine how their elopement would be viewed by the ton. He hadn't intended to ruin her life, to cut her off from everyone she'd ever known.

"Oh, dear Lord," she said, chiding his ignorance. "A scandal of the proportion *this* one is going to be? The love story they'll imagine is at the root of *this* runaway marriage? Your wealth? And your appearance?" she added unthinkingly, and saw again the small, upward quirk of his lips. "Give the gossip two months to ferment, and we'll be able to charge admission to the first dinner party." She glanced down at the paper he had handed her. They really had given her no choice.

"Let me worry about the ton, Mr. Raven. You worry about what horses you have in your stables that can beat my father's best in a race to the Border. I'll take care of the rest. It's what I was born to do," she asserted confidently. Having been bred and reared in the world he desired to enter, she was secure in her membership. She was already thinking of the best way to handle the necessary explanations when the time was right.

"I don't think that's what you were born for at all," Raven said, knowing exactly for whom Catherine Montfort had been created. His angel. His wife.

At that surprising comment, she looked up from the hated announcement. John Raven, however, was already striding through the door to make those arrangements that she had suggested were his responsibility in this merger they had undertaken.

Only a business arrangement, she reminded herself, her eyes resting again on the evidence of her father's treachery, which had driven her to this contract and to this man.

Chapter Four

Once the flight up the Great North Road had begun, they did not stop except to change horses. It seemed to Catherine that they flew through the darkness, the coach rocketing along the well-maintained thoroughfare. The horses Raven had arranged to be waiting at the various posting inns were not only fresh, but bred for stamina and speed. They finally reached their destination in less than thirty hours, without having seen any evidence of what she had been sure would be a determined pursuit.

Despite the inducements of the professional "witnesses," Raven sought out a real blacksmith shop. The ceremony over the anvil was quickly completed, an exchange of vows as stripped of pageantry as even, she believed, the American might wish.

Raven then took time to discuss with the smith the quality of the metal he had been using, before they'd interrupted him, to shape the products that came from his forge. Even the taciturn Scot responded to his well-informed comments.

"Aye, well, you're right enough about that, my lord," the smith said in answer to Raven's observation that nowhere in Scotland was wrought iron produced, which would be free from the impurities that often ruined an object of some hours' work.

"My name is Raven," the American had corrected, offering his hand, "and I'm no lord."

"Your pardon, then, Mr. Raven. I meant no offense," the smith said, smiling, his pale eyes twinkling at his joke.

"Offense?" Catherine Montfort Raven questioned.

Her husband turned, smiling, to answer her slightly affronted inquiry. "There are men," he explained, "who believe that to be accused of being English nobility is a deadly insult."

"Why?" she asked, never having encountered such a ridiculous prejudice. But then, of course, she had never before talked to a Scots blacksmith as he worked his forge.

"Because it implies uselessness, perhaps," Raven answered hesitantly. He had known instinctively what the smith implied, but he didn't intend to explain the insult to Catherine.

"Like my father, you mean," she suggested.

Without answering, Raven took her elbow to guide her back to the waiting carriage, scarcely able to believe that this incredibly beautiful girl, serenely elegant even after their long journey, was now his wife. His to care for and protect. And her comment had brought him back to the still-precarious situation in which they found themselves. The Duke of Montfort, when crossed, could be a very dangerous man. Despite the Scots' friendliness, Raven doubted they'd be willing to fight the duke's hirelings to defend a stranger who happened to know something of their trade.

He helped Catherine into the coach and walked back to the forge to wait for the mulled wine the smith's daughter had been dispatched to fetch.

"That girl's too delicate for marriage to the likes of you, Mr. Raven," the blacksmith offered, eyeing the foreigner's broad shoulders, which looked more than capable of handling the heavy hammers that were a part of his own trade. "She'll be whining and denying you after the first child. You'd best hope she gets you a son on her first swelling. Though, come to that, she don't look sturdy enough to bear a babe. Not up to your riding weight, if you get my meaning," he suggested, slapping his blushing daughter on her ample rump as she passed. "You need a fine Scots lass who'll welcome your lovemaking and bear you a houseful of strong sons. You'll soon be regretting this day's work," he said, becoming more daring in response to the hooting enjoyment of the men who had gathered to watch as he plied his bellows.

Even hidden from sight in the isolation of the waiting coach, Catherine was well able to hear the smith's comments. She felt the hot blood flowing upward into her cheeks, not only at the crudity with which he was discussing the consummation of her marriage, but at the contempt in which he obviously held her and her class.

"You may know a great deal about iron," her husband said, his voice coming to her as clearly as had the Scotsman's, although he had not raised it to entertain the listening crowd. "But I'm forced to tell you, sir, that you know nothing about women. My wife is, I assure you, the purest cast steel. You need have no doubts about her quality. Or," Raven added, "about anything else you've called into question."

At the burst of laughter and the catcalls that greeted his response—all made, surprisingly, at the expense of the smith and not the American who had so eloquently defended his choice of woman—Raven touched his hat, planted a quick kiss on the cheek of the smith's daughter as he took the stone bottle from her hand, and walked back to the waiting carriage.

Catherine's blush made it obvious, she was afraid, that she'd overheard the entire conversation. "They don't think much of the English, do they?" she commented, with what she hoped was a convincing display of nonchalance. "Or of me," she added almost bitterly, spoiling the effect.

"I told them they were mistaken," Raven said, smiling. When her lips moved slightly into a reluctant realignment, almost an answering smile, he finished, "About you at least."

Finally, she did smile. There was really no need to argue with him about the smith's assessment of the English nobility, an assessment she realized she had at times even shared.

She was also beginning to realize that she was no longer just a part of the world she'd always inhabited; she was, by virtue of the vows she had spoken, simple though they were, a part of Raven's. A world which, apparently, included vulgar Scots blacksmiths. She shivered slightly, whether from the cold of the morning air or from her acknowledgment that she belonged not only to Raven's world, but also, of course, to John Raven himself.

"Would you like some wine?" he asked into the uncomfortable silence that had fallen between them. "I can't vouch for its quality, but at least it's warm." He had wrapped his ungloved hands, their golden color reddened slightly with the cold, around the bottle, using it as a warming stone.

She tried to block the image of those strong hands moving over her body, one she was sure the Scotsmen whom they were leaving behind at the smithy were also picturing. She knew her life would never be the same. She had committed herself to this man who had promised her freedom, but now, in the swaying confines of his coach, she acknowledged that that was no longer the thing she most desired from him.

Raven watched the slender fingers smooth tremblingly over her arms. Somehow the sophisticated surety that had characterized Catherine Montfort since he'd met her had softened, had lessened in this unfamiliar environment. He could only imagine what she must be feeling now. She had committed herself to him without any certainty that he would honor their agreement. And if he broke his word, she would have no legal recourse. By virtue of the vows they had just spoken, she had given herself into his control. Because, he reminded himself grimly, he had promised her freedom.

"Here," he offered softly.

She looked up from the tangled emotions of the last few minutes, to find Raven holding out a steaming cup of the mulled wine. She took the tin mug, her fingers gratefully encircling its heat. As she sipped the comforting beverage, her frame still racked by occasional shivers, her husband's arm came around her shoulders. He pulled her, unresisting, to lean against the pleasant heat of his body.

At least he could hold her, Raven thought, as frustrating as he was finding the restraint imposed by the terms of their contract to be. For the time being he must be satisfied with the relationship he'd promised. A vow, his grandmother had taught him, was sacred and must be kept, no matter the cost.

Eventually he felt Catherine's breathing deepen, and he knew that she slept. Asleep in his arms. Her small frame sheltered by his. He would give his life, without hesitation, to guard and protect this woman who now belonged to him. At least in name, he acknowledged bitterly.

Catherine Montfort Raven, he thought again, feeling the pleasure of that stir hotly in his groin. Slowly and carefully he shifted his weight, trying not to waken her, but needing to find a more comfortable position for the painful hardness of desire. John Raven knew, of course, there was really only one position that would ever offer true relief for that particular ache, and he wondered how long it would be before he might be allowed to savor its sweet release.

Two months later

Catherine sat, nibbling the end of her pen, once again remembering that flying journey home from the Border. She had slept, exhausted, through most of the trip, and whenever she'd awakened it had been to the comfort of Raven's steady heartbeat, just under the hard muscles against which her cheek had rested. That was, however, the last time her husband had touched her, and in the months since their marriage, his apparent lack of interest had become almost unbearable.

He had promised her freedom from his interference, and it was a promise he had certainly kept. He had made a contract with her for certain services and then, surprisingly, he had scrupulously kept to its terms—terms that she had never believed he would be able to adhere to. She had expected to be courted, and instead he virtually ignored her existence.

She had occupied her time and energy during those weeks in staffing and furnishing the elegant mansion he'd purchased. Although her instructions had been carried out to the letter, the task of seeing that they were had been left to Mr. Reynolds, Raven's very efficient man of business, and his staff.

Her husband had taken no part in choosing the nearly priceless items she'd retained from the original furnishings, which she'd found stored, as he'd promised, in a vast warehouse near the East India docks. She had discovered that the warehouse was one of many London properties he owned, most of its space devoted to the temporary storage of goods that he imported from the Orient for the insatiable English market.

She had also been allowed to choose the finest of those imports for her new home. She had spent hours wandering among the bolts of newly arrived silks, the porcelains still in their straw-packed crates. Her skirts brushing against the Holland covers, she had examined countless pieces of furniture, paintings and objets d'art that had been purchased with the mansion, and which Mr. Reynolds's clerks uncomplainingly uncovered for her inspection.

She was conscientiously trailed by one of the banker's staff, and almost by magic, the pieces she had chosen from the warehouse, plus the additional ones she purchased from the manufacturers on Bond or Oxford Streets, arrived at the Mayfair residence and were set up in the rooms they were intended to grace.

And grace them they did, she thought with satisfaction, glancing around the small salon in which she was sitting. It was almost certainly the finest house in the capital. As it should be, considering the sums she had spent. But if she had been hoping for some comment on that almost deliberate extravagance from the man who paid the bills, she had been disappointed.

Now that the first task he had set for her was almost completed, she knew it was time to move on to the second—the introduction of her husband into the closed circle of the ton. She had carefully chosen the occasion at which they would make their first appearance together.

She had begun, of course, immediately on their return from Scotland, to mingle again with her closest friends. Catherine often attended the small, private entertainments that comprised the limited summer activities for those who were unfortunate enough to remain in the city. Her father might choose to treat her as an outcast, but her own clique's acceptance of her runaway marriage had been automatic. It had, however, been surprisingly tinged with curiosity and, she had come to recognize, a certain unspoken envy. Apparently she was not the only woman who had noticed John Raven's physical attributes.

"But an American, my dear?" Charlene Rainsford had questioned.

"An extremely rich American, if only half of what we've heard is true," suggested Amelia Bentwood.

"Well, Cat?" Charlene prodded with a graceful laugh. "You should certainly be in a position to verify the depth of your husband's pockets."

"I don't know," Catherine said, her own smile a mocking one. "I, for one, never listen to gossip."

They had been forced to accept her refusal to discuss her husband's financial status, but the questions about her marriage hadn't ended with that exchange.

"I have never thought men of that size attractive. So primitive, don't you think? All that vulgar brawn," Anne Aston said, her thin frame shuddering as she recalled the breadth of John Raven's chest and shoulders.

There was a distinct, though ladylike, sound of derision from someone in the group of women who had been sitting in Charlene's music room, languidly at their ease, long after the Italian soprano had provided the afternoon's entertainment. The response to that unspoken comment was a burst of extremely unladylike laughter.

"I don't suppose you would like to remark on your husband's size, either, my dear," suggested Lady Rainsford, with an air of resignation. "Something else you would certainly be in a position to discuss." Most of the ladies were aware of the obvious double entendre Charlene had thrown into their midst.

With what she'd hoped was an enigmatic smile, Catherine had discreetly lowered her eyes, as if that particular memory were too private to share.

But she had admitted to herself, as the talk had finally

*moved on to other topics when she didn't rise to the bait,
she could readily testify to the breadth of Raven's shoulders, having slept on the return from Scotland closely sheltered against them for hours. But nothing else.*

*With the exception of the Honorable Anne, who was still
a spinster and who, considering her unfortunate tendency
both to squint and to throw out spots, was likely to remain
one, everyone present had known what information Charlene had tried to elicit. Information Catherine could not
have shared, had she had any desire to, simply because she
did not know.*

"Forgive my intrusion," Raven said from the doorway.
Catherine had appeared so deep in thought he'd hesitated
to interrupt, but he wanted to see her. He had thought of
nothing but seeing her since he'd left London. He wondered
if she were unhappy, if the brown study in which he'd
caught her was as melancholy as it appeared.

She looked up in surprise. Her husband had seldom
sought her out in the weeks of their marriage, and it was
obvious from his apparel that he had just returned from the
business trip to the north of England on which he had been
engaged for the past week.

"I didn't know you were back," she said, straightening
the papers on the secretary to cover her momentary confusion.

She didn't know why simply seeing him again could
throw her emotions into such disarray. He was dressed for
traveling, his coat of Forester's green molding his upper
body. The tight pantaloons that fashion demanded did more
to delineate than to hide the muscles of his thighs. His
Hessians were lightly covered with dust, and knowing by
now his custom, she assumed he'd been traveling since
dawn.

"I hated to interrupt. You appeared so deep in thought."

Her eyes lifted quickly to his face, and she smiled involuntarily at the thought of the memories he'd interrupted. She hoped he'd never know that she had been daydreaming about him and the interest he'd aroused in the sisterhood of the ton.

"I'm working on the seating arrangement of the small dinner party you're hosting next week," she lied. She offered for his inspection the table chart she had quite truthfully been considering before her thoughts had strayed, as they did frequently, to the other member of this marriage of convenience.

"Good God," Raven said, refusing the offered paper with a shake of his head. "I hope you don't believe that I have any expertise or interest in that. Simply tell me where to sit and whom to talk to, and I shall attempt not to embarrass you."

"As long as you promise to refrain from talking to the ladies about coal," she advised, smiling.

"I assure you there's only one lady to whom I've ever mentioned coal," Raven said, his lips lifting in response.

"Then I suppose I should be flattered," she suggested. "Or insulted. I can't quite decide which."

"Well, I'll leave you to work that out."

Raven wondered what she'd do if he kissed her. Surely that was acceptable for a husband returning from a weeklong trip. But even as he thought it, he knew it was not acceptable, of course, in their marriage. He was no more her husband than he had been before those simple vows over the smith's anvil. Controlling his desire—something he'd had a bloody damned lot of practice at in the last few weeks, Raven thought—he turned to leave.

"But," Catherine said rather forcefully, reluctant to let him go, "there *are* matters that require your personal attention."

He hesitated in the doorway and then turned back, an expression of resignation masking his feelings.

"This *is* what you said you wanted," Catherine reminded him.

"My apologies. What must I do? I assure you I'm your willing victim."

"My great aunt Agatha is giving a rout, a celebration of another niece's birthday. She courageously sent an invitation, despite my father's refusal to acknowledge this marriage."

"And?" Raven asked, propping his shoulder casually against the frame of the doorway.

"She's also agreed to introduce us to her guests." Obviously the information meant less to him than Catherine had hoped. Seeing his puzzlement, she continued, "To introduce us as man and wife. Our first foray into the ton as man and wife."

"And what exactly will that involve?" he questioned, naturally suspicious of what would be expected of him.

"For one thing, leading out the first waltz. Along with my cousin and her father, of course," she explained, watching the lift of one midnight brow. "You do dance, don't you?"

"The reel," he admitted, beginning to enumerate. "And a passable Highland fling, which my grandfather taught me. I know a score of rather more exotic Eastern dances that I don't believe have ever before been seen in a London ballroom."

He paused, and the small movement at the corners of his lips should have warned her, but Catherine was concentrating instead on how much of the doorway his shoulders filled. And remembering again what they had felt like under the softness of her cheek.

"Then you must learn," she said decisively when it appeared he had finished his list of accomplishments. His inexperience was only what she had feared, and she was glad she had thought to plan for this eventuality. At least, now that she knew the worst, she could see to it that he was properly instructed.

"Very well," he agreed, fighting to control his amusement.

"I can have a dancing master here tomorrow," Catherine said.

"A dancing master?" he repeated. He hadn't considered that she might hire someone to teach him. "And will I be waltzing with the dancing master at your aunt's shindy?" he asked pointedly.

"I beg your pardon?"

"At the ball or whatever. Who will I be dancing with?"

"With me, of course. I thought you understood. We're to lead the dancing."

"Then you teach me," Raven suggested, his anticipation at holding her so great that he wondered how she could be unaware of what he was feeling. "I don't intend to prance around at the instruction of some hired popinjay."

"I don't know how to teach you to waltz," she argued, but the image of slowly circling the floor, closely held in Raven's hard, extremely masculine arms, was very enticing.

"Who taught you?"

"A dancing master my father employed."

"Then just show me whatever he showed you. It can't be that difficult. You'll find I'm an apt pupil," Raven said, the corners of his mouth again marked by his amusement.

"But I don't know if I'm an apt teacher," she reiterated hesitantly, her stomach fluttering with anticipation.

"I'll take my chances. And besides, it's that or nothing. I'm terribly afraid I shall have unbreakable appointments at whatever time you arrange for the dancing master to visit."

"Do you always get your own way?" she asked, smiling.

"If I can manage it," he admitted. "When shall we begin?"

"After dinner tonight?" she suggested. Surely that would give her long enough to get her emotions under some control.

"Are you dining in? Cook will certainly be in for a shock if that's the case," Raven said. "And Edwards. He'll be delighted. I keep talking to him while they serve my dinner. He never answers beyond 'Yes, Mr. Raven' or 'I don't believe so, Mr. Raven,' but I can tell it's a strain. I don't suppose he's ever had an employer who's tried to carry on a conversation before."

"You're not supposed to talk to the butler," Catherine said, but against her will, her smile was again pushing at the corners of her mouth. "It confuses the servants if you're too familiar."

"Are you trying to tell me that Edwards is ever confused? I've never met a more self-assured individual in my life."

"He is rather intimidating," she admitted, and watched Raven's blue eyes flick up to meet hers.

"I'm surprised he consented to lower himself to be our butler," he offered, matching her teasing tone.

"Well," she said, "you *are* paying him an enormous amount of money. Enough, I suppose, that he decided to condescend."

"Ah, that explains it. He probably refuses to speak to me because he's richer than I am."

Laughing, she watched him turn toward the door, and this time, having obtained his promise, she let him go.

It was not until she was gathering up her guest list and the seating arrangement she'd been working on that Catherine realized the significance of what he'd said. Raven had definitely indicated that he preferred not to eat alone, and more tellingly, that he'd noticed her many absences from their dinner table, absences occasioned by her deliberate attempt to accept as many social invitations as she possibly could. She had been carrying out her own redemption and reemergence into the folds of the nobility, a redemption she must complete before she brought her husband into that select world, given the shocking circumstances of her marriage. But, she decided suddenly, she would refuse any further invitations that would require her absence from her own dinner table, an absence her husband had just indicated he'd noticed.

"I understand, Edwards, that we're to be hosting a small dinner party next week," Raven said as the butler oversaw the removal of the final course.

"So madam has informed me," Edwards answered stolidly.

"I'm sure you'll be delighted to have something to do besides hover over my solitary dinners."

"Indeed, Mr. Raven, I have been very pleased to serve you," he said, a small flush creeping across his smoothly shaved jowls.

"And you've done so with remarkable skill. I don't believe I've told you how glad I am that you decided to work for us."

"I thank you, sir," the butler said, his spine rigid with embarrassment.

Raven had not been considering the effect of his teasing on the dignified Edwards. He had instead been watching Catherine across the table, wondering if his words were causing her to remember their meeting this morning and if she might be anticipating, as he had been all day, the promised dancing lesson.

"Edwards," Catherine interrupted the exchange, her russet eyes meeting her husband's, "if you would, please, fetch my shawl from the salon. There's a distinct draft in here.''

Raven watched the butler's retreat without comment.

''I told you you shouldn't carry on a conversation with the servants. You would probably enjoy teasing the lions in the menagerie,'' Catherine said when he was safely out of earshot.

''I probably would—except for the fact that they are unfortunate captives. Are you attempting to compare Edwards to the lions?''

''I'm attempting to compare you to a small boy who would pull the wings off flies. You embarrassed the poor man to tears.''

''That was never my intent. Do you suggest I apologize?'' Raven asked, sincere contrition in his deep voice. He certainly hadn't intended to show the butler any disrespect. The man had treated him with none, despite the fact that they both were well aware Raven had no idea how to get on with servants.

''Apologize to your butler? I shouldn't think so.''

''Not done?'' he questioned mockingly. ''The under classes are undeserving of an apology?''

''No.'' She tried to explain. ''Your apology would simply further the embarrassment. You would be acknowledging that you'd noticed his discomfort. Edwards would then feel he'd made a terrible faux pas by allowing you to read his emotions.''

''It must be very frustrating to have an employer who has no idea of how these things should be done.''

''I shouldn't be surprised if he decides to leave us,'' Catherine warned, watching her husband play with the fragile stem of the Venetian goblet. His fingers were not at all blunt as one would expect, considering his size, she thought. They were long and tapered, the nails very clean and closely trimmed, the skin darkly tanned. She remembered with pleasure their callused warmth holding her hand to bring it almost to his lips.

"I would," he said, replacing the glass on the table. "I checked on what you're paying him."

"He's worth every shilling. He adds to your consequence."

"I hope in proportion to what he subtracts from my bank balance," he countered, smiling at her.

"Cheeseparing already," she chided, returning his smile.

"I don't believe you can accuse me of that."

"No," she answered with some seriousness, "but I do realize that furnishing this house has been a very expensive undertaking. If you wish me to economize, I shall certainly understand."

"The house is perfect," Raven said, the first compliment he'd allowed himself to pay her. Fascinated, he watched its effect, the soft, becoming spread of color under the translucent skin of her cheeks. "And I'm not yet in dun territory."

"Despite my dressmaker's bill?" she asked, teasing him now.

"That I *haven't* seen," he said. "Perhaps I spoke too soon."

His hand had again found the stem of the elegant crystal, and her eyes unconsciously rested once more on the lean fingers.

"I hope you know," he continued, "that you've not yet strained my resources. You have simply carried out your part of our bargain exactly as I'd hoped. I am not quibbling over the cost of your success."

"Thank you," she said simply.

"But I *am* wondering if I passed?"

"I beg your pardon?" she asked, raising her gaze from the contemplation of that dark, graceful hand, so fascinating to her.

"I assumed your attention to my table manners was to ferret out any unacceptable habits before I fall under the less-kind scrutiny of the ton."

"My attention to..." she began, and then realized that he must have noticed her watching his hands. He was far too observant, and she, apparently, far too obvious in her fascination. Luckily he was attributing her near compulsion to look at him to some other cause entirely.

"Your manners are excellent," she said, "as you must know."

"I should have asked Edwards," Raven said consideringly. "His standards are certain to be higher than yours."

"You place your hand here," Catherine instructed, feeling the warmth of his palm against her back with a decided frisson of reaction. Her gaze rose to his face, to see if he had felt the energy that had leapt between them at the touch. She licked her lips, which were, for some reason, suddenly dry, and continued, "And take my hand."

The tall body moved into too-close proximity to hers, the hard muscles of his chest brushing against the softness of her breasts.

"Not too close," she cautioned breathlessly, and he obediently moved back a few inches.

"The music is in three," she began.

"What music?"

"To the waltz."

"Then we seem to be lacking something. Unless I am badly mistaken, there *is* no music." Raven made a pretense of looking around the vast, empty ballroom and even cocked his dark head as if listening for some faint strain.

"But there will be that night."

"Then wouldn't it be better to practice with music?"

"I don't believe we are at that point," she said rather briskly, fighting an inclination to laugh.

"You could hire an orchestra. Or a small string ensemble."

"Not tonight," she said sternly. "I believe that you are simply trying to postpone the inevitable. You *did* promise."

"I must have been thinking of something else. Are you sure this is necessary?"

"In three," she said, ignoring his delaying tactics.

"Why don't you hum?"

"All right," she agreed patiently, her palms beginning to perspire slightly at being this close to him. Unconsciously she took a deep breath, enjoying once again the pleasant masculine aromas that surrounded him. "I shall hum."

"Something I know," he suggested.

"I don't know what you know," she said reasonably.

"That's true. Then something they'll play that night. Could you tell them what to play? So I'd be familiar with it?"

"No, I could not," she said. "In three," she insisted again and began to move as she counted. "One, two, three. One, two, three."

"That's all?" he asked, following her steps as if in deep concentration, a little uncertainly.

"Except you turn, so you're not dancing in a line. Turn as you move. Surely you must have seen the dancing that night."

"The night you danced with Amberton and everyone else?"

"Not everyone. I didn't dance with you," she said, relaxing with the increasing surety of his movements.

"No," he agreed. "But you should have," he said, sweeping her suddenly in ever-widening circles across the polished floor.

Her eyes locked with his, and he smiled at her, mocking her surprise at his expertise. Eventually her lids drifted closed, and she savored the pleasure of moving in the embrace of a partner who knew exactly how to hold her and whose steps, despite his size, matched perfectly with her own. She could almost hear the music he obviously felt. They were one. At least here.

This was as near to heaven as he was likely to get, Raven thought—holding Catherine, who floated gracefully in his arms as if she belonged there. As if she enjoyed being there.

God, he wanted her. She was his, legally and morally, and he wanted her more than he'd ever wanted anything in his life. More than the money that, in his impoverished youth, he'd thought was so important. More than success or power. More even than the desire to create structures and industries that would exist long after he was dead and gone. Even after his children were gone. At the thought of a child of Catherine's, his body betrayed his iron control again. Like a damn schoolboy, he mocked himself.

He released her finally, knowing that if he didn't leave soon, he'd not be able to. She swayed slightly against his chest, as if reluctant to have it end.

"Will you save me another waltz?" he asked softly, and she opened her eyes to find him regarding her with something that looked very much like possessiveness. "Besides the one we'll be forced to share under the inspection of your friends."

"Yes," she promised, mesmerized again by being this close to him, in his arms for the first time in so long.

"Somewhere between the Reginalds and the Geralds?"

"You can tell me when the musicians play something you know," she teased, stepping back from the circle of his arms, before she betrayed herself by revealing how pleasant she had found having them hold her to be. "I wouldn't want you to be embarrassed."

Having chided him for making her go through this farce of a lesson, which had almost turned into something else, she curtsied as carefully as if they really were partners at a ball and then catching up the skirt of her gown, made her graceful way across the echoing emptiness of the ballroom.

She forced herself not to hurry, but when she was safely in the hallway and away from the steady scrutiny of that knowing gaze, she closed the door and leaned against it a moment.

Playing with fire, she warned herself honestly, wondering how much longer she was going to be able to endure the very inconvenient restrictions of this marriage of convenience.

Chapter Five

"Deserted already?"

Catherine looked up from her contemplation of the crowded floor of her aunt's ballroom to find Lord Amberton at her elbow. Since she had been wondering the same thing, she knew at once what he was suggesting about her husband's absence.

Raven had danced with her after her aunt's rather tremulous announcement of their marriage. He had not led her in the sweeping circles that they had made across the empty dance floor of their town house, but had guided her sedately over this floor's far smaller expanse, his performance polished enough, but without the flash that would have invited comment. The ton had been forced to watch without being given any additional reason to question the couple's inclusion at the small entertainment for family and old friends.

Catherine's husband had said and done everything that was required, and after he had completed the tasks she'd carefully laid out for him during the short ride to their destination tonight, he had disappeared, allowing her freedom to slip back into the flirtatious camaraderie she shared with several former beaus who were in attendance. Until now, however, she had not been called upon to talk to the Viscount Amberton.

"I doubt it," she answered, her tone sharper than she'd intended. She had not yet forgiven Gerald for his behavior the night Raven had abducted her. Intellectually she knew the viscount's lapse had been far more her father's fault for allowing Amberton to believe that she already belonged to him. But it still hurt that he'd so readily destroyed the friendship they had enjoyed, simply to prove his dominance. His comment had been apt, however. Her gaze *had* been moving around the room, unconsciously looking for the dark, towering head of her husband.

"He's in the card room," Gerald offered. "Apparently dancing isn't something our American visitor enjoys."

"He's hardly a visitor," she said, a trace of ice in her tone.

"Because he has a house in Mayfair and an entrée here tonight due to your aunt's senility? I assure you, my dear, he will *always* be a visitor," Amberton replied sardonically.

"And what does that make me?"

"Sorry?" he suggested softly.

"Hardly," she denied. "He's a very interesting man."

"He's probably told you all about his coal mines." And seeing her expression, he laughed. "By God, I believe he has. Probably nothing else to talk about."

"A successful marriage is not dependent on conversation alone," she said unthinkingly, and then, at his shout of laughter, blushed scarlet to the roots of her hair.

"I was sure there was some secret to his success. Not that I guessed *that*, of course. Somehow he doesn't appear to be—"

"If you'll excuse me," she interrupted, moving away.

He caught her wrist, continuing to hold her even when she looked down rather pointedly at his fingers, whitened with the pressure they were exerting against the kid of her glove.

"I think you should remove your hand."

"Such the proper matron," Amberton said, obeying. "So he's tamed you to the bit already."

"Tamed me?" she repeated, feeling a surge of anger.

"You weren't once so concerned about the conventions."

"And what makes you believe I am now?"

"You've not danced the last two sets, and you appeared to be trying to locate your husband. Hardly the behavior I should have expected from someone who was always the merriest hoyden of the Season. It's hard to picture you subdued and settled."

"Hardly *settled* because I am wondering where my husband is. Most women like to have an idea of their spouse's whereabouts. Raven doesn't have many acquaintances in this gathering."

"Wives who are concerned about their husband's whereabouts are usually up to mischief and don't wish to be discovered. But I hardly believe that to be your case. You seem far too enamored of your 'Raven,' as you call him. That's not a title, my dear."

"It fits him," she said truthfully. Perhaps because of the darkness of his midnight hair, she mused. And he *should* have a title. If anyone were arrogant enough to deserve a title, it was he.

"Shall I fetch him so you can play the dutiful little wife?"

"*That* title, however, doesn't fit," she responded tartly. She allowed her gaze to travel around the room, hoping Gerald would go away. Somehow she knew he'd had the better of this encounter.

"Then perhaps I might offer a different diversion."

She turned back to meet his eyes. He was laughing at

her, and she wondered what he had guessed about her marriage.

"Give me a game," he suggested. "You always loved a hand of cards. And since your lord and master is engaged elsewhere—"

"He is *not* my lord and master."

"Then if you are allowed such freedom, play with me."

"I'm sorry, but I'm not interested in cards. The room is always so crowded. Half of Aunt's cronies come for the whist."

"I wasn't suggesting the card room, but then I suppose a private hand is far too daring for the sedate Mrs. Raven," he taunted. "Why don't you ask him if it's all right to accept my invitation to a hand of cards? Maybe you can talk him into giving you permission to play."

"If I wanted to play cards with you, Gerald—"

"Oh, I understand completely, my dear," he agreed, his mockery clear. "I wouldn't want you to get into trouble."

"My husband and I don't have that kind of marriage," she assured him, realizing belatedly that she had made things worse.

He cocked his head, studying her face. "Then what kind of marriage *do* you have, I wonder? This is becoming more interesting by the moment."

"Raven doesn't attempt to restrict my activities."

"Is that why you married him? A very impetuous marriage, I might add." *And damn the bitch, bloody disastrous for me,* Amberton thought bitterly.

"I married him because my father had promised I should choose my husband, and then you and he decided to do it for me."

"What *are* you talking about?" Amberton asked with what he hoped would appear to be genuine puzzlement.

"I saw the announcement intended for the *Post,*" she said, but something in his tone had been very convincing.

Gerald had sounded as if he really *had* no idea what she was talking about.

"I must seem slow, but I'm afraid I'll have to ask what announcement." It was so easy to manipulate Cat, he thought. She was too honest herself to doubt the motives of others.

"It doesn't matter," she said, wondering for the first time if she had been gulled. *You belong to me*, Raven had said. Had he then set out to trick her, using the overheard conversation with Amberton to bait the trap? If so, he must have congratulated himself on how easily she'd been fooled.

No wonder there had been no pursuit in their journey to the Border, she realized suddenly. Her father had never intended to announce her betrothal and so, when she'd disappeared, he'd had no idea of why she'd run away or of where to search for her. No idea that she might have eloped to escape the marriage trap she believed he'd arranged. Instead, Raven had apparently tricked her into creating another trap, one of her own making.

"Then if you intend to stand beside the other matrons all evening, I believe I shall be forced to leave you, Cat, my heart," Gerald commented, interrupting her humiliating realization of how she'd been duped. "Boredom overtakes one so easily in the summer. It must be this oppressive dampness."

"I thought you mentioned something about cards?" Catherine asked, raising her chin. Damn Raven, she thought. How dare he trick her? She would never forgive him for that.

"I thought you'd decided to play the good wife."

"It's still a woman's prerogative to change her mind, I believe," she said, smiling at him with a warmth that caused his brows to raise slightly.

"Now there's my Cat. I'm afraid, my sweet, I really was beginning to believe he'd turned you into a tame tabby."

"Set your mind at ease. That's something no one will ever do. Not even Raven." Especially not Raven, she vowed silently.

"Do you suppose anyone else has discovered your aunt's solarium? Such a delightfully secluded room."

For the first time since she'd accepted his challenge, Catherine felt a small flutter of unease. This was certainly not what she'd intended. She had only wanted to show Gerald that she was still as daring as she had always been. And as for Raven...

She wasn't exactly sure what she wanted to show Raven, but she had a feeling, despite his promise not to censure her, that he wouldn't like her to be with Gerald in any "delightfully secluded room."

"I make that sixty points, my dear, and my game, I think. Your luck seems to have run out tonight."

Catherine took a deep breath, knowing that it was not her luck that was at fault. She couldn't seem to keep her mind on the cards. Her decisions regarding her discards had bordered on the absurd. She kept visualizing the ballroom below and a pair of crystal blue eyes searching the throng for her. Thankfully this was the last hand, and she would be free to escape.

"I'm really rather glad we decided on piquet. So much more challenging. And I believe, my dear, that your wager was..."

She met Amberton's look and knew again that he was making fun of her. Her lips tightened slightly, but she slipped the narrow diamond-and-ruby bangle, which Gerald had suggested would be an appropriate stake, off her wrist. When Raven had admired it earlier tonight, she'd thought with embarrassed amusement that he had probably not yet received the bill for it. She wondered if he would notice the loss of such a recent purchase, a purchase he had commented on. The first time, now that she thought about it, that he'd remarked on anything she'd worn.

"Unless..." Gerald began, and then hesitated.

"Unless what?" she asked, watching his face.

"I've just realized that the loss of a bracelet might be awkward for you. If Mr. Raven begins asking questions."

Since she had had the same thought, her betraying fingers hesitated in the act of placing the jeweled circlet on his side of the small gaming table at which they were seated.

"It's what I wagered," she said, seeing no way out.

"Well, I'm amenable to an alternate suggestion," Gerald said pleasantly. "I'd hate for you to get into trouble."

She flicked the bracelet angrily onto the gleaming wood of the table, and it bounced twice, the gems catching the light.

"I won't 'get into trouble.' It *is* my bracelet."

"And you may redeem it for a kiss," he said smiling at her. "One kiss between old friends."

"No."

"Well broken to the bit," he mocked. Come on, Cat, he urged silently. Get that famous Montfort temper up.

"That's not—"

"Afraid your dolt of a husband might object? Frankly, my dear, he doesn't seem to give a damn what you do. Rather a laissez-faire attitude. But he *is* a businessman, with what rumor suggests is a decided flare with money. He'll never miss the kiss, but I wouldn't be so certain about the jewels."

"All right," she agreed, fearing Gerald was correct. Anything to get this over and done. After all, it was not as if she'd never before been in Amberton's arms. But, her conscience reminded her, she'd never been there as a married woman.

How had she gotten herself into this? she wondered bitterly. She'd been married two months, had never even been kissed by her own husband, and she was about to allow another man that privilege. How could she have been so stupid?

"I'll send you word," Gerald said, rising and looking down at her. So easy. And now if the rest went as well, he'd be back where he'd been before the American had interfered.

"What do you mean?" Catherine asked, not understanding.

"You'll be hearing from me. When I want to collect." Smiling, he slid the bracelet back across the table. "I enjoyed the game, my dear. A very pleasant evening altogether, I must say."

Still smiling, he strolled to the door and, her eyes on the wagered jewelry, Catherine heard it close behind him.

When she was sure he was gone, she took the narrow bangle from the table and slipped it over her wrist. The beauty of the gems seemed to mock her as he had.

You'll be hearing from me, Gerald had said. And she had no doubt that she would.

"Did you enjoy yourself?" Raven asked on the way home.

Perhaps if he gave her the opportunity to tell him where she'd disappeared to, she would. By the terms of their contract, he had no right to ask. He had promised her freedom, he reminded himself bitterly, and noninterference in her activities.

Catherine knew she had been too silent, thinking about what had happened tonight instead of discussing the evening as he seemed to expect.

"Of course," she lied, trying to clear her mind of the circling recriminations. Why had she let Gerald convince her to go upstairs with him? She wondered for the hundredth time if anyone had seen them. And if so, had it been mentioned to Raven? Her husband had seemed exactly the same when, having made her furtive way down the servants' stairs, she had, upon reentering the ballroom, spotted him almost immediately.

Seeing his tall form, she had surprisingly lost all her anger about whatever tricks he'd employed to get her to marry him and had felt instead a sense of relief and of safety. He'd been talking to a group of gentlemen who appeared interested in whatever views he was sharing, but he'd turned his attention to her at once when she'd appeared at his side. At her whispered suggestion, he had immediately arranged for their departure.

"I looked for you for the waltz you'd promised," Raven said, hoping she'd relieve the pain eating his gut at the thought that she might again have been on some dark balcony in the arms of one of her former beaus, who had swarmed around her all night.

Catherine found that her hands were twisting the kid gloves she'd removed upon entering the coach, and she forced them to lie still in her lap. Guilt, she thought.

"Someone told me you were playing cards," she answered, turning to watch through the window the sweep of the elegant facades of the town houses they were passing, revealed by the brilliance of the moonlight.

"For a while. Some of the men I wanted to meet were playing. I managed to lose and then returned to the ballroom."

"Managed to lose?" she repeated, thinking of her own losses tonight.

"They really aren't very good card players."

"And you are?" she asked, smiling.

"Reasonably. It's all numbers. I'm good with numbers."

"I would have said it's mostly luck and intuition."

"And you probably lose more than you win," he answered, that small smile playing again over the stern line of his lips.

"You might be surprised."

"I might at that. Did you play tonight?" he asked casually, and she felt her heart stop.

"No," she managed to say, but even to her own ears, the whispered response sounded unconvincing.

"That's probably just as well. If you *really* believe it's all a matter of luck."

She waited through the remainder of the ride for the question she had expected and for which she still had no answer. *Where were you? Where were you when I looked for you to fulfill the promise of a second, more private waltz?* And she found herself regretting having missed the pleasure of that dance.

But he never asked. And, because she had thought he might care, she was perversely disappointed that she was *not* going to be called upon to explain her absence from the ballroom.

The days preceding the first small dinner she'd planned were crammed with last-minute preparations. Catherine resolutely put from her mind the events of her great aunt's party. She didn't allow herself to think about the threat of having to redeem her wager or about Gerald's seemingly genuine puzzlement about the announcement of their betrothal for the *Morning Post*.

She had found, on reflection, that it was rather flattering if Raven *had* taken the trouble to arrange that ruse. It must mean that he had really intended to marry her from the beginning and was willing to do almost anything to accomplish that. No woman could be very unhappy with that thought, whatever her husband's reasons for desiring the marriage. Especially, she was honest enough to admit, if that woman had fallen in love with the man who had gone to all that trouble.

She couldn't pinpoint the exact moment when it had happened, or even when she'd first acknowledged that it had. But there was no longer any doubt in her mind that she was, very unfashionably, in love with her own husband. She now knew how much she wanted their relationship to move into other directions, while he, it seemed, was content to allow their original agreement to stand. Of course, he didn't yet know a great deal about Catherine Montfort Raven. He had likened her to steel, and in the face of her determined decision to enchant him, it seemed an apt description.

Every night she faced Raven over the dinner table, listening with what had become truly fascinated attention to his quiet discussion, made in response to her encouragement, of his various business dealings and of the men whom he needed to win over in order to carry out those activities.

She found herself watching his hands or his mouth as he talked or enjoying the laughter in his eyes as he answered some perfectly ridiculous question she'd asked. Or as he teased her about why she might possibly want to understand the process by which steel was cast. But he answered her, patiently explaining and even reexplaining whatever she questioned. And if in those few days their time at table, under the watchful eye of Edwards, stretched far beyond the proscribed dinner hour, she was pleased to think neither of them minded.

The afternoon before the long-awaited dinner party had finally arrived and, carefully reviewing her arrangements, Catherine believed there was nothing else that needed her attention. She looked forward to a long bath and several hours in the skillful hands of her hairdresser and her maid.

Her dress had arrived the day before and, made up in blush taffeta overlain with cream lace, it was far more becoming than she had hoped. For the first time, she allowed herself to relax. She knew enough about her husband now that she had ceased to worry about how he would be accepted. His manners were as polished and his conversation as interesting, to her mind at least, as anyone she'd encountered in her long familiarity with the haut monde.

One of the maids tiptoed in, apologizing for interrupting her solitude. Catherine, seated at the small secretary in her bedroom, raised her eyes from the list she was checking off. She was still in her silk wrapper, having seen no reason to dress. Edwards would take care of everything downstairs, and she had thought he'd appreciate her being out of the staff's way as they made the arrangements she'd carefully gone over with him.

"What is it, Maggie?" she asked, wondering what could possibly have gone wrong with her meticulous planning.

"It's a letter, madam. They said it was urgent."

Catherine wondered if her father had changed his mind and decided to attend after all. His refusal had been expected and his response had obviously been composed by his secretary, but at least it had been polite.

"Thank you," she said, taking the proffered envelope.

She waited until the maid had left before breaking the wax seal, which she had recognized at once.

The words, after the first, began to run together, and with a growing sense of unreality, she was forced to reread what Gerald had written, the salient part of the message coming after the usual vows of friendship couched in rather flowery terms in the first paragraph.

…I now find myself strapped for funds for a minor undertaking. With my heartfelt apologies for any inconvenience it might cause, I thought it fair to tell you

I intend to apply to your husband for the repayment of the debt you incurred on Thursday last. He has agreed to a six o'clock appointment today. If, however, this arrangement presents a problem for you, I will, as a gentleman, be forced to accept the forfeiture we previously agreed upon. I look forward to hearing from you.

Yours faithfully,
Amberton

Faithfully, she reread with bitterness. The scoundrel. To think that she had been so foolish as to place herself in his power like this. And then, knowing that there was nothing to be gained by useless recriminations, she glanced at the clock. It was already past four, and the first guests were to arrive at eight. Apparently Gerald had planned his revenge with precision. And with some knowledge of her arrangements.

She wondered suddenly if it were a trick. Would Amberton be brazen enough to apply to her husband for payment of a wager he had won in their very clandestine and improper game? But, of course, the chance that he really didn't intend to meet with Raven was not one she could afford to take.

Reacting as decisively as she ever had in her life, she swiftly rang for her abigail, and before five she was in Raven's town coach heading to Gerald's apartment.

She had worked herself into a froth of rage by the time she arrived, and it wasn't in the least mitigated by the almost contemptuous fulsomeness of Amberton's greeting.

"My dear, what a delightful surprise," he enthused as he held open the door for her furtive entry. She could imagine what the wagging tongues of the ton would say if anyone saw her entering the apartment of an old beau less than three months after her runaway marriage. There would be a great many *I-told-you-so*'s exchanged across the ton's dinner tables if her visit today became public knowledge.

"How dare you approach my husband about a very private wager? Have you no honor at all, Gerald?"

"But you were quite insistent that your Mr. Raven didn't attempt to censure your behavior. And my financial need is, I'm sorry to say, quite pressing."

"How much?" she asked, opening her reticule, into which she'd stuffed every pound left out of this quarter's pin money. She knew that her useless anger was only playing into his hands and making this entire episode even more distasteful. Her temper had gotten her into this situation, and she must control it until she had gotten herself out. Whatever value he put on the bracelet she'd gladly pay, just to have done with this farce. In her head, a clock ticked ominously, measuring the brief hours before she would be expected to be at home, poised, assured and beautifully turned out, to play hostess to the beau monde. And the even briefer time until Raven's threatened arrival here.

"You surely didn't believe this to be a matter of money?" Gerald asked silkily.

Glancing up, Catherine was surprised to see a very smug expression on his handsome features. "Your letter indicated that you were strapped for cash."

"I assure you my pockets are not quite empty, my love. Though not, of course, as deeply lined as they would have been had you gone along with the plans for our nuptials. That really was too bad of you, Cat. I had such hopes for our union, an opportunity to see you really tamed. You always were such a hellcat. I wonder how your Mr. Raven is enjoying all that fire and passion."

Gerald paused, considering the effect of his comment. Because he did know her very well, he believed he could read the answer in her blush. What he'd begun to suspect about this very strange marriage was apparently true. It was a marriage of convenience, and not at all the love match the ton had proclaimed it.

"You never did anything by half measures," he continued smoothly. "And because of that, I don't believe anyone will be surprised that you've managed to become bored with your marriage to that barbarian after only a few short weeks."

"Leave my marriage out of this," she said coldly. "And he's not a barbarian."

"Oh, of course he is. That, and his unlimited funds, of course, are probably why you were attracted to him. He's rich enough that you didn't have to worry about whether he wanted you or your father's money, and you were always attracted to the bizarre. Your American husband certainly is that. Does he beat you, my sweet, when you make him angry?"

"*He's* never given me occasion to make him angry," she answered sarcastically, and was rewarded by the rush of furious color into the viscount's pale cheeks.

"Damn you," he said softly.

"If not money, what do you want? I have guests coming."

She hoped her cold display of rigidly controlled impatience was successfully masking her fear. Somehow Catherine knew that Gerald wanted to make her afraid. That it was part of the revenge he had planned to take on her for marrying Raven instead of him. He wanted her to be afraid of her husband finding out about the card game and afraid of what his own intentions were during this highly improper meeting, here in the privacy of his home.

"I think, my darling, you owe me what you promised. A kiss. If you're not giving those delightful embraces to that dolt of a husband, you might at least give the one you promised to me."

It was indeed what she had so foolishly agreed to. She

found it hard to believe Gerald had gone to all this trouble simply for a kiss, but she couldn't take the chance of refusing him. Unrequited love? Could that be motive enough for all this elaborate plotting? He had never seemed that passionate before, so it didn't really fit.

But whatever his reasons, she knew she had little choice. A kiss and then make her escape. She would still have time to dress and meet her guests with some modicum of composure.

"All right," she whispered. Seeing his smile at that small revelation of her distress, she said more loudly, "Let's get it over and be done with this business."

Business. Raven's word for their agreement. Here she was, again kissing Amberton, when all she really wanted was her husband's love. And that, of course, Raven had never offered. Only business.

"Such an eager lover," Gerald said chidingly. His smile was too smug, altogether too satisfied with his attempt to embarrass her. She wondered again if something else was going on, but her temper quickly overcame that whisper of suspicion.

"Never *your* lover," she answered mockingly.

She had gone too far, she knew, as he ruthlessly caught her wrists. She fought, realizing suddenly that he was not going to be satisfied with the chaste kiss she had intended to bestow. But he soon had her arms twisted behind her back, her wrists securely held in one of his hands.

He bent her uncomfortably over the back of the high sofa, pushing his body familiarly into hers. She struggled fiercely, even trying to kick at his legs. Her thin slippers made negligible impact against the leather of his high boots, and he ignored her. With that effort, however, she lost her footing and slipped farther back, her body totally in his hold now, only the tip of one foot still making desperate contact with the floor.

His lips descended with determination, but she turned her head away. He caught her chin with his free hand, his fingers brutal, gripping hard enough to leave bruises, she thought in panic, remembering the very observant people she would have to confront tonight. He turned her face until his wet mouth fastened over hers. He pushed his tongue past her lips, moving it against hers until she thought she might be physically ill with disgust.

Some inarticulate sound apparently made her nauseated response clear to him, for suddenly his mouth was removed from hers, and he lifted his head to look down on her in fury.

At least she was free from the subjection of that revolting kiss. But before her relief had fully registered, his fingers were digging into the bodice of her gown. His hand slipped under the globe of her left breast and lifted. For the first time, she felt terror replacing her fury. The cool air touched her exposed flesh, and then, unbelievingly, his mouth fastened over her nipple, biting and sucking.

At that painful contact, she twisted, bringing her knees up automatically in a protective gesture, and felt the right one connect sharply with Gerald's body. His reaction to that unintentional blow was startling. He released her with a howl, and unbalanced, she slid backward onto the seat of the sofa and then down in an unladylike heap onto the Turkish carpet.

She never even looked at Amberton or tried to guess the cause of the keening noises that were coming from his huddled figure. She scrambled to her feet, stumbling awkwardly over the skirt of her gown, which had caught under her knees. She heard the material rip, but nothing mattered except getting out of here. She was up and running, trying with trembling fingers to pull the material of her dress up over her breast, thankful that in his wrath Gerald hadn't torn the delicate muslin bodice.

She reached for the handle of the door, only to watch in dismay as it swung away from her searching fingers. She looked up to find her husband standing in the doorway of Gerald's small salon.

"Hello," Raven said simply.

She closed her eyes, hoping that when she opened them, the hallucination would have disappeared. Raven could not—oh dear God, she thought despairingly, he could *not*—be standing in the door of this room where Lord Amberton had just attacked her. But when she opened her eyes, her husband was still there, his slight smile touching his lips.

"You're leaving it very late, my dear," he said, his tone as relaxed as his greeting had been. "You have little more than two hours until our guests arrive. And I don't believe you're dressed for dinner."

With something approaching horror, her gaze fell, following the slow appraisal of his blue eyes. She found what had attracted that calm survey—her gown so disarrayed that the dusky rose areola that surrounded her left nipple was still exposed.

There seemed nothing she could say, and so she yielded to the impulse she had had since she had looked up to find him there. She threw herself against his chest and with unbelievable relief felt Raven's hard arms close securely around her.

Chapter Six

"May I see you home?" Raven asked.

Thank God she was safe, he thought. He had arrived in time to prevent whatever Amberton had been attempting. Catherine was trembling in his arms, but she was safe. That had been his only concern when he'd gotten the anonymous note inviting him to this address to witness his wife's indiscretion. Despite the terms of their agreement, he had been certain she had not come here to cuckold him, that something else had brought her to Amberton's apartment.

Unable to force a reply past the lump in her throat, Catherine nodded, her curls brushing against his shirtfront.

Raven's thumb and forefinger touched her chin and he raised her face to meet his gaze. His fingers were determined, but there was no painful pressure. He studied the tear-washed eyes, surrounded by the wet tangle of lashes. "You *were* ready to leave?" he inquired, and at the small, sobbing intake of breath that accompanied her nod, his lips lifted again in that slight smile. He had promised her freedom, and so he was honor bound to ask.

"I tried to leave," she whispered, wanting him to know that it was not by her choice that he had found her in this situation.

"Are you saying that he wouldn't let you go?" Raven asked, fighting his fury. He knew the bastard had somehow forced her to come here, and now she was telling him that Amberton wouldn't let her leave.

Something had replaced the calm with which he had greeted her, but, as always with Raven, Catherine was unsure about whatever emotion colored his tone. The adrenaline that had been sustaining her was draining away, and she felt almost faint in reaction to the security Raven's presence provided. Gerald was no match for her husband's strength, and she knew she was safe. But even as she thought that, she remembered with revulsion how Amberton's wet, loose mouth had closed over her breast. She retched softly, pressing her fingers tightly against her lips.

"Are you hurt?" Raven asked.

Controlling her nausea with the strongest effort, she looked up to reassure him. There was something very strange in the clear blue depths of his eyes. Fury, she thought, trying to imagine what he was feeling. He had every right to be angry.

"No," she said. "I managed to get away from him before—"

"Will you forgive me, Catherine, if I send you home with Tom?" Raven interrupted her to ask softly, knowing he was about to lose what tenuous control he had. "I believe I still have some business to conduct with Lord Amberton."

"He's had his kiss," she said unthinkingly. She didn't want him to give Gerald money. She'd paid for her foolish wager. She only wanted to go home and forget that Amberton had touched her. Whatever Raven wanted to do to her she deserved, and he was right about hurrying home. She wanted to be there, in the privacy of her own chamber, and to wash away, in the hottest water she could stand, the filth of what had happened this afternoon.

"I assure you I don't intend to give him another," Raven said. And when she glanced up, he was smiling at her—a real smile, the corners of his lips tilted farther upward than she'd ever seen them. "Go home and make yourself beautiful. I'll be there before the first guest arrives. I promise you."

At the quiet assurance in his deep voice, she nodded. He reached behind him and opened the door. On legs that continued to shake, she walked across the short expanse of Gerald's foyer to place herself into the competent hands of her father's former coachman, who had so willingly come to work for her husband.

"My lady!" Tom said, and she could hear the shock in his pleasant, country-bred voice.

"I'm all right," she lied. "Just take me home, please, Tom. You can return for Mr. Raven. He said he had some business."

"I should imagine he has!" said the coachman, putting his hand under her elbow and practically lifting her into the coach. In its dim interior she gave rein to the tears she had denied in front of Raven, and for the first time in her life she didn't consider what such a bout of weeping would do to her complexion.

"My wife informs me that, despite her attempt to leave, Lord Amberton, you tried to detain her."

Although the American's voice was perfectly calm, Amberton felt a flicker of unease. What he had planned had not gone off exactly as expected due to Catherine's painfully effective resistance and John Raven's surprising lack of infuriated response. But Gerald believed he could still achieve his ends if only he could goad the American enough.

"I would never be so ungallant, Mr. Raven, as to dispute

a lady's word," Amberton said mockingly, "but I would ask you to consider that I didn't abduct Catherine."

"My wife is free to visit whomever she wishes, but she should *also* be free to leave whenever she desires."

"You must know, Mr. Raven—"

"The only thing I *must* know, my lord, is why you chose to hold Mrs. Raven here against her will."

"Mrs. Raven?" Amberton repeated derisively. "I had almost forgotten. Poor Catherine always did have a penchant for eloping with unsuitable men. The first one, however, was both handsome and charming," he taunted, "and he swept Cat off her feet. But, of course, she was only sixteen. That time, I understand, the duke was more successful in saving Catherine from herself. You should be grateful Montfort didn't catch you. He tried to kill Henning, to whip him to death. Had to be forcibly restrained, I'm told. Rumor was Henning had managed to convince Cat her father wouldn't prevent their marriage if she already belonged to him in...some way," he suggested, allowing one eyebrow to rise and a small, salacious smile to touch his lips. "I'm sure you've already discovered the rather irreversible result—"

The mocking suggestion was abruptly cut off by the American's lightning-fast movement. Raven was across the space that had separated them almost before the viscount could raise the sword he had carefully concealed behind his right leg. He had taken the opportunity Catherine's greeting of her husband had offered to arm himself, the blade already prudently at hand.

God, the bastard was quick, Amberton thought, his body automatically executing the classic dueler's lunge that he'd practiced with his Italian fencing master for so many hours. The heavier blade affected his movement only slightly, but the American's reaction to the sword was as swift as his attack had been.

Raven couldn't avoid the point entirely; Amberton's lunge had been too well timed. The viscount had been waiting for his control to slip, and when the nobleman's taunting had achieved the result he'd wanted, he'd brought out the hidden weapon. Raven had time only to execute a small downward twist of his body to direct the shaft through the muscles of his shoulder rather than into his heart, which had been Amberton's target. He could feel the impact of the blow and even the slide of the blade into the muscle, its impetus driven by the viscount's graceful lunge.

There was no pain. Not yet, at least. And wouldn't be until he'd finished what he intended, Raven prayed. He blocked all thought of the sword and focused instead on the supple wrist of the man who held its hilt. "Release it," Raven ordered softly. His thumb found the vital nerve and exerted unbearable pressure. Without the viscount's volition, his fingers unclenched, surrendering control of the sword.

As soon as the hilt had been freed, Raven maneuvered the wrist he held, easily turning the Englishman's body and pinning his right arm behind his back. The position was so painful that an involuntary cry was wrenched from the viscount.

He could feel the American's breath on the back of his neck. More frightening than the steel of his grip was the fact that Amberton could see, out of the corner of his eye, the hilt of the sword that still impaled that massive shoulder resting on his own. Horrified, he realized he could even feel it move as Raven whispered, "Gossip, my lord, is for old women and cowards. If I ever hear that filthy lie on anyone's tongue, I'll come after *you*. And if I ever hear that you've touched Catherine again with your vile slander or with your viler hands, you may be very sure I'll kill you. Do you understand?"

Raven wanted to kill him now, had never been in a situation where he had wanted to kill a man more. The control he was exercising in not breaking this English bastard's neck would make his grandmother extremely proud, he thought. Almost without conscious intent, he jerked the arm he held upward as he released it. Although he hadn't anticipated it, the resulting snap of bone was somehow deeply satisfying. Uncaring of the damage he'd inflicted, he pushed the viscount away from him and stepped back. Fighting to control his murderous rage, Raven watched Amberton take a staggering step, trying to cradle the injured arm.

Allowing himself a small smile of satisfaction, Raven took another step backward, and with that movement was uncomfortably reminded of the viscount's sword. His eyes never leaving the ashen face of his adversary, Raven gripped the protruding hilt and pulled. Although the operation required more effort than he'd thought it would, he managed to prevent any expression of discomfort from touching his face. Nothing was allowed there other than a mocking smile as he held the Englishman's eyes.

When the sword was free, Raven threw it on the sofa, the dark blood marking the elegant cream satin. He allowed his gaze to rest on the viscount a moment more. Amberton huddled against the wall, his right arm held carefully by the slender, fashionably white fingers of his left hand, his mouth open in shock.

It was never wise to humiliate your opponent, Raven's grandfather had warned. Pride was something the Scots understood, and Raven knew he had damaged whatever pride Amberton had left. A dangerous enemy, Raven thought, but he didn't regret what he'd just done. Not when he remembered how Catherine had trembled and what the viscount had suggested. Turning, Raven let himself out, departing as calmly as he had entered.

Behind him, in the silence of the salon, Amberton shivered suddenly. He had never seen anything as cold-blooded as the American calmly removing that still-quivering sword from his own body, that damn strange smile playing over his lips. It was diabolical. Almost inhuman, he thought, shivering again.

"Bloody savage," he whispered bitterly.

Despite the heat of the bath water the servants brought up, Catherine found she couldn't stop shivering. Not only did she have to face thirty guests, but she had begun to think rather more clearly about Raven's actions this afternoon. She supposed he intended to knock Gerald down for what he had done, and he appeared capable of doing that with ease. But now she was far less worried about what he would have to say to her about her exploit and more worried about him. She knew that lesser offenses than the Viscount Amberton had committed today resulted in duels. The insult he'd offered her, even mitigated by the fact that she had gone to his apartment voluntarily, was certainly of a serious nature. Despite Raven's calm and his smile, she didn't believe he had taken Gerald's actions lightly.

He had, however, promised to return before the arrival of their guests, and not allowing herself to think about what possible explanation she could offer if he didn't, she permitted her body to be perfumed, groomed and gowned. When she found she was ready with a full five minutes to spare, she indulged in another finger of her husband's brandy. If she was unsteady in her movements tonight, she supposed that was to be preferred to giving in to a fit of vapors. That ridiculous performance was something she had never indulged in in her life, and despite all that had happened, she didn't intend to now. Fortified, she was able to sweep down the gracefully curving staircase seconds before Edwards opened the door to the first callers.

Catherine stood alone, automatically welcoming her

guests with a practiced warmth and a deliberate sparkle in her eyes that was intended to enchant those gauche enough to wonder about her explanation that Raven had been temporarily detained. In the midst of that refrain, made this time to Lord Elliot, a friend of her father's and a cabinet member as well, she felt Raven's warm, callused palm rest on her shoulder and slip caressingly down her upper arm. She leaned briefly against his strength and then stepped away, looking up into his face with a teasing laugh.

"You will have to make your own excuses, my dear," she said truthfully. "I'm afraid they looked askance at mine."

"To be candid, gentleman, I have had an experience that you should be able to sympathize with."

At his words, her breath caught. She met Raven's eyes, wondering if he could possibly be angry enough to betray her before the elite of the world he professed to want to impress.

"My valet ruined every cravat he'd prepared. I had to wait until he had heated the irons and readied another. I threatened him with my wife's displeasure should he manage to ruin this one."

He lifted long, dark fingers to touch the snowy linen, tied in the intricate folds of the *Trone d'amour*. Because she had been looking for any sign of what he had done to Amberton, Catherine's eyes examined the knuckles of that hand. Seeing her gaze on his fingers, Raven allowed his hand to catch hers and bring it to his lips.

"Am I forgiven?" he asked formally, his blue eyes lifting over their joined hands to meet hers.

"If our guests will forgive you, then I suppose I must."

"Be kind, my dear," advised Elliot. "You really have no conception of the demands on a man's patience an inept valet can make. I'm surprised, Mr. Raven, that you were in any condition to join us after a disaster of that magnitude.''

"As am I," Catherine said softly, and knew by the flicker of reaction in his eyes that her husband understood her comment.

"I'm generally a very even-tempered man," he said to Lord Elliot, still holding Catherine's fingers in the warm clasp of his. "It takes a remarkable event to unbalance my composure."

Aware that they had been playing their dangerous game of repartee for quite long enough, Catherine secured the freedom of her fingers and turned with a smile to the next guests. Her husband continued to talk easily to Lord Elliot for a moment, before he, too, turned to be introduced to the new arrivals.

Eventually the hardest part of the evening—the greetings and the introductions—were gotten through, and they were finally seated around the vast table, where the skill of Edwards's well-trained staff would carry some of the burden.

There were a few references made to her husband's interests in Durham and Tyneside, but he didn't dwell on those aspects of his business dealings. He might believe coal and the rails would be the key to whatever was going to happen in Britain, but he didn't seem inclined to talk about his commercial activities over his wife's dinner table.

He answered the inquiries politely and with the same serious attention with which he'd always responded to her questions, and then turned the topic to those more familiar to members of the quality. Racing and hunting, horses always being a safe subject, dominated for a while, as did the failures of the present government, which sparked a rather spirited debate between a gentleman with Whig leanings and Lord Elliot. When called on to offer his support, Raven presented a few well-informed remarks and again adroitly turned the talk in a less volatile direction.

When it was finally time to lead the ladies into the salon and leave the gentlemen to their port, Catherine knew that the evening had been a decided success and was relaxed enough to have stopped worrying about whatever would happen in the dining room when the feminine influence had been removed.

The gentlemen joined them in little more than an hour, the ladies not yet having exhausted their store of gossip nor their shared musical expertise. The guests eventually left in a pleasant babble of conversation, pledging to finish half-completed stories and interrupted *on-dits*.

When the door had closed on the last of them, Catherine found she didn't want to face her husband's censure to-night, however well deserved she knew it to be. She had dealt with enough for one evening, she thought, even though, she admitted, she had foolishly brought it all on herself.

When she turned, she found Raven leaning lazily against the door frame of the grand salon, watching her with those crystal eyes. Unwilling to meet what she was certain would be a rebuking stare, she made her way to the dining room, intending to congratulate Edwards on the success of the service and to ask him to pass on her compliments to the chef and, of course, to the staff, which had worked so hard to bring off tonight's triumph. She found the butler on his knees, a basin filled with soapy water on the floor beside him. Damp cloth in hand, he was scrubbing at a stain on the back of the chair her husband had occupied at dinner.

"What is it, Edwards?" she asked, and the dignified servant rose with an unaccustomed agitation, his body blocking her view of the chair, his smooth face flushing as it had when Raven had attempted to engage him in conversation.

"A stain, madam," he said, but he wouldn't meet her eyes. She wondered if he had spilled something on the imported silk.

"What sort of stain?" she asked, a delaying tactic while she tried to decide how to handle the situation. She knew he would expect her comment, but she was so genuinely grateful for the smoothness of the service tonight that she hated to spoil it by having to chastise him or some member of his staff for the careless destruction of what was a very costly piece of material.

"It appears to be...I believe, madam, although I might be mistaken—"

"I imagine it's blood," Raven interrupted matter-of-factly.

When she turned, Catherine found her husband standing in the doorway of this room, his right hand resting high on the frame.

"Blood?" she echoed. "But how would blood—"

"The usual way. Someone bled on it. And it's not the servants' fault. I'm only glad your guests are less observant than you and Edwards seem to be."

"It's not *their* embroidered silk," Catherine said, trying to think what he could be talking about. She stepped closer to get a better look at the dark stain, which almost covered the colorful peacock that had been painstakingly worked into the cream material. When the realization of what his words implied finally struck her, she turned back to find the doorway empty.

She found Raven halfway up the curving stair, which he was climbing much more slowly than his usual rapid, two-steps-at-a-time ascent. She hurried up beside him and caught his arm. She was afraid he might refuse to talk to her, but he stopped immediately, meeting her searching gaze without hesitation.

"What have you done?" she asked.

"Nothing to brag about, I promise you," he said, the blue eyes full of self-derision. "But I don't think you'll be bothered with Lord Amberton's attentions again."

He took a step past her, but her firm hold on his sleeve prevented him from moving farther up the staircase without rudely pulling his arm away.

"Did you kill him?" she asked, knowing very well the consequences of that to his business activities if he had.

"Did you expect me to?" Raven asked. "You led me to believe..." he began, and then stopped, his eyes resting on her face, wondering if he could have misinterpreted what had been happening this afternoon. "You know, I hope, that if you hadn't told me he'd tried to prevent your leaving, I'd never have touched him. Our agreement was that you might do as you please, up to a point. And I trust you to keep your word. Beyond that restriction, I recognize your right to entertain as many gallants as you wish. But I *thought* you implied that Amberton went beyond the boundary you'd set for him. Or was I wrong?"

"Of course, he went beyond those bounds!" she declared, hearing the doubt in his voice. "I would never have allowed the liberties he took. He..." Her voice faltered, because she thought she couldn't bear the humiliation of having to tell him.

"Then put him out of your mind. He'll never bother you again. And I didn't kill him." *I should have*, Raven thought, trying not to imagine what Amberton had done to make her look like that. *I should have broken his bloody neck.*

Controlling his renewed fury, he gently removed her fingers from the material of his sleeve and, once free, proceeded up the grand staircase before he said all the things he wanted to say to her, things he knew he had no right to say.

Catherine stood a moment, feeling distinctly deserted and wondering what she should do. Then, remembering with sudden fear the vivid stain on the Chinese-style chair in her dining room below, she followed the path the tall, dark figure had taken to his small bedroom on the second floor.

Raven never kept his valet waiting up to undress him. So despite the fact that his left arm hung rather awkwardly at his side, he was struggling to remove the dinner jacket. His back to the door, he didn't know that Catherine stood watching him.

"Let me get my scissors and cut the coat off," she said.

Raven paused in his efforts, and then, deciding that her suggestion made a great deal of sense, he nodded. He leaned against the high footboard of the bed, willing the ringing in his ears to cease. He hated his weakness. He hated being vulnerable. He hadn't wanted her to see him like this. He would never want anyone to see him like this, but especially not Catherine. She would surely despise his weakness, his inability to control the sensations the loss of blood was causing.

She ran to her room and rummaged among her embroidery silks for the small scissors. By the time she'd found them, her hands had begun to shake almost as much as they had after Gerald's assault.

When she reentered his room, her husband was standing exactly as she had left him. His slumped shoulders straightened slightly, however, as soon as she began to cut up the back of his jacket. When she had finally succeeded, having realized very quickly that the tiny scissors were not the ideal tool for the task she'd undertaken, she slipped the relatively unstained half of the coat off his right arm, allowing it to fall to the floor. She began to ease the blood-soaked left half off, but his right hand lifted and, gripping the ruined material, pulled it over his shoulder and down his arm. She was not pleased to notice that he didn't bend the left elbow, but held the entire arm as still as possible, given the nature of the operation.

The white, watered-silk waistcoat was far more revealing

of the amount of blood he'd lost than the dark material of the coat had been. Resolutely forcing herself to grasp the bottom edge of the sodden garment, she quickly cut up the back seam and freed him of that, too, revealing the lawn shirt. It was covered with the same dark color that had marred the chair in which he'd sat tonight, casually exchanging pleasantries about horses and politics with people he barely knew, while his blood seeped through shirt and waistcoat and even through the heavy material of his jacket.

"I can manage the rest," he said. He had been so silent throughout the ordeal that she jumped at the authority in his voice.

"What happened?" she asked, ignoring his suggestion that she leave him and beginning the struggle to cut the material of the shirt with the now-dull sewing scissors.

"I must have had my mind on something else," he said, and she heard again the self-derision in his voice.

"Did he shoot you?" she asked, finding it difficult to conceive that even Gerald would shoot someone in the back.

"He had a sword. I didn't notice it."

"How could you not notice a sword?" she exclaimed, beginning to peel the soaked shirt off his back.

"I told you. My mind was on something else."

"And he stabbed you in the back?" she whispered. Having removed the shirt, she could see the wound, finally revealed, a dark slit in the muscled brown shoulder, nastily oozing blood.

"No, to give him credit, he was quite straightforward about it. He went in under the collarbone."

The import of what he'd said reached her brain. Catherine moved around him to find a wad of blood-soaked cloth covering what she guessed was a matching slit in the front of his body.

"He ran you through," she said, her stomach heaving

once at the thought of the cold steel of Amberton's sword piercing the warm skin and cutting through the firm muscle of his chest.

"I believe that's the term. I confess I'm not very familiar with fencing. However, I suppose I must now admit to more than a nodding acquaintance with the art." Seeing the blanched features of his wife, Raven said, "It's all right, Catherine. I'm all right. A trifle embarrassed that I let the bastard stick me."

"But you weren't armed," she said, thinking how dastardly the honorable Lord Amberton had proved himself today.

"Not until I took his toy away from him," he agreed with a trace of amused satisfaction.

She glanced up and found that small smile again playing about his lips. But his face was too pale under the bronze skin, almost gray under the tan, and belatedly she realized she had forced him to stand while she cut away the ruined clothing.

"Sit down," she ordered, taking his right elbow, intending to help him to the small straight chair that stood near the bed.

He lifted his arm from her hand, smiling still.

"Feeling maternal, Catherine?" he asked softly, and she remembered his comment about the likelihood of that eventuality.

"Not about *you*," she answered with more spirit than she felt, thinking only of how secure in his masculinity he was and how reassuring she found his strength.

"Good," Raven said, searching her eyes for any disgust that he'd let Amberton catch him off guard. Only when he had assured himself that there was nothing in the russet depths except a natural concern for his injury did he turn to the chair she'd indicated.

She followed, wondering what she intended to do about

the wound. She had no experience with illness. Someone else always saw to those things. She supposed she should send for a surgeon.

"I'll have Edwards send for Dr. Stevenson. He's—"

"No," Raven interrupted. "Surely you realize what would happen if word of this got out."

"But I don't know what to do. I could ask Edwards—"

Again he cut her off. "Just bind it up. There's nothing else anyone can do. I couldn't reach the back, and it seemed to have clotted. I can only suppose the wound reopened when I moved my shoulder. I'm sorry I ruined your chair. I'll try to find a matching silk, or you can have the entire set redone."

"You can't really believe I care about the chair," she said hotly. "It's your house. You may bleed wherever you wish."

"Thank you, Catherine," he said, smiling. "I'm reassured by your consideration, but I don't believe I shall avail myself of the offer. At least, not if you'll bind this up. It's not so very bad. I haven't passed out on you yet."

"Don't you dare. Even Edwards couldn't get you up. You're too large," she said unthinkingly, tentatively touching the stiffened wad of padding that covered the entry wound.

"I'm sorry," he said. It was not the first time she'd referred to his size, so different, he knew, from the slim elegance of the London gentlemen she flirted with.

"What?" she asked, not even realizing he was answering her unthinking comment about his size.

"I should imagine," he suggested, "that you might begin with the other. It *is* still bleeding?" he asked.

"Yes," she whispered, feeling very foolish. The slit he had covered with a pad before he'd come down tonight had apparently closed. She put her hand against the hard

warmth of his shoulder, forcing him to lean forward enough
that she could see the one in his back, still welling blood.

"You'll need something to make a compress and strips
of cloth to bind it around my chest," he advised.

She wondered if he could feel her fingers trembling
against his skin as she studied the wound. "A sheet?" she
asked.

"If you can find the linen press. I couldn't. I'm afraid I
was forced to make do with something less appropriate."

She found it hard to believe that he could still mock
himself, but the amusement was clear in his voice. "Of
course I can find the linen press. This *is* my household,"
she said.

Curious despite the situation, she turned at the doorway
to ask, "What did you use?"

"One of the cravats my valet had laid out. He was very
puzzled as to why there was one less than he'd prepared."
Raven was still leaning forward in the chair, apparently
unwilling to take up her offer to bleed at will on her furnishings.

"He'll probably leave you. Disappearing cravats *and* not
being allowed to help you undress. You are really a most
unsatisfactory gentleman."

"I suppose Edwards will follow after the disaster tonight," he said. "You'll have your hands full keeping staff,
but I promise I'll try, from now on, not to scandalize your
servants."

"Concentrate on staying upright instead," she said. "I
don't want to have to explain a husband who's bled to
death."

"Then I suggest you hurry," Raven reminded her quietly, but again he was smiling.

He had endured her inept nursing with a calm patience.
Catherine had first cleaned the blood off his back as well

as she could with the cool water in his bedroom pitcher. She had decided to leave the wadding he'd pressed into the entry wound because she didn't want to start it bleeding again. He had lost quite enough blood as it was. She'd placed a thick square of cloth over the slit in his back and had bound it in place with long strips she'd torn from the remainder of the sheet. The white material she had wrapped under his arm and across his wide chest, covering both wounds, was stark against the dark skin. She had had to fight the urge to run her fingers caressingly over the reassuringly warm expanse of his chest as she'd worked.

Catherine had never before thought about touching a man's body. And she was surprised, given the events of the day and Gerald's behavior, that she should be attracted to the very masculine strength of Raven's. He could far more easily bend her to his will than Amberton, but she wasn't frightened by the latent power of Raven's body, strongly apparent despite the injury he'd suffered. Instead she was fascinated by the way the muscle shifted under the golden skin when, in response to her direction, he moved to allow her greater access to the wound.

"I think that's all," she said, stepping back to view her handiwork. The bandaging didn't look all that secure, and she hoped it wouldn't shift in the night. With that thought she realized that she should probably help him into his nightshirt.

"Do you want me to help you finish undressing?" she asked, not really thinking of what her offer implied. Since he was wearing only his trousers, that didn't leave much to remove.

"I don't think that's necessary," Raven said. He hadn't gotten up from the chair. He seemed to be waiting for her to leave before he disrobed for the night.

"Will you be all right?" she asked, feeling strangely reluctant to desert him. "I could ring for your man."

"No, Catherine. Go to bed. And thank you," he said, taking her hand in his. He pressed a warm kiss into her palm, then closed her fingers over the place he'd just touched.

Without her volition, her other hand was suddenly touching the raven gleam of his hair, smoothing back the dark strands. He didn't move as her fingers stroked his head, then under his ear and along the strong line of his jaw. She took his chin in her palm, her thumb sliding along the thin bottom lip. She thought he might react in some way, but he was perfectly still, unmoving under what was, she admitted, decidedly a caress.

She applied enough pressure under his chin to lift his face so that she was looking down into his eyes. Very slowly, giving him the opportunity, if he wished, to avoid her touch, her mouth lowered to meet his. He allowed the brush of her lips over his, but he didn't react in any way. He certainly didn't open his mouth and move his tongue, as Gerald had done today, and she found herself wondering what the hard line of his lips would feel like pressed closely over hers. What his tongue would be like, moving inside her mouth, against hers.

Finally, realizing that she had certainly broken the terms of their agreement, she lifted her head. His eyes had been closed, the long, dark lashes lying against the small network of lines beneath, and for some reason she was pleased. They opened at the desertion of her lips. Again there was something in the crystal depths that she couldn't read.

"I think you'd better go," Raven suggested softly.

Embarrassed by her display, Catherine nodded and turned to walk to the door, her knees again trembling, but for a very different reason from before. He didn't want her here, didn't want her kisses, she thought with a touch of bitterness. He had made very clear what he wanted from her, and it wasn't what she had just offered him. *I don't need a mistress,* he'd told her, and having been exposed to the beauty of his very masculine body, for the first time she was forced to think about what that declaration really meant.

The blue eyes of the man she had left in the small bedroom closed again, and he drew in a breath, so deep its force jolted agonizingly through the torn nerves and muscles of his shoulder.

It had been so difficult to let her go. She had kissed him, touched him, her fingers trailing across the darkness of his skin as if she found nothing to dislike in its color. And he had wanted to pull her down to him, to carry her to the narrow bed where he lay every night and dreamed of loving her, to finally make the temptations of those dreams a reality.

You made a promise, Raven, to give her freedom, his grandmother's voice reminded him through the dizzying light-headedness. *And no matter the consequences to yourself, you must keep it.*

Silently, in the dim solitude of his lonely bedroom that night, John Raven made another vow, as binding as the first. Only this time it was a promise he made to himself— that Catherine would be his in every way intended by the covenant they had made over the smith's anvil. Their souls would become one, the joining of the spirit as important in his heritage as the joining of the body. But with that thought, a harsh groan slipped past his control. He had ignored the pain, locking it away, during Catherine's tender and touchingly inept nursing. This whisper of sound was an acknowledgment of a far different agony, one that clawed his guts every time his fingers accidentally touched hers or their eyes met over the dinner table.

Tonight she had kissed him. He couldn't allow himself to hope that it had meant more than a recognition of the role he'd played in her rescue today from Amberton. But someday… Soon, my darling, Raven vowed again. Someday very soon.

Chapter Seven

For many reasons Catherine passed a nearly sleepless night. The longer she lay in her lonely bed, the more guilt she felt over the events of the previous day. She had allowed Amberton to put her in such a situation that her husband had been forced to defend her honor, suffering a serious wound for his efforts. And she had not even asked whether a challenge had been issued as a result of her foolish behavior.

She had reacted like a headstrong child to Gerald's taunts, but there had been nothing enjoyable about the outcome of her daring this time. She wanted to explain to her husband the convoluted path that had led to the predicament in which he had found her yesterday. Then if, in response to that explanation, Raven wanted to chastise her, she really couldn't blame him.

It was after eleven when she finally screwed up her courage enough to face him. She thought that discomfort from his injury might have prevented him from passing a restful night, just as her regret had interfered with her sleep, and so, she reasoned, he, too, might already be up. When she slipped through the partially opened door of his chamber, however, she found only his valet, who was straightening the room. He looked up in surprise at her entrance. She knew that nothing was ever hidden from the servants, and the knowledge that John Raven and his wife did not share a bed would certainly have been bandied about below stairs.

"Mr. Raven is in his office, madam," the valet offered.

She had enough presence of mind to take a quick inventory of the discarded clothing he'd gathered into a pile on the neatly made bed. There were no bloodstains visible on any of it, although the stack appeared to contain the requisite shirt and waistcoat and jacket along with the trousers. Raven must have gotten rid of the stained garments she'd cut off his body last night and replaced them with others from his wardrobe.

Apparently he intended to give the staff as little cause for comment as possible. Depending on Edwards's discretion, the ploy might have some chance of succeeding. After all, the butler might properly have required the maids to clean up the stain on the chair, and the fact that he hadn't seemed to indicate his concern that its origin not become common knowledge.

"Thank you," she said and closed the bedroom door.

Without allowing her guilty conscience time to find a reason not to confront her husband, she made her way resolutely to the room where Raven spent hours engaged in the unending correspondence necessary to maintain a financial empire the scope of his. Although he traveled extensively, she knew he still carried on a great deal of his business through the mails.

She stood a moment in the doorway, reluctant now that she was here. Raven seemed unaware of her presence, and it was not until he had finished whatever he was writing that he looked up.

"Come in, Catherine," he invited. "It's not often this

environment is graced with your presence. I don't believe you've visited my office before.''

''Not since you showed me Father's announcement of my betrothal to Gerald. Or perhaps I should say *your* announcement?''

She could hear the slight challenge in her voice, and from his puzzled expression, she knew he had heard it, too.

''*My* announcement?''

''Did you fabricate that entire scenario? Gerald indicated that he knew nothing about any plan to announce our engagement.''

''Then Amberton is a liar,'' Raven said calmly. Whatever story the viscount had told her probably had something to do with her presence in his apartment yesterday. ''Surely you aren't inclined to believe anything he asserts. Not after yesterday.''

''But, you see, I *did* believe it. On the night of Aunt Agatha's party. He implied that you'd created that announcement to trick me into a runaway marriage.''

''If you remember...'' He stopped, allowing her to complete his thought.

She did remember. She had been the one who'd suggested that flight to the Border.

''The announcement *was* sent, to the *Post* and the *Gazette*. Reynolds was barely able to prevent its publication. And I don't believe it was sent without Amberton's knowledge,'' he said.

''No,'' she admitted, convinced by the quiet sincerity in Raven's voice as he reiterated what he'd said the last time they had been together in this room. ''But I did believe him. That night. And since he'd already suggested that you'd managed to break me to the bit...I'm afraid I reacted very foolishly. He invited me to play cards. Not in the card room, but alone upstairs. And to prove that I wasn't under your thumb, as he'd said, I agreed.''

There was no response, either verbally or in the blue eyes. Catherine had expected that by this time Raven would have chided her for her actions or have made his disgust over them apparent, but there was nothing but polite interest in the lucid blue depths.

He doesn't care, she thought, and that idea was remarkably painful. Or I've destroyed whatever feelings he might have had about the impropriety of his wife's playing cards alone with a man by my far-more-improper actions of yesterday.

"And I lost," she forced herself to continue, swallowing the tightness that had begun to gather in her throat.

"I told you it was all a matter of numbers," Raven said, the corners of his mouth deepening. He hadn't really expected this confession. By the terms of their agreement, he had no right to an explanation, yet she seemed to believe he was entitled to one.

"I couldn't keep my mind on the game," she continued. "He suggested I wager my bracelet—the ruby-and-diamond one you'd admired on the way to the party. But when I tried to give it to him, after the game, he said it was something you'd surely miss. And you wouldn't miss...the other."

"The other?"

The question was very quietly spoken, but there was still no censure in Raven's face when she glanced up to answer him.

"A kiss. That was to be the forfeiture. And I *was* afraid you'd notice I'd lost the bracelet. You'd hadn't even had time to receive the bill," she said, her voice faltering slightly.

Raven looked down at his fingers, which had found the silver letter opener on his desk. He traced the handle's design with his thumb, trying to control lips that seemed determined to smile. Catherine had believed he'd rather she give up a kiss to that bastard than a bracelet.

He wondered for the thousandth time why he'd made this agreement. *Because that was the only way you could win her and you knew it,* he reminded himself grimly. At that unpleasant thought, he lost the inclination to amusement her hesitant confession had evoked. She was his wife, and she knew nothing about him, nothing about the way he felt. Especially the way he felt about her.

"And I missed our waltz," she continued, the non sequitur revealing, perhaps, how painful her recital was. But when his gaze lifted to her face, Catherine realized by the slight movement of the stern line of his lips that Raven knew exactly what she was talking about.

She took a deep breath, determined to finish. "And then he sent me a message. Yesterday. Just before I should have begun dressing for the party. If I didn't come to pay the forfeiture, he'd tell you about the wager. He said he needed the money."

"And so you went."

His eyes were once more on the movement of his long fingers, their darkness a contrast to the palely gleaming silver of the opener they held.

"Yes," she whispered.

"And he demanded more than his kiss," he suggested.

"He put his tongue in my mouth," she admitted, shivering at the remembrance of the disgusting slackness of Gerald's lips over hers. She wished suddenly that she hadn't told Raven that, but it was too late to deny what had happened. And the other was even more repellent. "And then—he put his mouth on my body," Catherine finished, determined to tell him everything. But if, as they said, confession was good for the soul, she wondered why she felt so awful. Her husband's face was completely calm, and when he spoke again, he didn't say what she'd expected.

"I have only one question," Raven said. "In light of our agreement, I don't understand why you didn't tell Amberton to call due the bet and be damned. I *did* promise not to restrict your actions, and nothing you've told me seems serious enough to warrant a breach of our contract. You certainly weren't entertaining a lover yesterday afternoon. It appeared that I'd interrupted a brawl rather than a romantic interlude."

"I thought you'd be angry," she said truthfully.

"Then I'd have violated the freedom I promised you."

"I suppose I never thought you'd hold to those terms," she said almost hopefully.

"I always honor my contracts, Catherine," Raven said, "no matter how unfavorable to me they may eventually prove to be. It's the only way to have your word trusted. If you break one agreement, then the person you've cheated will never trust you to keep your promises the next time."

Catherine reflected disappointedly that she really didn't want to hear a dissertation on contracts. Nothing had gone as she'd expected. She'd made her painful confession, and Raven had treated the entire incident as if she had been making mountains out of molehills. All he could talk about, it seemed, were contracts and agreements. What she wanted, on the other hand, was the comfort of his arms about her as they had been yesterday after Gerald's attack. Why did he never react as she expected him to?

"What did you do to him?" she asked, thinking suddenly that he'd never told her what had happened between them after he'd sent her home with Tom. Beyond the fact that Amberton had had a sword and he'd taken it away from him.

"Not, apparently, as much as you did. I think that's why he had to resort to stabbing me. He didn't have much fight left in him after you got through with him."

She could hear the sudden amusement in his voice, but she didn't understand its cause. "What *I* did?"

"I only hope, Catherine, that if I ever manage to displease you to the extent the viscount did, you won't resort to such desperate measures against me."

"I don't understand," she admitted.

He smiled at her confusion, realizing that she really didn't. Confirmation, had he needed any, that the story Amberton had told him was a fabrication. At least the supposed ending of that story had been fabricated by the viscount's vicious tongue.

"For all your professed recklessness," Raven said, savoring that knowledge, "you're a remarkably innocent child."

"I am *not* a child," she denied, stung by his evaluation. She was aware again of the difference in their ages and experience. Raven had traveled all over the world, and she had never even left England. He was the only man who always made her feel childish.

"No," he admitted, "you aren't. You are, however, a very beautiful young woman who's been confronted for perhaps the first time with the bitter lesson that people are not always what they seem. I hope it doesn't make a cynic of you."

"I should never have trusted him." She had fallen into Gerald's trap as easily as she had into that set for her two years ago by Richard Henning's charm. Too trusting by far, she acknowledged bitterly, of the gentlemen of her circle, who had, in the end, proved themselves to be far less than chivalrous.

"You have to trust someone," Raven said easily. "Next time you'll be wiser in choosing the object of your confidence."

Next time, he thought, perhaps she'd confide in him. If he taught her that he could be trusted. Knowing it was time to leave, Raven pushed himself up from the desk, an awkward effort, made with his right hand flat against the cluttered papers.

For the first time since she'd begun her confession, Catherine remembered his injury—an injury she'd been the cause of. Her eyes traced over his left shoulder, looking for any indication of the bandage that she knew concealed the wound made by Amberton's blade. The morning coat, however, seemed to fit with its accustomed smoothness over his muscular frame. Her gaze lifted from her examination of his body to find his eyes on her face.

"Try not to grow up entirely while I'm gone. I should hate to miss any of your further adventures," he said, smiling at her.

"Where are you going?"

"Manchester, and then perhaps into Scotland. I haven't quite finalized my itinerary."

"But I should think…" She hesitated, knowing that she had no right to question his plans. She couldn't imagine, however, that a jarring carriage ride would be very comfortable.

"I shouldn't be gone more than a fortnight," he continued, the clear blue eyes still resting on her face. "Reynolds will keep you informed."

"And that?" she questioned, lifting her hand in the general direction of his broad left shoulder.

"Is nothing for you to be concerned about," he said quietly.

His denial of her right to worry over him hurt. "But what if it becomes inflamed? And you're away from home."

"Home?" He repeated the word questioningly, wondering if her concept of a home was this politely distant relationship they shared. So different from what he'd hoped for, from the warmth of the home and family he'd known all his life.

Catherine couldn't read whatever emotion was hidden in that word. "This *is* your home, Raven. And I am your wife. Even if we intend to keep our relationship on a business basis, I should think you must know that I'm concerned about your welfare."

"Are you, Catherine?" he asked. And at her slight nod, he smiled at her again.

Altogether, Raven had smiled at her more today than in the entire length of their previous encounters, she thought. And that was very strange, considering that she had expected quite the opposite reaction, given the events of yesterday.

"I don't suppose your business could be postponed?" she suggested hesitantly. "At least until your shoulder's had an opportunity to heal."

"I think not," he said. "I told you not to worry. I'm well accustomed to looking after myself."

Reluctantly, she was forced to admit defeat. "Then I'll see you when you return."

Raven had moved very close to her, and she realized she was blocking his access to the doorway leading to the front of the house. She stepped aside just as he moved to go around her. Once again she found herself in breathtaking proximity to his very masculine body. Her hand lifted to find something to help her regain her balance, and what it found, quite naturally somehow, was the wide expanse of a muscled chest. Surprisingly, his right hand came to rest warmly over her left, which was lying now against the fine material of his coat.

"Try not to bring London tumbling down about your ears while I'm gone," he said softly.

She nodded, but she was remembering her head resting against this same chest yesterday and his hard arms reassuringly locked around her body. And last night... Most of the night she had spent remembering the feel of his lips under the caress of hers. And remembering his body, the width of his shoulders and the muscled chest.

Raven didn't say anything else for a long time, but there was no discomfort in the continued silence of their strange tableau. Only his hand was touching hers, which rested on the solid strength of his body. After a long time he lowered his head, moving very slowly, perhaps as she had done last night, giving her an opportunity to step back, to break the delicate connection between them. His lips touched against the smooth cream of the skin stretched over her collarbone, above the low neckline of her jonquil yellow morning dress. At the first electric jolt of sensation, her eyelids fell, closing suddenly in response to what he was doing.

His mouth moved without any pressure along the fragile bone that led to the slim column of her neck. The feeling of his lips gliding over her flesh was like nothing she'd ever felt before. There was no attempt at domination, no application of the unusual power of his body. Raven was touching her exactly as his strong, dark fingers caressed the frail stems of the imported crystal with which his table was set each evening. The fingers she had watched every night with such fascination.

She wondered what they would feel like against the rounded globe of her breast, their callused strength pleasantly abrasive against her skin. She must have taken a breath at that image, for she realized that she had forgotten to breathe before, holding her body still so that she wouldn't miss any of the sensations caused by the movement of his mouth. His lips hesitated, lifting away from her throat at that quick intake of breath, and desperate for their touch, she heard herself whisper, "Please."

Raven waited a heartbeat, evaluating the meaning of that request, but finally, hoping that he had rightly interpreted what she wanted, his mouth began again its slow, relentless journey. Up the slim column of her neck now, as she turned her head to give him freedom to touch her there. The caress slowed again when he reached the pulse under her jawline, nuzzling against the increased flow of blood through her veins caused by his nearness. She realized suddenly that he was running his tongue gently over the fluttering beat. She could feel the heat and wetness, and she had never felt anything more sensual in her life than the warmth of his opened mouth on her body.

It was nothing like yesterday. Nothing like Gerald's touch. It was as different as day and night, as dusk and dawn. The dawn of her recognition of just how much she had hungered for this. She hadn't known what she had wanted those nights she'd watched Raven's hands moving over the fragility of the glass he held so securely. Those times she'd studied the slight movements of his firmly chiseled lips. But her body had known. And it was responding to his touch now as if in those weeks it had simply waited in blind anticipation of this moment.

Raven removed his hand from hers, and she felt his thumb and forefinger against her chin. She opened her eyes as he lifted up her face. The blue of his eyes was more clear than she'd ever seen it, dazzling in the sharp brightness of his gaze. His mouth was not smiling, its hard line stern and set. And she wanted it. Over hers. Involuntarily, she moistened her lips with her tongue. His eyes followed its movement, and then his eyelids closed, hiding the blue flame. And in response to the unspoken invitation, his dark head lowered to find the moisture her tongue had left on her lips.

His mouth wasn't hard, as she'd expected from the thin, forbidding line in which it was too frequently set. Instead it was warm and gentle. Firm and knowing. He knew exactly how to touch her—not domineeringly, but with none of the disgusting slackness of Amberton's kiss. His lips settled over hers, moving, almost taunting her with their power to make her respond. Suggesting that there was more that she wanted, and now needed.

The expression of her need was running in shivering torrents through her frame. She moved against the hard body that was bending over hers, wanting to make contact with its power all along the length of hers. Somehow his arm was behind her, holding her so that she was firmly supported and free to think of nothing but what his mouth was doing. And of the movement of his body against her own. Raven was so vital, warm and real, and she wanted to touch his skin as she had last night. To feel it move beneath her fingers, a smooth sheath for the muscles underneath.

His mouth opened suddenly over hers, his tongue invading, hard and sure. As hard as the muscles she had just been imagining she was once again touching. As hard as the chest her breasts were crushed against by the power of his arm against her back. As hard as...

Catherine gasped a little under the shattering impact of the discovery that she was not the only one responding physically to what was happening between them—an occurrence so foreign to the arrangement to which he had scrupulously held in the long weeks of their marriage. This is what she had wanted, she now knew, but he had never before indicated that he had any interest in her body. As his was now clearly revealing that he did. She wondered why he had never before seemed to want to touch her.

I don't need a mistress, he had said so long ago. *What I need is a hostess.* The two roles had been clearly defined and separated.

So he already had a mistress. That, of course, was why he'd not shown Catherine his expertise at this art before. And expert he certainly was, she admitted bitterly. He had just forced her to forget what had happened yesterday in Amberton's apartment, and in doing so, he had left her trembling in his arms like a schoolgirl.

You're such a child, he'd told her. Apparently when it came to lovemaking, he'd been right. Or at least he'd reduced her to one. He was, she was forced to admit, far more experienced at this than she. Her mouth withdrew from the caressing touch of his tongue. She was embarrassed to remember how passionately hers had been matching the provocative movements of his—revealing, perhaps, in willingly following his instruction, how inexperienced she really was. The chaste kisses she'd allowed her beaux to steal on dark balconies and in the cunningly sheltered alcoves of a dozen ballrooms—kisses that she had thought so daring—had been nothing like this. Nothing to match what she had just shared with the man who was, and who was not yet, in any true sense of the word, her husband.

A business arrangement—that's all he had wanted from her. And she had practically thrown herself at his head. Raven had kissed her because she had made it obvious that she'd wanted him to. *Please,* she had begged, and he had accommodated her. In her embarrassed realization of what a fool she had just made of herself, she stepped back, removing herself from his embrace.

Raven let her go, but he stood watching her a moment. His high cheekbones were slightly flushed, the crystal eyes still lucidly shining in that dark face, and, Catherine was pleased to notice, his breathing was a trifle uneven.

"What's wrong?" he asked.

"I—I suppose I was remembering yesterday. What Gerald did," she said, grasping at any explanation he might believe, rather than the one that was really responsible for her retreat from what had been happening. From what she had been revealing about her feelings for him, feelings she knew he didn't share.

"Liar," he said, smiling at her.

"I don't know what you mean," she said, the conventional delay when one didn't have a response. Liar she certainly was. The memory of Gerald's assault had faded under the touch of Raven's lips, except as a contrast to how right this was as opposed to how wrong the other had been.

"I was afraid that bastard might have spoiled you for this. And then I was...delighted to find that I'd nothing to worry about. You aren't afraid of me."

"Of course not. You are my husband."

"Convenient," Raven said softly.

"I beg your pardon?"

"A convenient marriage. I believe that's the term you told me was used for our sort of arrangement."

Our sort of arrangement, her mind echoed bitterly. *The sort where you waltz off to Scotland while I sit at home thinking every hour about what you might be doing.* She wondered suddenly if he were going to Scotland at all. All these "business" trips... Very *convenient* for visiting some discreet address somewhere. Like an idiot, she'd never thought to question his travel. She wondered now how many of those journeys had been undertaken not to examine some coal mine or foundry, but rather to visit his mistress. The mistress he'd acknowledged quite openly.

"Scotland, I believe you said?" Catherine questioned.

"Lancaster first, and then perhaps across the Border."

Manchester, she thought. Raven had very definitely told her Manchester before. *Damn him, I was right. This isn't a business trip. And I suppose the interlude this morning was simply a warm-up to what he has in mind for later in the day. Or night.*

She took another step backward, away from the warmth and the now-familiar fragrance of his body, which, despite the confirmation of what she suspected, was so appealing. Her knees were still trembling with the aftermath of his touch.

"Have a good trip," she said, unable to hide the trace of bitterness at her discovery.

Raven's head tilted slightly, questioning that tone, and a small crease she'd never noticed before appeared between the sweep of his dark brows.

"Thank you," he answered, his attitude outwardly as correct as hers. "No goodbye kiss for your husband?" he suggested.

"I think you've had your kiss."

"Do you?" he questioned, his lips quirking slightly at her primness. "And by the rules, husbands are limited to only one?"

"How many are lovers limited to?" she asked, her anger making her bold.

"I don't believe there's a limit to lovers' kisses. I think they're allowed as many as they are able to steal. Don't you think that's probably how it works?"

"I don't know, I assure you. I've never had a lover."

"Good," he said. "Let's try to keep it that way, shall we?"

"And if Amberton calls?" she asked tauntingly.

was puzzled by her sudden shift in tactics. She a few minutes before been meltingly responsive ms.

d Amberton won't call. On that you have my word. And do you know, Catherine, I don't believe that husbands are limited to one kiss, after all. And if in England they are, that should certainly be changed. By an act of Parliament if necessary."

Even as he was speaking, he caught her up again into his embrace, his right arm moving commandingly behind her back and lifting her to meet his descending lips. There was no hesitation in the contact of his mouth over hers as there had been before. He had been afraid that Gerald's attack might have made her reluctant to endure a man's embrace, but her willing response had given Raven ample reason to know that was not the case.

His tongue pushed into her mouth, which, almost against her will, opened eagerly. Her tongue met his, matching the caressing quality of its movements. She seemed to be unable to deny him anything he wanted. Because, she knew, mistress or not, she wanted this, too. And had wanted it rather desperately now for several weeks.

Catherine couldn't have said how long his embrace lasted. Every bit of strength she possessed seemed to be draining from her body by the hard, sweet union of Raven's mouth with hers. She found that her hands had lifted to rest on those massive shoulders, holding him, not wanting him to leave when she had only just discovered how much she enjoyed his lovemaking. Perhaps if she became more adept at this, as he certainly could teach her to be, then he wouldn't want to seek out his mistress again. Maybe he'd choose instead to stay here with her. Maybe.

A vow, his grandmother's voice whispered into Raven's consciousness. Freedom, he remembered. He had promised Catherine freedom from this. Freedom until she wanted him as he had always wanted her. Gradually the movement of his tongue against hers stilled.

His mouth began to lift away, and unwilling to let the kiss end, unwilling to let him leave, Catherine clung damply to his lips with hers. Raven touched his mouth gently against those clinging lips, once, and then again, before he finally broke the contact. He turned his head so that his cheek rested, warm and wonderfully close, against hers. She could feel the slight roughness of his skin against the softness of hers.

"Manchester," she whispered.

"What?" he questioned, turning his face so that his lips caressed her eyelids, which were still closed.

"You said Manchester before," she said. *Deny it,* she prayed. *Make me believe that you're not rushing off to some other woman.*

"Did I?"

"Manchester," she repeated, nodding slightly against the movement of his lips over her face. They had now begun trailing warmly down her slightly retroussé and very fashionable nose.

"I must have been thinking of something else," he whispered. He kissed the tip of her nose and then lifted his head enough to look down into her face.

She opened her eyes, to find the startlingly bright blue of his own set in the beautiful stark planes of his face. And the golden bronze of his skin. She could see the pulse of the vein in his temple, the sheen of midnight hair, still unfashionably long and pulled back from those strong features.

"Then it is Manchester?" she managed to ask. What did it matter? she wondered. She was wasting the last few precious minutes he'd be here, asking ridiculous questions. She had no right to censure his behavior. This was what they had agreed to. He had never hidden the fact that he had a mistress. Most men of her class did. She had grown up accepting that reality. Gentlemen were entitled to their ladybirds as long as they fulfilled all the responsibilities of their legal bonds. But she had been forced to admit this morning that she didn't want Raven to hold another woman as he had just held her. Or to kiss her. Ridiculously gothic, she supposed, but true.

"Does it matter?" he asked, smiling at her. "I have interests in both. I didn't mean to mislead you. As soon as my plans are finalized, I'll have Reynolds inform you."

"You could write me," she suggested softly. She had no pride left. Next she'd be begging him to let her go with him.

"That may not be possible," he said. His eyes were no longer smiling, and there was something serious in the quietness of his deep voice.

"I understand," she whispered. And again she retreated, stepping back from the too-dangerous nearness of his hard body.

"Probably not," Raven said, touching his lips lightly to her forehead.

She raised both hands suddenly, her fingers caressing the dark hair that swept back from his face. Smiling into his watching eyes, she pulled his head down to move her lips against one lean cheek, delighting in the slight roughness of his closely shaved skin. His flesh felt too hot under the brush of her cool lips. On fire, she realized suddenly. And then he lifted his head abruptly and stepped around her and through the open doorway at her back. She listened without moving to the click of his boot heels striking decisively against the marble floor of the hall. And the murmur of voices, his and Edwards. And finally, her heart sinking, she listened to the closing of the front door.

Chapter Eight

When Oliver Reynolds had received the hand-delivered communication from his wealthiest client, he'd wondered at the abrupt instructions it contained. Despite his wealth, John Raven had never before ordered him to do anything, and certainly not anything as bizarre as this. Not the legal aspect, of course. *That* Reynolds had unsuccessfully sought to bring to Mr. Raven's attention on at least two occasions during the last three months. No, it was rather the location the American had chosen for the consummation of the business that seemed so unusual. As his coach stopped before the shaded doorway, Reynolds again wondered at the motives behind Raven's suggestion that they meet at this out-of-the-way hostelry, situated less than ten miles from the capital.

Slowly descending the narrow steps the coachman lowered for him, the old man felt the cost of this ridiculous journey in his aching bones. He had taken a few days longer than absolutely necessary to prepare the documents he carried today because he had found himself stubbornly thinking that, as rich as John Raven was, he did not control Oliver Reynolds. The man of business was too old to be at the beck and call of every client requiring his undivided attention. To give the American credit, however, he had, after the first, sent no more demanding letters of instruction.

Leaning more heavily than usual on the walking stick he liked to consider simply a fashionable affectation left over from his youth, Reynolds entered the low doorway of the inn. The hostess, having judged the quality not only of his attire but also of the carriage that stood under the shadows of the ancient oak from which the White Oak Inn had taken its name, approached, wiping her hands on her apron, which crackled softly with the starch her girls had laundered into it. She smiled at the banker and then shot a glance over her shoulder at her husband.

"I'm Oliver Reynolds," the old man said, fighting to keep his shortness of breath from being obvious. He was too old to be traipsing about the countryside, even at the behest of so valuable a client as John Raven. And he thought he might tell the American that. "I believe Mr. Raven's expecting me."

"Oh, sir," the woman said, her nervousness apparent in the work-reddened fingers now twisting a fold of the crisp cotton. "I swear I didn't know what I should do. Although as to that, Mr. Raven's instructions was clear enough, but it don't seem Christian somehow to leave him all alone. I brought him the willow, leaves and bark, like he asked me, and I even offered to help with the brewing, but he said no. I imagine if you're a friend, you know what he's like, right enough. Set on having his own way, it seems to me."

"Indeed," the banker said, thinking that he could with good conscience agree to that assessment, though, of course, he certainly did not intend to discuss John Raven's idiosyncrasies with the innkeeper's wife. "If you would be so good, Mrs...?"

"Hawthorne, sir. I'm Mrs. Hawthorne and that's my man that keeps the public house."

"Then if you or your husband would be so good, Mrs.

Hawthorne, to tell Mr. Raven I'm awaiting him in the parlor, I should be very grateful.''

The silence that greeted his very reasonable suggestion stretched, and still the woman made no move to deliver his message. ''He's upstairs, sir,'' she said instead, glancing again at her husband. ''He insisted he needed a fireplace, although with this awful heat, you'd think... And then there was the rocks, although he paid well enough for the carrying up of those, and to be sure, I'm not the kind to be begrudging a guest things that make him comfortable.''

Especially a guest with as generous a hand as he knew John Raven to have, Reynolds thought cynically as Mrs. Hawthorne continued.

''And I *offered* to call the doctor, but he'd have none of that, so I don't really know what else I could have done,'' she finished apologetically. ''But, I swear, as I said to my husband, it don't somehow seem Christian to me, despite what he says—''

''The doctor?'' the banker repeated, his hand suddenly arrested in the act of wiping the perspiration from his brow. Definitely too old to be traipsing around the countryside, he'd been thinking again when the woman's explanation had finally penetrated. ''For what reason should you summon a physician, my good woman? If ever in my life I've seen a man less in need of the services of a sawbones, it's John Raven.''

She hesitated, the brown eyes rich with concern, and her fidgeting fingers found another fold. ''That's what he said when I suggested it three days ago, but if you could see him now, Mr. Reynolds, you'd understand. I swear, as I told the mister just this morning, that shoulder's swelled like a cow with the colic. And he just sits there with his eyes closed and those rocks steaming around him. It's enough to make a body think...I don't mind telling you, sir, that I don't know what to think. Heathen's what I call it, but then he's such a gentleman. There's no denying that, no matter what strange ideas about healing he's got in his head. It's just that..." She paused, allowing the country shrewdness that had made her husband's business a success to show briefly in the dark eyes. "It's just that deaths ain't *good* for an establishment, if you take my meaning. They ain't good for business. The doctor's what we need, I said to Mr. Hawthorne just this morning. And I've had a mind, Mr. Reynolds, to send for one, orders or no."

The banker closed his mouth, which had fallen open, whether with the information just imparted or with the exertions of his descent from the carriage, he wasn't entirely certain.

"Upstairs," he repeated faintly. Rich or not, John Raven was proving to be a far-more-troublesome client than Oliver Reynolds had bargained for.

When Mrs. Hawthorne opened the door, steam wafted into the narrow hallway, curling whitely around the black serge of the banker's suit and wisping out of the way of the woman's determined entry. It was obvious she believed she'd found an ally in Mr. Reynolds.

A still figure was seated cross-legged before the blazing fire on the open hearth, where several dark rocks gleamed wetly, their sizzling moisture obviously responsible for the steam. As they watched, Raven's right hand slowly grasped a ladle that rested on the floor beside him and dipped it into the now empty china basin he'd taken from the washstand. When the metal rang sharply against the porcelain, the dark hand relaxed, releasing the ladle, which dropped again to the floor. The massive shoulders slumped and his head drooped, the black hair, loosened from its customary restraint, falling forward to hide his profile.

Oliver Reynolds walked the few steps that separated him from his client, and at the sound of his footsteps across the wooden floor, John Raven's head lifted, the fever-bright eyes blinking like an owl's as he tried to focus on the intruder. He realized only vaguely that this was what he had been waiting for, and the cracked lips opened to say the word he had imprinted on his brain, its normal intelligence seared by the heat of his illness.

"Will?" he asked hoarsely, and at Reynolds's nod, he finally allowed his lids to close in relief. There was something else he had to do, Raven knew. Something... He couldn't think. He had felt his mind slipping away into the steam. Something he had to do...for Catherine. And with her image, the task he'd been waiting to complete fluttered into the forefront of the darkness that was trying to rob him of the ability to think.

"Sign it," he whispered, but his eyes didn't open. At some level he was aware of the old man's trembling fingers touching his injured shoulder, but he couldn't really feel them against the familiar agony. That was something he had closed away four days ago, had locked outside of his consciousness and denied its ability to intrude on his prayers. Control of pain was one of the first lessons he had been taught, carefully instructed by the old woman, the ancient words whispering in his boy's mind like the drone of bees on a summer's day.

He had prayed to the All-Spirit, but the visions that had come, curling like the steam, had not been of strength and reassurance. He had defeated the pain, but the sickness that had entered his body through the hole Amberton had opened to the spirits would not be controlled. And there were, he had thought with regret, so many things he had wanted to finish.

He had allowed himself to hold her, to kiss her, knowing that if this time came, those memories would offer comfort. Catherine, he thought again, and knew he must have said it aloud when the old man spoke.

"I have it here," Mr. Reynolds said softly, but it seemed

to take a long time before Raven was aware of the pen pressed into his right hand. He couldn't see the document, its inked lines wavering before him, and when the banker finally understood, he guided his hand until it was done. Raven had to trust the old man that the instructions he'd written out so carefully that morning, some morning, had been followed. His holdings in New York were to go to his family, and everything else was Catherine's. Everything... Raven allowed his eyes to drift closed over the fire that burned inside them. So hot. But it didn't matter because... He couldn't remember why it didn't matter, but he knew that whatever he had been waiting for was finished.

The massive figure tilted gently to the side, and once begun, the momentum carried his body downward like a ship listing in a storm. And by the time his cheek was resting against Mrs. Hawthorne's gleaming oaken floor, John Raven was no longer aware of the storm that still raged through his body.

It had taken the combined efforts of several men called up from the taproom below, but they had deposited the American in the inn's best bed, and Mrs. Hawthorne had, for modesty's sake, found a sheet to spread over the wide, bare chest. The soft buckskin breeches he was wearing seemed unrestrictive and so they left those alone. And they left the poultice with its infusion of willow leaves that Raven had placed over the entry wound.

The physician had arrived in short order, perhaps hastened by the generous fee Reynolds had sent as an inducement, and the banker had thankfully left his client in the competent hands of the physician and Mistress Hawthorne. It was almost two hours later when the doctor emerged, carefully refastening the cuffs he'd obviously rolled up to perform some service for his patient. The banker felt his stomach clench when he remembered the grossly distended flesh underneath the poultice. Resolutely, he blocked that image and watched the physician shrug into his frock coat.

"How is he?" Reynolds asked when the man seemed disinclined to share any evaluation of the American's condition.

"Lucky to be alive," the doctor said bluntly. He had not learned a fashionable bedside manner at the University of Edinburgh, which was surely why he preferred a rural practice, tending to the honest injuries of farmers and farriers, than a more profitable London one, soothing the imaginary vapors of delicate gentlemen and fainting females. "I lanced the wound and bled him. For today, that's all that anyone can do. Alone in the world, is he?" he asked casually.

"I beg your pardon?"

The physician glanced up, shrewd hazel eyes assessing the old man's puzzlement. "I assumed there's no one who gives a damn whether that man lives or dies, given the fact that he appears to be well on his way to the latter, alone and uncared for."

Reynolds swallowed uncomfortably, remembering the unnecessary delay his pride had demanded before his delivery of the papers John Raven had asked him to prepare.

"He has a wife," he said hesitantly. Catherine Montfort, he thought again. He couldn't imagine how the American had brought that off, but the marriage was legal enough. Reynolds had made certain of that before he'd drawn up the will. However, he couldn't picture a woman he knew to be the acknowledged toast of London and a diamond of the first water sitting in a second-rate country inn beside a dying man's bedside.

The doctor's eyebrow lifted slightly. "Indeed," he said softly, a world of meaning in the single word.

"She probably doesn't even know..." the banker began, and then hesitated, wondering if that were true.

"Well, if she expects to see her husband again—her living husband, I should say—then I suggest you tell her." With that brusque opinion delivered, the physician picked up his satchel and descended the steps.

Taking a deep breath, the old man turned back to the door of the bedroom where the American lay. The devastating sarcasm of the phrase echoed in his head. *Her living husband.* It seemed he had no choice, but he supposed he owed it to his client to inform him of what he intended. As quietly as possible, he opened the door and almost tiptoed to the side of the bed that Raven's massive frame filled. The injury had been rebandaged, the poultice discarded, and the American lay unmoving under the spread of sheet and counterpane, their smoothness disturbed only by his slow, too-shallow breathing. Mistress Hawthorne sat in a straight chair near the curtained window.

"Is he conscious?" Reynolds asked.

"I don't know. He never made a sound through the whole ordeal, which was ghastly enough, I promise you. I've never seen as much vileness pour out of a wound as when the sawbones opened that one. Enough poison to kill a normal man, I should have thought," she said softly, shivering at the memory.

"The doctor thinks I should send for his wife," the banker said, looking down at the man on the bed. The black hair was fanned against the whiteness of Mrs. Hawthorne's linen, the golden skin stretched too tightly over the bones beneath.

The blue eyes slowly opened, bloodshot and unfocused with the fever. "No," Raven said. He licked parched lips, trying to think what he could say to prevent that. He didn't want Catherine here. *Feeling maternal,* he had asked her mockingly. *He* was the protector. That was the way it was supposed to be. He didn't want her to see him like this, too weak, he knew, to pretend strength if she came. But also too weak, he was afraid, to prevent them bringing her here.

"I don't want her," he whispered finally, watching the old man's face waver through the mists above him. That was not what Raven had meant to say. He wanted her, of course, but not to see him this way—brought down by the bastard he'd promised would never bother her again. She would never believe he could protect her from the likes of Amberton if she saw him like this.

"But the doctor thinks..." Reynolds began, and then thought better of telling him that truth.

The cracked lips moved upward slightly. "Don't send for Catherine," Raven ordered, imbuing his voice with all the surety he could command. "I'm not going to die," he said, remembering the vow he'd made. The solemn, sacred promise that Catherine Montfort Raven would be his. That she would be his wife in every meaning of the word. He'd be damned if he'd die before he fulfilled that oath. "I promised," he finished, and then the clouded blue eyes were slowly hidden by the downward drift of his eyelids as unconsciousness claimed him.

He'd had his instructions and unwilling to go against orders again, knowing that if he'd only arrived two or three days earlier, his client might not now be lying at the edge of death, Oliver Reynolds nodded. And it was not until much later that he thought to wonder about the past tense.

Despite the supposed dearth of society in London at the end of summer, someone who was very determined could find endless engagements to occupy what otherwise might loom as empty hours. And Catherine Raven was very determined. Because when she was not riding or dancing or promenading through the park, shopping or chatting away the afternoon with old friends, she was remembering the morning of her husband's departure.

As he had promised, Raven had had Oliver Reynolds send her word of his itinerary. She supposed the banker received written communication from his employer, but if so, none of it was ever passed on to her—only the briefest note to the effect that Mr. Raven had asked him to convey the information that he was now in Lancaster or Glasgow or Edinburgh. And eventually the days stretched beyond the fortnight Raven had suggested he'd be gone. Far beyond, to three endless weeks, and well into the fourth.

By then, of course, she'd relived a thousand times that morning's encounter, remembering not only the kisses they'd shared, but the feel of his body against hers. Its fragrance. And then, unbidden, would come the frightening remembrance of the hot, dry heat of his face against hers. As hot as if he were fevered. As if his wound were already inflamed with the inevitable infection that followed any injury that broke the protective covering of the skin. After the realization had come to her that the warmth of his skin that morning was not normal, she had remembered, too, the abnormal brightness of his eyes. She'd noticed them, of course, but she'd not assigned the proper cause to their nearly luminescent glow. Not at first, in any case.

And so she deliberately filled every moment of her day with almost hectic activity. She had found that if she were not surrounded by the most entertaining and lively members of her set, those who were still in the city, she found herself picturing Raven's body twisting in pain on some strange bed, the shoulder she'd so ineptly bandaged agonizingly swollen.

Men died from the effects of wounds far less serious than the one he'd suffered because of her. He could be dead even now, she had realized, and she would have no way of knowing. She had heard nothing in the last week, not even the unsatisfactory travelogue that the banker had originally provided.

I could kill you, John Raven, she thought illogically, *for putting me through this. If only you were here, and I could see to it that you were being cared for. That you were receiving proper treatment. That you were eating the things that would keep you strong through a debilitating fever.* Whatever those things were. Surely Edwards would know what to feed an invalid. Or the cook would. Surely *someone* would know in this vast staff whose wages he paid while he himself lay somewhere, dying perhaps, with no one of his own to look after him.

Her hand trembled suddenly, spilling the wine she'd barely tasted. Edwards was there immediately, offering a cloth. She touched it unthinkingly to the slight dampness of her fingers, and then, unable to bear the direction of her thoughts any longer, she rose suddenly, dropping the cloth onto the table beside her untouched plate.

"Thank you, Edwards," she said.

This was one of the few times she'd dined at home since her husband had left. How different tonight had been from the evenings she'd spent with Raven, discussing a hundred topics, even his businesses. Anything he said or did, she thought in self-mockery, was interesting to her. As sitting alone at his table certainly was not. He had been gone long enough that the chairs he'd ordered removed the morning he'd left had been returned, recovered in an elaborately embroidered fabric that had very closely matched the pattern she'd originally chosen. Standing by the table, arrested suddenly by the memory of the dark stain that had covered the back of his chair that evening, she lowered her head, fighting tears.

"Is something wrong, madam?" Edwards asked in concern.

"No, nothing, thank you," she whispered. Embarrassed

that she had given way to her feelings in front of the servants, Catherine turned and made her way out of the room and to the stairs that would lead to her chamber. And to another night that she would spend wondering where he was.

Sleep eluded her, as she had known it would. Sometime near dawn she slipped out of her bed and tiptoed, still in her night rail, down to the small room that served as Raven's office. She had done this before, sitting through the cold dark hours, her body curled into the chair behind his desk, somehow feeling closer to him here than in any other spot in the vast house in which he had spent so little of his time. Only here did he still seem real to her. And somehow present. And the hours she'd foolishly spent in his small domain this week had been the only comfort she'd found for her unreasoning fears.

The room was dark and silent. She stood a moment in the doorway, knowing that in less than an hour the servants would come upstairs to build up the fires in the kitchen stoves and to prepare breakfast. Just now the house was still deserted and quiet, and she had some minutes that she could stay here alone.

Raven was sitting in the darkness of his office when she entered, her body outlined by the dawn that was breaking through the tall windows of the salon across the hallway. She moved into the doorway, the material of her nightgown falling straight from its high waistline, the line of long, slender leg clearly revealed by its sheerness. She had left her hair unbound, and one dark red strand lay across her shoulder, resting smooth as a silk ribbon over her left breast.

He was unsure at first if he had conjured her here, if she were a phantom created by his desire. He had been savoring the familiarity of the small, dark room and envisioning

Catherine sleeping above, unaware of the battle he had waged during the past month. Unaware of his illness, because he had never intended her to know. The suffering hero was not a role he relished, and he had known from her halting confession that she blamed herself for his injury. He knew her well enough now to know that Catherine would have felt guilty over the result of Amberton's attack. Guilt and probably pity, he'd acknowledged bitterly, had she seen him as he had been only two weeks ago. Neither of those was the emotion he wanted to arouse in his wife.

"Good morning," Raven said softly.

Catherine's heart leapt in response to the quiet voice that spoke out of the shadows. "My God," she whispered, her heartbeat slowing because she had recognized the speaker.

"I didn't mean to frighten you," he said.

"What are you doing here?"

"I had *thought* this is where I live. Or has that changed?"

"No," she said, slowly shaking her head.

Raven was alive. Alive and seated in his accustomed place behind his own desk. The gladness that sang through her veins over that realization was almost impossible to contain. She wanted to laugh out loud. To hug him. Hold him. Touch the dark, warm skin. To be reassured that he was truly all right.

"Nothing has changed," she said instead.

"And in my absence, Catherine, have you taken to wandering around the house in your nightgown like Lady Macbeth?" he asked.

She was very thankful for the teasing quality that she clearly heard in his deep voice. She'd been so afraid she would never hear him tease her again. "Sometimes. And have you taken to sitting in the dark, waiting to frighten visitors to death?"

"Sometimes," he echoed. "Although I can't ever remember having had a visitor at this hour. Is something wrong?''

''I was worried about you.''

''About me? Why would you be worried about me?'' he asked, forcing the amused note into his question.

''Because I hadn't heard from you.''

''Surely Reynolds—''

''He would tell me where you were, but then you didn't come home when you had said you would. You've been gone a whole month, Raven. And this week I heard nothing. I thought you were sick, perhaps, or...'' She paused, afraid somehow to confess the hours she'd spent worrying about him. ''And even Mr. Reynolds's notes were so... He never told me *how* you were,'' she finished plaintively, knowing she was making a fool of herself.

''Why should he?'' Raven asked simply. ''I suppose he didn't realize you were worried. He had no way of knowing your imagination would suggest the delay in my return was because of some...danger,'' he suggested calmly.

She could see the quick gleam of very white teeth despite the shadows that surrounded him. He was laughing at her, she thought in sudden fury. ''I didn't *imagine* the damage Gerald did to you,'' Catherine said hotly. She'd spent nearly a month in the worst sort of anxiety, and he was belittling her concern.

''Damage that Gerald...'' Raven began, as if she'd mentioned some trifling mishap that had slipped his mind. ''Surely, Catherine, you didn't think Amberton had inflicted any lasting injury. I told you it was nothing.'' He prayed the lie was more convincing than it sounded to his own ears.

''I *saw* what he did, Raven. And then the day you left...''

Suddenly, in the face of his denial, Catherine was no longer so certain of her interpretation of the events of that morning. She reviewed the evidence on which her anxiety had been built. His skin had been hot and dry, his eyes too bright, so she had taken that to mean that he was ill, his shoulder inflamed.

"What about the day I left?" Raven's question floated to her out of the shadows, as if he, too, were attempting to remember.

"Your skin was hot," she said, trying to convince herself that she hadn't made up all the carefully constructed clues to the terrifying scenario she'd been living with.

"That *is* one of the side effects of passion."

"Passion?" she repeated. At least, she thought bitterly, she hadn't been wrong about *that*.

"I've never denied that I have carnal needs," he reminded her. "I'm afraid it had simply been too long since I'd taken the opportunity to satisfy them." He hoped that in her innocence she wouldn't recognize the absurdity of that as an excuse for fever.

"Then what happened that morning…"

"My apologies, Catherine. You may put that lapse down to blood loss. And to too prolonged an abstinence. I hope you'll forgive me for kissing you without your permission. It won't happen again. I intend to take steps to guarantee that it doesn't." Raven hoped she couldn't see in the darkness the involuntary lift of his lips that promise invoked.

"Steps to prevent such *prolonged* abstinence?" she asked bitterly.

"Yes," he confirmed. It was a simple statement of fact. That was one of the decisions he'd made during the tiresome weeks of his recovery. Despite the promise of freedom he'd given to convince Catherine to wed him, he intended somehow to court and to win his own wife. To make her want him with the same fierce desire that moved through his body whenever he even thought of her. That

was not against their contract. And it had been too prolonged an abstinence. Too damned prolonged.

"I see," she whispered.

No, my darling, you certainly don't see, Raven thought,
but you will. Soon, I promise you, you will. Aloud he simply
reminded her, "I *have* rendered my apology."

"Yes, you have," she agreed softly. How dare he apol-
ogize for kissing her? *Damn you, damn you, damn you*, she
thought fiercely. *How can it have meant nothing to you?*
And she wondered suddenly what his mistress was like.
Was she beautiful? Witty and charming? *Damn you, John
Raven*, she thought again.

"And what have you been doing in my absence? Besides
imagining me ill?"

Again she believed she could hear his amusement.

"I've managed to entertain myself," she forced herself
to answer, but the lie sounded brittle after the seriousness
of their conversation. "London in the summer's not nearly
so dull as everyone pretends. I think it's become fashionable to deplore the lack of society and adopt an air of ennui.
Pretending boredom makes people believe you're accustomed to far more exciting activities than the one you're
engaged in."

"You're probably right," he said.

Raven certainly sounded bored with what she was babbling about, and she didn't blame him. "Did you just arrive?" she asked, trying to get back to some topic that
made sense. The meaningless chatter her cicisbei found so
charming apparently left her husband cold.

"I arrived in London last night," he said. "It was very
late, so I decided not to disturb the household."

"Where did you spend the night?" she asked without
thinking.

There was a small silence from the figure hidden in the
shadows on the other side of the desk. Raven certainly

couldn't tell her he had stood for hours in the darkness of the street below, looking up at the window he knew to be hers.

"I'm sorry. You needn't answer that," Catherine advised suddenly, realizing where he must have spent the night.

"I told you that you might ask me anything, and that I'd never lie to you. Those rules have not changed."

"You don't have to explain. I'm quite capable of imagining that part of your itinerary on my own," she said coldly.

"Forgive me, Catherine, if I'm wrong, but you seem somewhat annoyed that I'm home. Shall I find some other business to call me away? I promise not to interfere in whatever flirtation you've undertaken to keep you entertained."

He wondered with sharp, cold jealousy if she *had* found someone in the month he'd been fighting to live, desperately determined, despite his body's infuriating weakness, to return to her. To fulfill his vow.

"Flirtation?" she repeated softly, thinking how different the image called up by his choice of words was to the nightmares she had been living with. "I haven't been engaged in a *flirtation*." She could hear the bitterness in her voice and knew that Raven was astute enough to detect it, too.

"Then you *must* have been bored," he said teasingly.

"I thought you were ill. I have been imagining..." She paused, angry that she'd admitted what he'd accused her of.

"I instructed Reynolds to keep you informed. I'm sorry if you've been distressed. It was never my intent to worry you."

"Of course," she said. All her concern had been for naught. She'd thought he was dying, and instead he had been arranging for the satisfaction of the carnal needs he had never even bothered to hide. "I apologize for interrupting your solitude."

"You sound almost angry that I'm not lingering at death's door. I told you I'm accustomed to taking care of myself."

"Yes, of course," she said calmly, sure now that he was belittling her concern for him. She was beyond anger. As he'd reminded her, he had never given her a reason to believe he needed or wanted her. "I should have known that you'll never need anyone's care. Especially mine," she said.

She turned and left the office, and despite the fact that she'd managed to have the last word, it was not a very satisfying one. Raven was back and that, too, had turned out to be far less satisfying than she had been imagining.

Raven took a deep breath and then expelled it. He didn't seem to be very adept at courtship. Of course, he'd never before undertaken to make a woman love him. He knew far more about iron and steel, about coal and mining, and far too little about courting a woman like Catherine.

Despite the knowledge that he'd badly mishandled this morning's reunion, eventually he allowed a slight, controlled smile, still safely hidden by the surrounding darkness. She had worried about him. Sometime between the routs and the balls and the rides in Hyde Park with the elegant Reginalds and Geralds, she'd worried about her inconvenient husband. In spite of the fact that Raven had never wanted Catherine's concern, would have rejected it had she expressed it, there was something very satisfying about that thought.

It was another chip on his side of the table, added to the two that had given him hope through his illness: she was already his wife, and somewhere, an ocean away, a fragile, indomitable old woman was sending up powerful prayers on his behalf.

The odds are definitely not in your favor, Catherine, my darling, Raven thought, allowing his small smile to widen.

Chapter Nine

Catherine managed to avoid any prolonged contact with her husband for the next several days. Raven was apparently occupied catching up on the correspondence that had arrived in his absence, spending hours closed up in that confined office. *Her* social calendar was really quite full; she made sure of that.

She saw him once in the front hall. She had been on her way to a drum, and he had bowed to her as she passed him in the foyer, as if they had been the merest acquaintances. Again that small smile had played briefly over his lips, but at the spark of anger she couldn't quite prevent from leaping into her eyes, he had made an effort at controlling his amusement and had made his very proper bow. As if she were a stranger instead of his wife. She'd taken satisfaction in knowing that, arrayed as she'd been in a new and daringly cut gown of bronze satin, she had looked her best. The fury that had resulted from that encounter had carried her through the next day, righteously determined not even to think about her husband, who was, she thought, probably busy planning his next *convenient* visit to his mistress. Whoever she was.

Catherine listened to the gossip that flowed around her

with a great deal more interest since Raven's return, knowing that if he *had* brought his demirep up to town, she'd be certain to hear of it. Someone would maliciously let it slip, but so far she had heard nothing and could only speculate on Raven's taste in women. An activity she found herself engaged in far too frequently for her own peace of mind.

Using Edwards as his messenger, Raven had asked her to arrange another dinner party and had even suggested this time some of those who should be invited. The invitations had already gone out, and she was sitting at a small table downstairs discussing the menu with the butler one morning, little more than a week after her husband's return, when he entered the room.

Under the observant eye of her majordomo, she couldn't retreat and was forced to endure the quick touch of Raven's lips against her forehead that he employed as his form of greeting. She even managed to smile up into those crystalline eyes, which clearly revealed that their owner was well aware of her true reaction to his almost paternal kiss. So different, she thought with regret, from the last time he'd kissed her.

She lowered her gaze to her list of instructions, trying to hide the pain of that memory from his discerning eyes. He greeted Edwards with his accustomed familiarity, and then, unbelieving, she heard him dismiss the butler. Anticipation tightened her stomach, and she fought to control her breathing.

"I wanted to talk to you," he said. "I hope I haven't interrupted something that can't be finished at a later time."

"Perhaps you should have asked that *before* you sent Edwards away," she said challengingly. She glanced up from her pretended contemplation of her list, believing she had her emotions well in hand.

"I'm sorry," Raven said. "Would you like for me to call him back and postpone our discussion until later?"

"No," she admitted, deliberately directing her attention again to her list. "It really doesn't matter. There's nothing here that can't be dealt with later. I simply like to have everything organized and every eventuality planned for."

"No surprises," he suggested. She could hear the smile in his voice, but knew that if she looked up, his face would be controlled. "You don't like surprises."

She did glance up at that. "No, I don't suppose I do. Not about a dinner party. But you don't leave anything to chance, either. You don't seem to like surprises any better than I."

"I don't know about that," he said, and he did smile then. "After all, I married you."

"And I surprise you?"

"Almost constantly."

"Because we're from such different backgrounds."

"Perhaps you're right. I had begun to think, however, that it was because you are not what I had expected your particular background to produce. You're not the typical product of your class, Catherine."

"I don't understand," she said truthfully. "If I've failed in some way to live up to what you require, you have only to tell me." She could feel the blush creeping into her cheeks. She had not really expected his censure for her foolish actions concerning Amberton at this late date.

"You haven't failed my expectations in any way. On the contrary, you've far exceeded them."

"Then you're not angry with me?" she asked, daring to hope that what had happened because of her foolishness in allowing Gerald to trick her might finally be forgiven if not forgotten.

"No, I'm not angry. As a matter of fact, I had thought,

since I've been back, that I had done something to make you angry, but I can't decide what it was.''

Apologized for kissing me. Put it down to blood loss. Brought your mistress up to town. Ignored me. The true reasons for her anger ran fleetingly through her head, but she couldn't admit to any of those, so she was left at a loss, an unaccustomed loss for someone usually so quick-witted in awkward social situations. And this one was very awkward. What did a wife say to a husband she was madly in love with when he admitted that he would seek her embrace only if giddy from a loss of blood?

"Catherine?" Raven asked softly.

"I'm not angry," she lied. There was really nothing she could legitimately chide him with. He had followed the rules of their agreement, with one very memorable exception. She was the one who wanted this marriage to become something they'd never agreed to, something he'd never indicated he wanted. Her fingers touched the list she'd been discussing with Edwards before Raven had interrupted. This was the only role he wished her to play in his life. He had certainly denied her any other.

"I don't think you need be so concerned with this. The dinner is still several days away," he said, taking the list from her hand and putting it firmly to the side. He pulled out the chair across the small table from where she was sitting and sat down in it. Her eyes must have expressed her surprise, because he smiled at her.

"Play cards with me," he said.

"What?"

"Cards. Whatever you played with Amberton that night. Whatever game he beat you at."

"Piquet," she answered unthinkingly. And then she asked, shaking her head, "Why should we play cards?" It was the middle of the morning. She had a luncheon engagement that she wasn't even dressed for. And Raven always spent his mornings busily engaged with his business affairs. And now...

"Because you lost that night. And that loss resulted in an unpleasant situation for you. I don't intend for that to happen again. Not if I can help it. I told you I'm very good with numbers. I thought I might teach you a few tricks."

"An unpleasant situation for *me?*" she asked pointedly, thinking of what Gerald had done to Raven.

His lips tightened slightly at her reminder, but he admitted, "And for me, if you will."

"I didn't mean for you to be hurt," she said, meeting his eyes. It was the most honest thing she'd ever said to him.

"I know. That was my own stupidity. Edwards told me you really were quite concerned while I was away. I'm sorry Reynolds didn't do a better job of reassuring you."

"I told you to write," she whispered.

"Yes, you did. Is that why you're angry?"

"I'm not angry."

"Liar," he said, and she remembered the last time he'd accused her of that. Her eyes fell before the certainty in his, but he ignored her lie and began to deal out their hands very professionally onto the small table.

"You have to calculate your odds," he said. "Not only with the play, but with the discards. Especially with discards," he advised. "Show me your hand."

He put his fingers over hers, which had automatically picked up the cards from the pile before her. Again their callused warmth left her breathless, causing strange sensations to move uncomfortably, yet enticingly, through her lower body. As if, she thought in wonder, as if he were somehow touching her there.

As his patient instruction continued over the next half hour, she found herself watching his hands, so dark and beautiful. Graceful. And his mouth.

"Think, Catherine," he commanded, and suddenly she came back to reality, back from the image of his hands moving against her body with the same sure skill with which he touched the pasteboards scattered between them.

She glanced at her cards, trying to remember what he'd told her, trying desperately to do the calculations in her head. She was a very good card player normally, but she had always relied on her instincts and luck. The things he had told her, while she was still in some condition to listen, had made a great deal of sense. Raven was, as he had claimed, very good with numbers. Taking a deep breath, she selected what she hoped was the right discard for the situation he'd set out and put it on the table.

"Brilliant," he said.

She looked up to find him smiling at her.

"You really are a very fine player," he continued. "I can't imagine how you managed to let Amberton beat you."

"I was thinking about how angry you'd be if you discovered I'd gone upstairs with him," she said truthfully. "My mind wasn't on the game at all."

"Never play cards if you don't play to win. And that takes concentration as well as skill."

"I know," she said.

"And I would have had no right to be angry with you. We have an agreement."

"I know," she said again, but she was afraid the bitterness had shown through despite her ready agreement with what he'd said.

"And I'm not easily angered," he added.

"It's a good thing," she answered, finally smiling at him. "I must be a sore trial to your patience. Getting you stabbed and then having the nerve to worry about you. What inexplicable behavior from your wife." She knew she was challenging him.

"Inexplicable, perhaps, only to me," he offered softly. "I told you that I'm unaccustomed to anyone worrying about my well-being. I honestly didn't know how to react. I hope you'll forgive me for not dealing with your concern any better than I did the morning of my return."

"You made fun of me," she accused. "For worrying about you. And I thought I had just cause. I didn't have any way of knowing that you're indestructible." His laughter was quick and soft, and she felt her lips move upward in an answering smile.

"I didn't intend to make fun of you," he said, taking her hand. "I intended to reassure you that I was all right. I'm sorry it came out wrong."

His hand was warm and hard and incredibly strong, like the man himself. And feeling that strength, she again felt very foolish for worrying about him. He did seem indestructible.

"Will you forgive me for that, too?" he asked.

I'd forgive you almost anything, she thought, her eyes still on her small hand resting in that strong dark one. "Yes," she whispered.

Raven's fingers tightened briefly over hers, a quick squeeze, and then he released her. He rose from the table, and she looked up in surprise.

"Are you leaving?" she asked. She was a little disconcerted by how strong her sense of disappointment was.

"I have work to do," he said, smiling down at her. "Not all of us are persons of leisure in this household. Someone must make the money to pay for all that folderol you manage to purchase every month. Reynolds says we shall soon have to wheel in your bills in a barrow."

Since she had spent almost nothing in the month he'd been away and very little since his return, she knew he was teasing her.

"Liar," she said in answer, and when his slight smile widened, she felt her heart turn over.

"Be careful or I'll become a slacker and let our fortunes go to rack and ruin. I'll spend the time I should be working playing cards with my wife or some such shocking activity."

"Should I worry?" she challenged, smiling back at him.

"As you please, Catherine. I'll never chide you for that again. As a matter of fact..." he said, and then he paused, looking down into her eyes. And he was no longer smiling. "I found the idea that you'd worried about me quite pleasant. Far more pleasant than I could have imagined it might be."

His tone was too serious for the discussion they'd been having, and she had no answer for what he'd just suggested. She finally began to breathe again, and then he reached down to touch her neck, his fingers moving slowly upward to a spot behind her ear. She had no idea what he was doing, but her head tilted automatically to lean against his hand. She wasn't even aware that her eyelids had dropped in response to his touch.

"Did you lose this, Catherine?" he asked. She opened her eyes as he removed his hand from her earlobe. "Your ear seems a strange place to keep something this valuable."

His fingers turned over as gracefully as a magician's, as if practicing some sleight-of-hand, to reveal on their outstretched tips a large blue gem. Its light hue was thrown into prominence by the dark gold of his skin. She blinked at the sudden, almost magical appearance of a stone that size. His hand, she was sure, had held nothing at all when he had first touched her.

"What in the world? Where did that come from?"

"Out of your ear?" Raven suggested helpfully.

"No," she denied, laughing. "That is certainly nothing I've ever seen before in my life."

He held it before her like an offering. The jewel caught the light in a strangely glowing way. Not like the glitter of a faceted stone. It was truly like nothing she'd ever seen before.

"Perhaps you should take a closer look. Just to be certain you don't recognize it," he said.

Catherine tore her gaze away from the pale depths of the gem to find the same compelling blue echoed in Raven's eyes, surrounded by their sweep of long dark lashes and his golden skin. Her breath caught and a blaze of some sensation, powerful and sensuous, moved through her stomach and then lower, searing deep and hot into areas of her body she'd never been so conscious of in her entire life. Intimate and seductive, the feeling burned and curled, and she wanted her husband in ways she'd never dreamed she could even think about a man. In response to her body's unbelievably physical reaction, she quickly glanced back at the stone resting on his fingers, trying to hide whatever might have been revealed in her eyes.

Her hand was very pale compared to the one she touched in order to pick up the gem he held out to her. To give her trembling fingers something to do, she lifted the stone to catch the light pouring in through the tall windows of the small salon and became aware for the first time of the pale streaks that marked the center of the orb she held. Like a star caught in the perfect blue of the sky that surrounded it.

"What is it?" she asked, her voice thready and breathless.

"It's called a star sapphire."

"I've never seen anything like it," she whispered, turning it back and forth in the sunlight.

"They're very rare. And, I think, very beautiful."

"Where did you find it?"

"In India. Kashmir. Beginner's luck, they told me."

Unable to resist, she glanced up and said teasingly, "I told you it was all a matter of luck."

He laughed, and she held out the stone to him. "It's very beautiful."

"I'm glad you like it," he answered politely, making no effort to take it from her. "I would have had it made up, but I wasn't sure whether you'd prefer a ring or a pendant."

"You're giving it to me?"

"Of course."

"But why? I don't understand. If you found it and it's very rare—"

Raven interrupted. "Perhaps it *is* all a matter of luck. Very rare," he repeated softly. "And I found it."

Aware that his words were intended to mean more than a simple repetition of hers, she closed her fingers suddenly around the stone.

"It's like your eyes," she said, unable to prevent the expression of the ridiculously romantic thought she'd had. Somehow the ease that had grown between them in the last few moments invited that very personal comment.

For a long time Raven made no response to what she had said, and eventually she felt a blush begin to creep into her cheeks. He was watching her with those beautiful eyes she'd just childishly remarked upon. *Like a lovesick school-girl,* she thought in disgust. But since he'd already admitted he thought her a child, she supposed it didn't matter how much more foolishly she behaved. Where Raven was concerned, she really had no pride left at all.

"Thank you," he said finally. When he turned and walked across the room, the Oriental carpet softening the sound of that decisive stride, Catherine closed her eyes. Finally, a reprieve from the intense examination his had just made. And when she opened them again, she also opened her hand and looked down into the depths of the priceless stone he'd just given her. He had presented it without any ceremony and with no fanciful words about his regard for her, it was true. He had, instead, plucked it from behind her ear like a conjurer at a fair. But he had given it to her.

And she thought again, looking down into its depths, that it really *was* very much like his eyes.

"But you can't believe that the workers are in favor of these innovations you're proposing as their salvation. You have only to look at the machine-smashing rampages of the Luddites," the Earl of Devon argued vehemently.

"Because they don't understand the machines' potential for improving their lives. They see them as taking jobs, not as—" Raven began to explain, only to be interrupted by Lord Elliot.

"Why shouldn't they? For most of them that has certainly proved to be the case. Jobs lost, families destroyed, land that could be in crop production used for factories."

"Surely you're not attempting to blame the lack of available farmland on the manufacturers? I should think you would more properly blame the greed of the landowners for that situation."

Her husband was treading on dangerous ground there, Catherine thought, since the gentlemen gathered around his dinner table were themselves large landowners.

"Enclosure, I suppose," scoffed Devon. "An old ogre."

"An old problem," Raven agreed. "One far more responsible for the dissolution of the family than the factories are. There they work together, I'm afraid, from the youngest to the eldest."

"Children?" Catherine asked. The ongoing debate had been waged with little contribution from the ladies. They had apparently decided this rehash of a favorite masculine subject would simply have to be endured.

"As soon as they are able to pick up lint from the floor in the textile mills," Raven answered, glancing at her.

Catherine had seldom taken an active part in these discussions, which were as lively, and often as heated, as those in Parliament, but she knew her dinner parties had become very popular because of them. No one seemed to mind what topics were introduced and threshed out over the exquisitely prepared courses her chef produced, the debates fueled by the flow of Edwards's carefully selected wines. She had been instructed by her husband to provide the best for those fortunate enough to be included on her guest lists these last few weeks, and she had done so unstintingly. And now an invitation to dine at the home of John Raven was one of the most sought after of the Little Season.

"It seems so cruel," she said, picturing such a childhood.

"Twelve- or fourteen-hour days. And the mines are far worse," her husband said.

"Mines?" repeated Lady Avondale. "Surely there are no children working in the mines."

"The smaller the better," Raven acknowledged. "The drifts are too narrow for the men. Women and children are employed to push the loosened coal up the inclines to the surface. And the owners prefer children because they can pay them less than a quarter of what an adult would make."

"But why would parents allow their children to go down into the mines?" Catherine asked, shuddering slightly as she pictured that dark, narrow tunnel Raven described.

"And if your choice were that or starvation for the entire family? What option do you believe you would have?"

"And your mines employ machines to do those jobs?" Catherine asked, almost forgetting the others listening to their exchange. As always, she was fascinated by the ideas her husband suggested.

"In several of the mines I own around Durham the coal is brought to the surface by machine."

"Then *you've* put workers out of their jobs," Devon pronounced, satisfied that he'd made his point.

"We've put *children* out of their jobs," Raven said patiently. "We've sent the children home."

"And the wages those children were bringing in? How have your workers endured that loss of income, Mr. Raven?" Lord Russell asked. There was simply interest in his question.

"Those particular mines are more productive than the ones around them—because of the machines, certainly. They're faster and they don't tire as the children do. And perhaps because the miners don't have to worry about their offspring. Because of that increased production, I've been able to raise wages."

"And I suppose your profits have remained as high?" Devon asked with sarcastic surety.

"No. To be honest, they've not," Raven acknowledged. "But they *have* been sufficient to allow me to undertake other innovations that will, in the near future, make profits even greater than they were before."

"That's well and good for a man of your resources, but there are owners who don't have the capital to bear the resulting loss of profit. What should they do?" Russell asked.

"Recognize that their ultimate success rests upon the efforts of their workers. On their workers' success."

"Bah," Devon said with disgust.

"Because the better paid they are, the stronger the workers are, the freer from disease, and the harder they're able to work. And the more interested they are in the success of what they're doing, in learning how to operate the machines that will eventually, I admit, take over some of the jobs. But by that time, the machines will also have allowed new mines to be dug, in seams that are now inaccessible. New foundries will be built to produce more and better iron. Iron rails and iron bridges will be built across England, gentlemen, and there will be a lot of manpower required to operate the machines that will build them.''

"I'm not such a skeptic as Devon, Mr. Raven, but I must confess that I can see no practical application of the rails and the locomotives you're so set on,'' said Russell.

"They are already being used to take coal from the mines to the canals and to the rivers, and I personally intend to run rails from my mines all the way to the foundries.''

"But why undertake that expense when the canals can transport your coal as easily, canals that are already in place?''

"Because the transport they offer is limited to the speed at which a horse can walk. And because of size differences, with a time-consuming transfer of cargo at the lock.''

"And by rail?'' Elliot asked, his fascination again evident.

Catherine was well accustomed to the spell Raven's conviction wove over his listeners. He'd shared his ideas with anyone who had professed the slightest interest. And to give the men of her class credit, more of them had been interested than she'd imagined before she'd seen the effect of Raven's words.

"Locomotives already exist that can run at over fifteen miles an hour. Compare that to the canals, gentlemen, and I think you'll see why I'm willing to go to the expense of building the rails to carry my coal and iron,'' Raven said.

"But you said the rails would spread all across England,'' Catherine reminded him. "Not just to carry coal?''

"To carry people. And anything else that needs to be transported quickly from one place to another.''

"People? Even women?'' she asked, smiling as if amused at the ridiculous idea of riding on a locomotive.

"I'll buy you a ticket on the first passenger run,'' her husband offered. "I assure you, you'll be perfectly safe.''

"Perfectly safe? But how disappointing," she said, smiling at him. The tension that had grown with the intense discussion was released in the appreciative laughter that ran around the table.

Catherine took the opportunity their amusement offered to signal Edwards to replenish the gentlemen's glasses, and she found herself again watching her husband's hand caress the fine hollowware.

"We're behind times in implementing that idea in this country," Raven suggested after the laughter had died down.

"Behind?" Viscount Templeton commented. "I thought Stephenson invented the thing."

"Trevithick, Hedley, Stephenson. Englishmen, or Scots, Welsh. But if we're not careful it will be the Americans who make the quickest use of locomotives. And they have as many iron and coal deposits as we do here."

"They're ahead of us in employing the rails?" Elliot questioned.

"More than ten years ago an American, Colonel John Stevens, acquired a charter to build a railway across New Jersey," Raven answered, his eyes on his glass rather than on the questioner.

"And did he build it?" the viscount asked.

"He did not. Not because the technology was lacking, but because of a lack of money. He couldn't find enough backers willing to invest what was, I must admit, a great deal of money."

"If you thought it to be a great deal, I'm sure the rest of us should be staggered," Lady Avondale suggested with a touch of asperity.

Raven smiled at Lady Avondale, and at the laughter her comment had aroused, without a trace of discomfiture.

"Certainly more than one man could afford to bear," he

agreed. "No matter the anticipated return. And that is perhaps where we have the Americans at a disadvantage."

"How so?" Lord Avondale questioned.

"Capital. *That* we have in abundance. And if enough people, gentlemen who can afford the investment, were convinced of the feasibility of rail transport, of its importance to the industrial development of Britain, and more importantly of the potential for gain it will offer them as investors…" Raven let the suggestion trail off.

Catherine knew that it was a compliment to his powers of persuasion that for several seconds no one spoke into the silence that fell. They were thinking about what he had said. And she knew that was all that he'd intended. For now, at least.

She glanced at him and found those remarkable blue eyes resting on her face. His lips moved ever so slightly in amusement at her expression. She had sat in on this same discussion, or one very like it, on several occasions, and no matter how many times he introduced these ideas, he always made believers of his listeners. Perhaps, she thought in fairness to her husband, because he himself believed so strongly in what he had just said. One dark, winged brow lifted, and knowing that was her signal, she rose.

"Ladies," she said, smiling openly across the table at her husband and then at the other gentlemen who were beginning to stand. "I believe we should leave the men to their port and their locomotives. I, for one, have heard all the steam I can bear for one evening."

Smiling slightly, her husband bowed to her, and amid the masculine laughter, Catherine swept the ladies out of the way of whatever else he might need to discuss with these very potential investors. This part of the evening was his business, and she was more than willing to leave him to it.

Chapter Ten

It was much later, as she sat before her dressing table, that Catherine decided she would finally share with Raven something she had been considering for weeks. The idea had grown more compelling with each dinner party at which she had listened to her husband's vision of the England he was sure would develop within the next few years, and finally she'd decided to act on it.

She knew Raven had been successful in finding men who were interested in supplying the capital he needed to begin the rail project, but not as many as he had hoped. He had acknowledged that disappointment to her on one of the few occasions their schedules had allowed them to dine together. And thinking of the little time she'd managed to spend with him in these last weeks, she sighed. It seemed nothing would come of the rapport they'd shared the morning he'd given her the sapphire.

She wore it often, always receiving admiring comments on the beauty of the stone, which she had had mounted as a pendant surrounded by diamonds. When she had come downstairs tonight, her husband's gaze had rested briefly on the sapphire as it lay just above the valley formed by the uplift of her breasts. His eyes had traced slowly over the skin exposed by the low neckline and had deliberately moved up to meet hers. There had been again something of the emotions of the morning he'd given her the jewel, and then he had turned to greet the first of their guests.

Catherine had long been accustomed to the adulation of the most eligible men of her world, and even Raven had seemed to find her decorative enough to be his hostess. But perhaps, she acknowledged disconsolately, it had really been only her position that had attracted him and nothing about her person. Looking at the woman reflected in the glass, she found herself wondering again, the most bitter of pastimes, about his mistress.

Knowing the futility of that train of thought, she rose decisively and found the silk wrapper her abigail had put out for her on the bed when she'd left. She drew it on and, without allowing herself time to reconsider, left the safe confines of her own room and walked the short distance to Raven's.

She lived in the same house with him. They had eaten dinner together surrounded by people who assumed that they were man and wife. They had even shared some brief moments of intimacy.

You may put that down to blood loss, my dear, Raven had told her, dismissing one of the most intimate of those memories. Catherine remembered also that he had sent her away the night she'd kissed him, the night she'd dressed his shoulder and had been allowed to touch the golden skin that shifted under her hands like warm velvet. But sometimes it seemed there was something in his eyes, something hidden in the lucid and open gaze, that made her wonder if he, too, spent sleepless nights remembering those moments.

She tapped lightly on the door to the small room he had selected as his own when he had chosen this house. She had expected to hear his voice, a spoken invitation to enter, but instead the door opened suddenly, and Raven was standing before her. He had taken off his coat and waistcoat, and his shirt was unbuttoned, revealing an expanse of golden chest and a tantalizing, mouth-drying glimpse of a flat, ridged stomach.

"Catherine?" he said, and she could hear his surprise.

"May I come in?" she asked.

The pause between her question and his answer was slight, but definite. She knew the terms of their agreement, and they didn't include midnight visits. And he had certainly never indicated that he wanted to modify those terms. She didn't understand why she kept putting herself in such a position that he would be forced to rebuff her.

"Of course," Raven said, moving away from the doorway and opening it to allow her passage. He had enough trouble keeping his hands off her during the somewhat formal moments they shared at dinner or at the theater. He wasn't sure his control was up to the challenge of entertaining his wife—his enticingly disrobed wife—in the intimate privacy of his own bedroom.

Catherine's eyes were drawn to Raven's disordered bed. The evening coat he'd removed had been tossed carelessly across the foot, and a glass of what appeared to be brandy stood on the small table beside it. A ledger lay facedown on the tumbled coverings, and from the arrangement of the pillows, she knew he must have been stretched out, studying it, when she'd knocked.

They stood facing each other for a moment, and she was again very conscious of the power of his body. She had to force her brain to dredge up the words that she had come to say.

"I'd like to invest in your railway," she said.

Some emotion disturbed the careful calm into which he had arranged his features while he'd waited for her revelation of why she'd come to his room in the middle of the night. And she realized only with that lapse of control what he must have been thinking when she showed up at his door.

"In my railway?" he repeated with a touch of disbelief.

"You *are* still seeking investors? That's why you were sounding out the men you invited here tonight?"

"If my tactics are that obvious, I had better rethink my plan of action," he agreed, amusement threading his admission.

"That obvious?" she repeated. "Obvious enough that even your *wife* knows what you're up to?"

"I didn't mean that as an insult," he protested, "but..."

"Your intent isn't obvious, I suppose, unless you've seen the same performance a number of times. As I have."

His laughter was quick and self-directed. "If *you* think it's a performance—" he began.

"Oh, I don't doubt you mean what you say. I'm here because I know you do. It's just that when you have the same discussion at every dinner, a discussion that leads to the same conclusion, it makes me believe it's by design. Eventually you'll find enough people interested that you won't need any more backers. And I wanted to ask you, before that happens, to let me in."

"You want to become one of my partners?"

"If you'll let me."

Again there was a pause, and finally, smiling, Raven indicated the chair he'd sat in as she'd bandaged his shoulder. "Then sit down, Catherine, and let's discuss business."

Always business, she thought with a trace of disappointment. But this was why she'd come.

When she was seated, Raven picked up the tumbler from the bedside table and arranged himself on the edge of the disheveled bed, waiting for her to begin.

"I have a trust. A rather...substantial trust. From my grandmother. It has just come under my control, and I thought I might use that money to invest in what you're doing.''

"Have you mentioned this plan to your father?"

"I told him what I intend to do, of course. But it *is* my money, Raven."

"And how did the duke react?"

She smiled. "Do you remember the day you told him you intended to marry me, no matter what his feelings were?"

"Vividly," he said.

The scar that had marked his cheekbone had faded, but Catherine knew he would always carry that reminder of her father's fury.

"I think what you saw that day would be comparable. Except this time he threatened to disinherit me."

"Do you mean he hasn't already?" Raven asked.

She could hear his genuine surprise that what she had told him would be the inevitable result of their elopement had not come to pass. She knew then that Raven had never even checked on the status of her inheritance, that he truly was as unconcerned about the potential wealth she would bring to the marriage as he'd maintained he was at the beginning.

"And the duke suggested I had coerced you into investing your money in a very risky endeavor," Raven continued.

"But you're investing," she reminded him.

"*Not,* I hope, everything I have. Not if I can find enough men of vision. Enough men willing to form the partnership it will take to carry out a design of this magnitude."

"I'm simply suggesting that I become one of the partners. If the size of my trust is comparable to what you're asking others to invest," she said.

"It's not the amount of your investment that I object to.

It's the idea of letting you risk everything that belongs to you personally in this scheme.''

"What's so objectionable about that?"

"I can imagine your father told you. Probably in great detail," Raven suggested with a slight laugh. "If the railway venture fails, every aspect of my holdings will be affected. If that happens, your trust fund looms more important as insurance that you won't be left destitute if anything were to happen to me. If anything prevents my rebuilding."

"But you're not going to fail," she argued. "And I hardly think my father would allow me to wander the streets of London if you did. Or even if something happened to you. It seems there are too many disasters that would have to occur for me to be in any real danger of destitution."

"If I lose my investment—" he began.

"Then you'll start over. You'll make *more* money," she insisted. "I think you told me it's all a matter of numbers."

"And if something happens to me before I can accomplish this financial rebirth you're so sure I'll be able to bring off?"

"Do you have enemies I'm not aware of?" she asked, smiling. "You seem determined to make an early end."

"If I have enemies, I'm also unaware of them."

"You seem healthy. And not so *very* old," she teased.

"Thank you," he said sardonically, with a slight deepening of the indentations at the corners of his lips. "However, I think you should keep your trust fund, Catherine. If anything happens to me, you may need it. If it becomes mixed with my capital, or if you become one of the partners, everything you own will be taken to repay my debts if the rail venture fails. If anything happens to my businesses or to me personally—"

"I thought you were indestructible," she said. Raven was giving her the same advice her father had, but without the coldly sarcastic fury that characterized her father's every reaction to anything that involved her husband. Raven was as bent on protecting her as the duke, despite the fact that she was sure her husband could use the money she was offering.

"Only from the Ambertons of the world," he answered lightly. "To other dangers, I'm as vulnerable as the rest."

"You don't seem very vulnerable to me." Catherine was aware of the personal note that had crept into her voice. She didn't seem to be able to conduct a business discussion with Raven. Her emotions always interfered. As they were now.

"Or very aged?" he said, his lips lifting slightly with his amusement. "Thank you, Catherine, for that vote of confidence."

There was the briefest pause. She knew she should leave. She had made her request and had been given all the logical reasons why he wouldn't accept what she had offered. And this business meeting should be over. But she didn't want to go. His eyes were on his brandy and not on her. He didn't want her here, she supposed. He probably wanted to get back to the fascination of those endless numbers that the open ledger represented.

"And I still seem very young to you?" she asked instead, prolonging the bittersweet indulgence of spending time with him.

Raven glanced up at the seriousness of her question.

"I've not been forgiven for that remark, I take it?"

"No," she agreed, but she smiled at him.

"Perhaps young wasn't what I should have said. Innocent. Protected. And none of those are meant as criticisms. They are what every eighteen-year-old girl should be."

"Nineteen," she corrected.

"You should have told me. I've missed a birthday."

"You were away."

"And you were imagining…"

"That you were dying."

"And that you'd be a nineteen-year-old widow."

"A very wealthy nineteen-year-old widow," she said, her smile widening. At his soft laughter, she knew this was what she had wanted, what she had come for tonight—his attention. His teasing response. For whatever happened to his eyes when he relaxed enough to laugh. She had been so hungry for him. A hopeless case, she thought, mocking herself. I'm in love with my own husband and am flirting very openly with him.

"And since you're not a wealthy widow yet, what can I do to make up for my failure to recognize such a milestone?"

She shook her head. "I didn't tell you for that. I'm not angling for a birthday present. I only wanted you to know that I'm not *quite* so young as I was when you married me," she said.

"I told you that wasn't a criticism," he answered.

He was still relaxed, and not unwilling now, she thought, to allow their conversation to continue.

"What did you do with the children?" she asked.

"I beg your pardon? Have we lost our children?"

She laughed at the teasing quality of his question, knowing his quick mind would have easily followed her tangent. "From the mines. Where do they spend the hours when their parents are working?"

He glanced down at his glass and then, lifting it, drained the liquid it held. When he'd done that, he looked at her again, meeting her eyes. His were cleared of laughter.

"I opened schools. They go to school until their parents come home. I'm also phasing out the role of the women in the operation of my mines, and I can imagine what the Earl of Devon would say to that ridiculous practice."

"And you pay for the schools. And the teachers."

He nodded, waiting for her reaction. Her mockery, she supposed. No wonder he hadn't mentioned this tonight. She, too, could imagine what Devon would say. What almost any of those men who had dined here tonight would say to that confession.

"They'll think you're mad," she warned.

"Hopefully they won't ever find out."

"That they've invested money in the schemes of a madman?"

"Are you going to tell them?" he questioned, but she knew that he was again teasing her. He'd never have told her unless he believed that she wouldn't be as appalled as his partners.

"No, but if they find out, you may need my trust fund, after all. And what do you plan to do for an encore to this insanity?"

"I was thinking about requiring safety inspections."

"A shocking waste of money. You act as if you think miners should survive the experience," she answered, smiling at him.

"That *would* be a novel approach in Britain."

"Certainly too novel for the Earl of Devon, but I don't suppose he'll ever become one of your backers."

"He's in for seventy thousand pounds. You'd be surprised what the promise of profit will do to a man's scruples."

"I probably would at that," she agreed.

She rose, knowing that although she might want to stay, that didn't mean he was having the same response to her presence. "Thank you for listening to me. And please know that if you ever need Grandmother's money, I am more than willing to invest in your ventures."

"Thank you, Catherine," he said, standing also.

"Good night," she said, turning toward the doorway.

"Do you still ride in the mornings?"

"Most mornings," she answered, turning back to him and savoring the promising direction of that inquiry.

"Do you plan to ride tomorrow?"

"I hadn't thought. But I suppose so, weather permitting. Would you like to join me?"

"If you're willing to have company."

"You're more than welcome. Do you still have the black?"

"Driving the grooms wild. I really should exercise him."

"At seven," she said, naming an hour far earlier than she usually rode. She knew Raven to be an early riser.

"Sleeping in?" he inquired silkily.

"Six, but not a moment before or you may ride alone," she amended, slipping through the door.

Behind her she heard his laughter. She was still smiling when she reached her room and chose the most flattering of her habits. And still smiling when she turned down the lamp.

The fog swirled around the horses' hooves, slightly deadening the sound of their passage over the cobblestones. No one else, apparently, had taken advantage of the inviting crispness of the fall morning to ride, and it seemed they would have the park's meandering bridle paths to themselves. They spoke little, Raven's attention, despite his unquestioned skill as a horseman, demanded to control the black. He knew the blame for the stallion's ill manners lay at his door. A lack of opportunity on his part to ride him, and the grooms too afraid of his diabolical tricks and stratagems to exercise him properly.

"So they leave him alone," he had said to Catherine, "and then when I finally have a chance to ride, he makes clear his resentment of that neglect."

"Then you should try *this* time to give him enough of a gallop to calm his temper for a few days."

"Do I detect a challenge?" Raven asked, glancing up from the maneuvers the black was using as his own form of challenge.

"No, but like the black, I'm afraid I'm feeling rather restless. I think I'm as much in need of exercise as he. And we seem to have the park to ourselves this morning. It's the perfect opportunity to work off some excess energy."

"Are you trying to tell me that the famous Catherine Raven, London's premier hostess and style setter, sometimes feels the need of excitement other than that provided by balls and parties?" Raven mocked.

"I don't find *you* making trivial conversation with people who've never had a thought beyond what they should wear to the next rout or with whom they should share the next liaison."

"I thought you enjoyed all that."

"Enjoyed?" she said in exasperation. "Surely you can't believe that I *enjoy* all those empty exchanges."

"Then why do it?"

"Because that was one of the requirements of our situation. I maintain our position in society…" She stopped, not sure how to word the remainder of that thought.

"While I provide the money that allows you to do so. If you're unhappy, however, I suggest you refuse the invitations."

"You need the contacts my mingling in society provides. Contacts with the men who dine at your table, for example. If I don't venture out to the entertainments they frequent, then they may accept other invitations for their presence at dinner."

"I honestly thought you enjoyed moving within the ton. You grew up accustomed to that, after all. And I thought it was every Londoner's desire to be immersed in the kind of activities that you seem now to be dismissing as trivial and boring."

"And you have *always* found them boring," she retorted. "I notice you're continually too busy to accompany me." She couldn't help chiding him.

Raven took a moment to smooth his hand down the black's massive neck, trying to decide how to react to Catherine's complaint. The stallion's restiveness had not abated, and Raven was exerting very strict control. The horse was already beginning to sweat slightly with the canter he was being held to.

"I thought that's what you'd prefer," he said finally, glancing up from his pretended concentration on the stallion.

"What I'd prefer?" Catherine repeated in bewilderment. "Why should you think I would prefer to go out alone, forever forced to explain why my husband is again unable to accompany me? I assure you the excuses I've offered are quite threadbare."

"You should have told me," Raven said, thinking of the endless nights he'd spent working or reading, trying to block out images of Catherine gliding across some dance floor in the arms of her latest courtier. Fighting his growing hunger simply to be with her, to touch her, to hold her in his own arms. If only he had had a hint that she'd wanted him to accompany her.

He had been trying to give her time to know him, to understand the kind of man he was and, more importantly, to realize that she could trust him. To discover that he always kept his word. And now she was apparently confessing to the same longings that haunted the lonely hours of his own existence.

"When?" she asked, anger creeping into her voice. "I never see you. You spend more time..." She stopped the bitter words. She had no right to censure Raven because he was doing what she'd expected him to do when they had begun their marriage. Except she had never thought she'd feel about him the way she now did. That didn't mean his feelings about their situation had changed, simply because hers clearly had.

"I'm sorry," she said.

"Are you implying, Catherine, that you would like to spend more time with *me?*"

Leave it to Raven to cut to the heart of the matter. And, indeed, what else could he possibly read into that bitter avowal? She had just complained, far too obviously, that she didn't see enough of her own husband.

"I'm implying nothing more than I've been shut up in drawing rooms and ballrooms too long. I'll race you, Raven. Like your black, I need a hard run."

She heard him call her name, but she had already touched her heel to the mare, and responding to that permission and perhaps to the sharp, clear air of the fall morning, her horse had left the black behind. Catherine smiled when she heard the pounding of the stallion's hooves following her, knowing her husband had accepted her dare. A contest she would lose, of course, but she was willing to be bested. It was enough to feel the powerful muscles beneath her and the wind trying to tangle her hair.

The race was tight enough that she wondered if Raven had reined in to give her a chance, but glorying in the freedom of the run, she didn't care if he had. The exhilaration of the hard-fought contest was too strong to quibble over technicalities.

When she drew Storm up beside the still-anxious black, she was laughing. Raven had beaten her, but not by much, despite the superiority of his mount.

"If you had a better horse, I should be looking to my laurels," he declared as she approached. There was a touch of red in the golden skin over his high cheekbones, and a few strands of the gleaming ebony hair had escaped their confinement. He raised an ungloved hand to smooth them back into place.

Her throat tightened at the image of that dark hand smoothing over her breasts, as his eyes had done last night. She could almost feel the sensation, the abrasive brush of callused palm and the delight of hard fingertips caressing her exposed flesh. She looked down in confusion. God, she was mad for him, and other than throwing herself into his arms, she didn't know what she could do about it. A mental image of his disordered bed and gaping shirtfront made her close her eyes hard.

She lived in the same house with him, and every night he retired to that room. A room separated from hers by only a few feet, she realized suddenly. There was no reason not to retrace tonight the same journey she had made last night—with her quite legitimate excuse—for a very different purpose. No reason at all except her pride and her fear. He had invited her into his room last night. Somewhere, despite all the doubts and fears, she knew with sweet certainty that Raven wouldn't refuse if she offered herself to him.

"What's wrong?" Raven asked. Catherine had suddenly gone still, her eyes downcast and the laughing exhilaration from the race wiped away.

She waited a moment before she answered, at last raising her gaze to feast again on the darkly beautiful, almost forbidding features of the man she had first married and then fallen in love with. As she looked at his face, she felt tears prick hotly behind her eyes, although she didn't understand why she wanted to cry. He was just so...

"Catherine?" Raven said questioningly. "What's wrong?"

She tried to gather control, to think of anything that might explain this ridiculous lapse in her ability to think.

"My stirrup," she offered, her voice thready, the emotion too powerful to deny.

Raven swung down with the fluid grace that marked his every movement. She watched the muscles of his thighs bunch and shift under the tight, revealing knit of his fawn pantaloons. She found herself wondering what those hard muscles would feel like next to the softness of her thighs. Found herself wanting them there.

Raven's strong hands lifted her booted foot out of the stirrup and then he bent to check the buckles. "There doesn't seem to be—"

He was interrupted when the mare leapt straight upward, her body twisting in midair. By the time her hooves touched the ground, she was away, tearing across the park like a beast gone mad. Raven saw Catherine's automatic reaction—her body stretching low against the reaching neck of the racing animal. But he also saw in his mind's eye, his heart suddenly in his throat, the small booted foot he'd removed from the single stirrup.

Raven had been aware of the crack of sound that coincided with Storm's leap. But even as he had identified that unmistakable noise, he had pushed it to the back of his consciousness, throwing himself into the saddle to send the black on the most desperate race of his life, a race Raven knew he had already lost.

Chapter Eleven

As the mare flew from the clearing, Catherine fought to remain in the saddle and regain command. Storm, however, was totally panicked, and nothing Catherine did could abate her mount's terror. Hang on and let her run it out, she commanded her body, her years of experience fighting her own panic.

When she realized they were approaching the stream, she knew this would be the greatest danger to both horse and rider. The mare was exhausted, already winded from the race with the black, but in her blind frenzy, she was still uncontrollable. The stream loomed before them almost before Catherine had time to be afraid. She began desperately gathering the mare for the jump, trying to instill a confidence that, horsewoman that she was, she knew was beyond the trembling beast. Then they were in the air, soaring. The reaching forelegs came down short, slipping on the slime of the opposite bank.

With time suspended, Catherine was aware of every quivering stumble in Storm's desperate attempts to recover. But despite their combined best efforts to right the situation, she felt herself flying over the mare's neck. She turned, trying to roll into the fall, but it all happened too

quickly to do much to prepare her body for its descent. Her
shoulder took the brunt as she had intended, but her knee
hit sharply against one of the rocks that lined the streambed
and then she struck her head, and she didn't know anything
else.

When she came to, it was to find Raven stooping beside
her. His hands were moving over her rib cage with the same
deliberate care he took in handling the crystal goblets at
dinner. She couldn't prevent the image, nor her lips from
lifting as she thought it. She tried to raise her head enough
to see what he was doing, but her senses swam as soon as
she moved.

"Lie still," Raven commanded softly, and because she
really had no choice, she laid her head back against the
bracken crushed by her fall and waited for her vision to
clear. When she opened her eyes again, he was tracing
down her right arm with the same gentleness he had used
on her ribs and hips, but he was watching her face while
his hands made their examination.

"I'm all right," she said. "This isn't the first time I've
been thrown. The most embarrassing, perhaps, but not the
first."

"Why the most embarrassing?" he asked, his voice relaxed.

"Because you were watching," she admitted. She closed
her eyes and rested her head again on the damp ground.
There was something very soothing about what he was doing. About the expertise of his hands. And the calmness of
his voice.

"Everyone falls," he said. "If you ride long enough,
you'll take your share of spills. Do you have any idea what
set her off?" he questioned casually, forcing his tone to
remain steady.

"I don't... She just..." Her voice faded because she had
no answer for the horse's reaction, and it hurt to think.

His hands had deserted her, and she was aware that he'd shifted position, no longer beside her. He began rearranging the skirt of her habit, and she felt the cool air touch her bared legs. Despite the fact that he was her husband, she reacted to that invasion with a very conditioned response. Absurdly, she tried to sit up, but she never completed the attempt. Raven was again beside her, holding her securely against the hard warmth of his body, when the mists cleared yet again.

"You seem determined to lose consciousness. I promise to be gentle, but I need to see if anything's broken."

"Nothing's broken," she said, leaning into his strength.

"There's blood on your skirt."

"My knee," she whispered. Her cheek was resting against the muscles of his chest. Like the child he'd called her, she felt most secure enclosed in his embrace.

"I need to see to it," he said. "I'm going to help you lie down again, and this time, Catherine, you damn well stay there. There is a place for modesty, and there is also a place for common sense. You're too intelligent to fight my taking care of you because of what would be false modesty in this situation."

"Because you're my *husband?*" she suggested, reminding him how far from reality that was.

"Because you're hurt," Raven said simply, and he gently lowered her back to the loam to continue his examination.

Incredibly, despite the throbbing in her head and her aching shoulder, she began to enjoy his touch. Raven's hands moved impersonally, but she couldn't help reacting to the warmth of his palms firmly tracing the line of bone upward from her ankles to her thighs. She gasped when he manipulated her right knee, and at her response the blue eyes lifted to meet hers. He smiled at her, and although the tears had gathered, unwanted, in her own eyes, she managed a rather tremulous smile in return.

"I think this needs a more professional inspection than I'm qualified to give," he said, finally rearranging her skirt to cover her legs. He allowed his hand to rest lightly on her thigh, its contact intended to be reassuring.

"Storm?" she asked, remembering her mare's stumbling landing.

"She's fine. She didn't go down."

"Thank God," Catherine said. She held out her gloved hand to him, but instead of taking it to help her sit up, he stooped beside her, placing his arm beneath her shoulders and lifting. She was allowed to lean against him again until the world stopped spinning. Finally, with fingers that still shook, she began to unfasten her veil, removing the small, jaunty hat she'd donned with such high spirits that morning. The autumn air felt refreshing against her brow, and she even thought about how unbecomingly disarrayed her hair would be, and then disregarded that concern as foolish, given the situation.

Raven's left hand lifted to touch her temple. His fingertips brushed over the thin skin, and she knew by the resulting pain that there was a bruise there. When his fingertips came away covered in blood, she felt her stomach clench despite her determination not to behave any more childishly than she had already. She knew she'd be very sorry tomorrow for this day's misadventure.

"You'd better help me mount," she said, gathering her resolve for the effort it would take to stand.

"Surely you don't think—" he began.

"You're horseman enough to know that's the best way. The sooner the better. There's nothing serious among my injuries. My pride's far more damaged than my body, I promise you."

"That may be true, but it doesn't mean you're riding home."

"And what do you suggest?" she asked, smiling. They were still alone in the park and probably would be for another hour or more. "It's by far the easiest way."

"Easiest for whom?" Raven asked, answering her smile. "Cast steel you may be, Mrs. Raven, but you're not indestructible."

"I suppose you're the only one who may lay claim to that."

He said nothing for a moment, and she turned her head so that she could see his face. He was looking down at her as she rested very comfortably against his massive chest. There was something in his expression she couldn't read. "What's wrong?" she asked, touching his lean cheek with her gloved hand.

"I think I'm beginning to understand what you went through when you believed..." She could feel the deep breath he took.

"That you were ill?" she suggested, at his continued silence.

"Come on," he said, refusing to answer her. He was still fighting the terror he'd experienced watching that terrible fall, helpless, pushing the black to his limits, and all the while knowing he would be too late. "However pleasant this may be, I think I should get you home."

"Pleasant?" she repeated, wondering, but her question was forgotten as he lifted her easily in his arms. She quickly stifled her small cry as he slipped his arm under her knees.

"Sorry, my darling," he said softly. "I won't hurt you again, I promise."

Shocked into silence by the unexpected endearment, she found herself relaxing. Raven carried her along the streambed despite the terrain and then across the footbridge that spanned it.

"Raven?" she said as he strode through the deserted park.

"Am I hurting you?" he asked, glancing down to smile at her.

"No, of course not. It's not so bad. A little sore."

"I can imagine it is," he said.

"I wondered if you intend to carry me all the way home."

"If necessary. But I believe we'll meet someone who'll be willing to take us up once we reach the street."

"And the horses?"

"Eating their heads off at the king's expense. They'll probably get colic and have to be put down. I may do it myself."

"Why?" she asked, smiling, knowing it was an idle threat.

"You need a steadier mount," he said simply. He knew it hadn't been the mare's fault she'd been hurt, but if he forgave the roan's panic, then that left only himself to blame. To blame for it all. He had been unable to push the black fast enough to reach Catherine in time. Raven couldn't bear the thought that he was responsible for hurting her.

"I don't know what happened to Storm. She's usually the most dependable of mounts. I promise to maintain a firmer control the next time."

"Can I trust you to keep that promise?" he asked.

"Have I ever broken a promise to you?"

"Have you ever made one?" Raven asked lightly, looking down again into her face. His mouth was arranged in its customary forbidding line, but there was something very tender in his eyes.

"Only one," she whispered, remembering their simple vows.

He was still looking down at her with that enigmatic

tenderness when a familiar voice hailed them from the street.

"Mr. Raven!" Lord Avondale's greeting was rich with genuine concern. "I say, is there something wrong?"

"My wife's been thrown. I wonder if I might impose upon you to take us up and drive us home."

"Of course. Only too glad. Shall I help you to..."

The offer was made ridiculous by Raven's ease in mounting the steps of the high phaeton, despite his burden.

"Mrs. Raven," said Avondale, nodding at her. Catherine knew she was blushing at having to face anyone in this embarrassing situation. Raven seemed immune to discomfiture. He acted as if he daily carried his wife through the streets of London.

When they reached the town house, Raven carried her upstairs, carefully placing her on the chaise longue in her bedroom. He left her to the care of her abigail and one of the maids, who removed her boots and, the operation painful in the extreme, her coat and stock and then finally the skirt of her habit. It seemed that Dr. Stevenson arrived in only a matter of minutes.

He confirmed her own claim that nothing was broken, but he was of the opinion that she'd severely bruised her knee as well as gashed it against the stone. Her shoulder was aching abominably by this time, but she didn't mention that to the doctor. The headache she'd been vaguely aware of in the park was beginning to throb with increasing violence.

"Laudanum to help you rest," the doctor said after he'd bathed her forehead and dressed her knee. He measured the dose in a glass of water, ignoring her protest that she really didn't need the drug. Despite its popularity as a nerve soother, Catherine had never liked its effects. But because she had grown up doing everything this prominent London practitioner instructed her to do, she drank the medicine under his demanding eye.

"And now I suppose I should let your husband know that you're really all right. A love match, I believe your father told me. And I should judge by Mr. Raven's concern that the duke's assessment was correct."

He pinched her cheek as if she were five years old, but since she had endured that exact treatment since she *was* five, she smiled at him and watched him walk out her bedroom door.

A love match, she thought in amusement, already beginning to feel the effects of the drug he'd given her drifting over her senses. She wondered what Raven had said to him to make him believe that. And then she remembered that it had been her father, surprisingly, who had originally offered that opinion. A rather astonishing revelation, she thought, closing her eyes.

She heard the door later, but it was almost too much trouble to respond. Her head had stopped pounding, and if she didn't move, she could forget the stiff knee and bruised shoulder.

"Catherine?" Raven said softly.

She opened her eyes, turning her head carefully to find that he was again stooping beside her so that his eyes were on a level with hers.

"Hello," she whispered, and she lifted her left hand to touch his cheek as she had in the park.

He caught her fingers in his and, bringing them to his lips, pressed the smallest kiss against them. "How are you feeling?"

"I told you nothing was broken," she said, closing her eyes against the disturbing sunlight that was pouring into the tall windows of her room.

"And I was delighted to have that information confirmed by a disinterested observer."

"How are the horses?"

"I sent Jem for them. I hope they've been abducted by highwaymen, but he'll probably find them just where we left them, waiting patiently for someone to come for them."

"Horses are really not very intelligent," she agreed.

"Then neither are we who trust ourselves to them."

She opened her eyes again to see his expression. Smiling at what she found in his face, she tried to shake her head. She gasped at the sudden stab of pain that resulted.

"I didn't mean to disturb you. I'll come back tomorrow—"

"Don't go." Against her will, in response to the drug's pull, she felt her eyes fill with tears. "Please don't go."

"Catherine," Raven said, brushing his thumb lightly across her wet lashes. He wondered if, despite the doctor's assurances, she might be more seriously injured than they thought. He had never seen Catherine cry. Except over the pitiful, shivering donkey he'd helped her rescue the day he'd met her.

"Don't go," she whispered again. She was shamelessly begging her husband not to leave, but she really didn't seem to be able to stop the words. "Stay with me, Raven, at least for a while," she added with a small catch in her voice. A watering pot, she thought in disgust, but she couldn't prevent the hot tears that continued to seep from under her lashes.

"Catherine," he said again. "Don't cry. I think you'll be more comfortable completely undressed and in bed. I'll get your maid, and then I'll come back and sit with you until you fall asleep." He stood up in preparation to carry out those actions.

"No," she protested, her fingers tightening their hold on his. He had called her a child, and she was certainly acting like one. With the greatest effort of will, she forced her hand to relax its desperate grip, but she couldn't seem to release him. "I'm sorry," she said. "I know you have things to do. Business to see to that is far more important—"

His soft laughter interrupted. "Guilt, Catherine? If I let you rest, then I'm once more the villainous husband who spends more time with his businesses than with his very beautiful wife?"

"Do you think I'm beautiful?" She forced her heavy lids open again to assess the truth of his answer.

"You surely don't need my affirmation of your beauty added to that of every eligible—and ineligible—man in London. Fishing for compliments?"

"Of course. Or I shan't have any. Not from my husband, at any rate." By the strongest effort of will, she took her hand completely away from his, curling her fingers under her chin. But her wide eyes didn't leave his face.

Smiling again, Raven shook his head. "Shameless," he said. "There's no weapon you won't use to get your own way. Let me get you into something you'll be able to rest in more comfortably."

"All right," she whispered. Still caught in the unthinking lethargy of the drug, she didn't realize that Raven had only intended, of course, to call her maid. Catherine began to unfasten the buttons of the soft lawn shirt she'd worn under her habit. Her hand didn't obey the intention of her brain very well, however, and in frustration, she felt the hated tears begin. She looked up to find Raven's gaze fastened on her trembling fingers, which had managed the top buttons, but were struggling with the one that lay just over the valley between her breasts.

"Raven," she begged softly.

His eyes, shimmering with some emotion she didn't understand—one she'd never been allowed to see before in their depths—lifted to hers.

Considering what she'd suggested in the park about

spending time with him, Raven wondered if she could mean... Slowly he denied that incredible possibility. Catherine was hurt. No longer the elegant sophisticate he'd enticed to marry him, she was as vulnerable now as an injured child. What kind of bastard would he be to take advantage of this situation, no matter how long he'd waited? Banishing the desire that had already begun to smolder deep in his body at whatever he had seen in the tear-misted eyes, he took over the task she was unable to perform.

Catherine marveled again at his fingers' dexterity and gentleness, despite their size. "Your hands are too large...." she began. For these absurdly small buttons, she intended to add, but somehow the thought didn't reach her lips.

He glanced up from what he was doing, the firm line of his lips straightening even further. "I can't help my size, Catherine. I'm sorry you find it distasteful."

"I don't find your size distasteful. Why would you say that?" she whispered.

"Sit up," he directed, instead of answering her question, his hand supporting her shoulders firmly.

He slipped the sleeve of the shirt off her left arm and then very carefully off the discolored right shoulder. His eyes examined the injury and then moved over the swell of her breasts, exposed by the low, ribboned neckline of her chemise. Again his body reacted, becoming painfully hard and tight. He wanted to press his mouth into the shadowed recess between those ivory globes.

Catherine saw his lips whiten under the pressure suddenly exerted to prevent that response, and then the breath he took before he deliberately lifted his gaze to her face.

"Put your arm around my neck," he forced himself to say impersonally, bending to lift her. He carried her as he had in the park and laid her on the high bed, where the covers had already been turned back. Too inviting. Too intimate.

She had controlled her reaction to the pressure on her injured knee by biting her lip, determined not to let any sound escape this time. She closed her eyes against the pain in her head. He had put her down as carefully as if she, too, were made of Venetian glass, one arm remaining behind her back to support her until he'd arranged the pillows to serve that same purpose.

Finally it was over, and she was in control enough to open her eyes and face him without any tears, tears he had accused her of employing to get her own way. And there was, of course, a great deal of truth in that assertion, but she would never have resorted to that stratagem to hold him if it were not for the uninhibiting effects of the laudanum.

"Would you pull the draperies, please?" she asked.

She watched him stride across the chamber, his masculinity out of place in its decidedly feminine atmosphere. He swept the draperies across the window, effectively shutting out the strong light and leaving the room in a dim, artificial twilight.

When he had done as she'd asked, he returned to stand looking down on her. She hadn't bothered to pull the sheet up. Since he had helped her undress, it seemed that in struggling to cover her body now she would certainly be guilty of the false modesty he'd accused her of. She lay very still, hoping the throbbing in her head would ease as it had before.

"Thank you," she said finally, thinking that perhaps he was waiting for permission to leave. After all, she had begged him to stay. She would explain that it was all the effects of the drug sapping her willpower, but now it was too much trouble. She'd tell him later, when she felt better. When everything was not so difficult and confusing. Later, she thought, the last conscious thought she would have for several hours.

"Just where you told me it would be, Mr. Raven," the groom said, running his hand over the mare's rump. The furrow he had been instructed to look for was raw and ugly, cutting across the gleaming hide of the horse.

"That old bastard," Raven said under his breath, feeling again the horror he'd felt as he'd watched the mare racing away from him. This fear was from the realization of the tragedy that might have happened.

"But why anyone would shoot at her ladyship—begging you pardon, sir—at Mrs. Raven, I can't imagine." Jem knew that was the title his mistress preferred. She had made that clear to the staff.

Shaking off the remembrance of his helplessness this morning, Raven met Jem's serious brown eyes. "They weren't shooting at her," he said softly. To test the truth of what he already knew, he aligned his body in the same position in which he had been standing after he'd dismounted. The bullet that had cut the long gouge in the horse's rump would have passed directly through his body had he not bent to adjust his wife's stirrup. The marksman had definitely not intended the mare—or Catherine—to be his target.

I'll see you in hell.... Catherine's father had threatened. *Damned fortune hunter!* The words had been echoing in Raven's brain for several hours now, ever since he'd put together this morning's attempt at murder with the proposal Catherine had made to her father about giving her trust fund to her husband. And having made that connection, John Raven knew with certainty who wanted him dead. Montfort had already tried to kill Henning for that same reason. *He'd shoot you, or hire someone to do it,* Catherine herself had told him.

Deliberately he pushed away the circling memories.

"See to the mare, will you, Jem. And keep your mouth shut. There's no need to worry Mrs. Raven." Turning, Raven stepped out of the stall and disappeared into the shadowed stable.

Behind him, in the pleasant dimness of the hay-scented enclosure, the groom ran a soothing palm over the mare's flank. Jem shook his head, a slow movement full of regret. He'd grown to like the tall American he had come to work for when his mistress had married. But as he had warned John Raven from the beginning, it didn't pay to cross the Duke of Montfort. Especially where his only daughter was concerned.

"Catherine."

Raven's voice seemed to come from a great distance away, but she had no doubt who was calling her. She forced open her eyes, finding the artificial gloom he'd created this morning had been replaced by the genuine darkness of evening.

"Catherine," Raven said again, and she turned her head to find him standing beside the bed. He had discarded his coat and was dressed only in a white shirt and pale blue-and-silver striped waistcoat above cream pantaloons. Surprisingly, his hair had not been pulled back into the neat queue in which he always wore it. It was loose, its slightly curling midnight blackness long enough to touch below his shoulders. She was fascinated by the transformation. Its surrounding frame softened the harsh planes of his face. She had always imagined Raven's hair would be straight and coarse, but its appearance tonight seemed to contradict that. She had a sudden impulse to run her fingers through the dark strands to confirm her impression.

"I thought it was time you woke up. I brought you something that will be more beneficial than what the doctor gave you.''

''Almost anything would be better…'' she began, and then stopped, embarrassed because she could vaguely remember clinging to Raven's hand, begging him to stay with her. ''What is it?'' she asked instead, attempting to sit up, only to feel her head swim.

''Be still,'' he ordered sharply, putting the cup he'd been holding on her night table. As he had this morning, he slipped his arm behind her back and held her until he could arrange the pillows to offer more support for her shoulders.

He picked up the cup to bring it to her lips, but even when her hand fastened around it, he didn't remove his. Instead he held it steady, her cool fingers trembling over his warm ones, allowing her to drink some of the acrid liquid the cup held.

''It's my grandmother's recipe,'' he said, and she heard but didn't understand the amusement in his deep voice. ''Willow tea. It will help your head.''

''How did you know my head hurts?''

''Because I've been thrown my share of times.''

''Somehow I find that hard to believe.''

''I told you. If you ride enough…''

Once again he raised the cup, resting its rim against her lips. ''Finish it,'' he commanded.

''I seem to be very trusting,'' she said, sipping the bitter concoction. ''I've never heard of tea made from trees. Maybe you're trying to poison me. Are you tired of your clinging wife already?'' Because she was terribly afraid he *had* found her tiresome today, with her tears and her demands, she raised her eyes to search his.

''How could I be tired of my wife? Since she thinks I spend so little time with her,'' Raven said, his lips lifting slightly.

''I suppose I deserve that. You have my apologies for

that remark. You may put it down to blood loss, my dear,"
she said, echoing his words to her on the morning he'd
kissed her.

"And I haven't yet been forgiven for that, either, I see."

"No," she admitted. Why deny the obvious? She had
just demonstrated that his words that day had made an impression.

"Unforgiven for the kiss or for the excuse?" he asked.

"I enjoyed the kiss," she whispered. Apparently all the
effects of the drug had not disappeared as she'd thought.
She couldn't believe she had told him that.

"Did you, Catherine?"

Wordlessly she nodded.

He replaced the cup on the table and sat down beside
her on the bed. She looked up to find the blue eyes studying
hers. He took both her hands in one of his large ones and
held them a moment. Raven was so close she could smell
him. Could feel the heat from his body. If she raised her
hand, she could discover if his hair was as soft as it appeared to be. Fighting that impulse, she lowered her eyes
from the contemplation of his face. She had already revealed so much today of what she felt. Feelings that she
had successfully hidden until now.

"May I take it you would like to try it again sometime?"
he asked.

Slowly she nodded, knowing how true that was and wondering if he might kiss her now.

"And our contract?" he asked very softly. "What should
we do about our agreement, Catherine?"

"Begin again," she suggested, raising her eyes to meet
his, daring to hope that that was what he, too, wanted.

"With new rules?"

"Without rules," she said, holding her breath.

"Are you suggesting that we might have a *real* marriage?"

"I know you think I'm very young."

"I think you're very beautiful. Especially now," Raven said. He touched her chin, and she turned her head, rubbing it against his fingers. "But I also think you're very vulnerable. And I'd hate to have you decide later that I'd taken advantage of that vulnerability. We could discuss this when you're stronger."

He wondered where he had found the strength to suggest that. *A vow, Raven,* his grandmother's whisper reminded him. Catherine seemed so fragile now—incredibly beautiful, but exquisitely fragile, in need of his care and protection. Not his lovemaking.

"You think I suggested that in a moment of weakness?" she asked, wondering if she would ever find the courage to tell him how long she'd thought about that possibility.

He raised his hand to touch with one knuckle the bruised temple, the evidence of her fall a livid contrast to the clear, translucent paleness of her skin. "A blow to the head can cause all sorts of complications," Raven said softly.

Such as making me fall in love? she thought. How he could fail to know what she felt? Or perhaps he *did* know. Perhaps...

"Catherine?" Raven said questioningly.

But suddenly she saw nothing of what was occurring here in her bedroom, remembered nothing of the closeness they'd shared during the last twenty-four hours. Instead she was recalling the careless phrase he had thrown at her before their marriage, as an enticement to marry him. No wonder he'd put her off with that ridiculous excuse! He didn't want her in that way. He had told her that. *I don't need a mistress.*

"What's wrong? Your head?"

She could hear the concern, undeniable in Raven's voice.

"It's nothing..." Her voice trailed off, the lump in the back of her throat growing too large to speak around.

"Are you going to cry again?" he asked, using his thumb to wipe away the single tear that was sliding down her cheek.

Swallowing, she shook her head. The resulting jolt of pain loosened a small, involuntary, sobbing breath. She put her hand up to her temple, closing her eyes. She felt Raven's hand close warmly over hers.

"Catherine?"

"I'm sorry. It's nothing. Just silly tears. I don't know why I can't seem to stop crying. I never cry. I despise women who weep," she said disjointedly, turning her head slightly to move it out of contact with his hand.

"I don't think anyone would deny your right to a few tears. And no one will ever know."

"*I'll* know that I'm turning into a disgusting watering pot. Please forgive me. And now if you'll excuse me, I believe I'll try to sleep again. I think your grandmother's tea has helped. Thank you, Raven."

He said nothing for a moment, his eyes again studying her carefully arranged features. Catherine was glad she was accustomed to hiding her true feelings. If nothing else, her experiences in society had taught her to school her face to reveal nothing more than what she intended it should.

"And our discussion?" he asked finally. She seemed to be backing away from the suggestion she'd made. Perhaps he'd been right. Too much emotion. Or the drug. The blow to her head.

"I think you're right. Perhaps we'd be wise to postpone any decisions until I'm feeling a bit stronger."

His lips tightened involuntarily, but Raven allowed nothing else of what he was feeling to show. He had promised her freedom, and by virtue of their marriage vows she was entitled also to his care. *In sickness and in health.* The rest could wait, as he had waited. Always it would be Catherine's decision to at last give *him* freedom. To free him from the constraint of his vow.

Catherine couldn't tell whether Raven was hiding a smile or was angered at her about-face. If only she knew what he was really feeling! But that always-controlled expression gave away as little as she hoped hers was now.

"Of course," Raven said, standing to follow her suggestion. "Sleep well, Catherine."

He bent and touched his lips to the darkened, abraded skin over her temple. There was no pain occasioned by the gentle movement of his mouth, but for some reason she felt hot moisture begin to sting her eyes again.

"Thank you, Raven," she whispered, closing her lids to hide that ridiculous reaction.

She was aware that he stood for a long heartbeat by the bed, but she never reopened her eyes to look at him. Finally she heard his footsteps cross the room and the sound of the door opening and then closing behind him.

Chapter Twelve

Catherine didn't fall asleep for quite a while after Raven left. She'd already slept too long. The pain in her head subsided and eventually the urge to cry had faded.

Lying in the still darkness of her bedroom, she had come to realize that the next step was really up to her husband. She had offered herself to him like the lovesick schoolroom miss he surely thought her to be, and now he would have to decide whether he wanted to fall in with the suggestion she'd made.

They had both known that eventually intimacy would have to find its place in their marriage. He had never denied that he would want an heir. And that was, of course, the major responsibility of every wife—to perpetuate the family line. Catherine's own mother had been guilt ridden by her failure to produce a son who survived infancy, and her father had been forced to lavish all his attention on Catherine, his only child. She wondered suddenly if her father had had a mistress during his marriage, especially during the long last years of her mother's illness.

Catherine wished there was someone she could talk to. She had a deep longing for her mother, dead now four years. There was no one to ask what a wife—a wife who had discovered she was very much in love with her husband—did when confronted by the painful reality that he had a mistress. Another woman who shared his attentions and perhaps even his affections. Who already shared, as Catherine had not, his physical responses.

Her thinking was no clearer with the light of dawn which she watched first brighten her window and then creep slowly across the polished wood to bring to life the rich colors of the oriental carpet. She would have to face Raven again this morning, she thought, remembering the painful images of his body in another woman's embrace, images that had played in her consciousness throughout the night, waking and sleeping. She was not, as were the other women of her class, sophisticated enough to dismiss the emotions aroused by those mental pictures.

She was, however, in control enough to speak pleasantly to the maid who brought her morning tea. She smiled against the rim of her cup at the remembrance of Raven's kindness yesterday. Kind and comforting to children, she thought, the smile fading.

"They said you were awake," Raven said from the doorway.

She glanced up at the sound of his voice and felt again the heat of pure physical reaction. The navy coat deepened the blue of his eyes. His hair was again neatly confined, emphasizing the hard, very masculine contours of his face, the high, white cravat a startling contrast to the bronze of his skin.

"May I come in?" he asked politely.

"Of course," she said, setting her cup on the night table.

He stood at the end of the bed and placed his hands over the curving footboard, studying her face in the morning light. "Feeling better?"

"Much better, thank you," she said.

The russet eyes met his with their usual serenity, the

small chin courageously raised. He had spent half the night praying that he would find Catherine recovered, again poised and in command. And the other half practicing what he wanted to say to her.

His lips moved slightly, and again she found herself wondering what he was thinking.

"Well enough to finish our discussion?" he asked, and this time his smile tilted the corners of his mouth.

"If you'd like," she said, knowing that she really wasn't sure what she could say. She had thought she would have more time to plan for this encounter, but she should have known better. Raven would always come straight to the point.

"I'd like it very much."

"You want to discuss—" she began, only to be interrupted.

"The provisions outlined in our original contract."

She couldn't prevent her own quick, almost resigned smile at that wording. *Contract*, she thought, shaking her head.

"Forgive me," he said, accurately reading the cause of her amusement. "I know I speak in the language of the business world. I'm not by nature given to flights of poetry, but I know, Catherine, that what we discussed yesterday…" He paused, and for the first time since she'd known him, he seemed unsure. "I know that there was nothing businesslike about what happened between us yesterday."

So apparently he, too, had felt some of the emotions generated by their intimacy. Or at least he had been aware of what she was feeling. "No," she agreed.

"I promised to give you the opportunity to rethink what you suggested. When you weren't feeling the effects of your fall."

"The complications of my fall?" she said softly, smiling. He didn't answer her smile or even her comment, but what he did say made her breath falter and her heartbeat begin to race.

"But I hope that you won't want to reconsider. Even if the idea developed in a moment of weakness."

"*You* hope? Are you saying that *you* want our marriage to become…" She paused, unsure why discussing the ideas she herself had introduced yesterday should be so difficult this morning. There was no shock of injury to hide behind. No drugs. No dim lighting to soften the reality of what she had asked him for.

"A real marriage. That was the term suggested last night."

His eyes were resting with calm attention on her face. *You may ask me anything,* he'd promised long ago. And what she wanted to ask him now would certainly strain the boundaries of that.

"And your mistress?" she asked, schooling her features and forcing her eyes to meet his without any trace of discomfiture.

"My…mistress?" Raven repeated hesitantly, as if he'd never heard the word before.

"You told me when you made your proposal that you needed only a hostess. That you already had a mistress."

He glanced down at his hands, still resting on the wooden foot rail. She watched, as he seemed to be doing, his fingers tighten and then relax against the unyielding wood. Straightening, he removed his hands and clasped them behind his back. When he looked at her again, she would have sworn there was amusement in the blue eyes. But his mouth was set in a line that was even straighter than his normal austere expression.

He's going to tell me that he loves her too well to give her up. Or that I knew the rules when we began this. That I have no right to ask, Catherine thought. The painful possibilities ran through her mind and a sudden sickness began to coil in the pit of her empty stomach. She wished she hadn't drunk the tea.

"When I told you that," he said, "there *was* someone." He paused, but his eyes didn't falter from hers. "Not perhaps what the word *mistress* implies in your world, but someone who..."

The pause was painful for her, but finding her courage, she completed his confession. "Satisfied your physical needs."

She expected nothing less than his agreement.

"It was not a relationship of long standing. But not, I would hope, as cold-blooded as you suggest."

"I'm sorry," she said, feeling a touch of anger at that. "I didn't mean to insult you."

"However that relationship might have been defined," he said, speaking as calmly as before, "it ended with our marriage. I was raised in a very traditional society, Catherine, and my values are different, perhaps, from those of your world."

"Ended?" She wondered why he bothered to make that claim. It certainly didn't fit with what he'd suggested before.

"'Forsaking all others.' I told you I *always* honor the terms of my contracts."

"But you told me..." She stopped, trying to remember exactly what he *had* said that dark dawn in his office. "You said you'd kissed me because of too prolonged an abstinence."

"Very prolonged," he agreed.

"You suggested you'd taken steps to rectify that situation."

"I had. I had married you. And I was hoping our marriage would, eventually, *rectify* a great many situations." His lips were curving again in his slight smile.

"Are you trying to tell me that you intended all along—"

"To make you my wife? In every sense of the word? Of course. I thought you understood that. I simply wanted to give you time to grow accustomed to the idea. And to me. And then yesterday…" Raven paused again, taking a deep breath. This was the hardest part. "Yesterday," he began again, "you led me to believe that's also what you wanted. That you were ready to modify our contract. Or did I misunderstand you last night?"

"You don't have a mistress?" she asked again, to be sure she'd not misunderstood him.

"No," he acknowledged.

She thought of the hours she'd spent visualizing the kind of woman Raven would want. And she realized suddenly that the kind of woman Raven wanted was, apparently, herself.

"And you want our marriage to become…" She found her voice unaccountably trembling over the simple question.

"Very much," he said, saving her the trouble of finishing. "I believe the question is if that's really what you want."

It seemed that every obstacle to what *she* wanted had miraculously disappeared. All she had to do was say yes—a far simpler decision than the one she'd made six months ago when she'd agreed to become his wife. Then he had offered her freedom. And what he was offering now was, she supposed, a kind of bondage—the creation of physical ties that she knew, even as inexperienced as she was, could never be broken lightly. The most intimate bondage on earth.

"Yes," she said, and unbelievingly, felt the ready tears of yesterday well again in her eyes. "Oh, damnation," she said in disgust, "I can't do anything but cry." She found the corner of the sheet and used it to wipe away the moisture. She found herself hoping that he'd take her in his arms. When she looked up, Raven was watching her with the same tenderness that had transformed his harsh features when he'd carried her from the park.

"Don't tempt me, Catherine," he warned softly. His hands were once again curved around the footboard, his fingertips white with the pressure he was exerting.

"Tempt you to what?" she asked, sniffing.

"To give you something to do besides weep," he said, and as she had when he'd entered her room, she felt the sheer physical response to what was in his dark face sweep through her body, causing a very peculiar sensation in the depths of her belly. Or, she realized, not exactly in her belly. Lower. Fluttering inside. Moving. Aching. As if he were touching her there with those graceful, skillful fingers that had impersonally examined her body yesterday. She remembered the callused strength of them moving over her skin, and she shivered slightly.

"Exactly," he said, watching her. "You have the most beautiful eyes," he added unexpectedly. "Like the beech leaves we rode under yesterday. Russet and touched with mist."

"Thank you," she said, sniffing again. She watched his smile begin. She could imagine how ridiculous she looked. Eyes red from weeping, a scrape over her temple, a bruised shoulder, wearing yesterday's chemise, which she'd slept in. And she couldn't begin to imagine what her hair was like. No wonder he was amused. She pressed her lips together tightly, trying to gather her dignity, and then she was forced to sniff again or be further humiliated by having her nose run.

"Will you promise to miss me while I'm gone?" Raven asked, and the worry she'd had about her appearance flew from her mind.

"Gone?" she repeated blankly.

"I have a meeting. Here, exactly a week from tomorrow. With the men who have committed to become partners in the railway. And I have to complete *my* part of our contract. I've already invested substantially in the land across which the rails will be laid, but I have to hire the men who will forge and lay them. And the engineers who build locomotives. And none of that, I regret to say, can be done from London."

"You're leaving," she said, finally understanding that he really intended to walk out after what they'd just decided.

"And by the time I return, you should be over most of the...complications of your fall. Not, I hope, all of them," he said, smiling at her. "I think it would be wise to postpone the...renegotiation of our contract until then. Since I have to meet my responsibilities to the men I've convinced to risk joining me in the rail venture, it seems the best solution to go ahead with my journey immediately. However difficult that may be."

"Why difficult?" He had said she might ask him anything.

"Because I'm finding it very hard to keep my hands off you."

"And you think that's necessary?"

"I think that would be best for you."

"Because you still think I'm a child," she said, hurt by his unexpected decision to leave just when everything between them had seemed to be moving in a very promising direction.

"If I'd thought you were a child, I'd never have married you."

"But you did marry me. And you seem to be suggesting... I don't know what you're suggesting, except that you're leaving."

"I'm suggesting that when I make you my wife, I don't want to worry about a bruised shoulder and a cut knee. Or a headache." For some reason, his lips quirked gently at the last item. "I'd like to be able to concentrate on making the consummation of our marriage as pleasurable as possible for you."

"And you're afraid it won't be...pleasurable?" she asked, wondering why he thought she wouldn't like having him make love to her. She knew enough to have some idea of what was involved. It had never sounded pleasant to her before, that was true, but the thought of Raven touching her with those hands she'd always admired, hands that she knew to be as graceful as she'd imagined them to be, made the prospect appealing. Extremely exciting.

"Forgive me, Catherine, and believe me, it has nothing to do with your age—with the difference in our ages—but you are..."

"Inexperienced?" she supplied, at his hesitation.

"Yes," he said.

"I'm sorry," she offered, the words falling on top of his.

"Delightfully inexperienced."

"Delightfully?" she repeated. "Then you don't mind."

"I'd want to kill any man who touched you before you belonged to me. The hardest thing I've ever done in my life was manage *not* to kill Amberton. I think he was aware of the struggle I was waging. That's probably why he stabbed me. He read murder in my eyes."

"Because he had...touched me?"

Raven hesitated a moment before he answered. There had, of course, been far more involved in his attack on Amberton, but Catherine didn't need to know what the viscount had suggested. Finally he said simply, "And because I hadn't."

"But you'd wanted to?"

"Since I'd met you. Since I saw you defending that donkey."

"Why didn't you tell me that?"

He smiled in self-mockery. "Because I was afraid you'd run like the hounds of hell were after you. I knew I was nothing like the men you admired."

She tried to remember the men she'd admired before she'd met Raven. No one was memorable enough among her previous suitors to offer the smallest challenge to his dominance of her senses now.

"I thought my only hope was to negotiate a contract you couldn't refuse, to give you what you seemed to desire most, to agree to whatever terms I thought you'd accept, and then gradually try to make you think about me in a different way."

"And how long were you prepared to wait for that to happen?" she asked, fascinated by his revelations. They were far more courageous, she supposed, than hers had been yesterday.

"As long as it took. The only problem was that I'd promised not to interfere in your flirtations. And I couldn't even bear to watch you waltz with someone else. I didn't want anyone else's arms around you but mine."

"Is that why you played cards at Aunt Agatha's?"

"Neither set of my ancestors was noted for tolerance where their women and other men were involved. Nor am I. I played cards as an alternative to playing the jealous husband."

"May I congratulate you on your skill," she said, smiling.

"At cards?"

"At deception."

"You never suspected?"

"No," she said, shaking her head. "Quite the reverse."

"You thought I was enamored of my mistress," he teased.

"And that you enjoyed discussing business more than conducting even a business relationship with your wife."

"And now you know that you were wrong. On both counts."

"I know what you've told me."

"Are you doubting my word, Catherine?"

"Which words? The words about undertaking a journey on the day that..." She paused uncertainly.

"We've finally admitted our feelings."

"Must you go, Raven?" she asked, fighting the urge to cry.

"I should have left yesterday. It's what I intended."

"Until I was thrown."

"And, of course, I couldn't leave until I knew you were all right. And you are all right, Catherine. Bruised and battered, but beautifully all right. I need to leave today if I'm to complete the arrangements that must be presented as a fait accompli to the investors. Since you need time to recuperate, it seemed best to get this journey out of the way while you do so."

"And I'm supposed to be the understanding wife and smilingly bid you goodbye."

"I had hoped that you would." His eyes were on her face, his small smile still touching that firm mouth.

"Goodbye, Raven. I hope you have a very pleasant journey," she said, raising her chin slightly. And then she smiled at him, slowly and deliberately, a small upward tilt of her lips that she knew to be very becoming and very provocative. She'd practiced it often enough before her glass.

"That's a good child," he said, teasing her.

"I'm not—" she began.

"A child," he acknowledged. "And I think I might have time to verify the truth of that before I go."

"I thought you were going to wait until your return to…" She paused, and her eyes fell to where her fingers were twisting the ribbon that fastened the low neck of her chemise.

"A week seems, suddenly, a very long time."

"I believe you told me husbands are allowed one kiss."

"A rule that hardly seems to apply in our situation."

She glanced up to find that he was no longer at the foot of the bed, but was standing beside her.

"Our situation?" she questioned. His eyes, looking down into hers, were again starred like the sapphire he'd given her.

"Lovers," he reminded her softly, "are allowed as many as they can steal. Don't you remember anything I've taught you, Catherine? Shall I be forced to begin all over again?"

She was once more mesmerized by him, by the powerful body, his voice, the piercing crystal eyes. And his beautiful hands.

Her fingers had played with the narrow satin ribbon until the bow had loosened. Now her hand stilled under the spell he was weaving. He placed his palm over her fingers. With his forefinger he stroked the hollow at the base of her throat. She swallowed suddenly, feeling the soft pressure of his touch against that movement. The long dark finger began to slide slowly down her chest and into the rift between her breasts. He carried her hand down with him, out of his way, so the opening at the top of her chemise, which the ribbon had once secured, was now unobstructed. With his thumb he pushed the material away from the swell of her breast. His eyes never left hers, compelling her to allow this. And she had no strength, in the face of his, with which to deny him. She lay against the propped pillows, acquiescent and more than willing for him to touch her.

He eased down to sit beside her on the bed, his thumb continuing the slow rhythm it had begun, smoothing over the soft, milk white skin of her breast. She knew he could feel her heartbeat, running too rapidly, like a frightened hart, just under the heel of his hand. And her breathing, uneven, coming in shuddering inhalations. And he was barely touching her.

His fingers slipped under her breast and lifted gently. Her eyes closed with the impact of the sensations moving through her. He held the heavy globe a moment, his thumb never stopping its now-familiar stroke, from the darker valley up onto the curving ivory swell and back. His fingers began to spread out under the weight of her breast, to glide upward until the callused edge of his forefinger was under her nipple. And then over it, sliding across with a sensuous abrasion that sent sensations shuddering through her stomach and between her legs, which moved involuntarily, loosening, waiting for what, she didn't know. Wanting.

And then he allowed his fingers to catch her nipple between them. She gasped softly, her eyes flying open to find his. Reassuring. Steadying. Telling her without words that this was what she had waited for so long. So long when she hadn't known what she'd wanted. Only Raven.

She waited still, and when his fingers moved again, pressing the small, sensitive nub between their strength, her eyes closed and her hips writhed uncontrollably. Pushing into the bed, seeking. Still innocent of what they sought.

His hand shifted, the hard palm again cupping under her breast and lifting it. His fingers pushed the soft cotton of her chemise away, the air suddenly shocking against the dark warmth his hand had given her skin. She felt his breath—hot and moist, tantalizing—a second before she realized what he intended. His lips touched where his fingers had been, enclosing the peak that had grown taut and aching under their relentless demand. That demand was now replaced by the caress of his mouth, soft and sweet. Wet and hot. Moving over her nipple. Pulling. A dark embrace. Lifting her skin into his mouth. Suckling gently.

And all the nerve endings nature had so generously supplied in that place responded, acting according to divine design. A spectacularly emotive reaction. Building and tearing down. All the barriers destroyed. All the preconceptions rearranged by the reality of what it meant to have Raven's mouth on her body.

As she moved, her hips arching again without her conscious volition, she never once remembered Amberton's touch. There could be no parallel between what had happened then and what was now taking place under the exquisite command of Raven's lovemaking. Her lips breathed his name, a sighing surrender. Her fingers tangled in the blackness of his hair, finding it as silken as it had appeared last night, loose then, unrestricted as she wanted it now to be.

At the sounds that began in her throat, torn, almost, from lips that had opened at the first contact of his mouth over the reaching peak of her breast, he allowed his teeth to close very gently over the rose nipple. Teasing. Then his tongue's caress replaced that nearly painful tension, circling, pushing back and forth across the hard tip.

She couldn't breathe. There was no more air left in the universe. Their universe. No one else had ever inhabited this world or ever would. His teeth grazed her flesh again, biting softly this time. Nibbling on the edge of pain. She was aware of the heat building between her legs, burning and yet so wet. Needing.

The feel of his mouth was primitive, dark and elemental. And somehow elegant, like what happened to her body when she danced or rode. The movements awakening something inside that demanded a response, just as his lips were demanding. And her body was trying to respond, moving against the bed, lifting as if to find his. As if to meld her softness into that hard strength.

"Raven," she begged, because she didn't know anything else now but him. There was nothing in her experience to help her. He had taken her far beyond what was familiar and into a realm that was unexplored. And she was lost without his guidance.

At something in those whispered syllables, at what was very obviously a plea, Raven responded. The pressure of his mouth and teeth eased until he was holding her only with his lips. And then, lifting his head slightly, he released the distended nipple. The sudden breath of cool air against the moist skin that his mouth had been warming was harshly invasive, another almost-painful sensation. She whimpered at the loss of his touch. At that pleading sound, his lips caressed the peak he'd so lovingly created and then deserted. Caressed as gently as he'd kissed her nose the last time he'd deserted her.

He eased away from her body, sitting up to look down into her face, which was softened with passion as it had never been before. She no longer cared that he could read what she was feeling. And, of course, she couldn't have hidden what he'd done to her even if she *had* desired any longer to keep her emotions hidden. But she didn't. She was his and she had no will to hide her feelings from him ever again.

"I told you," he said. "Very rare."

She couldn't speak. Not yet. It was too new, whatever bond he'd forged between the masculine beauty of his body and the small, seeking softness of hers. And so she lay, watching him. Drained. Exhausted by emotion. And he'd only touched her.

"You, Mrs. Raven, are indeed very rare."

Her smile was not practiced. She was too far beyond the

boundaries of flirtation. Too far into a place she'd never before entered to be able to command her features.

"Why?" she whispered. She raised her hand to touch the single strand of dark hair that had escaped confinement. It was as soft as before and as enticing to her trembling fingers. She wanted to loosen the ribbon that held the rest and feel its curling length run like silk threads through her hands.

"Because little girls aren't supposed to react like that," he said, answering her smile. She didn't resent, this time, the suggestion that she was very young. She felt very young, especially when confronted with his obvious experience.

"And how are little girls supposed to react?"

"Shocked?" he suggested softly, his smile widening into small creases that broke the hard plane of his lean cheeks. She shook her head.

"No?" he asked, his fingers rearranging the edges of the chemise and, graceful despite their size, retying the small ribbon.

"I like your hands," she said.

He looked up from his task, and his soft laughter was very pleasant. She felt her mouth responding with a smile, answering his laugh just as her body had answered his caress. So in tune to his every movement.

"I thought you said they were too big."

"No," she whispered. "I like you big."

Raven's amusement deepened, suddenly breaking through his normal control. He laughed, full and rich, and without self-consciousness, revealing very white teeth against the golden skin. Although she wasn't entirely sure what had caused that response, she laughed with him. Because she belonged to him.

"I hope so, my sweet darling," he said finally, the laughter still lurking in the lucid depths of his sapphire eyes. "Dear God, I certainly hope so."

"Goodbye, Raven," she said bravely, exactly as she had before in response to his request. *Before,* she thought, shivering. "I hope you have a very pleasant journey."

"And I wonder if you know how impossible that's just become. How impossible you've made the likelihood of that."

"No," she said.

"Will you try to stay out of trouble while I'm gone? No more card games with lecherous bastards and no water hazards?"

He took her fingers and brought them to his lips, his eyes meeting hers as he allowed his tongue to trace over the fine porcelain skin on the back of her hand. She followed the movement with her eyes, remembering the previous journey of his tongue over her breast, as he had, of course, intended.

"Recuperating." She forced the word through dry lips.

"What?" he asked, dropping a small kiss between each finger.

She swallowed, trying to find the breath to answer him. The sensations in her lower body were beginning again. Simply because he was touching her hand, she realized with wonder.

"I'm going to be recuperating," she said, fighting the urge to tighten her fingers over his, to try to hold him to her. God, she didn't want him to leave, now that she had just discovered how very much she desired him.

"Good," he said softly, placing her hand carefully against the sheet. "And I'm going to be remembering. Miss me," he said, and she wasn't sure if it was a question or a command.

"I miss you already," she whispered truthfully. She missed his touch. The feel of his mouth against her skin.

"Close your eyes," he commanded. Willingly she obeyed. She felt his weight leave the bed, and then unexpectedly and very gently, as if she really were as fragile as the Venetian goblets downstairs, he kissed her forehead.

And the hated tears were already welling when the door closed behind him.

Chapter Thirteen

"But if you think that Mrs. Raven—" the groom began.

"I don't think Mrs. Raven's in any danger. I'd never undertake this journey if that were the case," Raven explained patiently. "The doctor has ordered at least a week's recuperation, which should preclude any activities outside the house. If she does venture out before I return, I want you with her. And I don't think she's in danger." Raven wondered for whom he'd made that repeated assurance. He knew, however, that *he* had been the target of the attack, and the farther away from Catherine he was, the safer she should be.

"But Mr. Raven—"

"Don't let her out of your sight, Jem. I'll be back on Sunday. I'm trusting you with the most precious thing I possess," Raven said, placing his hand on the shoulder of Catherine's groom. "Don't let me down."

Jem nodded, his eyes meeting his master's in perfect understanding, and Raven's lips relaxed into a softer alignment. This man would protect Catherine with his life.

Intellectually, Raven might know for whom that bullet had been meant, and that the last thing the old man would want was to hurt his daughter. Whatever estrangement might have been caused by her marriage, Catherine was still the Duke of Monfort's only child. Raven would never leave if he believed his wife's safety was threatened, but to be certain...

"One stop," he instructed the coachman as he mounted the narrow steps of the carriage that would carry him north. His hand touched the fine line of the scar on his high cheekbone. He imagined his welcome this time would be even colder than when he'd last visited that elegant town house. And as he remembered, it had been remarkably unwelcoming then.

Montfort's butler recognized him. Raven could see the same fear reflected in the man's eyes that had been there before. Especially when the American pushed open the door of the Mayfair mansion, despite the servant's resistance.

"But his grace isn't expecting—" Hartford began.

"He damn well should be," Raven said, easily breaking away from the trembling hand attempting to grip his arm. He threw open doors until he found the duke, seated at a rosewood desk.

The old man looked up from whatever had been occupying his attention, lifting the gold lorgnette he had been using and focusing its glass on the massive figure of his son-in-law. If he was surprised by this invasion of his office, that emotion was not evident in the expression with which he regarded the American.

"I'm going to assume you have a reason for being here," Montfort said.

"You may be certain, your grace, that I'd never put myself in the position of having to be civil to you without reason."

"Civil?" the duke taunted softly at Raven's tone. One white eyebrow climbed cynically. "But perhaps our stan-

dards are different," he suggested with more than a trace
of condescension.

"Very different," Raven agreed, his words as mocking
as his father-in-law's. "*I've* never ordered anyone shot in
the back."

"Indeed," Montfort said, his lips twitching in amusement. "I'm very relieved by that confidence. If, however,
that is the extent of the information you desire to impart..."
Pausing, he waved one bejeweled hand at the stack of documents on his desk.

"I'll fight you or your hirelings any time you wish, your
grace," Raven said, anger building at the dismissal, "but
if you ever hurt my wife again, I'll gut you like the animal
you are."

The boredom in the midnight eyes remained a fraction
of a second before the import in his words reached the
sharp brain behind them. Something shifted in their glittering depths, and Montfort repeated, his voice no longer
taunting, "*Hurt* your wife?"

"Your assassin missed, as I'm sure he informed you.
What he didn't tell you, I suppose, is that his ball grazed
Catherine's mare, which as a result bolted with her."

There was a long silence. Montfort said finally, his eyes
never wavering from the cold fury in Raven's, "And my
daughter?"

"Catherine was thrown."

There was another long, silent heartbeat. Raven could
hear his own, pulsing too quickly, frightened as well as
furious at the renewed images of what might have happened.

"I assume you intend to tell me the outcome," Montfort
suggested. He had lowered the lorgnette, the thin, elegant
fingers of both hands playing with it restlessly, so that
Raven periodically caught glimpses of gold. Unbidden, the

surety came again that the old man had never meant to hurt Catherine.

"Bruises," Raven admitted, watching the white fingers pause suddenly. The duke's mouth tightened, and then he set the quizzing glass on the desk. When the midnight eyes glanced up from under those intimidating brows, they were again politely amused.

"How fortunate," he said. "If you are unable to protect my daughter, Mr. Raven, perhaps it might be better if you allowed—"

Raven didn't bother to listen to whatever suggestion the old man was about to make. "I'll protect Catherine from the devil himself," he promised softly. And then remembering what Jem had told him, he released his own lips from the rigid line in which they'd been set. The Devil Duke, the groom had called the old man. How bloody apt.

"Don't hurt my wife again," Raven said. "I'm warning you."

He turned on his heel and started across the room. The butler was standing in the open door of the duke's study, backed by four burly footmen. Raven met the majordomo's eyes with nothing but contempt in the cold blue ice of his own. The servant's glance flicked to his master, and at whatever silent communication passed between them, the butler stepped out of Raven's way, sending footmen scattering behind him. For a moment Raven allowed his amusement to show before he strode across the wide foyer.

As he reached for the front door, it opened before him, and for the first time in months Raven found himself confronting the Viscount Amberton, the sartorial elegance of the bottle green morning coat he was wearing almost matching the duke's. Birds of a feather, Raven thought, his lips moving at the mental image of two strutting male peacocks. Still smiling, he bowed slightly to the English aristocrat, who had stepped back with the same alacrity just exhibited by his grace's servants.

"Don't worry, Amberton. I'm not going to hurt you," Raven promised, amusement again allowed to tinge that assured voice.

The viscount's blue eyes met his, revealing in their depths an emotion Raven identified correctly as unadulterated hatred.

"Family business?" Amberton asked, recovering his aplomb, his own mockery very clear at the idea that the coal merchant and the English duke might have any other business in common.

"Exactly," Raven agreed calmly. Nodding, he stepped around the viscount and into the clean sunshine of the London street.

When the door closed behind the American, Amberton's lips whitened and a small muscle twitched beside his mouth. Realizing finally that the servants were watching, the viscount strolled across the foyer with his usual languid grace and entered, unannounced, the office where the duke sat.

Montfort had been tapping the lorgnette he held lightly against his cheek. The dark eyes came up at the nobleman's entrance. "Tell me, Amberton," his grace said, "do you know anyone for hire with, shall we say, a disposition to violence?"

Raven closed his eyes and rested his head against the leather of the carriage seat, exhausted by what he'd accomplished in the short time he'd been in the north. He had spent the last four days pretending interest during endless meetings, and additional hours at night writing out the terms that had been agreed to in contracts to be signed the following day. In the dim quietness of his lonely rooms, in which he seldom had the opportunity to rest his head against the pillow of the undisturbed bed, the memories of a very different bed intruded.

Catherine. He savored again the unexpected responses she'd made to his touch, welcoming his hands and even his mouth against the soft, smooth fragrance of that porcelain skin. Raven's body would harden against his will, against all his determined intent, torturing him with the promise of what awaited his return.

And even here in the confines of the coach, bound finally for London, he could feel that painful reaction to the unending fantasies he had of making Catherine his. Of finally being allowed to show her what he felt, what he *had* felt since the day he had first looked up into those russet eyes misted with unshed tears. Exactly as they had been the morning he'd left.

As his heritage had compelled him, he had honored the vow he'd made to Catherine so long ago, when they had begun this inconvenient *mariage de convenance*. And now, finally, he would honor, too, the promise he had made only to himself.

The noise that shattered the intensity of his memories was as recognizable as it had been the morning in Hyde Park. Harsh commands and then shots, sharp and clear, disturbed the cold upland air. His orders to Tom, however, had been explicit. John Raven was no one's fool, and he'd known that another attempt to put an end to his life and, therefore, to his unsuitable marriage, might be made on this journey. The mate to the pistol that was now held competently in Raven's right hand had been given to the coachman in anticipation of just such a challenge. And Tom had been told to drive on, no matter what.

The coach swayed more strongly, the tiring horses prodded with the whip to outrace the men who were trying to stop them. Raven wondered if this assault had been that carefully planned—the site well isolated and yet near the next post station to ensure the team's fatigue. And remembering the shrewd mind behind those midnight eyes, he knew that nothing had been left to chance.

The road was dangerously narrow, the coach rocketing between the sweep of wind-gnarled trees on one side and a rock-strewn drop on the other. Raven fired methodically, exposing himself briefly at the window as he squeezed off his careful shots, then retreated inside to reload, his hands automatically performing the necessary procedure. He could hear their pursuers, shouting to one another and their occasional shots. He never knew which of those had the desired effect, but Tom would, of course, have presented a stark target for the following riders, his body silhouetted against the leaden sky of the north country.

The horses plunged onward, now without the familiar guidance of experienced hands on their reins. Legs trembled from exhaustion and panic, and eventually there came the fatal stumble, throwing off the steady cadence that had sustained the chase. The break in rhythm began to unravel the confidence of that precise team that had strained in unison for miles. Dangerously out of synchronization now, the horses faltered, allowing the carriage to career too close to the hillside along which the roadway had been cut. The outside leader lost its footing in the rubble, struggling frantically to regain its stride, but it was too late. The rear wheel of the coach rounded the curve well off the road. It collided with one of the boulders that edged the decline and splintered, ending any prospect that the horses might, in their exhaustion, have slowed enough to allow the man inside, waiting his chance, to attempt the hazardous climb to the empty box.

Instead, pulled by the resulting tilt of the damaged vehicle, the outside pair first and then the entire team were dragged over the edge with the heavy coach, onto the rocks below. At the initial impact with the boulder, Raven had braced his body in the protected space between the facing seats. The fall seemed to take an eternity, the vehicle rolling end over end to the bottom of the decline. Eventually the shattered carriage came to rest, one wheel still spinning drunkenly, the traces attached to the carnage of broken and dying horses.

Raven was not aware when the crushed door was forced open by his pursuers, who had willingly made the treacherous climb down the rock face. After all, they had been very well paid to make sure the American never reached London. Very well paid indeed.

The long hours of Saturday trudged by without any sign of Raven's arrival. Despite her determination to react with calmness, Catherine had started, her heart in her throat, at every sound of carriage wheels in the street. She stayed up very late waiting, not even bothering to offer an excuse for her behavior to Edwards, who unobtrusively kept watch over her vigil. When she had finally surrendered to her disappointment to begin the long climb upstairs, the butler himself had lighted her way and had bid her good-night with an almost paternal kindness.

Sunday was an endless succession of hours that she spent going through the motions of living. Foolishly, that night the tears came again. She remembered her anxiety the last time Raven had been away, but then there had been some excuse for her behavior. This was sheer lovesickness. She wanted Raven here, teasing her, his blue eyes glinting with hidden laughter and the stern line of his beautiful mouth controlled. Until it touched her and left her uncontrolled. Lost without his guidance.

The boot that prodded Raven's ribs was not gentle, but compared to the other sensations his body had endured in the last hours, not particularly brutal. The journey up the incline, and then the endless ride draped across the back of the rough-gaited cob they'd thrown him over, hands and feet tied, dangling like an ill-arranged pack of tinker's wares, had been far worse.

He had drifted in and out of consciousness, pain almost defeating his ability to plan, to think, to care anymore what happened. All he wanted was to stop the agony. His will to endure, trained and instilled from childhood, had been lost with the cataclysm in his skull. Only by focusing on the one image that remained, untouched by what was happening to his unprotesting body, could he retain a desire to survive. Catherine. Again he allowed her picture to superimpose the agony in his mind, to block it. He had made a vow, and had been so close to fulfilling it. So near that he could feel her slenderness beneath his driving body, arching upward into—

"Time to wake up," a voice said, interrupting that fantasy.

He was lying on the ground, with rocks embedded in the muscles of his back. He forced open the one eyelid that still functioned, and watched the wavering outline of a man appear between him and the graying sky of twilight. Hours must have passed since the coach had crashed.

"Why?" he whispered, the one syllable all he could manage.

"Because someone don't like you very well," the disembodied voice affirmed. "And he's willing to pay to have you disappear."

"I'll give you ten times—" Raven began, the offer cut off by his captor's laugh.

"He said you'd try that, but honor among thieves, you know. I have a contract. And, I understand, you ain't got that much money anymore. All your ready gone in some worthless scheme to build a railway." Again the laugh jarred in Raven's skull. "Some folks'll believe anything," the man said mockingly.

"What are you going to do?" Raven asked. It was almost idle curiosity. Trussed like a dressed fowl, there wasn't much he could do to prevent whatever they intended.

"I'm going to make you disappear, Mr. Raven. And I thought of the perfect way—a way that gives a little justice to men like me. You want to put miners out of their jobs, I hear. To use machines in your mines, and let the folks that have always worked them starve to death, along with their babes."

"That's not true," Raven said, anger imbuing his voice with strength. They didn't understand. No one understood the potential of the machines to ease human suffering.

"You ever been in a coal mine, Mr. Nabob? Ever had coal dust ground into your skin so it don't wash off no matter how hard you try? I thought you might like a taste of what a mine's like."

Raven swallowed the sudden fear, fought its control. He was beginning to win the battle to think, to fight the lethargy left by his injuries, but if they threw him down a shaft...

"You can cooperate or we can throw you in. I don't have no stomach for killing a man all tied up. Not quite sporting, it seems to me. But eventually, time will accomplish the same end. It ain't a real mine, just a test hole. And if it rains, you'll have some time. A few days to think about the miners you've put out of work, their starving families. There may even be some water down there from the last rain. Uncomfortable being cold and wet, but I don't imagine you'll mind after a while. Get him up," the man ordered, and rough hands callously accommodated him. Someone fitted a loop of rope around the toes of Raven's boots and then put the trailing hemp into his hands.

"Hold on now, Mr. Raven," the one who had done all the talking commanded. "Let's see how you like the dark."

Three of them picked him up, swinging his body over the edge of the pit. Raven was afraid suddenly that they wouldn't be able to hold the rope with the pull of his weight, but when they began to slowly lower him into the increasing blackness, he wondered why he had worried about living through the descent. Wouldn't it be better to die quickly, to fall to death rather than to starve, prolonging the torment of dying, alone and in the darkness?

The rope was released suddenly and he dropped a short distance, his boots striking the ground first and then his knees banging painfully onto the damp, unyielding hardness. His hands, tied palm to palm, automatically broke the rest of his fall. He felt the remaining rope drop over his back and shoulders.

"Goodbye, Mr. Raven," the voice said from a very long way above his head. Despairing, he closed his eyes, and before him, again, was the image of Catherine as he had left her that morning, her lips parted slightly and her eyes, wide and dark, locked onto his as he touched her.

You made a vow, his grandmother's voice echoed inside his head. *And you must keep your promise, my dark and beautiful Raven. All your promises.*

He rolled slowly onto his back, and despairing, watched the light fade from the sky far above his head and the stars gradually replace the dusky dimness of twilight with true night.

"But the situation is extremely critical, Mrs. Raven. I must impress upon you—" Oliver Reynolds argued, wondering why he had believed it might be beneficial to visit his client's wife.

Since the disastrous meeting with the investors this morning, a meeting at which John Raven had failed to appear, the banker had tried to decide upon the best course of action. He had, he supposed, been a fool to allow the bank to become involved in a scheme this speculative. Visions of the profits that would accrue if the American nabob succeeded had blinded him to the risk. That and the character of the man himself.

It had been in remembering John Raven's character that he had made his call, uninvited and unannounced, on Catherine Montfort Raven. A last hope. A desperate gamble for information. Information which he now knew she didn't possess.

"What's *critical,* Mr. Reynolds, is the fact that my husband seems to have disappeared. And you're far more concerned with protecting your investment than with determining what might have happened to him," Catherine retorted angrily.

"*His* investment as well. I assure you, Mrs. Raven—"

"Have you sent out inquiries? Do you have people looking for my husband?" she interrupted again to ask.

"I hadn't..." Reynolds began, and then paused, wondering if he dared tell her what had been suggested today as a reason for her husband's disappearance. Montfort's daughter, he thought again. That devious old bastard. And judging by the steel in the girl's voice, she had inherited some of the old man's temper. "No," he finished simply, meeting the steady brown eyes.

"And why not? If you're so concerned about Raven's—"

"It was suggested Mr. Raven might not *wish* to be found."

The movement of the slender fingers tearing at the lace edging of her handkerchief was arrested. She waited a moment, the mind behind those remarkable eyes obviously also owing something to her father.

"Suggested?" Catherine finally asked, her voice controlled.

"By one of the investors."

"But why? Why would Raven want to disappear?" she asked, thinking of the morning he'd left. Of the promise that had been in the flame of those blue eyes. She shook her head. Her lips lifted slightly, knowing how ridiculous that was.

"Mr. Raven carried with him to the north a rather large sum of money. Other such sums have, in the past weeks, supposedly been used to secure the land and to make the necessary—"

"Supposedly?" Montfort's daughter repeated coldly.

Oliver Reynolds could feel the perspiration beginning to dew his forehead. He removed his own handkerchief and dabbed at the moisture before he answered, "Your husband's accounts are dangerously low, depleted, he said, to finance the venture. The investors, however, whose moneys are also involved, are not so certain of that situation. It was suggested," he said again, thinking how to word what could only be an insult, "that Mr. Raven's disappearance at this juncture is too...coincidental."

"Implying Raven has absconded with the investors' money?"

"I am simply repeating what was said. This morning. At a very important meeting your husband failed to attend."

"And what did these partners suggest you do about it?" she asked bitterly. She could hear the anger building in her own voice, but was pleased to believe that the old man was unaware of it. How dare they accuse Raven of stealing their damned money?

"They want an accounting of your husband's remaining holdings. They're demanding to be repaid."

"But you said Raven's funds were tied up in the land he's bought, in the contracts he's made for the railway. If they pull out now..." She was beginning to realize the extent of that potential disaster. No wonder the banker was so upset. "Then it's over. It collapses. And Raven loses everything," she breathed aloud. This was what he had warned her about. Everything he owned would be taken to pay off his partners.

"Exactly," Reynolds agreed, relieved that she'd arrived at that point on her own. He wiped his face again and then stuffed the cloth back into his pocket. "I thought he might have told you...something of his intentions."

"His intentions to steal from men I lured to my dinner table so they could be fleeced?" the girl asked, her lips again curved in a small, knowing smile. "No, Mr. Reynolds, I assure you my husband didn't impart anything of that plan to me. What he did tell me, and what you may be very sure is the truth, is that he intended to return to London on Sunday. And since he has not yet arrived, I can also assure you that something has happened to him. And I intend to discover what it is."

"But how will you—"

"I'm going to do what you should have already done. First I'm going to send out search parties. And then I'm going to consult my father. I imagine he'll want a list of the investors. If you would be so good as to provide one?"

Thinking about handing the Duke of Montfort a list of the gentlemen who had only this morning been screaming for John Raven's head on a platter sent a tremor through the banker. He was too old for this, he thought with despair. "Your father?" he repeated, just to make certain he'd not misunderstood.

"The Duke of Montfort," Catherine said, smiling at him. It was the provocative one she'd practiced so often at her mirror. "After all," she assured the old man, "this is a family matter."

* * *

When Oliver Reynolds finally stood on the stoop of John Raven's town house, he again wiped his brow. At least it was no longer his problem alone, he thought. Montfort's daughter had been extremely efficient, once informed of the situation. As businesslike as her husband when it came to making decisions. And that was surprising in itself, given her age and her class. Women of her circle were supposed to be highly decorative and nothing else.

What the banker had found even more surprising than her intellect was Catherine Raven's unshakable faith in her husband's intentions. Everyone in London might be convinced of the American's duplicity, but his wife's calm amusement that John Raven could have planned anything remotely dishonest was the most reassuring thing the banker had heard today.

Now, however, he must prepare the information she had requested for her father. The Devil Duke himself, the old man thought again, remembering all the stories. A bad man to cross, they said, and Reynolds couldn't imagine Montfort being willing to bail out a son-in-law not of his choosing. The gossipmongers had been quite specific about that. The Viscount Amberton had been the horse the duke had been backing, and the banker could imagine what his grace had felt about his daughter's runaway marriage.

There had been something else, Reynolds remembered, following that train of thought. Some rumor about Amberton. Something financial, he believed. He couldn't remember exactly what those whispers had concerned, but it would come to him, he knew. He never forgot anything dealing with money.

"Excuse me, sir." A voice interrupted his effort to remember.

Cap in hand, Jem had stood respectfully waiting for the old man to notice him. It seemed to him that someone should know what had happened, now that Mr. Raven had disappeared. The responsibility the groom had been given for Mrs. Raven's safety loomed as a task beyond his ability, especially with the master missing.

"You *are* Mr. Raven's man of business, aren't you?" Jem asked, hoping he was doing the right thing.

The old man nodded, wondering what kind of household the American had put together, where a schoolroom chit gave orders about business and the grooms addressed callers.

"Then there's something, sir, I think you should know. Something that happened before Mr. Raven left London," Jem said, "and some right disturbing things I've noticed since."

The groom's relief, now that he had made the decision to unburden himself, hurried the careful recitation he had planned. And eventually he found it very gratifying that he had such an avid listener.

Chapter Fourteen

Catherine watched her father scan the list Oliver Reynolds had prepared. She already knew the names it contained. Devon, Cumberland and Avondale. Russell and Elliot. Templeton and the Earl of Surrey. Even the Duke of Exeter. There were one or two she didn't know very well, but all were friends of her father's.

Because of that friendship, they had come to her home to meet her husband. And now that Raven had failed to keep his appointment with them, it appeared he had intended to cheat them all along. She understood the men of her class well enough to know that whatever plans her husband had had to involve these gentlemen in future projects would now be doomed.

"You must be joking," her father said, his thin lips curled in a very self-satisfied smile. In spite of the fact that she loved him, Catherine felt the urge to wipe the smirk off his face with the flat of her hand. She had been forced to deal with this business while almost frantic with worry about Raven. And she knew that her father was enjoying very much the idea that he had been right about John Raven and she had, again, been quite wrong.

"Why should I guarantee an extremely risky scheme

concocted by your husband to divest some of my more gullible acquaintances of their money? Surely you know me better than that, Catherine. Just because he's managed to take you and these idiots—''

"Raven hasn't taken any one in. He offered them an opportunity to become partners in an investment that promises a very high rate of return. He himself has invested far more than any of the others. Probably more than all of them combined."

"You may convey my thanks for that opportunity to Mr. Raven, my dear, at the same time you convey my regrets. My funds are all tied up in legitimate and quite practical ventures. And now if you'll excuse me..." He raised one brow.

"No, I won't excuse you. I need your help," she said angrily. "Why else do you imagine I would give you the chance to gloat as you're doing? And I must tell you, it's most unbecoming."

They had always struck sparks off one another. Too strong willed and too much alike to deal easily together, they had been bound by the fact that neither had anyone else. And she realized for the first time that in her case it was no longer true.

"Forgive me, but I still don't intend to invest. You must have known that when you came. I'm surprised at you, Catherine."

"I had no choice," she admitted.

She knew she would have to tell him the truth and throw herself on his mercies. He was, after all, her father. And no matter how strongly he'd threatened her with his displeasure in the past, his anger had never withstood their mutual affection. He needed her, she knew, as much as she needed him. And loved him, she admitted. She hadn't stopped to think what her marriage and their estrangement would mean to him before today, and she had been shocked by the changes these few months had wrought. He was an old man, and he looked his age. Stubborn and proud as always, but older than she'd ever realized before.

"No choice?" he questioned, his black eyes studying her.

"Raven went north to finish the arrangements for the rail system before last Monday's meeting. He intended to return on Sunday, but...he hasn't yet come home." She refused to put into words the reality; that he had disappeared. "And now the partners are demanding to be repaid, but with the expenditures he's already laid out for the land and the rails, the contracts he's already signed..." She hesitated, but was forced by the situation to admit the rest. "Even if Reynolds sells what he can and uses my trust fund, there won't be enough capital available to repay the investors. If they pull out now, the entire venture will collapse, and Raven will lose everything. Unless you convince them that Raven's railroad is still a sound investment, and..." She paused before she finally found the courage to suggest, "And that you're standing behind your son-in-law."

"What do you imagine has happened to your husband, Catherine?" her father asked, his eyes still on her face.

"I don't know. I can't imagine. It's so... But I know something's happened to him. He promised..." Her voice faltered, but again she forced herself to continue. "I've hired people to look. To follow the route he took, but so far there's no word. I don't know what else to do," she admitted. That admission was very painful. An admission of her failure.

"Let me arrange a divorce," the duke suggested softly.

"A divorce?" she gasped, unable to believe that was his response to her plea. "I don't want a divorce. Why would you believe that I want a divorce?"

"It seems apparent to me you've been deserted, my dear."

"I haven't been deserted. That you could suggest such a thing shows how little you understand. Raven would never..." Knowing the futility of continuing that line of argument, she shook her head. What could she say about their evolving relationship that would make the duke as certain as she that her husband had not voluntarily walked away from their marriage? "Raven always honors his contracts," she ventured finally, knowing as she said it that words would never convince her father.

"I would imagine Elliot and the rest are finding little comfort in that claim," he suggested cynically.

"Then they don't know him as well as I do," Catherine said, meeting his eyes with conviction in the depths of hers.

"Not, perhaps, in the biblical sense," her father agreed, his thin lips moving slightly. "Admit it, my dear. You've simply made another mistake. Whatever you've done, however outrageously you've acted in the past, you've always been just this certain that you were right. And clearly, again, you were wrong. But because I'm your father, I am willing to help you. More than willing, if you'll allow yourself to be guided by me."

"To divorce my husband? To make a more suitable match? With someone like Amberton, I suppose," she said bitterly, remembering the announcement to the *Post* and the viscount's subsequent actions. But given Raven's disappearance, it would be hard to persuade her father he was the one who had been wrong.

"I haven't heard much from Lord Amberton. At least not since their confrontation. Broke his arm, you know."

"Raven?" Catherine asked, fascinated. She couldn't imagine how her father could possibly know about that incident, but she wasn't surprised to find out that Raven had hurt the viscount, given Gerald's actions that day. "No, as a matter of fact, I didn't know. But I'm not surprised. He stabbed Raven. With a sword. And Raven wasn't armed."

"Apparently to deal with the viscount, he didn't need to be," the duke said, the trace of amusement still in his voice. "What happened? Did you lead Amberton on to make your husband jealous? Lead him on enough that it became a blood feud?"

He knew her too well, Catherine thought. He knew her recklessness would have had something to do with the incident.

"Gerald objected to my marriage to Raven. He had expected I'd marry him. You had led him to believe I would, and that such a union would have your blessing."

"I thought you liked Amberton."

"I didn't want to *marry* him. Especially..." She remembered Gerald's actions at the dance, and how he'd treated her in his apartment. And how he'd stabbed Raven, who hadn't been armed.

"Especially after you met the coal merchant and fell in love," her father finished for her.

"No," Catherine admitted, smiling at him for the first time. "Our marriage, in the beginning, was a business arrangement."

"And now?" he asked softly.

"And now..." She hesitated, remembering. "Now it is something very different. I don't know what's happened to Raven, but I do know that he hasn't disappeared by choice. He wouldn't do that."

"What do you want from me?" Montfort asked.

"Help me find Raven. And until we do, protect his investment by agreeing to come into the partnership."

Raven forced his body up from the cold dampness of the stone floor. He knew as he moved that it had been a mistake to allow the brief respite. His swollen knees and the cramping muscles of his thighs had convinced him that a few moments of precious rest would enable him to go back to the task he had stoically accepted as the only way out, the only hope that he might escape. Now, however, he knew what a serious mistake that pause had been.

He had believed his hands had lost all feeling. Had feared it. In the back of his mind had stirred the horror that the condition might be permanent, but he'd pushed the possibility away, realizing that even if that were true, he had no other choice. Not if he intended to fulfill the vow he'd made.

He had finally found, inching carefully on his knees around the pit into which he'd been lowered, a small, rough outcropping. He had then spent hours, still on his knees, working the rope against the sharp edge of rock.

And now, with the first renewed abrasion, he was forced to acknowledge that there was still a great deal of sensation in those damaged hands. Swollen far more grotesquely than his knees, bleeding and raw with their continual contact against the rock face he was using to sever the ropes that bound him, they still, definitely, had feeling. The edge of rock that seemed to have so little effect on the hemp had abraded the flesh of his hands extremely well. There was only one position in which they would fit over the narrow outcropping and allow it to make contact with the rope— at least, now that the rock had removed a great deal of flesh from his hands.

He closed his eyes, pushing the pain again toward the small dark circle he began to create inside his head, to be swallowed and lost in the darkness. The fakirs in India could do this—destroy their consciousness of sensations that should be too painful for human flesh to bear. As his grandmother's people had been trained to do. Raven tried to remember the lessons she had taught him so long ago. Tried to close off the unending agony of forcing his mutilated hands over and over against the rock.

He allowed the sibilant whispers of the old woman's

voice to circle in his mind, fighting the pain and fear. He could destroy his hands, will his mind to allow that destruction, in spite of screaming nerves and raw flesh, but he had no control over the rope. No control over how long it would take its strands to fray and part. No control. Only prayer. And a remembered vow.

Catherine's father had proved a valuable ally during the days following Raven's disappearance. The shattered coach had been found by the searchers, and Tom's body brought home, but there had been no trace of the American in or near the wreckage. The duke expanded the search Catherine had begun, sending his agents to areas far from the route Raven had taken.

Although she believed she had held up remarkably well under the pressure, Catherine was beginning to fear they wouldn't find him. Indestructible, she constantly reminded herself. Raven was indestructible, but she came to dread the entrance of one of the servants and felt an almost euphoric relief when the interruption turned out to have been caused by some household question.

She had racked her brain for any explanation for Raven's disappearance, other than the one everyone else believed. She had found herself remembering the fight with Amberton and her husband's subsequent disappearance. Gerald's attack had been done in fear, a reaction to Raven's anger; one might even argue that Gerald had acted in self-defense. She imagined that a furious John Raven would certainly produce terror in most men. Amberton was physically no match for her husband. When she suggested to her father the possibility that Raven's disappearance might somehow be laid at Gerald's door, he was reassuring.

"We have no reason to believe Amberton harbors any ill will against your husband. They both suffered from their encounter. Gerald has been peacefully tending to his own affairs. I can't think of any reason to connect the viscount with this business."

"And *I* can't forget the cowardly way he stabbed Raven when he was unarmed. That alone speaks to the character of the man."

"The man I intended you to marry?" her father reminded her.

Her lips lifted in a small, twisted smile, but she didn't reproach him. She was surprised when he went on.

"My apologies, Catherine. I was mistaken in that intent."

It was unusual for the Duke of Montfort to admit to being wrong about anything, but owning that he'd erred about a matter of such importance was almost unheard of.

"Thank you," Catherine said. "I hope..." She paused, thinking that all she had hoped might now never come to pass.

"What is it, my dear?" the duke asked, and at the kindness in his tone, she felt her eyes burn with tears, which were nearer the surface with each passing day. Resolutely, she had not allowed herself to shed them. Except in the dark loneliness of her bedroom, the last place she had seen Raven.

"I just thought that I would like you to know Raven. I would like very much for the two of you to be friends."

"We may never be friends, Catherine," Montfort replied, his tone amused. "Not given our past relationship."

She had a brief mental image of his raised hand bringing her crop down across Raven's face and knew he was right.

"But," he continued, "if we are successful in locating your husband, I will attempt to make amends for my previous behavior."

It was quite a concession for a man as proudly stubborn as His Grace, the Duke of Montfort, and Catherine was well aware of what an about-face it represented.

"Thank you," she said again. "I would like that. I'd like for you to know Raven as I do." And then realizing what her father believed about her relationship with her husband—a relationship that had not yet become conjugal—she amended, smiling at him, "Not, of course, in the biblical sense."

The staggering figure blended with the shadowed twilight that had crept over the back garden of the Mayfair mansion. There was no stealth employed in the approach, so that the Duke of Montfort's hireling had been aware of the man who transversed the alley behind the town house since he'd appeared on the edge of John Raven's property. His grace had employed the watcher to be alert to just such an event as was unfolding. As the intruder left the shadows to cross the broad expanse of lawn, which would give him access to the vulnerable doors at the back of the house, the duke's man moved silently into position behind him.

John Raven paused before the completion of this endless journey, a journey that had begun at the bottom of the hell-hole the old duke had intended to be his tomb. He looked up at the welcoming glow from the windows of his London town house, feeling his throat close with emotions he had forced himself to hold at bay until now. He had won, and he stood at last on the threshold of his own home. He blocked from his mind the toll he'd paid for that escape. Blue eyes lifted to find the windows he knew were Catherine's, and finally he allowed himself to imagine what she might be doing in that room as he stood below.

The point of the knife biting into his back was totally unexpected. He was a fool, Raven suddenly realized, to think that Montfort would not have planned for the possibility of his reappearance—would not have prepared for *every* eventuality. Panic clawed in his belly at the thought that he might have come so far, might have given up so much, only to now be denied.

No, damn it, you old bastard. Not when I've come so close, Raven swore. As that resolve formed, his body automatically began the graceful series of moves he had been taught during his years in the Orient. A downward twist accompanied the hammering blow of his elbow into the gut of the man behind him. Knowing he had already exceeded the limits of his strength, Raven also knew that if he did not succeed in his first attack, this would be a fight he would ultimately lose.

The remembrance of the old man's insults flashed into his head. *Your stench offends me,* Montfort had taunted. And so the two kicks with which Raven disarmed and then felled his assailant were fueled more by the idea of how satisfying it would be to assault his elegant father-in-law than by any anger against the duke's hireling. Gasping, Raven watched as the man dropped, but his opponent had already been forgotten. *Your time will come, Montfort,* he found himself thinking instead.

Threatened now only by his own exhaustion, Raven leaned against the wall of the coach house, watching his attacker for any sign of returning life and wondering what he thought he could do if the man did revive. But when a hand reached out of the growing darkness and touched his arm, Raven reacted to the new assault with the same unthinking skills he'd used to free himself before. Sweeping his attacker's legs out from under him, Raven threw him to the ground, even as a belated recognition swam to the surface of his mind.

Jem lay on the smooth lawn, looking up at him as if he belonged in Bedlam. "Mr. Raven," the groom whispered, his voice full of concern.

"Get that man up, Jem," Raven ordered, making no effort to hide his condition, but not acknowledging the anxiety he had heard underlying the groom's shock. "I have something I need to ask him." The henchman's answer would only be confirmation of what Raven already knew, but made now before a witness.

Unquestioning, from astonishment or from force of habit, the groom obeyed, pulling the man Raven had downed to his feet. Raven stepped behind his attacker and, using the advantage of his height, positioned his forearm around the man's throat, exerting as much upward force as he could without snapping his neck.

"Who hired you?" he asked.

"Go to hell," the man gasped through a windpipe he expected to collapse like rotten fruit under the pressure. In answer to that foolhardy bravado, his head was suddenly jerked upward, so that he strained on his toes, desperate for relief. He'd seen enough public hangings to know what was happening—his face darkening, tongue protruding as he fought for air.

"I'm sure they know you there. *And* your master. I want you to tell me his name, and this is your last chance," Raven warned.

Something must have broken through to the thug, so hardened by violence and deprivation he had believed he had no fear of death. Suddenly confronted by someone who promised it with such quiet conviction, he found he very much wanted to live.

"Montfort," he acknowledged, and felt the blessed air trickle through his bruised throat.

"Get out," Raven ordered, releasing the pressure he'd been maintaining with the last of his strength. And more than willing to obey, the man disappeared into the shadows. Startled by the unexpected command, the groom darted after him, realizing almost immediately that he had no chance of finding his quarry in the gathering darkness. Giving up,

Jem returned, to find his master leaning, eyes closed in the sunken sockets, against the wall.

"You shouldn't 'a let him go, Mr. Raven. We should have—"

"He'll report to the old man."

"You want *him* to tell Montfort you're back?" Jem asked, puzzled by that idea.

The blue eyes opened, full of amusement. "Someone will have to. Let him bear the brunt of his grace's displeasure. I should think that would be punishment enough for his role in all this."

"Displeasure?" Jem echoed. "But—"

"Get Edwards," Raven said, allowing his eyelids to fall again. Slowly the aching muscles of the legs that had carried him so far gave way to the weakness he had fought, and finally the abused knees bent. As the groom watched, the massive body folded as gracefully as a lady's fan, and John Raven slid down to lie on the comforting grass of his own back garden.

Catherine could never remember exactly what Jem told her, but by the time she arrived in the garden, her knees were trembling uncontrollably. The fear engendered by whatever the groom had said wasn't lessened by the sight of Edwards bending over the figure that lay collapsed on the lawn.

She was kneeling by her husband's side in a heartbeat. Edwards had slipped one of the maids' cloaks, a makeshift pillow, under his head. Raven's lashes were resting against the parchment gray of his skin; she had never before realized how long and thick they were. His hollowed cheeks were stubbled with a heavy beard and his lips were cracked and slightly parted.

"Raven," she whispered, touching his temple with her hand.

His lashes flickered, as if responding to her voice with the greatest effort, and then finally his lids lifted, revealing the heartbreakingly beautiful blue eyes trying to focus on her face.

"Catherine?" he breathed, and as she watched, the lids again begin to drift downward.

"What's happened, my darling?" she whispered. Glancing up, she found Edwards's eyes reflecting the same anxiety she felt.

"I tried so hard to reach you," Raven whispered, his voice faltering. She had to lean close to hear him. "I can't..."

His lids fell, hiding the unfocused paleness of his eyes.

"No," Catherine said. Her hands framed his face, turning his head. She could feel the thrust of cheekbone, too prominent beneath the gray-tinged skin. "No, damn it. Don't you dare die on me, John Raven. Don't you dare," she ordered in terror.

The lids lifted again, and this time there was something behind the dazed irises that he eventually succeeded in focusing on her features. Something that she recognized, with shocked relief, as amusement. He met her eyes. His lips began to move upward into the curve that passed for Raven's version of a smile.

"Not dying," he said, his voice slightly stronger than before. "I didn't come all this way to die. I promise you that, Catherine." His voice faded again, and the heavy lids dropped to cover the blue. But she believed him. Her shoulders heaved once, and then she gathered her courage, wiping at her tears with fingers that still trembled slightly.

"Get a doctor," she ordered.

"I've already taken the liberty of dispatching one of the footmen for him, Mrs. Raven," Edwards assured her.

She looked up to find a circle of faces surrounding them, the servants in various stages of dress and undress.

"We have to get him upstairs," she said, trying to think.

"May I suggest, madam, it might not be wise to move Mr. Raven until we know the extent of his injuries," the butler said.

"Of course," Catherine agreed, realizing the logic of that. "Thank you, Edwards."

"You are very welcome, madam," the butler said. "And if I might also suggest…"

"What is it?" Catherine asked, glancing up.

"With your permission, I should like to send the staff about their business. It really would be best, Mrs. Raven."

"Yes, of course," Catherine agreed, knowing that there would already be a wealth of gossip from tonight.

She turned her attention again to Raven's crumpled body, barely hearing Edwards's efficient marshaling of his staff back to their quarters or on various duties to prepare for the master's care. For the first time she began to take in the details of Raven's appearance. He was wearing trousers and boots. His own, she decided, although considering the gathering darkness and their begrimed and tattered condition, she couldn't be completely sure. But at least they fit. As the filthy garment that partially covered his broad chest and massive shoulders did not. It gaped in several places, revealing many shadowed bruises and abrasions on his upper body.

Again fighting tears, Catherine looked up into the eyes of Jem, who had come to kneel on the opposite side of her husband's sprawled body.

"It's his hands that's hurt the most. I tried to take his hand to help him up, but he cried out." Dark with concern, the groom's eyes looked into hers. "What do you suppose he's done to them?" he asked, trying to imagine, as was Catherine, what sort of injury could make a man like John Raven cry out.

"I don't know. But the doctor will be here soon. He'll

see to everything. Raven promised me he wouldn't die,'' Catherine whispered, her voice breaking slightly. And then, forced by an incredible act of will, she finished the thought she'd been holding on to. ''And he always keeps his promises.''

It seemed that the doctor's examination took an eternity. He had finally given permission for Raven to be carried upstairs, and then he disappeared into the master bedroom for another eternity.

Catherine paced the hall outside the closed door, fighting for control. Finally the door opened and Dr. Stevenson emerged.

''A dreadful business,'' he said, shaking his head. ''Dreadful to think something like this could happen in England. I don't know what this country is coming to. Damned ruffians. I swear it's not safe to go out of doors anymore without an armed escort. And that's exactly what I told Mr. Raven.''

''How is he?'' Catherine asked, less concerned about what had happened than about the consequences for Raven's well-being.

''Nothing that a few days of rest and good nursing won't cure,'' he said.

Catherine closed her eyes in a brief prayer of thanksgiving.

''I've left laudanum. He'll not sleep with those hands. They're by far the worst. But even so, I believe there'll be no permanent impairment. Damned lucky at that. I beg your pardon, my dear, but it's the most bizarre tale I've ever heard. And Catherine...'' He paused as he began to make his way down the curving grand staircase.

''Yes?'' she said, turning back from the door it seemed she had finally been given permission to open.

''See that he takes the laudanum. Despite his denials,

he's in a great deal of pain. Never seen anything like it. Self-inflicted. Says something about the determination of the man, although I'm not sure exactly what.''

The doctor's voice faded with his descent. Catherine took a deep breath and, without knocking, opened the door to the bedroom.

Chapter Fifteen

The light was very low, and it took a few seconds for her eyes to adjust. Gradually she was able to make out Raven's form. His face was turned toward the door, the long lashes fanned over the shadows that surrounded his eyes like bruises. She could smell the pleasant aroma of the soap he always used. Someone—Edwards or his valet—had used that same soap tonight to bathe and shave him. She stood a moment looking at him, savoring the fact that she was finally able to do so, despite his obviously battered condition. At last, unable to resist the urge to reassure herself that he was truly all right, she brushed her fingers against the midnight blackness that swept back from his forehead.

"John," she whispered, willing him to respond to that entreaty. She needed to hear him speak to her, and then she'd be able to believe Stevenson's assurances.

His lashes rested against his cheeks, unmoving, but his mouth began to curve. "If you've taken to calling me John, I must be in worse shape than your sawbones admitted," he said.

She felt her own lips tremble upward in relief. If her husband could tease her, he must, as the doctor had tried to assure her, not be seriously injured.

"Raven," she amended, and was rewarded by the slow opening of his eyes. The starred sapphire gleam seemed unchanged.

"That's better," Raven said. "But you're crying. I thought you despised women who weep."

"And I thought you liked to comfort them."

"You have me at a disadvantage. I can't even hold you."

"It's all right," she whispered, stroking the dark hair.

"Give me a few days."

"As many as you like."

"What I'd like..." he began, and then he deliberately banished that thought, realizing the impossibility of doing what he'd *like,* what he'd dreamed about for months, given the state of his hands. "Damn," he said softly, closing his eyes again.

"Shall I get the laudanum? Dr. Stevenson said that you'd—"

"I don't need Stevenson's drugs. I need you. I've needed you so long."

"And I'm here," she said. "So there's nothing—"

His eyes opened again, the self-mockery clearly revealed in their depths. "I want you here, Catherine. Make no mistake. But that's not *exactly* what I meant."

"Oh," she said, suddenly understanding. Color flamed into her cheeks, but she leaned down to put her lips against his forehead. "Do you want to..." She hesitated, having no idea what to suggest in response to that unexpected confession. Her thinking had not yet made the adjustment from fear that Raven was dying to a remembrance of the passion that had flared between them. As his obviously had.

"Bloody bastards," he said softly. He shifted his body carefully, easing toward the center of the bed. She heard the small intake of breath occasioned by that movement. "Sit down," he ordered. "If I can't hold you, at least I can look at you."

She sat on the very edge of the bed, moving as carefully as he had, unwilling to add to his discomfort. He raised his hand to touch her neck, the thick bandaging making the usually graceful strength misshapen, alien. In unthinking response, she touched the thick linen strips that had been wound professionally around his palm and over the back of his hand. Only the tips of his fingers emerged from their cocooning protection. Putting her fingers carefully under the bare tips of his, she brought them gently to her mouth, placing a small kiss on each. Still supporting his hand, with pressure only against the fingertips, she glanced up to smile at him.

"As long as you're safe," she said, "the rest can wait."

"I *have* waited. Too bloody long," he said. "Thinking. Imagining. The whole time I was in that hole, I was thinking about you. And about how long I'd waited, wanting you. About what a fool I'd been to walk out that morning. I should have stayed here to look after you until you were well. And then I should have made love to you. Really, finally, made you mine. Instead—" He stopped abruptly and removed his hand.

"And instead you went to build a railroad," she accused, but she let him see her smile. "Business," she finished, shaking her head, "always business."

"I'm sorry," he said.

"And while you were away, you realized that business wasn't as important to you as I was?"

"You've always been more important—"

She laughed suddenly, too glad to have him back to even pretend to be angry. "I never believed I'd play second fiddle to a coal mine. Or to a locomotive. I really don't know why I'm willing to put up with it."

"Because you know how much I love you. Or at least I hope you do," he suggested softly.

"And how should I know that? Because you've kissed me? Twice in the six months we've been married?"

"But you have to admit, they both were very satisfactory kisses. Confess, Catherine."

"Very satisfactory. When do you suppose we might try for a third?" she whispered. Her hand had again found the sweep of dark hair, damp from the ablutions his servants had arranged, in order to return their master to a state more in keeping with his wealth.

"There's nothing wrong with my mouth," Raven said, his eyes locked with hers. "It's only my hands. I can't hold you, my darling, but if you want a kiss..." he suggested, his lips curving upward again.

As she had downstairs, she allowed her palms to frame his face. Too thin, she thought again, wondering what had happened to return Raven to her in this condition. She was too glad he was here to bother him with questions. They could come later. Now was the time to simply relish that he was once more with her, teasing her. Demanding, both emotionally and physically.

She lowered her head until her mouth met his. As if the intervening days had never interrupted what had happened between them, when her tongue met the hot caress of his the reaction was as strong as it had been before. Her lips cherished his, trying to tell him all the fears of the last weeks, the joy at having him here again. She deepened the kiss, hungry for whatever fulfillment they could find in clinging mouths and melding tongues. She wanted so much more now, as she knew he did. She wanted his lips on her body, commanding, teaching, urging her response. His hands caressing, the sensations building inside her. And instead, she remembered the bandages. Raven, she thought bitterly, what have they done to you?

"Bloody bastards," she said, softly echoing his invective when the kiss ended. She raised her head to find the blue gaze shimmering with emotion. She knew his frustration was as great as her own. And there was no need to tempt him with what couldn't be accomplished tonight. She had seen the marks on his ribs and stomach—livid bruises and scrapes. She didn't want to cause him any more pain. And she wasn't a child. She could wait.

"Not very ladylike, my lady," he said.

"Jem called me that tonight."

"*My* lady," Raven whispered. "And you always will be."

"Very confident, Mr. Raven. I'll have you know my father offered to arrange a divorce should I desire a husband less prone to extended journeys. He seemed to feel I'd been deserted."

Raven had pushed the thought of her father to the back of his mind. He hadn't wanted to deal with that. He didn't want to imagine what the knowledge that it had been Catherine's father who had arranged for his "journey" would do to their relationship.

"And what did you tell him?" he asked finally.

"That we had a contract. And you never break a contract."

He laughed softly, the sound tinged with bitterness. "You must be the only person in London who believes that."

"I don't understand."

"I missed the meeting. With the partners. They're not likely to forgive me."

"It's all right. My father took care of it."

The laughter faded from the blue eyes, and he was very still. Suddenly the inclusion of her father into Raven's project didn't seem the painless solution she'd thought. Catherine had believed that appealing to her father, groveling before him to beg his help, had been the most difficult thing she'd ever done. But faced now with the question in her husband's eyes, she wasn't sure that was true. Including her father into Raven's investment no longer seemed so minor nor so wise, now that her husband was back.

Her gaze moved to the small white scar that marred his cheekbone and rested there uncomfortably while she tried to think. She didn't know why this had become so difficult. She had done what she had to do to prevent Raven's losing an incredible amount of money, losing everything. And after all, her father was simply another investor. Why should Raven care whose money saved his railway? Again the image of the crop descending on his dark face intruded.

"Why?" Raven asked, almost to himself, remembering the fate the old man had arranged. Why had the duke gone in on the investment? Because Catherine had asked him? Raven knew Montfort would have had less altruistic reasons for that action.

"The other investors were reassured by my father coming in," Catherine said. "That's the only way..." She paused, hating to tell him that they had lost faith in Raven himself. She glanced up to find the blue eyes resting on her face, their color shading to ice. He didn't attempt to touch her now. His bandaged hands rested quietly against the sheet that concealed the bruised ribs. A coldness was beginning to grow in her stomach to match the coldness in his face. So she forced herself to finish it. "They would stay, hold to their financial commitments in the project, only if he agreed to join the partnership."

"And he guaranteed the investment? Out of the goodness of his heart, I suppose?"

She flinched mentally from the ice in his tone. "Of course. He *is* my father, your father-in-law. And it was the only way. They were demanding to be repaid, and Reynolds said there weren't enough assets to manage that. The project would have collapsed."

"And so your father intervened?"

"Yes," she said. Why did she suddenly feel guilty? Raven should be thanking them. They had between them saved the rail system, and he should be grateful. But she knew he wasn't.

"Because he believed so strongly in the railway?"

"Because he's my father. And I asked him."

"I see," Raven said softly.

"There was no other way," she argued.

"How do you know that?"

"They were demanding their money."

"They know my reputation. They were involved in the first place because they want to make money. And they believed that I would. That the railway would."

"You weren't here," she said, suddenly angry at his continued condemnation. She had thought that what she had done had been clever. Mr. Reynolds had been pleased at the duke's intervention. Grateful. Catherine had thought that Raven would be proud of her, and instead he seemed bitter that her father had agreed to help.

"Not because I chose *not* to be here. And in light of what's taken place in my absence, I'm beginning to understand..." Raven paused, thinking that now it all made sense. The old man had arranged not only his death, but to take over a venture that anyone as astute as the duke would surely realize would eventually be highly profitable. That sly old bastard. *Catherine's father*, Raven reminded himself, wondering if the old man's scheming had left any hope for this marriage.

"What?" she asked, when he didn't finish the thought.

His eyes held hers for a long moment, wondering if he should tell her what he suspected about Montfort's motives and his role in his disappearance. But finally Raven simply shook his head. "It doesn't matter," he said, his expression closed.

Catherine recognized that something was very wrong,

but she didn't understand why he was so furious. All she knew was that the closeness that had been growing between them was broken. Raven had become again the controlled stranger she had married.

"It matters to me," she said angrily. There should be nothing between them but joy that he'd returned from whatever ordeal he'd undergone, and instead there was this cold bitterness. "You promised that I might ask you anything and you'd tell me the truth. We have a *contract* to that effect. So I want to know, Raven. What do you think you understand? Just what are you suggesting has taken place in your absence?"

Raven said nothing for so long she began to believe he intended to break that particular vow, but finally the blue eyes met hers. "I'm wondering exactly what role your father played in my abduction," he said quietly.

The shock of what he'd said held her speechless a moment. "My father?" she repeated finally, incredulous at what he seemed to be suggesting. "What the hell does that mean?"

"It means that he would have gotten his way."

"His way about what? What are you talking about? Damn you, John Raven, you tell me just what you're accusing my father of."

"Of attempting to rid himself of a highly inconvenient son-in-law, whom he believed was a stain on his family's honor. Of getting back into his daughter's good graces. And even of taking control of a venture that's bound to make him a great deal of money. All in one fell swoop. Very neatly done, Catherine. You have to admire his boldness. Only I'm afraid I put a spoke in the cogs of that particular machination. I wasn't supposed to return. I was supposed to die in that bloody shaft, a singularly unpleasant death. Starvation or drowning, depending on the duration of the next rain. I promise you he'll be extremely annoyed that I've shown up here tonight.''

"Are you suggesting that my *father* tried to kill you? In order to take over the railway? My God, you must be insane.''

"Complications from a head injury?" he mocked. "No, Catherine. It all fits.''

"It's ridiculous! And you must know that. My father would never do something like that.''

"Pardon me if I doubt the duke's goodwill. But I have no reason to believe that, as he openly told me, he wouldn't like to see me in hell. He made his feelings about both my stench and my unsuitability to be his daughter's husband very clear that day.''

"He was angry. Enraged. But for you to suggest... How can you possibly believe that? He's my *father*,'' she argued, desperate to make him realize how ridiculous that suggestion was.

"And he again has you eating out of his hand. Well-tamed to that bit, Lady Montfort. As you always were.''

"I don't intend to listen to you blacken my father's character any further. You should be very grateful to him for saving your project, and instead—''

"Pardon me for not kissing his feet. Perhaps when I've recovered from what his hirelings did I'll be able to react more calmly, but for now, my dear, if you'll forgive me—''

"No, I certainly won't forgive you. This entire conversation is unforgivable. But I'll be glad to leave you alone so you can think about how stupid this is. My father hasn't tried to hurt you, Raven. I'll see you again when you come to apologize for that suggestion, and not before.''

She had risen sometime in the midst of their argument and it didn't take her long to cross the expanse between the bed and the open door to her room, which she slammed angrily behind her.

By the time she had changed into her nightgown, she knew she had reacted childishly. With anger instead of logic and calmness. He had no reason to trust her father's goodwill. She herself had told Raven that the duke had tried to arrange for their divorce while he was missing, suffering deprivations and injuries, the extent of which he had not yet shared with her. And it would be natural for Raven to doubt the duke's motives, given the events of their one meeting. Instead of trying to convince her husband rationally that what he had suggested could not possibly be true, she'd railed at him and demanded apologies. She had acted like a shrew and not at all like a loving wife.

"You're right," Raven said softly.

She looked up in surprise, as if her regret had somehow conjured him up. He was standing in the connecting doorway between their rooms, wearing only a pair of cotton drawers, which made his masculinity far more obvious than even the tight pantaloons had done. The bandaged hands hung loosely, slightly curved, at his sides. He was clearly waiting for her response, but instead of managing to formulate any answer, she found her eyes irresistibly drawn to the front of his body.

"I couldn't manage my trousers," he said, his tone revealing a trace of amusement at her fascination with his near nudity. "I promise you I tried. And I'm sorry."

She glanced up to find his eyes no longer rimmed with ice. "Sorry for not putting on your trousers?" she asked, the teasing light in her eyes matching the returning warmth in his.

"And for accusing your father of trying to murder me."

Raven was sorry he had told her that. Whatever he knew about the duke's plotting, it wasn't fair to expect Catherine to accept those ideas about her own father. And Raven had no proof to offer her. Nothing tangible.

"He didn't. He wouldn't do that. And I think he has

even begun to accept the idea of having you as a son-in-law. He told Dr. Stevenson we'd made a love match."

"Do you think he could possibly be right?" Raven asked.

"Yes," she whispered.

"We didn't act very much like it tonight."

"I know. I was just about to come and tell you I'm sorry."

"Were you, Catherine? I'm glad."

"And I'm glad you're home. And safe. But you haven't told me what happened," she said. "While you were gone."

Raven shifted his weight to lean against the frame of the door. He glanced down at his hands, unconsciously lifting them, holding them up as if examining damage he could no longer see.

"I told you I was used to taking care of myself. Apparently I wasn't as apt at that as I believed."

"Not indestructible," she suggested.

He looked up, letting his hands drop. "Not entirely."

"I'd really like to hear the story, if it's not too painful."

"It's not the story that's painful," he confessed, smiling.

"What did they do to your hands?" she asked, although she found she preferred not to know. Eventually she would have to be told what had happened during those weeks he was missing, and the injuries to his hands were sure to be a major part of the story.

"To my hands?" he said, sounding surprised. "*They* did nothing. Beyond tying them."

"But...then why... I don't understand."

Raven looked down again, his hands making that almost involuntary turn, palms up, as he remembered what he himself had done to them. The only way to get home. And now, instead of what he'd envisioned... He took a breath, but still he didn't explain.

"Raven?" she said.

He didn't respond in any way.

"Are you all right?" she asked, worrying again.

"Of course," he said, his head still lowered.

She waited, as unmoving as he was.

"Except..." She watched him take another deep inhalation. "Except tired. And still a little..."

"A little?" she prodded carefully, watching him.

"Could we continue this conversation next door, Catherine?"

"In your room?"

"You're perfectly safe," Raven said, looking up suddenly, the laughter back in the blue eyes, despite their tiredness. Despite the dark shadows and sunken cheeks she'd almost forgotten when faced with the obvious strength of his body.

"I doubt it," she said, but she rose and walked past him toward the bed he'd left to make the apology she'd demanded.

Moving with more assurance than she felt, Catherine threw back the counterpane and straightened the bed until it lay smooth and inviting. She plumped the pillows hard, a very small cloud of feathers flying out to surround her. When she had completed the task she had never before performed in her life, she turned back to find him standing in the open doorway watching her.

Neither of them moved for what seemed an eternity as the feathers drifted slowly back down to settle on the bed. She blew one away from her nose, and the corners of Raven's mouth began to tilt. She knew he was trying to control his amusement at her attempted housekeeping, and that he was about to lose the battle. She sent him a rueful smile.

"Come on, Mr. Raven," she invited, patting the mattress. She lifted the edge of her gown and climbed up onto the high bed. She sat on one side, her legs crossed like a red Indian at his campfire, leaving more than half of the wide expanse for Raven to stretch out on. "Come to bed."

"You don't know how long I've waited to hear you say that," he said softly. He began to walk, more slowly than she had ever seen him move. A trifle unsteadily, he maneuvered his body onto the edge. Using his elbows, he levered his big frame entirely onto the bed and lay back, his wide shoulders propped against the pillows she'd stacked against the headboard.

For some reason she was very disconcerted by the look those sapphire eyes were now directing at her, their color darkened and intensified by the dimness.

"Come here," he suggested.

"I don't want to hurt you."

"You're not going to hurt me, Catherine. Come here."

Raven stretched his right arm along the top of the pillows, creating a space for her body to fit next to the powerful solidness of his. It took her less than a second to respond to that repeated invitation. She doubted the scramble with which she transversed the small distance between them was graceful, but she really didn't care. And from the strength with which Raven's arm enclosed her, neither did he.

He pulled her to him, the muscles of his chest hard against the unconfined softness of her breasts. His mouth roamed over the loosened auburn tendrils at her temple and then across her forehead. Her fingers pressed into his warm, golden skin, moving languidly across the breadth of his shoulder and upper arm. Finally she was again where she wanted to be.

"I missed you," he whispered softly, lips against her brow.

"I missed you, too. And Raven?"

"Hmm?"

"I worried about you."

"Did you?"

"I know you think that's ridiculous."

"Maybe not. There were a few hours I spent worrying, too. I'd thought I wasn't ever going to be allowed to do this."

"This?" she asked, brushing a light kiss over his lips.

"Hold you. Make love to you. Make love to my wife."

"Don't think about that. You don't have to tell me what happened. Not if you don't want to."

"Nothing happened that's to my credit. I allowed myself to be taken captive, tied up and left to die. Not a very attractive list of accomplishments."

She heard the derision in his voice. "And you don't know who did it?"

"They tried to stop the coach, but I had ordered the coachman not to slow down for anything." Raven didn't tell her about the attempt on his life in the park, which had prompted that precaution. "I used the pistol I always carry, but there were too many of them. They shot Tom, and then the carriage went over the edge of the road and onto the rocks below."

The quiet voice paused, and his lips again touched her hair. She lifted her hand to his cheek, but she didn't try to look up to read whatever was in his face. To see if it matched what she could hear in the deep voice. Her face rested still against the bare skin of his chest, listening to the steady rhythm of his heartbeat. She knew he'd finish the story in his own time. He would face the memories, the bitterness of being taken. The humiliation of whatever they'd done to him. Raven wasn't a coward, and so she knew he'd tell her. Eventually.

"I didn't think then to wonder why they didn't shoot me, too." Again he paused. Her fingers, finding the fall of dark hair, were gently combing through its silken softness.

It was dry now and curling against his shoulders. "I suppose I was too disoriented by the accident. They had tied me up before I regained consciousness, and then they took me to the shaft." He drew in a breath, but his quiet voice continued, his calm tone never varying. "They seemed to think it was poetic justice."

"Why?" she whispered.

"Someone had led them to believe I was putting miners out of their jobs by employing machinery in my mines. The same logic the Luddites used to stir up their riots."

"You take care of your workers. That's so unfair."

"I don't think they were concerned about fairness."

"Maybe they really believed that. At least it offers an alternative…" She couldn't bring herself to repeat the accusation he'd made against her father.

Raven didn't have the heart to deny her that possibility, especially not with the warmth of her small body pressed closely along the length of his for the first time. They would deal with all the painful realities later. Not tonight. He didn't want to think of anything tonight but holding Catherine.

"How did you get away?"

"They'd left me tied, hand and foot, at the bottom of that hole. I realized I had to first get my hands untied."

She waited again, her fingers caressing, as he paused, letting him tell it without prodding him with questions.

"There didn't seem to be anything to use against the ropes. There was nothing down there except the walls and floor—no discarded tools. Nothing. I'd probably inched my way around the shaft a dozen times before I found it—a narrow little outcropping, a couple of feet off the floor, the stone rough edged. I began to rub the rope against it, trying to abrade it enough that I could break it."

"And you did."

"Eventually," he agreed. There was another long silence

before he added softly, "They make damn fine rope in this country, Catherine."

"That's how you hurt your hands?"

"I thought the bonds were shrinking because they were so wet with blood, but my hands were swelling and finally I lost feeling in them. I suppose that was good. At that point. But it made the climbing a nightmare."

"You *climbed* out of the mine?"

"It was only a shaft. A test hole. It was like climbing up a chimney—feet and elbows, like the sweeps. It was wider, of course, and if I weren't as tall as I am, I'd never have done it. And they'd left me my boots. I guess they thought it wouldn't matter. They never expected me to walk anywhere."

"They *knew* you were alive? When they left you there?" she asked, horror coloring her voice.

"I'm sorry. I should never have told you this. We should concentrate on the here and now. A very pleasant here and now that I was afraid might never happen."

"I want to know. I *need* to know. And Raven, I'm not a child. Did they leave you there, knowing you were alive?"

"They tied me up, Catherine. You don't worry about dead men walking out of the grave you've dug for them."

She shivered suddenly at the fate they'd intended for him. She found it hard to believe that anyone could treat another person with such inhumanity. But then, as Raven had told her, she had been very protected from the realities of human misery the world contained.

His arm tightened comfortingly around her shoulders.

"It's all right," he said softly. "It's over."

"Once you were out, how did you get home?"

She felt his laugh lift the solid muscles of his chest.

"I'd thought that would be the easy part. After I'd finished the climb. After I reached the outside. But I had no idea where I was. The hole they'd lowered me into was part of a site that had long been abandoned. There were no cottages nearby. I hadn't eaten in days. At that point, I had no way of knowing how many days. My only thought was to get back here as quickly as I could. But even when I eventually stumbled on a village that offered some semblance of civilization, no one wanted to help. And considering the way I looked, I guess I understand their reluctance. I tried to convince them that if they'd arrange for my transportation to London, they'd be amply rewarded. You can imagine their reaction.

"So I ran. And then walked. As long as I could. I stole food and someone's shirt. Eventually a carter took me up. By then I was afraid all the effort was going to be wasted because I was going to die by the road. I still don't know why he stopped. But he saved my life. He gave me water and something to eat, and then he brought me to the outskirts of the city."

"We'll have to find him," she said, thinking how grateful she was. Human kindness given without hope of reward. It had returned Raven to her, and despite the horror of what his attackers had planned for him, he was safe and holding her.

"I don't know his name or anything about him. But you're right. We'll find him."

They said nothing for a long time. By now the great house was totally silent, even the excitement over the master's return and the doctor's visit fading as the tired servants sought their own beds and well-deserved rest. Catherine could hear the tall hall clock and Raven's heartbeat and nothing else in the peaceful stillness of the London night.

Eventually she felt her husband's breathing even into a regular rhythm and she knew he was asleep. She thought briefly about returning to her own room in order to allow him to rest undisturbed, but the arm that enclosed her was strangely compelling, even loosened and relaxed in sleep. She closed her eyes and lay in the darkness, and before she slept, she thankfully acknowledged the divine intervention she'd so fervently prayed for in the days he'd been gone for sending Raven back to her.

Chapter Sixteen

When Catherine awoke the next day, she was alone. She closed her eyes again, savoring the fragrance of Raven's body, his scent caught in the sheets of the bed they had shared, surrounding her as his arms had enclosed her last night. She wondered briefly where he was, and then acknowledged with amused resignation that he was probably in that small office downstairs, again overseeing the business empire she had guarded until his return. She and her father. Remembering the duke's kindness, she wondered how her husband could possibly believe—

"Mr. Raven thought you might like breakfast in bed, madam."

Catherine opened her eyes to find Edwards holding a tray on which a teapot and cup reposed along with a covered silver dish. Raven was again issuing orders to the staff.

"Thank you, Edwards, but just the tea, I think. I'll have luncheon downstairs with Mr. Raven."

"I believe Mr. Raven's in his office. And he's eaten. Shall I tell him you wish to see him?"

"No," Catherine said, still smiling. "Don't bother him."

She needed to let her father know about Raven's return. She remembered again Raven's bitterness last night and his accusation. The duke needed some warning that the emotion John Raven entertained about his investment wasn't gratitude.

"Thank you, Edwards," she said aloud. "If you would, return in half an hour, please. I'll have a letter to be delivered to my father."

"I'd be delighted, Mrs. Raven."

When the door closed behind the butler, Catherine rose and, putting on her wrapper, sat down at her secretary to compose the difficult letter she knew she must write.

The afternoon seemed endless to Catherine as she waited for Raven to rejoin her. The door to his office remained securely closed. She knew that because she made several otherwise unnecessary trips downstairs to check. She'd see him at dinner, she assured herself more than once when he didn't reappear. Raven would surely join her at dinner. Her thoughts went back to the early months of her marriage, those private moments at the huge table and the daylong anticipation of being with Raven the only comforts that had sustained her then—as they must now.

The hours crept by, but she forced herself to work her way through the pile of invitations that had accumulated, unopened and unanswered, during Raven's absence. Her hands trembled suddenly if she allowed any of the images to form in her head—Raven standing in the doorway last night, or his mouth against her breast on the morning he'd left. Her body reacted to that last memory, the sweet, hot ache of desire tormenting her.

She entered the dining room that night with that same fluttering anticipation. It had taken her an hour to decide on the gold satin gown, which seemed to create answering highlights in the upswept auburn hair and to give a glow like candlelight to the clarity of her skin. The mirror in her bedroom had been complimentary, and she entered the room with the same provocative smile she had practiced before its reassuring reflection.

She allowed Edwards to seat her, never questioning that Raven would join her. He always informed her when he was going to be absent from the dinner table, and today she'd received no such message. It was probably taking longer than he'd anticipated to dress, given his injuries. It was not until the first course was served that she realized something was wrong. She turned to Edwards, standing silently behind her chair.

"Mr. Raven—" she began, only to be interrupted.

"Mr. Raven has dined, madam," the butler said simply, but there was something—some unexpressed thought—behind the impenetrable calmness.

"He's already dined?" she repeated, all the pleasant expectancy collapsing. "Here?" she asked.

"In the kitchen," Edwards affirmed. For some reason, a dark flush was beginning to stain his cheeks.

The answer she sought should not come from her majordomo, Catherine realized in embarrassment. Whatever had compelled Raven to desert his own table would be better explained by the man himself. Not waiting for Edwards's help, she pushed back the heavy chair in which she was sitting and rose, leaving her napkin and the untouched food. She didn't notice the small smile Edwards allowed before he directed removal of the first course.

Catherine walked purposefully to the room where her husband had been sequestered most of the day. The office was as dark as the morning she'd made this same journey, clad only in her night rail, to find Raven in the chair behind the desk. The master suite that connected to hers was also empty, the counterpane stretched smoothly over the huge bed. There had been no preparations for occupation of this chamber tonight. Which meant, of course...

Without allowing herself to think about the possibility

that Raven might not welcome her intrusion, she retraced her steps down the upstairs hallway to the door of the small chamber in which, until last night, he had slept since before their marriage. She listened briefly at the door and then, knocking softly, she entered without waiting for permission.

The two men occupying the room looked up in surprise. The valet had just removed his master's waistcoat. He stood behind Raven, frozen by the shock of her unexpected entrance.

"Thank you, Browning. That will be all," she said, holding her husband's eyes, daring him to countermand her dismissal.

The valet looked quickly to his employer, and never glancing at him, Raven nodded, his gaze unmoving from Catherine's face.

She was made aware that the valet had left by the click of the latch. They were alone, but still the silence stretched.

"Did you come to ask me something, Catherine?" Raven inquired. She had come here the night before she was thrown. Before their agreement to rethink the contract they had made for this most inconvenient marriage of convenience. Before he'd left on the journey from which he'd almost not returned.

"No," she said. "I didn't come to ask you anything."

"Then…?" Raven allowed the question to trail off.

"I have been waiting to be with you all day. At dinner, if you couldn't break away from business before. And then at the table, Edwards said you'd eaten. I had so looked forward to having dinner with you, Raven." She broke off that confession, fighting childish tears of disappointment.

"I ate in the kitchen," he said.

"Why? Why didn't you tell me? I could have joined you."

"No," Raven said simply. The firm line of his lips tightened, but he didn't explain. His eyes fell, and his hands began a small upward movement, the palms turning. Suddenly the gesture was halted and the bandaged hands were allowed to slowly return to his side, but his eyes didn't lift to her face.

"I don't understand," she said, but she knew something was wrong.

"Someone had to help me," he admitted softly. He had hated the dependence. Hated every mouthful Edwards fed him, the butler's features carefully arranged in the mask of the perfect servant. But Raven would have hated even more to have Catherine watching. To see him helpless as a child.

Of course! Catherine thought. What a fool she had been not to have realized all the restrictions those damaged hands would impose. But she should have been the one. It wasn't fair that someone else had been allowed to help Raven.

"Who?" she asked, fighting jealousy. "Who helped you?"

Raven's eyes came up at whatever was in her tone.

"Edwards, of course. I think he felt it was his province." The small, controlled smile that was uniquely Raven's touched the line of his lips.

"It was *my* province," she said bitterly. "*My* place, and you denied me that right. And what about after dinner, Raven?"

"Forgive me—" he began, but she cut him off.

"You're still avoiding me. And I can't imagine why. Given what you said last night."

She paused, waiting for him to deny what she'd suggested. "Raven?" she said softly.

There was no response.

"What's wrong?" she asked. "It's not that you don't want me here. You told me last night…"

He looked up at her hesitation, reading in her breathless

whisper the sudden fear that she might be wrong. That he might have changed his mind.

"I want you," he said, his features still perfectly controlled, the stern line of his mouth now giving nothing away.

"Then why...?" she began. "Why are you here instead of in the room we shared last night?"

"Last night," he echoed. He shook his head slightly. "Forgive me, Catherine, but I don't believe..." She saw the depth of the breath he took. "Last night I was exhausted, and our sleeping together then was possible. But tonight..." Slowly his eyes met hers. "I don't think I can *sleep* with you tonight, my darling."

"I don't understand," she said. What was different about tonight? He had held her last night, curled into the solid warmth of his body, held her as if he never wanted to let her go.

Correctly interpreting her unhappiness, Raven knew he would have to explain. Despite the painfulness of that confession, he would have to tell Catherine why he had come here and not to the bedroom where last night he had finally been allowed to touch the woman who had haunted his dreams since the first day he had looked into her eyes.

"Because tonight I want far more than to hold you," he admitted softly. "And because that's not possible."

"Why?" Catherine asked, trying to comprehend.

Again a brief smile slanted the hard mouth, holding no trace of amusement. This time Raven deliberately lifted his damaged hands, held them out between them, palms up, as if they explained everything.

"Because of these," he said, looking down on the bandages, fighting the bitterness and frustration. Abruptly he turned and walked to the bed, its smoothness marred by the stacked pillows.

"You'll let Edwards help you. And your valet," she said to the expanse of broad shoulders, "but not me."

He turned at the pain she had just revealed, that had trembled in the strained confession. His eyes were full of regret at hurting her.

"I can help you," she argued, unable to prevent the entreaty that echoed clearly in her tone.

"Not with this. Not given our situation," he said.

"I don't understand. You could tell me what to do...."

He glanced up at that suggestion, his lips moving quickly in involuntary amusement.

He was laughing at her ignorance, Catherine thought. And against her will, the hot tears burned. She blinked to control them, but it was a battle she was destined to lose. She despised women who wept, but he could reduce her to tears with a smile.

"Catherine," he said gently, comfortingly.

"Tell me why!" she demanded, swallowing against the building lump. Despite what he had said, he didn't want her. *I don't need a mistress,* an echo in her heart taunted bitterly, but she knew now that there was no other woman. Raven didn't lie. He didn't lie! She closed her eyes tightly, fighting for control.

And felt his lips on her forehead, warm and sweet. "There's so much I want to show you. Things I've wanted to teach you since the beginning—" He broke off that thought, but his mouth touched against her eyelid, caressing, even as he continued. "All those long months I watched you. And I wanted you. Meeting you in the hallway on your way out to dance with some other man. Or to ride. And I thought only about making love to you. Slowly. Touching you. Teaching you to *want* my touch. Wanting to show you all my hands could tell you about what I feel. And now..."

He rested his chin briefly against the top of her head.

And then he stepped back, the spell he had woven deliberately broken.

"Raven?" she whispered, the word as full of pain as his broken confession had been.

"I can't. Don't you understand? If we had been lovers... If I had taken you before... If you weren't—"

"If I weren't so inexperienced?" she finished bitterly.

"I don't want to hurt you. You don't deserve a clumsy lover. I don't intend that for you. And so...we wait."

"And if I don't want to wait?" she challenged. She had to show him none of this mattered. He wanted her. All she had to do was convince him that what they both wanted was possible.

She closed the small distance he had created between them. He watched unmoving as her fingers lifted to the front of his shirt. She held his eyes, smoldering blue flames, as she began to unfasten the buttons. Finally she tugged the material out of his trousers to complete the task she'd undertaken.

She took a step backward to look at him. The soft cotton hung loosely from the massive shoulders. The ridged stomach and the deeply muscled chest were exposed by the opening she'd created, so totally masculine that something inside her shifted, aching with the realization of the difference between the hard strength of his dark body and the soft, pale weakness of hers.

Tentatively, she lifted her hand and, using one finger, touched the hollow at the base of the wide brown column of his throat. His skin was warm beneath the coolness of hers. She smiled at him, but the careful alignment of his features didn't change. He was waiting. Watching her.

She let her finger slide downward, following the line of bone that divided the swell of muscle on either side, barely exposed by the opened shirt. Down to the concavity below his rib cage; down the channel that bisected his flat stomach. Gently into the small cave of his naval, her nail touching into the center and then downward again. Fascinated by the dark hair her fingers encountered at the top of the trousers that rode low on his hips. Having reached that barrier, she pulled her finger across the band that blocked its descent. To the right and then slowly back to the left.

His breath trembled suddenly, sighing through nostrils that were slightly distended. Encouraged by the evidence that what she had instinctively done had had some effect, Catherine slipped both hands into the gaping front of his shirt, moving them, palms flattened, to his sides. And then upward, skimming ribs and iron-hard bands of muscle, to the dark nubs of nipples that she could feel but couldn't see. She turned her hands, allowing her fingers to capture the hard peaks between them, and the breath Raven took then was a gasp, his body jerking under her fingers.

But he hadn't asked her to stop. And the shuddering breathing she could feel vibrating under the smooth, golden skin she was touching was exciting, revealing a power she hadn't realized she could have over this strong body. Her hands smoothed upward, finding the line of collarbone, following its rim outward to the knot of bone at the top of his shoulders. She opened her hands, lifting, thumbs up, until they caught the material of his shirt and peeled the edges open and then down, pushing it off his upper arms so that his chest and shoulders were exposed. Skin—golden velvet that she had touched once before—stretched over muscle and sinew, sleek and tawny like the hide of a great cat, warm and smooth under her fingers.

At his small, quick inhalation, she looked up into his face.

A tiny nerve jumped at the corner of his mouth, but his lids had fallen, hiding his eyes. Her palms skimmed down the outside of his arms, thumbs pausing to caress the sensitive skin inside his elbows, but his shirt was in her way.

She unbuttoned one cuff and eased the sleeve over the bandaged hand. And then the other, allowing the lawn garment to fall, discarded, to the floor.

"Catherine," he whispered, a plea.

"Do you want me to stop?" she asked, not really worried any longer that he might deny her. Might deny them both.

"No," he said hoarsely, surrendering. "Don't stop."

Smiling, she bent her head, and as he had the day he had introduced her to passion, she touched her lips to the small nipple rimmed with brown against the surrounding bronze. Again his body jerked. Reacting. His hand came up to find the back of her head, cupping gently to strengthen the contact between them.

She nibbled, teeth delicately teasing, her tongue at the same time tasting the dark warmth. She suckled, pulling the hard nub, lifting even the brown ring that surrounded it into her mouth.

His hand found her shoulder, and he asked, his voice ragged with the unevenness of his breathing, "Do you have any idea what you're doing to me?"

She slowly lifted her mouth away from his chest. Looking down, she could see the moisture her tongue had left on his nipple glinting softly in the candlelight.

"Tell me," she commanded, using her thumb to wipe away the trace of dampness that was almost too intimate to contemplate. He flinched at the movement of her finger across the hardened nub.

"Damn bloody bastards," he whispered. He rested his forehead against the top of her head, his eyes still closed.

"Tell me what to do," she suggested.

He hesitated so long she thought he intended to deny them both the release they so desperately needed. Whatever happened between them, whatever awkwardness was inevitable, she knew they could wait no longer. They belonged to one another. And only the joining of bodies remained, necessary to complete the joining of spirits that had already taken place.

"Tell me," she urged. She turned her hand and slid her palm downward toward the barrier she'd hesitated to force before. This time she pushed her fingers between the slim, hard belly and the material of his trousers. She could again feel the coarseness of the dark hair under their sensitive tips, and then the unfamiliar contours of his body. Almost involuntarily, it seemed, he pressed into her touch, arching upward into her hand. Wanting her. She hoped that desire would be strong enough to overcome whatever reluctance he felt about making love to her.

Please want me enough, she prayed silently. Her fingers slipped farther downward, exploring, entreating.

"Catherine," he breathed against her hair.

"Tell me what to do," she whispered.

"They fasten at the sides. There's a flap. To close the front. Help me, Catherine," he begged softly.

"Of course," she said, her fingers quickly moving to unravel the mysteries of masculine attire. "Of course I'll help you, my beautiful Raven. You had only to ask."

When she had tugged the tight trousers down, kneeling to slip them off his feet, she found herself grateful that the valet had already undertaken the job of removing the Hessians. She glanced up to find the sapphire eyes considering her, watching her exactly as Aunt Agatha's tabbies regarded the sparrows they stalked, safely separated by the glass of the windows.

"And the rest," he suggested. She hesitated, realizing the incongruity of his near nudity compared to her fully dressed primness. She was afraid that if she allowed him to sense her reluctance, he'd again retreat behind the excuse of his hands.

Reaching up blindly, she stripped the knit undergarment

down the slim hips and over the muscles of long thighs and calves. As he had with the trousers, he stepped out of it at her guidance, the tips of his fingers pressed into her shoulder for balance. She found herself nervously smoothing both garments across her lap with hands that shook. She was afraid to look up, and she was certain he must know what she was feeling.

"Catherine," Raven said softly, a command.

Steeling herself, she raised her eyes, slowly skimming upward from broad, bare feet, finely made, to ankles and shapely calves, and then to his knees, the right one slightly bent with his stance. Bravely her gaze moved to the deeply delineated muscles of his thigh and finally higher. Her heart rocketed into her stomach at the evidence of how much he wanted her. And then she forced her eyes away, upward to meet his. She expected amusement at her obvious fascination with his masculinity. She had known, of course, from a childhood spent on her father's country estate, what to expect, but until faced with the startling reality of Raven's body, she had not known how very little she understood. She should be frightened by his sheer size, she supposed. But this was Raven. And she could never be afraid of Raven.

She smiled at him, a small, trembling, upward slant of her lips. And suddenly it was all right. Nothing mattered but that she was with him, and she knew he'd care for her with the same protective tenderness he'd always shown. When his lips lifted in response to her smile, she felt none of the resentment his amusement had always caused. Not even when the teasing note in his question lightened the tension that had been between them.

"Do you think you might join me?" he suggested.

Wordless with the intensity of anticipation, she nodded. Awkwardly she rose from her knees, still holding his clothing.

"Drop them," he said, and at what was in his face, she obeyed, letting the garments fall to the bare wood of the floor.

She stood before him, fully dressed, holding her eyes on his by sheer force of will. Hers wanted to move downward, to touch again that compelling, essential difference between his body and hers. She began to struggle with the buttons and laces of her dress, as clumsy as if her hands were impeded by the bandages that wound his. Fingers trembling, she knew she was making a fool of herself. Too young. Too unfamiliar with this. And too obviously disconcerted by his blatant masculinity.

When she had finally managed the business of gown and slippers and petticoat and was clad only in the thin chemise, she looked up, trying to assess his patience with a process that had seemed to her both endless and endlessly embarrassing. Whatever she had expected Raven's expression to reveal, it was not the emotion that marked the harsh planes of his face. They were very still, but the skin had been stretched by his ordeal too tightly over the bones to hide what he was feeling. And what he was feeling, what was reflected in the shadowed eyes and the stern line of his mouth, was not impatience with her clumsiness or annoyance at her lack of experience. It was desire. Even in her innocence she was left with no doubt that he wanted her, that he found her body enticing and her hesitancy provocative rather than annoying.

"You are so beautiful," he said.

Well used to compliments on her truly remarkable beauty, accustomed to the adulation of the best-looking men of her exclusive circle since childhood, she found herself tongue-tied at the simple avowal. The poised and sophisticated society hostess, unable to formulate any reply, shook her head mutely.

"Take down your hair," he commanded, still watching her with those crystal eyes.

Her hands lifted to remove the pins that held the elaborate chignon. Unthinking, she saved the hairpins as she removed them, holding them in one palm until she had loosened the entire mass. Running the fingers of her other hand through the heavy strands, she let the perfumed cloud of rich red-brown fall over her shoulders, the vibrancy of its color a contrast to the maidenly whiteness of her chemise and the cream of her skin.

Raven said nothing in response to her obedience. He offered no other suggestion, so the stillness again echoed between them. Frightened, finally, that he had once more decided this was a mistake, she opened her hand and allowed the hairpins to cascade to the floor, a few of them landing on the small pile of masculine garments and some bouncing across the wooden boards.

She found the ribbon that laced the bodice of the chemise, and as she had before, she loosened it, quickly sliding her thumb under the narrow, crisscrossing satin. With the release of tension on the fabric that covered her breasts, she slipped the straps off her shoulders, guided the soft material to her waist and then, bending, pushed it down her hips. The garment puddled over small, arched feet. She resisted the urge to cross her arms over her breasts in that primitive gesture of femininity. Instead she bravely raised her head, finding his eyes still lowered, having followed the drop of the last of her clothing.

His eyes traveled upward, as slowly as hers had done. Up the smooth, slim length of leg his callused palms had once traced, exactly as his gaze was doing now. Over the width of very feminine hips and the slender shaft of her waist. To the high breasts, rose tipped and peaking in the cool air of the small, shadowed chamber. Touched and softened by the lamplight.

"So beautiful," he said again.

At that invitation, she took a step out of the pool of white at her feet. And then another. His arms opened, inviting. She moved against his body as if she had always belonged there, and when he enclosed her in his strength, she knew that she had. She wondered why she had been embarrassed before, why she'd hesitated in enjoying the incredibly sensuous sensation of her bare skin against the warmth of his. Every inch of that muscled body fitted hers, as if it had been made to meld into her smoothness.

Her hands found his shoulders and, as if reading her mind, he moved the hardness of his chest teasingly against the tips of her breasts. Some inarticulate sigh escaped with the rightness of that abrasive contact and with her pleasure in the contrast of his body to hers. While she was still savoring that, he bent his knees and then arched upward, so that the heavy masculinity that had so fascinated her made a tentative union with her body. She was the one who gasped at that, shocked by the feel of Raven's virility in such intimate proximity. But when he eased back, afraid he'd frightened her, her hips instinctively moved with him, to repeat and prolong the contact he'd briefly allowed.

"Yes," he said softly. "Very rare."

Ignoring the awkwardness of his hands, he lifted her, as easily as he had in Hyde Park, and deposited her on the bed. He stood a moment looking at her, blue eyes shadowed in the low lamplight.

Smiling now at what was in his face, she lifted her hand and ran the back of her knuckles along the length of his arousal. His eyes closed, and again that shuddering breath shook his body.

"Come to bed, Mr. Raven," she invited. And this time there was no doubt of what she intended.

And now, long after she'd whispered that suggestion into the darkness, Catherine Raven woke to the weight of her husband's leg resting over her thighs. Her body was pale cream against the golden ruddiness of his, Raven's massive frame, work hardened, a contrast to the slimness of hers. Yet they were one, no longer joined, perhaps, in sexual passion. They had slipped, unaware, into the relaxed intimacy of lovers, familiar and uninhibited.

Catherine's toes traced slowly the long, hair-roughened muscle of Raven's calf. Eyes still closed, she moved carefully, turning her body more snugly into the inviting warmth of his. She was aware of, and ignored, the slight soreness between her legs. The pain of Raven's entry had been negated by his determination to pleasure her exactly as he'd promised. And this small, telltale evidence of her lost virginity was not something to regret, but a memory to cherish. To hold to her heart as she had held Raven's body, its strength controlled and dominated by his desire for the enclosing frailness of hers.

She realized he was still asleep, the strong features vulnerable as she'd never before seen them. She resisted the urge to touch his lips, parted with the soft exhalations and inhalations of his breathing. She was afraid she'd wake him, and despite the fact that he had, being Raven, made no reference to the suffering he'd undergone during his abduction, she remembered that there had been injuries beyond the damaged hands.

Her fingers wanted to caress him, to feel again his responsive reaction to their touch, but they were forced to wait. She allowed them to move over her own breast, lightly tracing across the rose nipple, remembering the touch of his lips.

Denied the use of his hands, Raven had employed what tools his expertise allowed. His warm mouth drifting with sure experience over and then into all the small, provoking contours and silken crevices of her body. His tongue darting quickly to explore, to touch, to suggest. And then returning, hot and sensuously slow, stroking and building. Heating to flame the tinder that was her body.

She had known the first time he'd touched her that her responses to his lovemaking pleased him. And that they were apparently unusual in a woman uninitiated into these arts. Tonight he had again made obvious his delight in that so easily evoked responsiveness. She lifted her head to look down with remembered pleasure at the intimate position they shared.

Their bodies, still entwined, lying among the stained sheets of the high bed, were clearly marked with the evidence of their first joining. Suddenly embarrassed by that realization, Catherine began to move carefully out of Raven's embrace, only to feel the muscles of that confining leg tighten over hers, his knee squeezing downward, effectively holding her prisoner.

"What's wrong?" he asked, his lips lazily caressing her temple. "Are you trying to leave me already?"

She knew by the teasing tone of the question that he certainly didn't understand her sudden discomfort.

"I just thought I should..." Somehow she couldn't find the words to finish that embarrassing confession.

"You should what?"

His mouth moved, slightly opened, along her cheekbone and down the slender slope of her nose, finally stopping over hers. His tongue dipped inside and then retreated, to trace slowly around the outline of her lips. When she didn't answer his soft question, Raven propped himself on one elbow to look down into her face.

"What's wrong?" he asked, studying her features.

Her eyes fell, and she shook her head. Despite all they had shared as he'd made love to her, despite the fact that he had worshipped delicately but thoroughly at each of the shrines to Eros nature had erected in its design of her body, she was hesitant to confess that she wanted to get up to wash off the embarrassing evidence that she had given him her virginity.

"I told you that you could ask me anything," Raven reminded her, still smiling. "Or tell me. What's wrong?"

"I thought I should clean up," Catherine whispered, feeling the heat moving under the translucent skin of her cheeks.

"You're getting up to clean the room?" Raven asked, amused. He turned to survey the clothing scattered in shadowed mounds across the gleam of the polished wood.

"No," she admitted. Her eyes again found the dark smears, so obvious she wondered why he didn't understand.

There was a long silence. Finally, his gaze followed hers, his lips lifting in understanding. "Catherine?" he said softly.

She looked up, to find the planes of Raven's face highlighted by the lamplight, the hollows darkened with mystery. Only his eyes were readable, and in them she found the same enigmatic tenderness with which he had always regarded her innocence.

"To my grandmother's people the first blood is holy, as sacred as baptism. And the honor of cleaning your body should be mine."

He said nothing else, although she waited another eternity. She was fascinated by his concept of something she had felt could only be an embarrassment.

"The honor?" she repeated finally.

"The first act of caring for a wife," he said. "The promise of eternal protection."

She felt again the quick burn of tears at the images he'd drawn in the soft dimness of this English bedroom, so far removed from those who had devised that ritual.

"Your grandmother's *people?*" she whispered, suddenly wondering at the strange phrasing.

"They called themselves The People," he said, smiling down at her puzzlement. "My grandmother is Indian."

"Raven," she said, thinking aloud, finally understanding so much. "That's...Indian?"

"My father took her clan name. It was a matriarchal society. Since she and my grandfather were never married except by tribal ceremony, my father had no right to call himself MacLeod."

"And so you became John Raven."

"By choice," he explained softly. "The old man, my grandfather, wanted me to be John MacLeod. But like my father, I chose to retain the ties to the other part of my heritage. My mother's family were also Scots. They had come to America as indentured servants. My mother fell in love with my father too quickly to worry about his background. She thought, as you did, that Raven was simply his name. Until she met my grandmother."

Catherine could hear the love and humor in his tone. An often repeated and beloved family story, she imagined, the inevitable confrontation between two different ways of life.

"I never even thought to wonder," she said, touching again the bronze skin of his shoulder. That heritage explained so much. The dark, angular beauty of Raven's features. Even, perhaps, the way he wore his hair, deliberately clinging to his American ancestry in the face of the fashions of London society.

"And your eyes?" she asked, running her thumb across the black brow, arched like a raven's wing, above the piercing blue.

"My inheritance from the Scots side of my family tree."

Slowly the corners of her lips began to lift at the thought of His Grace, the Duke of Montfort, acknowledging an Indian half-breed as his son-in-law. "I don't think we should tell my father until *after* the grandsons have appeared. I'm not sure he's quite ready for that revelation."

Raven didn't answer, knowing, as she could not, how far from acceptance Montfort's feelings for him were. Instead he lowered his mouth to nuzzle softly along the underside of her jaw and then over the slim column of her throat. His lips found, eventually, the small peak of her breast, and he began to tease gently until he caught the hardened bud between his strong, white teeth. He pulled, his eyes laughing into hers at the whimpering response that escaped her lips.

"Could you..." she began, and then paused, unsure of how to ask. "I mean could we... Would it be possible to..."

With a laugh, he released his captive. "I believe that might be arranged. Given that my wife is again willing to help."

"Of course," she said softly, feeling, despite the soreness, sweet anticipation at the thought of all the ways he had touched her last night, in spite of his inability to use his hands.

"And this time..." Raven said, rolling onto his back.

Surprised, she lifted herself on her elbow to look into his face.

"This time," he whispered, cupping that bandaged hand on the back of her tangled hair, "you do most of the work, my lady."

She still didn't understand until he told her, in whispered phrases, what he intended. Because there was no barrier to his entry and because she had always enjoyed controlling her own affairs, the experience proved even more satisfying than before.

And when it was over, she lay limply against the massive body beneath her, feeling each breath he took, harsh and deep and then easing, slowing, until they both were still and still one.

"I love you, Catherine," he said, whispering the words

into the darkness. But she heard them most clearly in the ear that lay on his broad chest.

"I love you, too, John Raven." She touched her tongue to the small dark bud of his nipple. "Every inch of you."

"Are you measuring me, Catherine?"

"No, but I told you I liked you big. And you laughed," she teased, remembering.

He laughed again, the intimate noise vibrating under her cheek.

"Always happy to oblige a lady." As he said the strange American expression, he arched his hips under hers ever so slightly, so that she realized what he was suggesting.

"Raven?" she whispered in wonder.

"We are taught endurance," he said softly, lifting once more. "And patience," he whispered, his body arching into hers, slowly advancing and then retreating. "But I've waited for you a long time, Catherine. A very long time through this most inconvenient of marriages. And to-night..." The movement of his hips was stronger now, thrusting upward, so that her nails tightened into the red-gold skin of his shoulders with the growing, sweetly shattering sensations moving through her body.

"I thought Indians were also taught silence," she suggested daringly, raising her upper body away from his. But she was smiling down into the gleam of starred sapphire eyes as she said it. And slowly she again began to move above him. Helping him, as he had taught her.

Chapter Seventeen

His grandmother's voice whispered from the darkness. He was again in the shaft, stretching far above him into the starred sky, matching its blackness. He could feel the rock's abrasion against the unyielding rope and the too-yielding flesh of his hands. To fight the pain, he filled his mind again with the images that had sustained him there, their promise overlain now with the perfection of fulfillment. With the remembrance of Catherine's body arching in trembling response beneath his, he fought his way out of the net of the dream.

Bothered by the clarity of the nightmare, Raven sat up in the wide expanse of the bed. The relaxed form of his wife lay beside him, still secure in the comfortable, protected world he had promised her. But underneath the quietness of the London night, Raven could sense something moving, dark and evil. Something that should not be in this place was here, in his home.

An Englishman feeling that same cold breath of dread against the back of his neck might have denied the premonition, given in to a practical man's disregard of any hint of the supernatural and put a pillow over his head to return to sleep. Or turned again to the welcoming embrace of the woman who slept beside him. John Raven was not far enough removed from a society in which heeding such warnings meant the difference between life and death. There was this time no snap of breaking twig, no whisper of undergrowth, no sudden silence of the night birds—nothing that he could point to as significant. But still the hair all over his body was rising in the age-old precursor of danger.

He glanced at Catherine's small form, and the line of his lips softened, but he did not allow himself to think of touching her to wakefulness. Spoken or unspoken, his vows had included the promise of protection, and that was what he must concentrate on now, rather than the panting sweetness of her responses.

He pushed off the sheet, slipping out of bed silently to stand naked on the oriental rug. On broad, bare feet he crossed the room to the small chest he had not opened since his arrival in England. The memories it held were too emotionally weakening for a man so far from all that he held dear, so far from home. But now this was his home—the small, hesitantly guiding fingers, the gasping reaction to his touch, the fragrance of Catherine's skin trembling under his....

He pulled his mind away from the seduction of those memories and with the tips of his fingers released the simple catch on the box. He knew he could manage none of his London clothes. He thought, however, that the softness of the buckskin tunic and breeches his grandmother had made for him so long ago would allow him to pull them on, despite his ruined hands.

He didn't let himself consider what he intended to do if the danger was as real as his prescience warned. He had fought Montfort's man in the garden without using his hands. Whatever the duke had planned this time Raven was more than willing to face. He was tired, however, of dealing with his father-in-law's henchmen. Despite what it would do to Catherine, he knew the day of their personal confrontation could not be put off much longer.

Slipping his arms into the sleeves, he allowed the tunic to fall over his head, fitting his body as smoothly as it had when the old woman had given it to him. It covered the massive shoulders without a wrinkle, the finely tanned skin tightening over his flat belly and then ending in a fringed edge that touched against the muscles of his powerful thighs. The breeches took him more time, but finally they were secured on the slim hips, fitting loosely over his legs. The laces made the moccasins impossible, he knew, and so he left them in the bottom of the chest.

He stepped back to the bed, almost hidden in the shadows. Only moonlight illuminated the chamber now. Using the tip of the finger that protruded farthest from the bandage, he touched the curve of Catherine's hip. She didn't stir, and not knowing what threat he might face downstairs, Raven didn't wake her. He stood a moment in the darkness, looking down on her, barely able to see her in the dimness of the bedroom, remembering. And then he disappeared into the blackness of the hallway.

He glided like fog, ghostlike, across the grounds of the London town house, blending into the darkened contours of broken light and patterned shade. Hidden by the shifting moonlight and the drifting shadows cast by floating clouds. Noiseless and patient, Raven examined the mansion's environs, using eyes that had been trained from childhood to make use of whatever light the night allowed. And he found nothing. No threat to the woman who slept above.

Some instinct guided him to the expanse of glass that backed the main salon. His senses still screaming alarm, he reentered the house through one of those tall Palladian windows. He knew his entry had been noiseless, but the man seated in one of the chairs Catherine had chosen to compliment the soaring dimensions of the room seemed remarkably unsurprised by his presence. There was no betraying start of the graceful hand.

His Grace, the Duke of Montfort, allowed his glass to complete the journey it had begun to his thin lips. He sipped, and then savored the excellence of his son-in-law's brandy.

"Come in," he invited softly.

"Since it *is* my home," Raven agreed, stepping down from the low sill onto the gleaming oak of the floor.

"Would you care for a warming draught against the night's chill?" Montfort asked, lifting his own glass in invitation. The crystal caught a moonbeam and flickered briefly in the dimness.

"Thank you, no," he replied, his tone as polite as the duke's.

With his long, graceful stride Raven moved halfway across the salon, to where he could see the old man clearly. He was dressed in full evening dress, its elegance and cut in keeping with the current mode. The size of the diamond in his cravat and the scattered fobs, however, proclaimed that the duke belonged to a generation whose tastes had formed before Brummel's strictures had forbidden such evidence of wealth.

"You wanted to see me," Raven suggested, waiting. The next move was Montfort's, and apparently he had come here to make it.

"Not particularly," the old man answered, smiling.

"Then why are you here?"

"Unfinished business?" Montfort mocked, one brow arching.

"No hirelings?" Raven asked, his tone as sardonic.

"I didn't think I'd need them. Not to eliminate vermin."

Raven's lips involuntarily tightened at the insult, but he

controlled any other reaction. It was no shock that Montfort hated him, the old man had been open about that from the beginning. The only surprising thing was that the duke himself was here tonight. But, Raven acknowledged with some satisfaction, his hirelings had proved less than dependable, so apparently the old bastard had decided to take things into his own elegant hands.

At that thought, Raven's eyes found the frail white fingers and found them once again gently caressing the object they held. Not, this time, the gold lorgnette. A pistol appeared fleetingly under the restless movement of the duke's exquisitely jeweled hands. Raven's gaze lifted to meet the dark, unfathomable gleam of Montfort's eyes.

"Because I'm not good enough for your daughter?" he asked.

"No one ever was. All they wanted was the money, like the bastard who tricked her before. Making her think he loved her, and that I'd accept the match. Fortune hunters. Bloodsuckers."

"So you tried to kill him. When you caught them."

"Catherine told you the story?" The duke sounded surprised.

"No," Raven admitted. "It was my lord Amberton who shared that particular...gossip." He remembered the viscount's suggested ending to the escapade, an ending that he knew now, without any shadow of a doubt, had been a lie.

"What did he tell you about my daughter?" Montfort asked. His tone had changed subtly, the mockery erased.

"Whatever he...suggested, I promise you he paid for."

"Is that why you broke his arm?"

"Yes," Raven said, his lips lifting in remembrance of how satisfying that encounter had been, despite its cost.

"Not because he stabbed you, then."

The blue eyes refocused on the duke's face. "How did you know that?" Raven asked.

"I've made it my business to know all about you, Mr. Raven. I thought I had a vested interest in acquiring that knowledge."

"Because of Catherine."

"Yes."

"And then you decided to get rid of me."

The old man didn't speak for a moment, the movement of his hands on the pistol again drawing Raven's attention.

"To free Catherine and allow her to marry someone more suitable," Raven continued.

"That was my original intent," Montfort agreed.

"Rather ineptly handled. I'm surprised at you, your grace. That's not your reputation."

"It's so difficult to get good help these days," the old man murmured, smiling slightly.

"And if Catherine doesn't want another husband?" Raven asked, moving closer to the chair where his father-in-law sat.

"I've always believed I know more about what Catherine requires for happiness than she. She's innocent of the evil that walks the world, still inclined to romance rather than reality."

"Making her a widow is your idea of an introduction to reality?" Raven asked mockingly, as he took another step closer to the chair. "Have you asked your daughter what she wants?"

"I believe I know."

"Amberton," Raven suggested.

"Amberton made himself very agreeable, always a willing and acceptable escort for Catherine. A friend and companion to me."

"But there's one problem. She's not in love with Amberton."

"In our society being 'in love' is not generally considered a requirement for a successful marriage."

"A marriage of convenience," Raven suggested, smiling. Just as he had promised Catherine. When all along his intentions had been quite different.

"As was yours. At least, in the beginning," the duke said.

Raven was beginning to register the surprising fact that the Duke of Montfort possessed that information about his daughter's marriage, and then he watched as the pistol in the frail white hand began to track upward toward his body. He was not close enough to rush Montfort before he could fire, not close enough to dislodge the weapon with a kick. He could see the muzzle, a dark eye, move unerringly toward his heart.

"*Now*, Mr. Raven," the duke ordered.

Reacting to that command, a threat that was also a warning, Raven dived sideways, throwing his body in a controlled roll across the salon, even as the echoing report shattered the quiet.

The movement that brought Raven to a crouching stance, hidden in the most deeply shadowed corner of the room, was simply a continuation of that which had taken him out of the path of the duke's bullet. Adrenaline pouring into his bloodstream, his big body poised for whatever threat the duke would offer now, Raven waited, the blue gaze fastened on the small, satisfied smile that touched the thin lips of Catherine's father. The light caught the enormous ruby the duke wore on his right hand as he laid the smoking gun on the small table beside his chair.

"It's very gratifying to find that one hasn't lost all one's skills to age," Monfort said musingly, his hand now caressing the smooth translucence of the glass that held his brandy. The ball that had shattered the filial of the chair in which the old man sat had come within an inch of his head.

There were small splinters of dark wood caught in the shining white hair.

Taking a deep breath, Raven's gaze followed the duke's across the wide expanse of the room to the same window through which he had entered earlier. The sprawled body of the Viscount Amberton rested half inside and half out. The fingers of his outstretched arm were locked around the dueling pistol that lay on the edge of the oriental rug. Even in the shadowed dimness, the gleam of blond hair was unmistakable in the moonlight which spilled from the sweep of glass behind the body. It touched also the still-open, rapidly glazing eyes of the English aristocrat.

"Amberton," Raven whispered.

"Of course," the duke confirmed. "He had far more reason to want you dead than I. I'm surprised you failed to realize that."

"Because I broke his arm?" Raven questioned, his eyes coming back to Montfort's reactive smile.

"Because you took from him everything he had worked so hard to acquire. Catherine. Her trust fund. And eventually, of course he believed, the control of my wealth at my death. When you married Catherine, all of that disappeared from his reach. He had spent years insuring that those things would be his. I always did think he was a trifle toadying. However, one becomes too accustomed to that. Until I met you, I'd almost forgotten what it was like to encounter someone unintimidated by my money and position. It was rather refreshing," the duke admitted.

"Refreshing," Raven repeated, finally remembering to breathe. Amberton and not the old man. And he realized the echo he had heard when the duke fired had not been an echo at all. It had been the viscount's shot, aimed at his own unprotected back.

"Damned coward," Montfort said, his gaze again on the dead aristocrat he had once chosen as his son-in-law. "I knew when Catherine told me he'd stabbed an unarmed man that he would never do. And then when Reynolds explained the financial situation—''

"The rail project?" Raven asked, trying to follow.

"Amberton's situation," the duke said impatiently. "He was dead broke. Had been living on his mortgages for years. And then when we signed the marriage agreements, he'd taken out an additional, rather substantial loan from the moneylenders, secured solely by my signature on those documents. Only—''

"The marriage never occurred because Catherine eloped."

"And Amberton was left with no prospects and too many wasted years. Apparently, the situation embittered him enough that he became...unbalanced, which led to his repeated attempts to kill you. He thought that if he got rid of you, things would return to the way they had been before. The way they *should* be. He would become my son-in-law."

"And Catherine's husband," Raven said, thinking of that bastard's hands and mouth again profaning his wife's body. He blocked the image from his mind with the greatest effort of will, wondering what would have happened had he not escaped from the shaft.

He suddenly remembered the man who had greeted him in his own garden on his return. Montfort's henchman.

"Then why did I find your hireling on my grounds?" he asked.

"I told you if you couldn't protect my daughter, I would."

"He was here to guard Catherine?"

"Of course. I employ a large number of people, and I use them however I see fit. To guard this house. To spy on Amberton. That's how I knew what he intended tonight. I pay quite well for information. Amberton would have liked to hire another assassin, but unfortunately he was out of funds. His creditors were closing in, the threat of Newgate very real, and there was nothing he could do. Except, perhaps, take revenge on the man who was responsible.''

"I thought you were the one hiring assassins," Raven said.

"Why should I want you dead, Mr. Raven? I believe that Catherine..." The duke hesitated, always hating to admit an error. "I think Catherine has grown to like you," he finished finally, but he had the grace to blush at Raven's laugh.

"I believe you might be right, your grace."

"And your marriage is no longer a business arrangement."

"Catherine said you wanted to arrange a divorce."

"That was before she told me what she felt. My first consideration has always been Catherine's happiness."

"I'll take care of her," Raven promised. "I always—"

"Keep your contracts," the old man finished for him. "So I've been told. And since I believe Catherine is waiting upstairs..." He smiled.

"What about Amberton?" Raven asked, his eyes moving back to the man who had tried on at least three occasions to kill him. As he had come here tonight to do. Raven could feel no regret for Amberton's death, but there would be the necessary cleaning up, explanations to the authorities as to why the viscount's body had been found in his home and who had fired the fatal shot.

"A wedding present?" the old man suggested. "I owe you one, I believe. I think I have enough influence to handle the explanations. And if not, I certainly have enough money."

Hard blue eyes met the fathomless dark ones. Their gazes held, and slowly the blue ones softened and the stern line of Raven's lips relaxed enough to move into a controlled smile.

"Thank you," he said, and watched the graceful incline of the erect white head. "And now, if you'll excuse me…"

"Of course. Pressing business, I suppose…which will be less pressing shortly, I imagine." The duke's lips twitched quickly and then were still. He lifted his lorgnette to survey the figure of the man who stood, relaxed and unintimidated as always, before him. Montfort's gaze drifted over the supple skins that had been used to fashion the long tunic Raven wore over the matching leggings.

"Remind me, Raven," he said, "*not* to ask your tailor's name, a gentleman whose acquaintance I prefer not to make."

Raven laughed suddenly, the straight white teeth a surprise in the bronze face. "Do you know, your grace," he said, still smiling, "I believe you're mistaken. I think you would enjoy meeting my…tailor. You and she are, I think, two of a kind."

The duke's head tilted slightly, questioning the comment. But Raven had already turned, his long strides carrying him swiftly away from the old man's presence. He crossed the salon, and when he had left the room where his father-in-law continued to sip his brandy, he began to move with greater speed.

By the time he reached the grand, curving staircase, he bounded upward, taking the stairs two at a time, his mind no longer occupied by images of the stiffening body or even by the old brigand he'd found sitting at ease in his salon, but on the woman that he'd left sleeping above when he'd dressed and set out on his mission tonight. Only on Catherine.

She was lying as he had left her, in the center of the vast bed. The width of mattress that stretched on either side of her slightly curled figure emphasized her smallness.

His throat closed with emotion as he stood looking down on her. He had wanted her from the first time he had seen her in the noisy London street. And he wanted her still. He could feel desire for her welcoming embrace move painfully through his groin. He would never tire of touching her. Of holding her, possessing her and being possessed by her.

And eventually there would be far more: the intimacy of the mind, shared stories, laughing remembrances of growing up. Separated in experience by the vast differences between the worlds into which each had been born, they would begin to bridge the gulf between them by talking, by sharing memories. Lying in this bed, night after night, they would begin again to find the ease of companionship of those long-ago private dinners, which he had been surprised to discover Catherine seemed to relish as much as he. Those quiet meals had provided the hope he had lived on during those empty months. And now here, again, they could talk—long conversations interrupted by lovemaking, unhurried and relaxed. Or shatteringly urgent.

My wife, he thought, with the same amazement that had sometimes possessed him as he looked across the dinner table lined with high-ranking guests and watched her insure the success of the evening for everyone present without seeming to exert herself in the slightest. He remembered the innocence she had revealed about her own body and about the mysteries of his, mysteries that she was rapidly unraveling. Child and woman. Assured and then so charmingly uncertain. Sweetly and seriously questioning. She hadn't minded his delighted laughter last night when a query caught him off guard. She had laughed with him, pounding a small, ineffectual fist against his chest. Until, laughing, he'd pulled her to him, carrying her down into the softness of the mattress to hold her captive beneath his body.

Raven struggled awkwardly out of the tunic. Its fall to the floor was followed eventually by the trousers, until finally he stood nude once again, looking down on the small sleeper. He placed one bandaged hand gently over the smoothness of her upper leg, against the pale perfection of her body.

At his touch she moved, turning so that she could look up at him sleepily. She put her warm, soft hand over his forearm, avoiding the bandage. Remembering and caring.

"You're so cold," she said. "Come back to bed." But her eyes closed again even as she made the suggestion.

Raven lay down beside her, his hand still resting on her thigh. She eased her body back into his.

"Did you have to get up?" she questioned.

He didn't answer, and because it was such a pointless question, she let it go, cuddling into the hard strength behind her, preparing to return to sleep.

But the bandaged hand began to move upward, drifting over her hip bone. Her eyes opened in the darkness, and she waited. The abrasive cloth that swathed his palm brushed slowly over the small mound of her belly and then slipped lower, his bare fingertips edging nearer the hidden area between her legs. Unthinkingly she parted her thighs, her bones suddenly molten at the simple promise of Raven's touch. She eased onto her back so she could look at him. He was propped on his left elbow, his chest elevated above her, his damaged hand still making its slow and inexorable journey. She closed her eyes suddenly, her breath released in a soft gasp as he stopped that movement and began another. As he touched her with one finger, his hard mouth lowered to her throat. Her hands found either side of his head, tangling in the long dark hair, holding his mouth captive against her body. His lips moved against the tip of her breast. Almost with that same motion, he suckled, pulling strongly, and her hips arched into the compelling movement of his finger.

"Raven," she said, her own fingers tightening in his hair. He bit gently and then withdrew slightly. His tongue circled the pearled nipple, and then he suckled again. Harder. Already her breathing was heavy, her lungs gasping, seeking enough air. His mouth deserted her breast and found her lips. He thrust his tongue against hers, blocking the small moaning noises she hadn't even been aware she was making. She had forgotten to think why his skin was so cold, moving over the warmth of hers. She didn't wonder anymore where he had been. She couldn't think of anything but the demands he was making on her body. He could make her mindless in seconds. If he were not Raven, she would be frightened by how easily he could control her responses. Frightened by what he could make her feel.

His mouth left hers and returned to her breast, pulling and teasing. Wet and hot and hard. His tongue against her body. Demanding. Giving what she wanted. And what she knew he wanted.

He stirred in the darkness, his mouth again removed from the aching contact with her breast. She wanted him there, and she wondered why he was deserting her. And then, with his shift over her, she knew. His face was against her hair. She could hear his harsh breathing beside her ear, and he was no longer touching her. Instead she felt him slip into the wanting moisture he had coaxed from her. At the heavy sensation of his body filling hers, she moaned again.

He held his weight off her slenderness with his elbows. She could feel the movement of his knees against her legs and the shattering entry and retreat of his body, into and then almost out of hers. To the edge of no return. Slowly retreating, and then the sure, hard invasion. Rocking her. The hammering intensity of the sensations surging upward through her body. Wave after wave of force, building in a power that she could not deny, even had she wanted to. And then she exploded, her body arching under his, almost faint with what she felt.

This was not, of course, the first time he had carried her here. But before, he had stopped, easing the pressure and letting her rest with the ebbing tide of sensation. Now he continued, allowing no rest, no luxury of release while he had waited, patient with her pleasure, waiting for her to rejoin him in fulfilling his own need. This time the demand was relentless, and she felt the sensations begin again. Her fingers tightened into his back, nails biting as the surging peak built yet again. So quickly this time. Her body bucked under the power of his, but she was too small to force him to stop. And when the sensations began to grow again in the center of her body, she knew she didn't want him to stop. She thought she might really lose consciousness she was so lost in sheer physical response.

When the explosion of release came this time, she cried out, lifting again and again at the relentless, inexorable demand his body was making. She heard the echo of her own wordless ecstasy somewhere inside her mind, but she was unaware enough of its reality to be surprised when Raven's voice whispered, "Shh, my darling. Your father will hear."

She couldn't imagine why Raven thought her father would hear her. Or why he cared. Or thought she would. To make him stop talking to her and concentrate on what her body wanted, she bit into the damp skin of the broad shoulder that was against her mouth. Bit hard. And was rewarded by the pulsing thrust of Raven's body into hers. Deep, so deep. And again.

She cupped her palms over the hard muscles of the driving buttocks, feeling them contract with each movement. Her nails dug, urging him inside, pulling him to her. Wanting him. She felt the shuddering explosion everywhere. Inside her. Under her hands. His body slamming downward into her stomach. Bone beating into bone. Hard and exciting. She heard the harsh, guttural shout of his release, and thought fleetingly of what he had said about her father. And then finding, in the midst of his spiraling emotion, her own release, she thought about nothing at all. Not for a long time.

Again they lay entwined, exhausted. Drained. They were learning each other. How to trigger the most intense passions, the deepest responses. If there were no longer mysteries, there were still surprises, as this had been. Not in the fulfillment, but in the degree. In the profoundness.

They were still joined. Raven had rolled over, pulling her on top of his still-heaving body as soon as he could think about some reasoned movement. Protecting her from his size. Careful of her comfort even at the height of his surrender.

"Cold," she whispered, her lips moving against the dampness of his skin.

He held her shivering slimness against his heat. He was so warm now. He felt so good against her trembling body. So strong and secure, keeping her safe. Her lips lifted at the thought of any threat defying Raven's strength. When she was a child, her father had protected her. And now Raven did. She wondered idly if there were any other woman in London as fortunate as she. He had promised her freedom, so long ago. And he had kept that promise. But she knew now that what she had believed to be freedom was so incomplete. Now she was complete. Free to belong to Raven. Free to confess that belonging.

"I love you," she whispered.

He said nothing. Only his lips moved to answer that acknowledgment of his power over her. Power he never used to control her. For, of course, she could exercise a like control over him. Bondage.

For a man born to a freedom few in this confined society

could understand, a freedom of open vistas, unpeopled and unexplored, Raven had recognized long before she had the intimate bonds of marriage. Had recognized them and still had sought them. And would never regret giving himself into her hands.

Turning into his body, she moved to guide him, offering help. He relished the feel of small fingers willingly handling his body in the most intimate of ways. He whispered something then, phrases strangely sibilant, their softness lost as his mouth brushed across her temple to find her eyelid.

"What did you say?" she asked, her hands still moving against him.

"A vow," he whispered in English. "The marriage vow."

"I think you're a little late for wedding vows," she said, laughing. "I believe we took care of that legality in Scotland."

"There are legalities," he said, his lips over hers, "and then there are marriages."

"I don't understand."

"*Marriages* are forever, vows or no vows. Didn't you know?"

"I do now," she agreed, lifting to match his movements.

"I love you, Catherine Montfort MacLeod Raven," he whispered.

Smiling, she once more gave herself willingly into the sweet bondage of Raven's love.

Epilogue

One year later

The scarred fingers suddenly unclenched their grip on the crystal tumbler. Finally, from the floor above, the soft wail of a newborn had drifted down. Raven closed his eyes in a quick prayer of thanksgiving, and then realized that the birth of the child did not guarantee the safety of the mother, which was for him, of course, the more important consideration.

"Congratulations," the Duke of Montfort said, raising his glass in salute. "It seems that Catherine has finally made you a father."

"I have to know she's all right," Raven said, putting the brandy down and standing. Surely now he would be allowed into the sanctum of the bedroom. He had been banished, first by Stevenson, when the fashionable London practitioner had given them no hope of the safe delivery of the too-large infant or the survival of the slender mother who struggled so valiantly to give birth, and then by the stern but loving command of the old woman he had at last gone to for help.

His grandmother's unexpected arrival at the door of the

Mayfair mansion a week ago had been a shock. Although Raven had urged his family in America to join him in London, now that he knew this would be his home, he had never dreamed that the matriarch of that beloved clan would be the one to undertake the hazards of the incredibly long journey.

Catherine, uncomfortably in the last stages of her pregnancy, had made a charming effort to be the welcoming hostess, but the old woman's unfathomable black eyes had simply watched her, studying her every move. As if she were evaluating her suitability to be Raven's wife, a worried Catherine had confessed privately to her husband.

As Raven bounded up the stairs, he met his grandmother halfway down, the child held securely in her arms.

"You have a son, my Raven. A strong and beautiful son." She pulled back the swaddling to reveal the baby, the tiny head covered with the same black hair as his father. After glancing at the small, perfect face of his son, Raven's eyes came back to his grandmother's.

"Catherine?" he asked.

The wrinkled features softened, the dark eyes smiling into the sapphire blue. "I delivered *you*, John Raven, and you were bigger even than this one. I would not let anything happen to your Catherine."

Raven took a deep breath, the first real breath, it seemed, in the long hours he had been waiting. He knew that the old woman would never have given him that assurance unless it was true. The long, still-elegant fingers of Raven's scarred hand reached out to caress the head of the babe. He dropped a kiss on the child's forehead, and then his gaze moved to the top of the stairs.

"Go," his grandmother said. "She has been asking for you."

"Thank you," Raven whispered, and they both knew that it was not gratitude for that permission. It was acknowledgment that she had again been the one who had protected John Raven and those who belonged to him.

"You chose well, my Raven," she said. "A woman worthy of what you are. Worthy to bear your children."

"I think, perhaps, I had some...help," he suggested.

The old woman's thin lips moved, the enigmatic smile very much like Raven's own. "A small intervention," she agreed. "For your own good, of course."

"Would you do one other thing for me?" Raven asked. "Catherine's father is downstairs. Would you show him the baby?"

The dark eyes held his for a moment, again evaluating. "I will show this English lord what fine sons the Raven clan makes," she said. "And you will go and hold the brave girl who waits for you."

The room was shadowed. The draperies had been drawn to allow Catherine to sleep, but the russet eyes opened as soon as he knelt beside the bed.

"Have you seen him?" Catherine asked, her voice hoarse with exhaustion.

"He's perfect," Raven said. He bent to touch his lips against the sweat-dampened curls at her temple. "Although I had hoped he might have the wisdom to take after his mother..."

"Perfect," she whispered, denying the idea that anyone could be disappointed in a child so much like her beautiful Raven.

"I hope your father will think so. I asked my grandmother to take the baby down. I thought it was time they met."

She wondered what her father would make of the old woman, and then, her lips tilting, she thought about how much she would have liked to see that particular meeting.

"She was so kind to me, Raven. I was afraid that she'd be disappointed you'd married me, but...I don't think that's true. It was like having my own mother here. And unlike Dr. Stevenson, she didn't make me afraid. Suddenly, I knew that I could trust her to see to it that everything would be all right.''

''You don't have to worry about her approval. After all, Catherine, she chose you,'' he said.

The question was in her eyes, but despite her desire to understand, her mind had begun to drift. Everything was perfect. The baby. And Raven was here. She'd ask him what he meant when she woke up, when she wasn't so tired.

The Duke of Montfort lifted the gold lorgnette to survey from head to foot the strange figure which had entered the formal salon where he and his son-in-law had awaited Catherine's delivery. Despite the woman's obvious age, her braided hair was as long and as dark as Raven's. The eyes were different, of course, almost black in the seamed face, but as unintimidated, despite his deliberate attempt to intimidate, as his son-in-law's.

''This is your grandson,'' she said, holding out the baby for his inspection. ''Born of the clans Raven and MacLeod.''

One of the duke's white brows arched, and then he said simply, employing a tone reserved for those whose conduct approached familiarity, ''Indeed.''

The calm black eyes met his, and she moved across the room to stand before him. Because she had known that the girl would need her help, she had this morning donned the white ceremonial dress, made of the finest doeskin and decorated with beading that had required hours of careful work, so that she might be properly attired for the important events of this day. And she was too old and far too wise to be impressed by this Englishman's title or his posturing.

Finally the duke glanced down at the child. Despite his intent to allow nothing of his emotions to be revealed, he touched the small fingers very gently with the tip of the glass he held.

"You may hold him," the old woman offered.

Montfort raised his gaze to her, desire to do just that warring with his arrogant pride.

"He will be the comfort of your old age," she said very softly, looking into his eyes. "The son you never had. And like his father, he will be a builder. The new has come home to the old. New blood—rich and powerful—to blend forever with the strength of yours."

The soft syllables had slipped into a smooth singsong, almost mesmerizing Montfort with the force of their conviction, and their power held him speechless for a moment.

"Indeed," he said finally, fighting to keep the customary sarcasm in place, despite the emotional pull of that promise.

A small enigmatic movement of the thin lips was the only answer she made, still holding the child out between them.

The duke gestured her dismissal with a quick upward movement of the lorgnette. She still watched him a moment, and then she inclined her head with all the dignity of her own royal line. She turned, carrying the babe she intended to instruct as she had instructed his father. This man could choose, as he wished or no, to be part of that circle. When she reached the door, the duke's voice stopped her.

"And the clan Montfort," he offered. A challenge which they both recognized.

She turned back and looked at the English aristocrat whose blood also flowed in this baby's veins. "Raven and MacLeod," she said again, and then she added. "*And* the clan Montfort."

The old man smiled and, picking up his glass from the table, raised it in silent salute to the mingled heritage of the child she held. And to the future.

* * * * *

Babies are en route in a trio of
brand-new stories of love found on the
way to the delivery date!

Labor of
Love

Featuring

USA Today bestselling author
Sharon Sala

Award-winning author
Marie Ferrarella

And reader favorite
Leanne Banks

On sale this July at your favorite retail outlet!

Only from
Silhouette Books

Silhouette®
Where love comes alive™

Visit Silhouette at www.eHarlequin.com   PSLOL

Double your pleasure—
with this collection containing two full-length

Harlequin Romance®

novels

New York Times bestselling author

DEBBIE MACOMBER

delivers

RAINY DAY KISSES

While Susannah Simmons struggles up the corporate
ladder, her neighbor Nate Townsend stays home baking
cookies and flying kites. She resents the way he questions
her values—and the way he messes up her five-year plan
when she falls in love with him!

PLUS

THE BRIDE PRICE

a brand-new novel by reader favorite

DAY LECLAIRE

On sale July 2001

MONTANA MAVERICKS

Bestselling author

SUSAN MALLERY

WILD WEST WIFE

THE ORIGINAL MONTANA MAVERICKS HISTORICAL NOVEL

Jesse Kincaid had sworn off love forever.
But when the handsome rancher kidnaps
his enemy's mail-order bride to get revenge,
he ends up falling for his innocent captive!

RETURN TO WHITEHORN, MONTANA, WITH

WILD WEST WIFE

Available July 2001

And be sure to pick up
MONTANA MAVERICKS: BIG SKY GROOMS,
three brand-new historical stories about Montana's
most popular family, coming in August 2001.

HARLEQUIN®
Makes any time special®